MW01172247

TEN
TEMPLE MAZE LEVEL THREE

ANNA FURY

© Anna Fury Author

Paperback ISBN: 978-1-957873-96-1

Hardcover ISBN: 978-1-957873-95-4

Editing - Kirsty McQuarrie of Let's Get Proofed

Proofreading - Marcelle of BooksChecked

Cover - Books N Moods

Map - Darren DeHaas (@theadventurousfuryk)

❀ Created with Vellum

A QUICK NOTE

Ten is a dark omegaverse romance, and omegaverse often deals with difficult topics like generalized violence, possessiveness, physical dominance, recreational drug use, consent and more. This book has all that in spades. Sprinkle in the on-page and remembered death of multiple loved ones, and Ten is intended for mature audiences due to dark themes.

It's never my intention for a reader to feel triggered by something in these pages. If you're worried about anything more specific than what's listed above, please reach out!

author@annafury.com

MONSTER GUIDE

While I made up some of this world's monsters, a few are loosely based on existing entities. For the sake of those not familiar with monster lore, I'll quickly lay out the monsters you'll see and hear about in this book.

Vampiri - humanoid with exceptional senses, incredible speed and occasional psychic ability. They are pale-skinned with black claws, lips and fangs. Vampiri are venomous and drink blood.

Manangal - loosely based on the mythical filipino manananggal, a vampire-like winged creature that could separate it's lower half from it's upper to fly in search of prey.

Naga - Half human and half cobra, naga have humanoid upper bodies with a flared hood behind a distinctly snake-like face. Their lower half is that of a snake.

Gavataur - I made these up. Vaguely humanoid body with two arms and legs, but very tall and thin with saggy skin and a bull head, complete with horns. Ancient, wilder forms of the more modern minotaur. They are cannibalistic and non-communicative with hybrid monsters.

Velzen - Velzen are the vampiri court's version of a guard dog. Imagine a thinner version of a greyhound and fox mixed together, but all black with occasional white spots

Mermaid - We're not talking about Ariel, y'all. These mermaids have long, spindly limbs, rows of razor sharp teeth and hair/scales in all the beautiful colors of the sea. The mermaids in this book are carnivorous and hunt anything they can.

Carrow - A near-extinct monster spirit that can live inside any other monster breed. Identifiable only by a pale tattoo along the monster's jawline. Carrow have the ability to read intent and heart, and can vanish into a cloud of smoke to move through walls.

Volya - Volya are ancient creatures from deep within the Tempang Forest. Ten feet tall, their bodies are thin enough for their bones to be visible. A wide mouth features rows of conical teeth. Where eyes should be, a flat expanse of bone crosses their foreheads and then curls up and behind their heads. Horrifyingly, they've got leathery, claw-tipped wings as well.

PRONUNCIATION GUIDE

Ten - TEN-uh-briss
Onmiel - AHN-mee-EHL
Renze - renz (like friends)
Jet - JET
Achaia - uh-KYE-uh
Noire - Nwar
Diana - die-ANNA
Cashore - CASH-or
Ascelin - ASK-uh-lin
Vampiri - vahm-PEER-ee
Naga - NAH-guh
Gavataur - GAV-uh-tar
Manangal - mahn-ANG-ahl
Lombornei - LAHM-bor-NAI
Tempang - TEM-payng
Siargao - See-ar-GAH-O
Rezha - RAY-zhuh
Vinituvari - vin-IT-u-VAHRI
Deshali - deh-SHAH-lee
Dest - rhymes with west

PRONUNCIATION GUIDE

Sipam - SAI-pam (like dam)
Nacht - KNOCKED
Arliss - ARR-liss
Dore - Door
Velzen - VELL-zehn
Volya - VOLE-yuh
Evil - eh-VEE-zehl
Zakarias - zak-uh-RYE-uhs
Okair - oh-KAYR
Garfield - like the cat
Zura - ZUHR-uh
Kraven - KRAY-vehn
Anja - AHN-juh
Lahken - LAY-kehn
rahken - rah-kehn

ZURA'S LAND

TEMPANG FOREST

CARROW
VILLAGE

NACHT

MOON PROVINCE
LIBRARY OF PENGSHUR

the Adventurous Jurgh 2023

A SHORT HISTORY LESSON

In the early days, the continent of Lombornei was ruled by humans, and it was lawless. Monsters kept to the shadows of the Tempang forest, living far from the human element and never mixing.

Eventually, a direwolf and a human woman fell in love. The wolf shifter sired a son, and the first alpha was born. Those hybrid genes spread quickly, and other monster crosses emerged as humans and monsters bred for the first time in history.

This new generation was less content to remain in the Tempang, and they desired freedom to roam and settle across all of Lombornei. Hybrids were bigger and stronger than humans, and within five hundred years, every province on the continent was a mixed region of monsters, hybrids, and humans together.

Most provinces lived in relative harmony, but not all monsters were thrilled at this new world order. Hybrids and humans built the province of Deshali on the edge of the Tempang forest, right within claws-reach of every dark shadow that remained in the forest.

A SHORT HISTORY LESSON

The villain of our story was born and grew up in Deshali, her soul twisted and torn by life among true monsters—eventually turning her into the very worst one of all.

CHAPTER ONE

TENEBRIS

I've died a thousand deaths since I ripped my mate's head from her shoulders.

Snarling, I shove overwhelming anger away only to have it rush back over me in waves so heavy and hard I fall to one knee in the scorching sand.

Rocking onto my heels, I lift my head to the sun, willing the intense heat to burn away the pain in my chest. It's so cutting and sharp that I can barely breathe around it.

Tenebris, get your ass back here. My older brother, Noire, barks into our family bond, calling me like a lost pup.

I suppose that's what I am.

Growling, I hop to my feet and sprint across the dunes instead. I'll run until I can't hear his voice. Until I can't feel my other brother, Jet's, pity. I'll run until Noire or one of his lackeys drags me back, clawing and kicking like every other day.

Noire's pack alpha command hits me straight in the gut as he demands my return again. Ignoring it, I rip my clothes off and shift into my direwolf, picking up the pace across the hot desert sands of this desolate province, so different from my own. I'm far faster in this larger form, sprinting over searing dunes as sand peppers my face. It stings, and yet I don't care.

My mind jerks me back to before I killed her, my omega mate. I drift to a memory of pinning her to the wall, both hands above her head while I knotted her. I remember the way our bond was so clear and full of pleasure. I remember burrowing my head between her breasts after the ecstasy faded, kissing her tenderly, her long, elegant fingers stroking my jawline before demanding another kiss.

An enormous flying shadow comes out of nowhere, barreling into me as all the air is knocked from my lungs. We tumble over a dune and down the other side. I lash out with my claws as the shadow swirls around me, a low chuckle emanating from within its inky depths.

I flop onto my back, shifting into human form, lips curled into a sneer.

The shadows reform as a hand reaches out for mine. "You look like shit, Tenebris," the bulky, older male croons.

I take a moment to look up and scowl at Arliss. He's nearly as big as I am but far, far older. Sapphire blue eyes flash as his black lips part in a wicked smile. Noire warned me about the devious carrow. He takes "every man for himself" to the extreme. Not that I really need the warning. Years of hunting prey in the Temple Maze tell me this male is a predator to be wary of.

He's vicious enough in human form, but in carrow form, he can read intent and travel around on a wisp of smoke. He is beyond dangerous.

Arliss tsks sensually, licking his lips when I get up. Standing, I'm half a head taller than him—and still naked.

"Don't look at me like I'm a piece of meat," I snap, slicing out with a claw-tipped hand.

He catches my wrist smoothly; he's been fighting for hundreds of years. Or so he says.

Arliss rolls his eyes. They're so striking against the pitch-black of his skin and hair. "You cannot continue running, Tenebris. You achieve nothing, and Diana worsens by the day."

My one-time savior. My brother, Noire's, mate. My pack omega.

My mind helpfully supplies a memory of her entering the Temple Maze to free our pack and the vampiri clan.

That feels like a lifetime ago, before the day I realized our captor and the maze's creator was my fated mate.

Before I *killed* her...Rama.

Another memory assaults me. Opening my eyes after being kidnapped by her, only for her to smile at me. It was so real, so genuine, so godsdamned gorgeous. "*There you are,*" she'd said. And I knew what she meant. I was hers, bondmates in the ways of our people. True bondmates are rare, even among direwolf shifters.

And I *had* that, even if it was for a short time.

A sob leaves my throat, and the first tear falls as I grit my teeth tightly together.

Arliss crosses his arms. He's a silent sentinel as the tears come hard and fast. He doesn't yell at me like Noire or try to hug it out like Jet. He simply waits for it to pass, and when it does, he jerks his head back in the direction of his remote, desert compound.

"Let us return, Tenebris. I have something for you."

"I don't care," I manage. I don't care about anything anymore, apart from running to escape the pain that clenches my heart so tight it feels like it'll burst at any moment.

"You will," he retorts, grabbing my hand as we disappear in a swirl of black smoke.

I scream into a tornado of wind and sand, falling to the ground when Arliss stops whatever the fuck he just did. Looking up, I see we're back at his home, the only building around as far as you can see in this wasteland of a province. There's nothing but sand and rocks for hundreds of miles until you reach the Tempang Forest on the northern end of Lombornei.

Staring at the long bridge that leads to the compound's entrance, I notice burn marks mar the double doors, and there's still a giant hole nobody's bothered to fix.

"She did that, you know," Arliss reminds me. "She liked chaos

ANNA FURY

and control, Tenebris. Which is precisely why she drugged you to keep you with her, despite being your bondmate."

"If everyone could stop reminding me what a psychopath she was, I'd appreciate it." I can't stop thinking about how she infused me with a serum that did...something. She was mine, but she didn't trust me enough to allow me to be hers without drugging me, it seems.

Not that I can ask at this point, what with her being dead and all.

Without waiting for Arliss's response, I stalk down the steep dune and across the metal bridge.

Heads pop out of the water as the moat's mermaids watch us. Hair in every possible shade is matted from the murky, filthy depths. Long, pointed ears, wide eyes, and rows of sharp teeth are enough to keep me squarely in the center of the bridge.

"Beautiful, aren't they?" Arliss whispers as a chorus of snarls rings across the water. "Hush!" he snaps. "I will return you home soon enough, as promised."

The captive mermaids fall quiet at that, returning below the water's surface when I glance down at them.

A shuffling sound brings my focus back in front. In the hole blown into the front doors, a black-clad figure stands with her thin arms wrapped behind her back. She says nothing until we reach her, and then she gives Arliss a haughty, condescending look.

He reaches out to stroke Ascelin's cheek, but she swats his hand away like a bug. "Arliss, I have seen you fuck dozens of men and women on every surface of this compound. I am not your next conquest."

It's on the tip of my tongue to share how he looks at me the same way he looks at her, but I say nothing because I don't really give a fuck how Arliss feels or what either of them wants.

He laughs darkly but disappears in a puff of black smoke.

Ascelin, the beautiful vampiri warrioress, rolls her all-white eyes and slips her hand through my arm, clacking her long, onyx-colored nails together.

4

"I fucked him once," she whispers conspiratorially in my ear. "Just like I fucked you."

A shudder wracks my frame, but her sensual words don't spark desire as they would have before Rama. When we were escaping the maze, there was a time that I took what I needed from Ascelin's body. But all that was before I fully realized what awaited me outside the maze's walls.

Rama, my bondmate.

Ascelin's pale hand wraps firmly around my bicep as she guides me through opulent, sun-drenched halls and across tropical court-yards. There are obvious signs of a recent fight here too. The walls are singed, and scorch marks are all over the tiled courtyard. I don't really remember the actual fight, though.

She's silent, and I'm thankful that she doesn't remind me how terrible my mate was like everybody else feels the need to.

I absentmindedly rub my chest.

"Do your wounds hurt?" Ascelin questions. "Or is it deeper?" Her voice is gravelly but comforting, reminding me of how we formed a near friendship escaping the Temple Maze. She tried to save me during that final fight when Rama took me. Not that I wanted saving, exactly.

"*Everything* hurts," I whisper. Rama drugged me with a mechanical spider filled with some sort of serum. I'm still healing from ripping it off my chest once I realized what she was doing. If the serum vial hadn't broken during that final fight, I'd still be under its spell. I don't know how I feel about that.

She squeezes my bicep tighter, stopping us in place. A few hall-ways ahead, I hear the rest of my pack speaking in low tones.

Ascelin grips my chin, forcing me to look into her eyes. "You will overcome this, alpha. Eventually, you will find a new normal."

"There is no normal, Ascelin," I say, pulling away from her touch. "I tore my mate's head from her shoulders to protect everyone on this godsforsaken continent. There is no coming back from that, not for me."

Her white eyes fill with sorrow as she gives me a long, calculating look. Finally, she nods. I think she gets it more than the rest of my pack does. I had to do something unthinkable because the reality is my mate was an awful person—horrific, even. I knew that, and I made the choice to rid Lombornei of her, knowing I was killing myself at the same time.

My mind circles back to another memory of waking her with my tongue between her thighs. To the way she woke so slowly and then ravaged me in our bed.

Ascelin must sense she's lost my focus because she disappears into the hallway's shadows, leaving me to my thoughts.

A tug in my chest reminds me that my brother requires my presence. I always expect a sermon from him; it's what he did in the maze. But finding his own mate, Diana, changed him. Now he reads my emotions and intent better than ever, and there's a *slightly* softer edge to Noire that wasn't there before.

Although, as the youngest of the four Ayala brothers, I didn't experience his wrath as much as my older brothers since I was the pack baby. Noire was far harsher on the older two, pushing and shoving them to become the designations he needed for a strong pack. I was never meant to be part of his leadership crew. My three older brothers doted on me, even when I came of age.

That thought sends heat spreading through my core because when I came of age, Rama began to send me books and trinkets in the maze. It's when she started a seductive semi-courtship that lasted until I escaped. I didn't really understand it until I saw her for the first time in person. That's when I realized she was mine.

Growling, I shake my head to expel the demons of my memories, but, if anything, my body is even more focused on my dead mate, on the time we had together before I—

I shut that train of thought down, hard. When I enter the dining hall, conversation ceases, and everyone looks at me. Arliss is already there, seated at the head of the table. He steeples his fingers and gives me an appraising look.

"Your brother has plans to make, Tenebris."

I shrug my shoulders and sit at the far end, away from my pack. Jet turns and gives me a look, sending a tickle of affection through our family bond. The thing is, none of it sinks in. I don't give a fuck about making plans. Right now, my only plan is to keep putting one foot in front of the other to try to survive.

CHAPTER TWO
ONMIEL

"Onmiel, are you listening to me?" A low, teasing voice breaks through my thoughts as I look over at my mentor, Zakarias. His dark brows knit together over piercing eyes as he purses his lips. The very corners turn up, though, so he isn't mad. Of course, he's never mad at me. I'm his favorite Novice.

"I'm always listening," I chirp, pushing my reading glasses farther up my nose as I give him a haughty look.

"You said listening, but I believe you meant 'daydreaming,'" he corrects in a kind tone. The glare he gives me is equally haughty. He's full of shit.

"Yes, Daddy," I snark back, batting my long eyelashes. He's always joking about how he's older, despite the fact we aren't *that* far apart in age.

He snorts out a laugh, gesturing to the quiet book stacks surrounding us. "You are incorrigible," he mutters, mostly to himself.

"I'm also your favorite Novice," I whisper, looking around the library as he gives me a second warning glance.

"I have no favorites," Zakarias hedges.

"You do; it's me."

"I would never admit such a thing aloud."

"Don't need to. The eyes say it." I laugh. "Plus, you've let me deeper into the archives than any of the other apprentices. Just admit it." I sigh, leaning on my ornate wooden chair to rest both arms along the back. "You adore me."

Zakarias smirks but says nothing. And that's how I know I've got him.

Chuckling, I gesture at the giant, dusty tome on the wooden table in front of him. "How long are you going to stare at that ancient writing before realizing you can't read it?"

His happy smile falls, black brows dipping into a vee as a faint, anxious sentiment emanates from him. Ah, he is terribly angry about the perplexities of this particular book. "It reminds me of something, Onmiel," he says in a near-whisper. "It is on the tip of my tongue, and I cannot place it."

"Shall I take a look?" I offer quietly. Novices are not generally allowed in this section of the library without accompaniment by a First Librarian, but I'm miles ahead of the other Novices in my chosen topics of study—monster lore and languages.

Still, there seems to be some unspoken rule of the library—some books are simply off-limits to those of us who have not progressed through the training to officially become a First Librarian of the Ancient Library at Pengshur.

Gods above, that's a fucking mouthful.

But it's been my dream to become a First Librarian since I was much younger, maybe even the Master Librarian one day when I've learned enough to qualify.

Zakarias seems to consider it, then shakes his head. "Good as you are with languages, there is something off about this book, and I'd rather not. You have a way to go, young one."

I bristle a little at the comment, even though I know he means nothing by it. I'm not *that* young. I'd estimate Zakarias to be just twenty years older than me, and I've been through plenty of shit. I feel far older than my twenty-two or so years.

Not that he knows any of that.

Still, I can't push him into allowing me to take a peek. I know because I've tried in the past. He gets all bristly and weird, and there's just no point. I'd rather he remained in my corner for a time when I actually do bend the rules. Because that happens a lot, and he's always been willing to go to bat for me.

He must sense my frustration because his eyes soften, plump lips parting into a kind smile. His smile is his best feature—it lights up his face.

"You are learning quickly, my future librarian. It will not be long before you take up the official mantle. When you do, the entirety of the library will be at your disposal. I have complete confidence in you."

I nod absentmindedly, distracted by a ray of sun that comes through the plate glass window to my right. It highlights every mote of dust in the air, and I watch them twirl and dance as I put my chin in my palm. Next to the window, a light shines down on the column of books below it.

The entire continent of Lombornei has been without electricity for seven long years, but it was suddenly and inexplicably restored everywhere this week. Most of the librarians are scrambling to figure out how it happened. Plenty of theories are going around through the usual gossip channels.

I rather preferred it when our world felt a little more prehistoric and wild. People reading by firelight, not being connected to screens everywhere. It was heavenly for me. Technology is not my friend, so being unable to use it was awesome.

Zakarias stands and closes the dusty book gently, snapping his finger. I watch the book disappear into thin air and sigh. It's an odd ability that First Librarians develop once they're officially titled.

"Stuck it in your keeping room, eh?" I joke.

"I'll need to revisit it soon," he confirms.

I cross my arms. "Gods, I wish I could visit your room. I'd love to know what else you've got squirreled away in there. To be able to snap my fingers and magic me and my books away to a secret room? Hells, yes!"

Zakarias laughs. "Sometimes, I take Okair into my private room just to fuck him atop the books. It is *glorious*. That'll be you one day, Onmiel."

I give him a stern look. "Fucked atop your library stacks? No, thanks."

His dark skin flushes as red steals across the tops of his cheeks.

"Not *my* stacks, of course. I simply meant…"

I chuckle. "I know what you meant; I'm joking. I just want my own private keeping room, full of the things I want to read, where nobody can bother me. That and a nice coffee is all I need."

"It is a heavenly place to hide away from the world for a bit," he agrees.

We fall silent as we continue to pore through our books, cross-referencing data with the current paper we're researching. Occasionally, I look up at the long rows of tables lined between soaring stacks of books. The library is so tall that I can't even see the ceiling in this section. I imagine all the knowledge kept here and cannot wait to soak up every ounce of it. The Pengshur library is full of secrets and ancient magic, and I am obsessed with learning every last thing there is.

Onmiel, First Librarian of the Ancient Library at Pengshur. Here I come!

~

Hours later, I follow Zakarias along the wooden row table, looking at other First Librarians hunched over books of every size, color, and shade. I ache to know what they're reading, what they're researching, and what they're *doing* with all the knowledge they gain. Most librarians are knowledge-seekers, but First Librarians often serve the leaders of the realm as advisors. Still, anyone can come to the library and request to be assigned a librarian for a research topic. Some of the research programs go on for years and years.

Gods, I'd love to get assigned to one of the language-focused programs. Right now there's a whole First Librarian team cataloging a newly-uncovered ancient naga language. It's so fascinating.

My attention returns to the library around me. The only sounds are the faint page turns and the occasional rustle of clothing as we come to the exit. At the wide double doors that mark this section, a naga librarian slithers up to us, tapping Zakarias on the forearm but ignoring me entirely.

Ugh. One day, I'll have the distinctive triangular facial tattoo marking me as a First Librarian, then they won't ignore me like a bug. Stupid, ridiculous hierarchy.

This particular librarian has always been a conundrum for me. Naga don't love to mix with other monsters or half-breeds, and his huge, snakish body must be so unwieldy in the narrow rows of the library. I look up at the humanoid top half of his figure, only belying his naga heritage with the circular hood that flares at the back of his head. Slitted, catlike green eyes narrow on Zakarias as he crosses his muscular arms over his chest. He wears only a vest rather than the black tunic that would normally mark his rank.

"I need to speak with you, Zakarias," he begins. Just as I imagine a snake man would, he draws out the end of Zakarias's name into a long "s" sound, his forked tongue flicking out to lick his lips. His tongue is black, just like his hood and the snakelike portion of his body. He's always creeped me out a little bit, honestly.

Zakarias's voice is firm but calm. "Anything you wish to say to me can be said in front of my Novice."

Slitted eyes flick to me as the naga nods once, uncrossing his arms to hook his thumbs in the vest's pockets. He looks...uneasy? Behind him, the giant coils of his body draw tight together, as if he'd prefer to dive into them and hide from the world.

"I believe Rama is dead," he says abruptly, not taking a beat before he continues on quickly, "I cannot be sure, but…"

Zakarias and I hiss in matching breaths.

"Onmiel and I were discussing this yesterday," my mentor murmurs in a low tone. "We have all assumed that with the electricity back on, something happened to her."

The naga nods. "I was just speaking with Master Librarian Garfield, and he assumes it to be so. I'm considering leaving Pengshur as a result. What if this is another of her games?" The big librarian huffs, looking around as if Rama might have operatives hiding behind every musty stack of books. "I watched the nightly hunts she hosted in the Temple Maze. Now, the electricity is back when she cut it off for all those years. I cannot shake the feeling it might be time for me to return to my home province, far away from her and anything she might be plotting to do now."

What he says is very possible. She's psychotic enough to do that, I've heard. The reality is that for some reason that nobody is entirely sure of, Moon province, where Pengshur is located, is one of the few places Rama never attacked or even visited. I heard whispered voices once that she requested books from the Pengshur library, but who knows?

Zakarias looks up at the naga, straightening his chin. "If it's true that she is gone, then we are better off for it. It felt like only a matter of time before she turned her sights to Pengshur. Just imagine, for a moment, if she put her attention on the library…" Tears fill his eyes as he frets about the knowledge that could be lost if Rama brought her endless wars and bullshit here.

The naga doesn't look at ease as he lets out a soft hiss. "Perhaps she is gone, but something worse is coming."

His tone is ominous as Zakarias places a protective arm around my shoulders. "What could possibly be worse than Rama, Evizel?"

The naga shakes his head, his hood flaring wide as his forked tongue pokes out again. He looks down at me with a frown. "I do not know, Zakarias. But I cannot shake the feeling that this is the beginning of our issues."

I suppress a shudder as his emerald eyes narrow to slits. Without another word, he slinks back into the library's shadows and disappears behind a stack of books.

If there's something in Lombornei that's worse than Rama, I hope I never meet it.

CHAPTER THREE
TENEBRIS

N oire ignores my lackluster entry, focusing on the petite, dark-skinned woman seated at Arliss's right. His sister, Elizabet.

Her eyes go soft when she sees me look at her, but unlike everyone else, she's never treated me like I'm made of glass. I look away.

My big brother clears his throat, waving his hand for Elizabet to continue whatever she was saying when I came in.

She nods and leans forward over the glossy wooden table. "I can't heal Diana. I think we all realize that. I've tried everything I can think of, but she needs something I can't provide."

"Speak plainly," Noire barks.

Next to him, Diana stiffens but reaches out to place a hand on my brother's shoulder, her blond hair hanging limp against her thin shoulders.

A tic starts in Noire's jaw. I recognize the focused, predatory look on his face. It's like he thinks the cure is somewhere inside Elizabet, and he's ready to strip every bit of flesh from her bones to find it.

I should probably care.

Well, Arliss should care. He seems to be close to his sister.

It occurs to me that Elizabet wouldn't have lasted ten minutes in the maze. She'd have been ripped to shreds in minutes. I grit my teeth, thinking about it.

She lifts her chin and continues. "You need to go to Pengshur to the library there. They have healers and access to thousands of years' worth of research. Diana's injury is not commonplace. We need information that can only be found there."

"I'll accompany you, of course," Arliss decrees.

"A fucking library?" Noire's voice is barely above a snarl as he rises, planting both hands on the tabletop and looming over it. It's too wide for him to actually hover over Elizabet. Still, she shrinks back in her chair anyhow, casting a nervous glance at her sibling.

Arliss's expression goes cold and distant. "Sit *down*, Noire."

A ragged roar leaves Noire's throat, and it stabs like a dagger through the muscle of my chest. It reminds me of when Rama died, of how I screamed then. How it was full of anguish and emotion and horror.

That's the sound Noire makes now. His muscles tense and quiver. Elizabet stands and steps behind her brother's chair, never taking her eyes from my pack alpha.

"Noire, we need *help*, brother."

That's Jet—always the voice of reason, ever the strategist.

I'm barely involving myself, yet I'm exhausted thinking of how to control Noire and his temper. He's a flame that dances between pieces of dry kindling. Anything could spark Noire into a rage. He was always like this. He's the most calculating person I know.

My oldest brother jerks his head to Jet, and something imperceptible passes between them.

They don't bother to share it in our pack bond.

Not that I care.

Arliss unsteeples his fingers and rolls both eyes skyward as if he's thinking. Eventually, his focus returns to Noire. "I have a friend at Pengshur. He runs the place. Let us call and arrange to assign you a team to look for a cure. Garfield owes me a favor. I'm happy to collect on that now."

"And what'll I owe you after this is done?" Noire barks, defaulting to how he would have been in the maze, where nobody ever did anything for free.

Arliss grins. "Does it even matter, Noire? Diana's life is at risk. So, if I say you will owe me everything, will that stop you?"

There's a drawn-out, heavy pause. "No," Noire huffs. The glare he levels at our host would drop a lesser man to his knees.

"As I thought." Arliss grins, big white teeth making a show from behind ebony lips. "Let's go to my command center. We'll call Garfield."

"And then you've got another little errand to run, isn't that right?" Jet's mate Achaia's voice is fierce when she directs the question at him.

Our host rolls his eyes and huffs in irritation, shrugging his muscular shoulders.

"How could I forget, with you here to remind me so sweetly and repetitively." His voice is pure sugary sarcasm.

Jet's other mate, Renze, slips in a wisp of smoke across the room and reappears with a dagger pressed to Arliss's jugular.

"Speak to my mate thus another time, and you will lose your tongue, carrow. Perhaps without it, you will learn to be more pleasant."

Arliss's blue eyes narrow and focus on Achaia. He moves the dagger from his throat with one fingertip, shifts forward, and stands. When he jerks his head to the door, beaded braids tinkle around his broad shoulders.

I watch my pack and the vampiri follow him out of the room, but Jet lingers behind. He joins me and claps one hand on my shoulder.

"Come with us, Ten?"

I pause for a moment, trying to summon the energy to give enough of a fuck to stand up.

After a long beat, I do, trailing Jet and the rest of the pack through darkening halls. We head deep into Arliss's sandy compound until we reach a room full of monitors. Many of them are broken and trashed from Rama's attack. I was drugged then, so I scarcely remember it. Was I part of the group that blew holes in Arliss's home? Did I stand beside Rama when her soldiers threw every member of Arliss's family to the carnivorous mermaids in the moat?

I search my memory, closing my eyes as everyone finds a spot to stand or sit. But...I can't remember. It's hazy, like a lot of my memories these days. Even off whatever drugs she pumped me with, I can't seem to find clarity.

A beeping sound breaks through my thoughts, and a new voice echoes out of a speaker at the front of the room. A cracked screen blinks to life, and an older human-looking male with salt-and-pepper black hair appears. He squints at the screen momentarily and then smiles, but it looks forced. "Arliss, old friend. Haven't seen you in an age."

Arliss chuckles. "I'll write up the story of the last seven years of my life and gift it to the library. It would make for excellent fiction."

Noire bangs his fist on the desk in front of Arliss. "Get the fuck on with it."

When Noire appears on the screen, the male on the other end hisses in a breath. "Alpha Noire. So, it's true. You escaped the maze. We couldn't tell from what was televised."

Noire's focus turns to the male. "I'm coming to Pengshur, and I require your assistance."

Arliss shoves Noire back into his seat, and for a moment, I think there will be a scuffle. Again, Diana reaches for him, laying a hand on his chest.

Noir's focus turns to his mate. He pulls her carefully into his lap and buries his face in her neck, huffing softly. Our family bond is so tight it feels like splintered glass ready to shatter. I sense Jet's need to comfort our pack alpha. When I try to summon the same sentiment, I find I can't.

Arliss looks at the human again. "To make a very long story quite short, Alpha Noire's mate, Diana, was injured by a monster from the Tempang. She needs healing, and we cannot provide it here. Her injuries are extensive."

Garfield licks his lips and looks over at Noire, who's now glaring at him again. "Of course. The library has an excellent team of researchers, and we also work with local healers. But…" his voice trails off. I suspect what he's going to ask before the words leave his mouth, but it's still a knife to my gut that twists and turns when he says them. "You've escaped. So, is Rama dead? There are rumors."

For some reason, I force myself to stand there, wondering how Noire will explain what happened. Will he tell this man that I killed her?

"It's…complicated," Arliss hedges.

Noire breaks in. "If you cannot heal my mate, Rama will be the very fucking least of your concerns."

The male, Garfield, gulps and nods. "Of course, Alpha Noire. Please send any data you have about your mate's injury, and let me know when you'll be arriving. I'll pick my best team."

"See you soon," Arliss chirps in a cheerful tone.

Garfield grimaces, nods, and clicks off. The screen goes dark, and the room falls silent.

"You didn't want to tell him?" our host questions my pack alpha.

Noire snarls and rises with Diana in his arms. "I want him off-guard and worried. I don't want him to think the threat has lessened because Rama is gone. I will be Garfield's worst godsdamned nightmare if he doesn't find answers. And I want all of that at the forefront of his mind every second of every fucking day."

My older brother turns to me, his features twisted with frustration. "I need you to make this trip, Ten. You know about Pengshur. You've always been interested in that place. I'm counting on you to tell me if they try to fuck us over."

I glance at Diana, but her head lolls back in the chair. She can't stay awake for more than a few minutes at a time. So I nod and leave the room. I can't stay and listen to this any longer.

I'm just so fucking tired.

❧

Hours later, Ascelin joins me on the porch as the sun sets behind the dunes. For a split second, all I can think of is my home province of Siargao. This province is hot, but it lacks the humid resplendence of Siargao. A pang of homesickness overtakes me. Ascelin hops onto the stone railing, resting her hands gracefully on both lean thighs.

I look up to find her smirking at me, all-white eyes flashing with mirth. It still surprises me to see her smile. She was my enemy for seven long years in the maze. Being something close to friends now is…weird.

"Diana is not well enough to travel to Pengshur, but I will accompany you," she states as if it's the simplest thing in the world.

I shrug. "You mean you're coming to babysit me?"

"Not hardly," she purrs. "You are a grown male, Tenebris. But Arliss wants something from that library, and per usual, he's not forthcoming about it. I want to know what he wants, and so does Noire. So, I'm going with you."

"Gods, this reminds me of the maze," I grumble. "Everyone's got an agenda. Nobody trusts anybody. It's fucking exhausting. Why do we even give a fuck what Arliss wants?"

Ascelin's smile falls. The maze was kind to no one, which reminds me that my godsdamned mate created it in the first place. It was Rama who imprisoned us there and tortured us for seven years. I grew up in the fucking Temple Maze until Rama realized what I was to her. Even then, she didn't let me out. I had to escape on my own. What does that even say about her?

I shake my head as I struggle to reconcile what I know to be true about my mate from my brief experience as her lover.

"Tenebris?" Ascelin's voice is gentle as she reaches out to pat my arm. When I look back up, she gives me a soft smile, translucent black teeth glinting in the faint light. "You have not seen a library in years, my friend. Will you not be excited to visit the most revered library in Lombornei? All they do there is read, learn, and advise rulers and leaders. It seems like something you would enjoy."

I grit my teeth and nod. I don't need to tell her how the first time I took my mate was in a library in her quarters. A library she built for me with books taken from the famous Pengshur collection. A library I fucked her in dozens of times, spilling my seed as she fell apart on my knot, screaming my name, our mate bond ablaze with violent ecstasy.

The familiar ache reappears in my chest, and I rub at it, wondering absentmindedly if broken mate bonds can ever be healed. Or gods, maybe even turned off? But that train of thought leads me down a circuitous route of thinking. If I turn off my broken bond, will I forget her? Will I forget the perfect connection we had for such a brief time? Do I want that?

I don't know what I want, to be honest. I want to not be tired.

Ascelin must sense she's lost my attention for the second time today. She pushes off the railing and disappears inside. I don't need to focus to hear my pack talking about me just inside the doors.

"Ten."

Achaia's soft voice breaks through my thoughts as she joins me on the balcony. Goddess, it's one person after another, a steady stream of well-wishers hoping to convince me everything will be fine.

I look over at my brother Jet's beautiful mate. Luscious red hair falls in waves down her back, her green eyes sad when she smiles at me.

"Your mermaid form is so different from this one," I muse as I attempt to return the smile.

She winks conspiratorially. "To be honest, I miss the boobs in mermaid form. The boobs are really nice to have."

"That's not what I meant," I bluster, feeling a flush spread across my cheeks.

"Oh, I know." She shrugs, laughing as she leans against the railing. "I just think when someone experiences a loss, those around them tend to treat them like victims all day, and that shit gets old.

Sometimes, you just need one person to act like the sky didn't fall on your head, and that one person is me."

A bit of relief threads through my system as I turn to her, leaning against the railing to match her stance. I can't ask her about what she lost because that'll lead to more stories about how crazy and vicious my dead mate was. Achaia tried—and failed—to kill Rama more than once after Rama decimated her clan. She's another person who lost literally everything because of my bondmate. Her victims are so numerous I can't turn without seeing one.

It's hard to wrap my mind around that most days.

"I could use your help with something," she says after a long beat. "I need someone big and strong."

I glance over my shoulder at my brother Jet, but he's currently wrapped in his other mate's arms. He passionately kisses Renze, the graceful vampiri warrior, sitting on the edge of the dining table.

Achaia follows my gaze and grins at them, then trills her fingers along my forearm. "Will you help me for a few minutes?"

I shrug again and gesture for her to lead the way. I follow her through lengthy, sunny halls until we come to a vast airship work-shop I've seen once or twice. Arliss and Elizabet are there already. Elizabet holds a clipboard as she marks something off, checking a list. Arliss dwarfs her much smaller figure as he clips a giant glass box together at the corners with creaky metallic locks.

Elizabet's plump lips split into a smile when she sees us. It lacks the devilishness of Arliss's grin, but everything about him seems deviant, whereas Elizabet is a breath of fresh air. She's a scientist at heart, though, and Arliss is just…Arliss.

"Ah, you've found a helper. Thank you, sweet friend!" she says to Achaia. I wonder how the women have become so close so quickly, but I haven't been paying attention. Then again, Achaia seems easy to be around. She's thoughtful, kind, and strong. I'm glad Jet has her, even though it crushes my soul to see happy people continuing on as if my world wasn't decimated by a single moment.

Arliss gestures to the giant glass box in the middle of the room. "Tenebris, help me move this."

I stride across the junk and tool-filled space, picking my way over random pieces of shrapnel left over from Rama's attack.

"What's the box for?" I question as I shove against it, helping him move the entire thing to the far wall, which opens into a courtyard of sorts.

"Nothing just now," he grunts. "It will be full of mermaids soon. We will return them to their home sea on our way to Pengshur."

"That's right, and what else?" Achaia presses in a stern tone, following us with her arms crossed.

Arliss rolls his eyes exaggeratedly but winks at me before turning to her. "And I will apologize for accepting them as a gift, entrapping them with a spell, and keeping them in my shithole of a moat for seven years."

"And what *else*, Arliss?" Achaia presses further, green eyes flashing as she crosses her arms. "Don't make me threaten to shift and level this place. I could, you know…"

The hint of a smile tugs at my lips. Mermaid queens can let out a shriek that can obliterate armies with a single sound. It's a last-ditch protective effort, although I know Achaia leveled Rama's home province once before my mate took the pearls from her crown and stole that ability. Achaia's crown is full now, though.

I turn to her. "Mermaids swim great distances so fast. Can we not release them in the closest sea and allow them to return home more quickly?"

"We're not *that* fast," she mutters. "And they'd have to swim all the way down the coast and around Siargao just to come up the other side of Lombornei. It makes much more sense to deliver them with the airship. It's the least Arliss can do after keeping them in that—"

"Muddy, filthy, disgusting moat. I *know*," he cuts in, throwing his hands up. "I have already apologized twice to you and thrice to the other mermaid queen."

"And I don't believe you meant a single word of it," Achaia snarls. "So, while I'm here, I will advocate for them until they are safe and away from your clutches. It's not natural for mermaids to be trapped in such a small body of water. The conditions they're living in are—"

"Deplorable. Yes, I *know*," Arliss hisses. Somewhere across the room, Elizabet chuckles. Achaia and Arliss fight like this every day, and I think the big male's sister finds it highly amusing.

"Mermaid cities typically cover several square miles," I think aloud. "And it's not uncommon for a mermaid to travel as far as fifty miles in a day. They'll be glad to be home, I'm sure."

Achaia shoots me a thankful look.

One of Arliss's dark brows raises. "How do you know about mermaids?"

Pressure crushes my chest inward, but I stand tall and cross my arms. "I wasn't born in the maze, Arliss. And there was a library in my room."

He opens his mouth to say something else but seems to think better of it.

"I'm going to bed," I murmur. The sun isn't even down yet, but I've lost any energy I had trying to muddle through this conversation.

"Come to dinner, Tenebris," Achaia encourages, stepping forward to stare at me with those shocking green eyes.

For a long moment, I look at her, truly look at her, this wondrous person mated to my brother and Renze. And I know I should *want* to get to know her. She's not a direwolf omega, but she's my brother's mate, which means I'm connected to her, too. If I listened hard enough, I'd hear her in our growing pack bond.

But I ignore that because I don't want to hear all the whispered worries and concerns in the bond these days. I don't want to join in on the fear everyone has for Diana's life.

I just want to go to sleep.

CHAPTER FOUR
TENEBRIS

Morning comes too fast. Sometime in the night, Jet packed a bag for me. It's sitting by the door to my room, and his scent is all over it. Early morning sunrays filter through my room's open balcony window. Noire tugs at me insistently through our family bond.

Asshole.

Groaning, I roll out of bed and change. I grab the bag without looking inside and head for the open-air dining area. Noire feeds Diana small pieces of meat, glaring at me when I show up. Jet and his mates look on in concern, whether for me or Diana, I couldn't say.

When I catch Ascelin's attention, she schools her heartbroken expression into something more neutral.

Ah, Diana then. The vampiri king connected with her in the maze. Of course they're worried for her. Even though he's gone.

Sort of.

I manage my way through a breakfast I don't care to eat.

Ascelin, Elizabet, Jet, and Achaia leave to load up the mermaids. Noire and Diana focus on me from across the table.

There's an impossibly heavy tension in our family bond.

"I'm counting on you, Tenebris," Noire begins.

Next to him, Diana's already pale face is more drawn than ever, her long, blonde hair hanging limp against her skull. She looks like a dead woman walking, and even in our family bond, she feels faint.

Noire almost looks like he's about to beg for something, but he continues on, his voice low.

"We three brothers are the future of Pack Ayala. It is our duty and gift to rebuild it. I want us *all* to have a chance to do that, Tenebris. You included, one day. When you're ready."

I shake my head. "I can't think about that, Noire, I—"

"I know," he interrupts. "I'm not asking you to. But you're still *here*, Tenebris. Your fate, your future still lies ahead of you. Not behind."

"Easy for you to say," I snap.

"No," he barks in a furious tone. "It's not easy for me to say that. Nothing about our journey has ever been easy, brother. Escaping the maze just brought us new godsdamned issues. We have to face them together."

Diana's blue eyes focus on me, and she gives me a reassuring smile. It's easy to see she's with Noire on this one.

"We appreciate you, brother," she says, her voice barely above a whisper. It sounds cracked and broken like it's hard for her to even speak. "We love you so fucking much, Ten. We're here for you, too, you know."

"I don't need anything," I bark.

"We need one another, now more than ever," she counters, her tone growing fierce despite her obviously waning strength. "We trust you, Ten, just as we always have. And you can trust us, alright?"

For a moment, I can't think of how to respond. Eventually, it becomes awkward, so I stand. I round the table and lean down to brush my cheek against Diana's with a soft purr. Despite everything that's happened, she's still my pack omega. I'm still drawn to protect her.

She leans into that touch, brushing her soft cheek against mine.

Warmth steals through our family bond. There's satisfaction from Noire that we're connecting, and there's elated pleasure from Diana.

But being this close to her, I smell sickness. It seeps from her in inky, insidious tendrils that seem to creep around the room and congregate in the shadows.

She doesn't have long. I can sense it the way a direwolf senses any sick packmate.

When she pulls back, Noire takes her place and pulls me into his arms for a brusque hug.

"Love you," he says in his usual gruff tone. "Always have, always will, baby brother."

"You, too," I manage, wishing like hells I could snap my fingers and appear somewhere where we aren't exchanging heartfelt emotions. I can count on one hand the number of times Noire has told me he loves me.

I manage to extricate myself from his embrace and make my way to the front of the compound, where the long, metallic walkway leads over a dirty-looking moat. The water's surface roils, dozens of scaly bodies flipping and swirling. On the far side, resting on the dunes, is the enormous glass box from Arliss's workshop. Today, it's filled with clear water. Arliss and Elizabet stand in front of it.

Achaia and Jet stand next to them, and Achaia looks pissed. I head toward them, and by the time I get there, she's shouting at Arliss.

"You're such a godsdamned bastard, you know that?"

"You've said," snaps Arliss.

Next to them, Elizabet frowns at the water.

Jet taps me through the family bond. *Apparently, the mermaids arrived under some sort of enchantment that kept them from transforming to their two-legged form, and that's how he kept them trapped in the moat. Achaia wasn't fully aware of how it worked and she's going to rip his guts out through his nose if he doesn't fix it soon.*

I hadn't thought about why the mermaids didn't just shift and walk away from Arliss, or attack him in his sleep, but it makes sense if they're enchanted. I know Achaia can shift between mermaid and human forms, I just didn't give thought to why they *didn't*.

"I thought Elizabet sorted it already," Arliss grumbles.

Arliss's sister sighs, taps at her temple, and looks at Achaia. "I think I can actually fix this. Although Arliss failed to mention it earlier." She gives him a dirty look and jogs up the metal walkway past me.

Arliss groans as she goes, kicking at the sand with one booted foot.

When I join the group, Jet greets me with a toothy grin. "As soon as we figure out how to get the mermaids out, we'll be on our way."

I nod and head for one of two compact airships parked just beyond the moat, tossing my bag onto a metal bench inside. Jet and Achaia are going to accompany us as far as returning the mermaids and then they'll come back to try to stabilize Diana to come to Pengshur, if possible.

Ten long-ass minutes later, Elizabet returns with a vial of purple liquid. For the first time in days, I find myself interested in how this will go. I haven't spent much time with Arliss's sister—or anyone, for that matter—but I've learned she's something of a science whiz. It's why Rama kept her at the city of Nacht, forcing Elizabet to run experiments for her.

I grit my teeth as a memory of Rama backhanding the smaller woman assaults me.

Elizabet kneels down at the water's edge and dumps the purple vial out. Immediately, the viscous-looking liquid spreads across the surface, bubbling as water vapor rises off the surface. I leave the dark confines of the airship to rejoin the group for a closer look.

A crown rises up out of the water, covered in iridescent pearls of varying sizes. Wide, slanted eyes and a flat nose appear next, along with tapered, pointed ears. The mermaid queen swims to the edge and reaches out with spindly, claw-tipped fingers. When she reaches the sand, she hisses and sucks in a breath of air.

She jerks her head over her shoulders and lets out a string of hisses and clicks that remind me of Renze and Ascelin's language. I wonder if there's a common ancestor somewhere between vampiri and mermaids…

But then there's movement where the water laps at the sand, and that pulls my attention back to the current moment.

The queen drags herself up onto the sand. Obsidian scales shimmer and disappear, and her long, twin-tipped tail becomes two slender, shapely legs. She wiggles her toes with a gleeful smile and then stands, lifting her chin high. In this form, she reminds me of Achaia, but she's taller and thinner.

Behind her, nearly two dozen other mermaids begin to leave the moat, shaking off dirty, smelly water as they struggle to stand for the first time in who knows how long.

The predator in me realizes we're outnumbered, but that the mermaids are probably off-kilter, having not been on two legs in years. Even so, I widen my stance and ball my fists, ready for an attack if there is one. If the maze beat anything into me, it was to always be prepared.

The queen's fierce gaze flicks over to me and she turns, stalking across the hot sand. It must burn her feet; this province is hotter than the seven hells. But if it does, she pays it no mind. She comes to a stop in front of me, but Achaia steps between us and reaches out to place one hand on the other queen's shoulder.

I don't understand the words that leave Achaia's mouth next, but the queen's focus flicks to the behemoth glass box and she nods. Achaia gestures to a ladder on one side of the box. The queen strides on shaky legs to it and waits for the next woman to follow her.

I shift closer to Jet and Achaia, ready to protect his mate if something happens. These are her kind, but I don't trust anyone who isn't bound to me in some way. Achaia reaches out, loosens my fist, and threads her fingers through mine, pulling me close.

Touch.

A gentle, soft, woman's touch.

I never knew that with Rama. There was never any of that even in the middle of our mating. She was pure and violent delight, and not a shred of anything else. She hated anything soft, absolutely despised it and declared it as being weak.

I think I'll hate Achaia holding my hand, but I don't push her away. Jet says nothing in our bond, but there's a slow and tangible sentiment of pride. My formerly broken brother is proud of his woman.

I hate that. I'm not proud of mine.

I pull my hand from Achaia's.

The first mermaid climbs up the ladder and dives into the enormous tank. Nearly two dozen more follow. After long minutes, the queen stands at the base and a final head pops out of the water, a smaller one next to it. A child.

An ember stirs in the cold, dead fires of my heart. I don't give a fuck about anybody who isn't related to me, and even then, I'm having trouble giving a shit. But children have always been a soft spot. Maybe it's because I was a child myself when I saw every kid I knew massacred by Rama's goons. Maybe it's because I was a child myself when my godsdamned mate threw me in a maze of monsters to kill for her. Maybe it's because this world is a piece of shit, but children are the single shred of light and hope for me.

The woman and child leave the water, but when the child touches the sand, she squeals and leaps back with a pained cry.

The mermaid queen and I move as one, but I get there first, swooping the girl up into my arms. The mother and the queen scream at the same time, but I ignore them, focusing on the galloping heartbeat of the merchild I hold frozen to my chest. When I reach the tank, I heft her halfway up the ladder and stand to make sure she doesn't fall. She topples into the water, shifting back into mermaid form and pressing herself against the glass. One hand comes flat to it, and she gives me the tiniest of smiles.

The queen and the mother join us. She hisses at me, and I step back. She and the mother ascend the ladder and follow the child into the water. The tank is so full. It's not nearly big enough to comfortably hold two dozen mermaids, but it'll have to do, I suppose. Mermaids are always more comfortable in their natural form. Achaia will have requested the tank for them, rather than having them sit in human form. Truly, I think the only reason she stays in human form so much is for Jet's and Renze's sakes.

I watch the queen cross her now-spindly arms and glare daggers at Arliss.

He rolls his eyes and presses a button on a remote. Tracks on the bottom of the tank creak and groan as he moves it toward the larger of the two airships. He maneuvers the tank inside and secures it to the metal floor with giant chain hooks.

When I follow Jet and Achaia into the second ship, Renze appears out of nowhere. He stands, stroking Achaia's face as he kisses her.

Ugh.

Might wanna head to the other ship, brother, Jet says helpfully in our bond. *We'll be a minute.*

Wrinkling my nose, I leave my brother and his mates. When I turn to look at the compound one final time, Noire, Diana, and Ascelin stand in the hole in the gate. Ascelin looks to be saying her goodbyes. Diana lifts one hand to wave at me. Noire glowers, but that's his normal face.

Be safe, brother, he huffs into our bond.

Ascelin hoists her backpack over her shoulder and hugs Diana one last time. Then she turns and paces across the long bridge, striding into my airship and seating herself next to Arliss at the controls.

"Hello, pretty girl," he croons. Elizabet and Ascelin groan at the same time, but then Elizabet kisses her brother on the forehead and leaves the airship, waving goodbye to the mermaids and me.

Great. Third wheel with the couple who refuses to admit they're together. Fun times lie ahead for me.

I strap myself into a seat in the vaulted back with the mermaids. It doesn't take long for us to get under way. It takes even less time for Ascelin and Arliss to get into a shouting match.

I manage to drum up a notepad from under one of the seats, and I play tic tac toe with the mermaid child for an hour before she tires and swims into her mother's arms to rest. The queen watches me from the corner, eyes narrowed and dark blue lips pursed together.

There's no energy in me to engage with her or any of the rest of them, so I let my head fall back against the curved metal hull of the airship. Sleep overtakes me, despite having woken up not long ago.

Sometime later, I wake to the sloshing of water. Rising, I join Ascelin and Arliss at the front of the ship. Ahead of us lies a crystal-clear turquoise sea. Giant, blue waves splash up against pitch-black craggy rocks. The mermaids grow agitated, flipping and spinning, sending great sloshes of water onto the ground.

"Pipe down!" Arliss roars. "You'll be home soon enough," he tacks on under his breath.

Ascelin rolls her white eyes at him and punches one of the controls. A metallic croak echoes out from underneath the ship. Landing gear, maybe?

Five harrowing minutes later, Arliss lands the airship on a large rock with the back facing the water.

He stands and gestures to the mermaids. "Get out, fishes. You're home."

Ascelin stands and grips a fistful of his braids, yanking his focus to her. "Can you not see the rocks look sharp as daggers, you asshat? Get them close to the water, at least."

His blue eyes narrow on her. "Did Achaia put you up to this?"

Ascelin doesn't bother to answer, but drops his braids as if they're venomous snakes. She grabs the tank remote from the dashboard and hands it to him. "They were promised front-door service, I believe." When she crosses her arms, Arliss leans in and snarls, backing Ascelin against her seat.

Shocking blue eyes drift down to her lips as he snarls. "It is high time to stop pushing me, vampiri. Fuck me or don't, I care not at this point. But press me further and you will see a side of me you do not care for."

"Been there, done that on all accounts," she barks, shoving him out of her face as she slips in a stream of smoke to the back of the airship.

Their banter makes me want to find headphones and go back to sleep.

Arliss uses the remote to maneuver the mermaid tank out of the airship. The scent of salt water fills my nostrils. It reminds me vaguely of Siargao, but it lacks the undercurrent of fried fish and that unique scent that's riverwater versus seawater. Gods, I think I miss home.

Jet and Achaia join us. They reek of cum and slick. Achaia's cheeks are flushed, and there's a sated, hazy look on Jet's face.

Gross.

I can't wait to get to the library if only to stop seeing mated couples every-fucking-where I turn.

By the time Arliss gets the tank to the very edge of the rocks, the mermaids are in a literal frenzy, spinning and whirling around the tank, crashing against the thick glass panels.

Arliss gives Achaia a haughty look. "Perhaps I should simply shoot out one side of the tank and splash them in?"

"Try it," Achaia snaps. "Maybe I'll just shove you in with them." She gives him a condescending look and heads to the tank, standing at the base of the ladder as the queen pulls herself out of the tank and descends it. They press their foreheads together and speak softly.

The queen stands guard as her people make their way to the edge of the rocks. They leap in with cries of joy, appearing with their heads above water to wait for her to join.

Two things happen almost simultaneously.

The queen lets out a shriek that splits my skull like a hammer. It shatters all four walls of the tank, and a giant shard breaks free and knocks Arliss backward.

Then, with seemingly inhuman strength, two of the mermaids snatch Arliss by the braids. He shouts and falls on his back, his head banging against the craggy rocks. There's a hissed intake of breath, and the mermaids drag him to the edge and over.

He lets out a raging bellow as he disappears from view, blood coating the rocks where they took him.

There's a moment of silence, and then Ascelin screams. I rush forward to look over the edge at the waters below. Blood blooms bright and red in the water, and her screams become wails of anguish.

I wonder if they're eating him.

Seems like it.

Or will they just rip him to shreds and leave him for the sharks?

Achaia joins us with a neutral look on her face. She looks neither surprised nor displeased at this turn of events.

Ascelin, on the other hand, is losing her mind and looks like she's about to throw herself into the expanding circle of red blood. She slips in a trail of black smoke to the edge of the rocks, wringing her hands.

I place my hand on her shoulder and push her back before she can do something stupid, something like I'm about to do.

Will they tear me apart if I toss myself in, too? What would that feel like?

I want to find out.

I kick off my shoes and leap over the edge into the roiling water.

∽

Warm, tropical water covers me, muting sound as I enter the water. I open my eyes but can barely see anything. The mermaids roil madly around me, but I let out a roar that grabs their attention.

Arliss slashes out, but his movements are sluggish and heavy. He's drowning. There's a splash next to me, and Ascelin appears in the water with a dagger in each hand. A third splash reveals Jet and Achaia. Jet swims for Arliss, shoving mermaids away from the fallen male.

Blood fills the water.

So much blood.

Closing my eyes, I wait for a strike. A hit. Anything. Will they eat me too?

When nothing happens, I open my eyes, squinting them to try to see.

The mermaid queen glares at us, deprived of her revenge and her meal.

Achaia lets out a string of hisses and clicks. The other queen's gills flare angrily but she nods. She seems to decide it's not worth the fight because she lets out a horrible hiss and flits off into the darker turquoise water.

Death has no plans for me today, it seems.

I swim to Jet's side, grabbing a fistful of Arliss's shirt. Ascelin joins us, and together we manage to get him above water. It takes all three of us since he's heavy as fuck, but we're able to lug him to where we parked the airship.

We lay him flat on his back. Ascelin throws herself across his prone figure and starts mouth to mouth. He's bleeding from dozens of slash wounds to his torso.

Jet throws a furious look at me as I watch Ascelin trying to save the monstrous carrow.

"What the fuck were you thinking, Ten?" Jet snaps. "Diving in after him. You could have been killed. Is this the kind of help we can expect when you go to Pengshur? Because if this is what you've got to give right now, I'll go instead."

His fury is a slap in the face.

I wasn't thinking about Diana. I wasn't thinking about anyone. I just wondered what might happen. It was instinctive, more than anything, to follow Arliss in.

When I open my mouth to say something, nothing comes out. Jet glares at me, but I can't summon a response.

A coughing sound behind us draws our focus to Arliss, who chokes up seawater as Ascelin lays across him, seemingly trying to hold back a sob.

When he sits up, she slaps him across the face.

He grunts, whipping his head back toward her. He grips her cheeks, squeezing them together, and then he plants the most tender of kisses on her dark lips, falling to the ground with her in his arms. It's like they don't even know we're here. Ascelin sobs into the kiss, Arliss grunts in pain, and I watch on as he bleeds from dozens of deep-looking wounds.

Jet clears his throat, but I don't want to see this shit.

I turn and head back for the airship, dripping water and blood in a stream behind me.

CHAPTER FIVE
ONMIEL

I'm sitting on my apartment's small balcony, looking down the street at the southern entrance to the library when a sudden pounding at my door makes me leap up. Hot coffee spills down my legs as I hiss and grumble, pushing my glasses higher up the bridge of my nose as I stomp to the door.

When I swing it open, Zakarias stands there, out of breath. He steps into my cramped apartment, one palm placed dramatically over his heart.

"Onmiel, now that the electricity is back, *kindly* turn on your computer. I've been pinging you on the library's messaging app for half an hour."

My face flushes. He's told me this twice already. But to be honest, not only do I not like technology, I'm not that great with it either. I didn't grow up with it, and I'm not accustomed to how it works. I much prefer the days when someone who needs me would pick up a phone or knock on my door. Like…a week or so ago.

"Sorry," I murmur, grabbing napkins off the kitchen counter to wipe the coffee that's dripping down both legs.

Zakarias ignores that completely. "Get dressed quickly. We've got an assignment as a team!"

I jerk my head up at that. "An assignment? As a team?"

Zakarias's dark lips split into a grin, white teeth showing as the smile broadens impossibly wide. "A team! Meaning this is your final test before they grant you the mantle of First Librarian. ML Garfield wants to see us straight away."

"Oh my gods!" I shriek, throwing my hands up in the air and dancing around. "Are you serious?"

"As a heart attack," he mumbles, rubbing at his chest. "I ran all the way from the archives when Master Librarian Garfield called me in to tell me."

"Garfield called you himself?" I'm incredulous. ML Garfield rarely comes out of his keeping room, except for librarian meetings, I'm told. I've only ever met him a few times, and he looked through me like I was a wisp of wind.

"He did." Zakarias preens as he straightens the lapels of his collared shirt. "And he told me I could pick any of my Novices to assist."

"Knew I was your favorite." I wink.

Zakarias points toward my bedroom. "Get dressed quickly. He rang me half an hour ago, so..." His brown eyes dip pointedly to my robe.

That's all the hint I need to haul ass into my room and change.

I throw on my umber-colored Novice tunic, tying a sky-blue belt at my waist. Looking in my window, I fluff my shoulder-length peachy ombre waves, throw on a little matching lipstick, and thank the gods I took a shower this morning.

Tossing my notebooks and pens in my bag, I sling it over my shoulder and head for my small living room. Zakarias stands in the doorway, tapping his foot impatiently. The broad male looks so out of place in my pink and turquoise living room. I'd giggle if I wasn't so excited for his news.

I jog past him and out the door, hearing as he clicks the lock for me, and then we speed up the cobblestone streets toward the archives and the Master Librarian's Study, the long hall where ML Garfield's office is located.

Normally, I appreciate Moon Province's tropical beauty, but today, my mind is squarely on the gothic building that looms at the end of the high street.

"What do we know so far?" I question my mentor as he power walks past bustling shops, just as focused as I am on the library ahead.

"He was unusually cagey," Zakarias gripes. "Said he'd give me the details once we got there."

I grit my teeth but excitement fills me so fast I can barely stop from screaming with anticipation. I'm humming by the time we make it to the glossy black double doors that mark the archives, the non-public section of the library. A lone guard tips his white hat to us as we pass through the security station and head down a long, sunny hallway.

Zakarias makes a hard left down a hall I've never been down, the hall ML Garfield's office is on, and most of the First Librarians'. A gilded sign at the entryway marks it as the Master Librarian's Study. It's completely off-limits to Novices unless you've been requested and are accompanied by a First Librarian or the Master himself. The hall is lined with fancy, painted portraits of former Master Librarians. There are dozens of famed names I recognize from my Novice training.

I'm giddy with anticipation by the time we reach the end of the sun-drenched, windowed hall.

A giant maroon door looms before us, a white placard indicating we've reached the Office of the Honored Master Librarian Garfield.

If I can say one thing about the Library at Pengshur, they've got pomp and circumstance down. Everything about this place is designed to give it an air of dignity and academic excellence. I want into the inner circle so bad I'll do just about anything. Today marks a huge day in my slow-but-steady progress. I've been in the Novice program for eight years—it's definitely time to take the next step.

Zakarias reaches over and straightens my tunic, giving me a once over. I smile wryly. It's just as important to him that I be successful—not only because he adores me, but because it reflects well on him, too. I'm really fucking good at what I do, and he chose me for that reason.

My mentor takes a deep breath, then knocks twice.

"Come in," rings out a voice from inside, the tone gruff and impatient.

I wince as Zakarias swings the door open and sails through. Following behind him, I resist the urge to stare around at the office I've been dying to see inside for ages. Instead, I make direct eye contact with ML Garfield.

He sits behind a desk, except it's not a desk; it's more like a platform. It almost looks like where a judge sits in a courtroom. Stairs lead up to it from both sides, and the entire front is wood so I can't see what's behind it.

Garfield looks every bit the angry judge ready to mete out punishment.

Shit, I really need to learn to use the paging system.

Garfield's human, but his role at Pengshur is so important that he seems larger than life to me in his navy tunic, the scrolling Master Librarian tattoo visible on his pale cheek. Salt-and-pepper hair is slicked back effortlessly. If I wasn't freaking out about having made us late, I could definitely be ogling ML Garfield and his silver-fox good looks.

"I'll get straight to the point, as the clients are waiting," he begins in a harsh tone.

Next to me, Zakarias shifts from one foot to the other, but I lift my chin higher. This isn't the time to apologize or make excuses. I can offer a sincere apology after we get the assignment.

Garfield's sharp gaze moves to Zakarias. "Zakarias, I'm assigning you to a request from an old acquaintance of mine. His name is Arliss. He is looking for information on healing. Apparently, one of his companions was injured by a monster from the Tempang."

I open my mouth to ask a million questions. The Tempang? Nobody goes there, except Rama, who lived right on the edge until she built her city in the sky and flew that around instead. Shit, I wonder if this is connected to how our electricity came back on?

TEN

Garfield continues, "Arliss was unclear about their exact needs, but given your expertise in ancient methods of healing, I feel you're the best librarian to assist him. You chose this Novice as your second?" Eyes the color of the deep sea flash to me.

Zakarias nods. "Onmiel is exceptionally skilled in not only healing knowledge but languages and—"

"Good," Garfield interrupts. "I'll tell you now, he'll be accompanied by two of the monsters from the Temple Maze. You'll probably recognize them from the broadcasts, assuming you watched. One is a vampiri warrioress, and the other is Alpha Noire's youngest brother, Tenebris."

"Shit," blurts out Zakarias. "It's true, then. Rama must be gone? And the monsters are out of the maze?"

"I'll be blunt," Garfield mutters, ignoring the outburst. "Arliss is a wily asshole, and even though we have a long history together, he was not forthcoming on the details around the monsters escaping the maze. However, for the safety of the library and its librarians, I'd like to know more because I couldn't turn down this request. Arliss has been a Pengshur benefactor for a very long time. Assist as you can and find out what you can about the current situation with Rama and the maze's monsters. I want to know why and how the electricity is back on, and what future state I can expect for this province."

"You want us to spy on them?" I blurt.

Zakarias steps on my foot as Garfield sits back in his chair, steepling his hands together.

"I want you to *support* them, Novice Onmiel," he clarifies. "But find out what you can and report it to me. You wish to be a First Librarian yourself, do you not?"

When I nod to confirm, he opens his arms wide. "Your duty is not only to me, but the entirety of the librarian community. Arliss was vague on their needs. I know far less than I'd like, and while the library's duty is to assist, I cannot help but feel there is more to their story. That somehow, Rama herself is involved."

"Rama always left us alone, though," I counter because I feel like there's a hole in his tale and it's making the hair on my nape lift. "She never attacked us here, never took anyone from here. She focused on other provinces. Why worry now?"

ML Garfield stands, looming over the edge of his desk as he scowls at me. "Did she, Onmiel? If you feel that's the case, then I did my job of protecting the library very well."

Chilly fingers trace a path down my spine as I shudder and shrink back under the weight of his perusal. Is he saying what I think he's saying, that Rama was more involved here than I thought?

Zakarias steps in front of me. "We are up to this task, of course, ML Garfield. Are the clients in the Solarium now? We'll go immediately."

Garfield nods and gestures at the door. "There's a band for your novice just there. See she keeps it on while on assignment."

I dart to the door and grab the band, slipping it over my sleeve as I mutter a quick thank you. Then I follow Zakarias out without a backward glance. Even so, Garfield's eyes are on my back the entire way.

I can feel him.

~

"Onmiel, you must learn to hold your tongue," Zakarias chides the moment we're out the door.

I turn to him with a heated look.

"This assignment is huge," I agree, "and I'm grateful, but Garfield just dropped some very random information in our laps, Zakarias. You aren't the slightest bit worried? The monsters being out of the maze could mean a lot of things…" I think back to Evizel, the naga librarian, and how worried he was about what's happening.

Zakarias gestures impatiently up the hallway as we set off at a blistering pace.

"Yes, Onmiel. It means answers to the questions we've been asking ever since the power came back on."

"But—"

He cuts me off by raising a hand and giving me a warning look. "A First Librarian's duty is to the library, then to their partner librarians, and finally to themselves. In that order. Or have you forgotten our motto?"

"I haven't," I grumble as we pass through the entryway, where the motto is engraved over the door back out into the street. I give the engraved words a haughty look and fall quiet as we come to the steps of the eastern wing. We ascend them quickly and enter double doors, nearly jogging up the hallway until the Solarium comes into view.

The giant domed room sits between the archives and the First Librarian Hall. I love the Solarium, and it's the perfect place to meet the library's clients.

I sense monsters before I see the group. There's something about even half-breeds that sends butterflies tumbling around my belly. A sense of collected, barely-contained wildness hits me square in the chest as we round the corner. Three beings stand in the giant glass-domed room, looking up at the plate ceiling and the rain that's beginning to pour from the sky in buckets.

The first one to turn is a gigantic black male with long, braided hair. Bright blue eyes sparkle as thick, ebony lips part into a devious grin. His gaze travels from me to Zakarias and back, and the smile deepens.

I lift my chin and give him a polite smile. It is my sworn duty as mentee to a First Librarian to aid Zakarias in helping this group find what they came in search of. And I suppose to dig for answers for Garfield as well, although I'm not sure how I feel about taking on that mandate.

Next to the black male stands a striking vampiri woman with black braids that travel up over her scalp and down the side of her neck. They confirm her status as a vampiri king's First Warrior. I never watched when Rama broadcasted the nightly prey hunts in the maze, but I've heard the hushed whispers from other librarians. This female has killed dozens of beings in the last seven years, if she's who I think she is.

I resist the urge to shudder because she looks every inch a predator with her sharp, jet-black claws and focused, intense gaze. In person, her skin is nearly translucent. Her eyes are pure white, although I know a pupil and iris lie behind the protective covering. Thin, black lips purse into a frown when she notices my perusal.

The male smirks at her and reaches out to shake Zakarias's offered hand. "I'm Arliss, and this is my companion, Ascelin. That one..." He points to the third figure. "That is Tenebris, Alpha Noire's brother. Noire will be along in a day or two."

I turn to say hello but stop dead in my tracks at the third figure. He towers over the vampiri by a head or more, his huge body stacked with layers of muscle. I've never met a direwolf alpha in person, but nothing I've read about them prepared me for the way he dominates the room.

Broad, powerful shoulders taper to a trim waist. And gods, his ass is a work of art. Swallowing hard, I watch as he stares at the rain above us. It pelts the glass ceiling and slides down in giant rivulets. I know it's intoxicating; I've found myself doing the same thing from time to time. But I'm surprised he hasn't said anything or even noticed we've arrived.

"Tenebris?" The vampiri's voice is gentle as she addresses him, like he's a wounded bird.

Perhaps he's the one who was attacked, and they're hoping to find an answer here. Not all injuries produce visibly obvious wounds.

I straighten my shoulders, determined to be as helpful as possible.

The alpha male cocks his head to the side, and I catch a flash of amber eyes before he turns the rest of his body. Time seems to slow, or maybe it just does for me as I gaze at how fucking gorgeous he is from the front.

A thin tee does nothing to hide thick pectoral muscles or the dips and valleys of every visible ab. My throat goes as dry as the deserts of Dest, but I manage to drag my eyes quickly back up. Shit, he's looking at me. I expect to find wry amusement in his gaze, maybe wary interest, or even anger that I was staring at his beautiful midsection...but there's nothing there.

His pale eyes are blank of any emotion at all. Dark lashes flutter, framing how shockingly beautiful he is.

Where most men who meet me for the first time would at least give me a quick once-over, this male does nothing of the sort. Those stunning eyes move from me to the vampiri, who claps him on the shoulder.

"Tenebris, these are the librarians assigned to help us."

He nods once, but then those eyes go right back up to the rain as it pours onto the glass ceiling.

The vampiri sighs and grits her teeth.

I'm not sure what the issue is, but I am godsdamned determined to make my first assignment a fruitful one. These beings came here with a need, and so help me, I will fill it.

CHAPTER SIX
TENEBRIS

I don't know what sort of greeting I expected at the famous Pengshur library, but after Noire's threats, I half expected a red carpet. Or at the very least, the help of the Master Librarian himself. Garfield, I think his name is. Instead, we're presented with a First Librarian in a black tunic and his Novice, if I'm remembering their color system correctly. She looks barely my age, although she stands with the confidence of an older woman.

The rain pounding on the glass ceiling of the Solarium suits my mood. It mutes other sounds, soothing the pressure in my chest. I always loved the rain as a child, but then I didn't see it for seven years in the maze.

Somewhere along the way here, I've gone from inconsolable grief and exhaustion to anger, and that anger has set in good and hard. I'm furious at myself, furious at my mate, and furious at the world that fucked her so badly, she became the monster she had to be to survive.

So, I do something I started on the way here in an effort to distance my mind from her death.

I didn't see the rain for seven years because *she* imprisoned me.

She imprisoned my family. *She* was an utter and complete asshole, and I had to kill her.

Still, thinking that feels disloyal, and it sends jagged strikes of pain through my gut so cutting I resist the urge to drop to both knees.

I grit my teeth and try to follow along, but it's hard to focus. The librarians introduce themselves. The male is Zaka—something. I don't catch the female's name at all. They gesture for us to follow them out of the room we're in. Ascelin paces behind me, watchful and wary as ever. She's worried I'm falling apart and unpredictable, especially after the scene earlier with Arliss.

She's right, of course.

When I was younger, I'd have given anything to make a trip to see Pengshur and visit the famous library. Now? Now, I don't fucking care. I'm somewhere between numb and enraged, but my emotions flip-flop one minute to the next. I think if I stop moving, everything will come crashing down, and I'll fall to the ground. I might never get back up if that happens.

The tall male librarian leads us down a long, windowed hall away from the big room they called the Solarium. Outside, foliage spills from hundreds of terra-cotta pots in a garden.

Diana would love it.

The thought enters my mind and dashes away again.

But then it comes back, curling around my consciousness.

Diana who faked her way into the maze under false pretenses, knowing my brother Noire was hers. Diana who screamed for me when Rama's monstrous machines dragged me up into the sky and away from my pack. Diana who's fighting against a terrible wound the Volya inflicted on her while I struggled to understand why my own mate would drug me.

Grinding my teeth, I let the anger flow through my system, and I visualize my pack omega. She's never done anything but try to help my family. She risked her life to save mine over and over again. She came onto Paraiso, Rama's sky island, to get me back.

I can do this for her. I can focus on finding a cure. If anyone in my pack is capable of understanding the knowledge here at Peng-shur, it's me. Because the truth is I studied monsters for a long time in the maze, and my mate fed my addiction to knowledge by sending me books I'd enjoy.

I soaked up that knowledge, and now I need to use it to help.

Ascelin is a quiet presence behind me, but I wish she'd stop. I'm not going to take off running. I'm done trying to escape, for now at least. I'll help find a cure for Diana. But I don't know what I'll do after that. Maybe I'll take one of Arliss's many vehicles and go on a road trip, just disappear for a while.

Maybe I'll go back to Nacht, Rama's mountain city. It's where we spent our first nights together. It's where we cemented our—

I banish that thought the moment I have it, shaking my head. I can't go back to the dark, ominous city, right on the edge of the Tempang. I can't stand in the spot where I ripped her head from her shoulders. I don't think I'll ever be able to see Nacht again without thinking about killing her.

A door opens ahead, and when I lift my eyes, the female librarian is smiling at me as she holds it open, indicating I should go through.

She only comes up to my lower chest, but her face is uplifted as she smiles at me. Her eyes are kind. They're a shocking shade of pale gray, a weird combination with hair that starts at her scalp as a dark orange but fades to peach at the tips. It sort of matches her dark orange Novice tunic. I wonder if she did it purposefully. Maybe librarians have a whole style code I'm not aware of.

She tucks a strand of it behind one ear absentmindedly. When I step through the door, our eyes meet. Hers don't go to the ground, but she nips at the edge of her lip.

Sighing, I look from her into a tiny courtyard. It's full of plants, too. They burst from every surface, even covering the ground like a carpet. There's a large stone table in the middle of the room, and the male librarian sits at the head. The female rounds the table to hover at his side, grabbing a notebook from a bag slung over her shoulder.

Ascelin leans against the only spot in the wall with no plants, but Arliss and I sit. I guess they want another meeting.

The male opens his arms wide. "We'll quickly sync on your project here, and depending on any additional details you provide, Onmiel and I will begin our work. Master Librarian Garfield has already apprised us of what you're looking for at a high level." He gives us a concerned look. "But we need more information. I understand you want to know more about healing, but we need to know about the injury itself. How was it inflicted? How long has it been? What healing have you tried? Any details you can provide would be most helpful in directing our research."

Arliss sighs and steeples his fingers. "Volya. Just over a week. We've tried everything, and I have an extensive array of healing options at my fingertips. She heals because she's an omega, and then a day later, the wounds reopen. She is weak and does not have much time."

The librarian nods, but at his side, the female seems frozen at Arliss's words. When I narrow my eyes and observe her, her muscles relax, and she begins writing in her notebook.

"Not much is known about the Volya," the male librarian shares, glancing over at his assistant. "Onmiel, you're excellent with monster history. What do you think?"

She looks up, seemingly surprised he asked her opinion. But she turns to us with a serious expression, one scrawny forearm resting on the table as she lightly taps her pen. "The Volya are secretive. There's never been a half-blooded Volya to anyone's knowledge, for instance. They've always remained in the Tempang, so anything we have on them is from ancient travelers who braved the forest before the monster-human wars began."

Arliss huffs. "Are you saying there aren't answers to be found here? That would certainly be a first."

She shakes her head. "There are mentions of Volya scattered in hundreds of books throughout Pengshur, but it will take some time to find them." She looks directly at Arliss. "May I be blunt?"

"Please do," Ascelin purrs, pushing off the wall, "because my Chosen One's life hangs in the balance, and if we cannot find help for her here, we need to try something else."

The Novice purses her lips but nods. "It's possible there is help here, I can't be sure because I've never deeply looked into the resources we have on Volya. If the knowledge exists anywhere, it'll be here at Pengshur. But the reality is that your best bet is probably to find the Volya who hurt your friend, and to bargain with them for a cure."

"Not possible," Ascelin snaps. "We need another way."

There's a tense moment of silence, and it's so filled with worry for Diana that I feel my own mind receding back into the corners of my headspace. I'm trying to be angry, to push myself into that next stage of grief. But I keep drifting back to exhaustion.

"There's something else," Ascelin murmurs, tossing a paper on the stone tabletop. "A prophecy about the Chosen One. We always thought we knew the whole thing, but it turns out there were two halves. The second is in a language so ancient, there is not a vampiri alive who knows it. I'm hopeful it will tell us something that can save her."

The male, Zakarias, frowns. "How is a direwolf omega your leader?"

"You watched us in the maze, I presume?" Ascelin's voice is tense as I roll my shoulders and close my eyes to ward away the memories. When the male doesn't respond, she snarls.

"Then you'll have watched Diana risk her life to save her mate and his pack. And somewhere along the way, she found it in the goodness of her heart to save my court, to save younglings who have never seen the light of day. She carries my king's spirit, and so we will tear this place apart if it means finding an answer for her."

I open my eyes, sensing focus the way all predators do. When I look to my right, the peach-haired librarian is looking at me, but then she flicks those gray eyes over to Ascelin.

"I'm excellent with languages, so I'll start there." She looks at her mentor. "Zakarias, is that okay with you? I think I can be most helpful with that. You're better on the healing front."

He nods once but still looks uneasy.

If this obviously terrified male is the best Pengshur has to offer, I'm less than impressed.

"Does it bother you that we were in the maze, and now we're out?" My tone is laced with alpha edge. He shrinks back on his stool, shaking his head.

I focus on his gaze, or rather the lack of eye contact. He's looking everywhere but at me.

This male gives off a very prey-like aura, which makes my natural predatory instincts thump in my chest. Standing, I loom over him. He looks up, pupils flaring wide as his heart pounds in his chest. I'd almost swear he's about to start running, and I haven't chased prey since the maze. I'm surprisingly ready to run someone down, to rip someone to shreds. I want the destruction I mete out to match the way I feel inside.

I'm surprised when the female librarian steps in front of him, placing a hand on my chest. She pushes gently against me, the faint hint of a warning, until I look down at her. When I do, peachy lips tip into a smile.

"The library's systems are still coming back online now that the power is back. It will take Zakarias some time to find books on the Volya. Why don't I give you a quick tour and show you where you can work? Then we can tackle the prophecy issue."

For a moment, we stare at one another. I dare her with an imperious glare to push me again. But unlike the cowering male, this woman's smile simply grows broader. She's either incredibly brave or incredibly stupid.

Ascelin snorts. "You're just going to tackle the prophecy issue like *that*?" She snaps her black-clawed fingers together.

The librarian laughs. "Well, it's not likely to be that quick, but I'll do my best to impress."

Ascelin's black brows tilt upward.

Arliss rises to a stand. "A third request, then, once the first two are fulfilled."

That I pay attention to. I know Noire's curious why Arliss wanted in on this mission. It seems he's about to tell us.

The male librarian seems to have gathered his wits at that point, and he stands to match everyone else. "How can we help, Arliss?"

Arliss's normal leer is gone, replaced by a neutral look. "Information on carrow, if you have it."

Both librarians hiss in a breath, but it's the female who speaks first, her tone urgent.

"Why?"

Arliss shrugs. "My reasons are my own. But I'd like to learn more."

There's an awkward moment of silence before Ascelin snaps her fingers again "Let us go. Time is short, and Diana is fighting for her life."

Her life.

Those two words rush through my system like a dagger stabbing right into my heart. I think about how I watched the confusion and hurt and life die out of my mate's eyes. Lives are such finnicky things. They can be long. They can be short.

And I can't seem to find the energy to care about mine.

CHAPTER SEVEN

ONMIEL

This assignment is getting more interesting by the minute, although I sense Zakarias is deeply unsettled by our clients. We work with monsters and half-breed librarians all the time, but this group is different. Raw power ripples from them. I'd give my left arm that the black male is a carrow or suspects he is and wants to confirm it. I haven't seen him up close enough to tell if he carries the typical tattoo, but carrow are such an obscure and unusual monster to request information on.

I try not to envision these monsters killing people in the Temple Maze, but it's hard not to. They're dangerous, and their predatory awareness is obvious in the way they keep an eye on their surroundings. Plus, the way Tenebris loomed over Zakarias? I thought my mentor might shit his pants and run. It's unlike him to behave that way around a client.

Still, this is my first official assignment, and I'm really fucking excited.

I have so many questions for the group. How did they escape Rama's Temple Maze? Is Rama actually dead? How and who killed her? Is that why the power's back on? Then there's a long line of questions about the Volya. Volya don't leave the Tempang forest in the north of Lombornei, so how did they come into contact with the monsters? I'd wager all of the answers are tied together by some neat and pretty bow, but it doesn't seem they're going to be forthcoming.

Holding back my enthusiasm, I smile at our clients.

Zakarias grabs my hand and pulls me just outside. He looks terribly worried as he glances back through the door at them, then down at me.

"I'm concerned about this assignment, Onmiel." He peeks around the doorframe a second time, and I imagine all three monsters looking over at him.

"They can hear us," I remind him in a whisper. "And I'm not afraid. This is an excellent chance to help the pack that might have saved our continent from a psychopath. We should be grateful to them, right?"

He rapidly blinks several times , but his big chest heaves. I never took Zakarias for a weenie, so I'm a little surprised to find him so reticent right now.

When I nod my assent, he straightens his black tunic.

"I'll head to the archives and see about digging up books on the Volya, and we'll go from there. Are you sure you want to remain on this assignment, Onmiel?" His voice is wry and weary as if he's already tired from what lies ahead of us.

"Absolutely," I confirm, turning back into the room before he can remind me he thinks this is a terrible idea.

Opening my arms wide, I smile at the clients again. "FL Zakarias is off to start his research, so let's do a quick tour, grab a working room, and get you settled."

The vampiri woman grunts, and gestures toward the door. The males look at one another, and something unspoken passes between them.

Sighing, I fold my hands in front of my stomach. "This will go far better if you're open and honest with me about your needs. I sense you're holding back, but if there's critical information, it could help us find an answer quicker."

Arliss looks up at me with a shit-eating grin, the type of smile I'm sure has wooed many women into his bed. But that's not me, taken with a man who's so overtly sexual. I'm into nerdy, so he's barking up the wrong tree.

"You'll forgive us if we have trust issues, Novice Onmiel," he purrs. "If a time comes when you need to have additional information, we'll provide it, then."

I hold back a harrumph as I purse my lips and turn to the vampiri because of these three, she seems most focused on their injured packmate. When I lean in close, her all-white eyes narrow, black lips parting to reveal translucent black fangs. Gods, I bet she was terrifying in the maze. Vampiri hunt in packs, and I can just imagine her ripping someone to shreds with those teeth.

For the millionth time, I'm glad I never watched the televised nightly hunt. Hearing about it in hushed tones was enough.

She doesn't frighten me. "I trust you to know when I need further information, First Warrioress. You'll let me know, even when they're being dumb?"

She lets out a barking laugh, throwing her head back as the sharp noise slices through the air. When she's done laughing, she claps me jovially on the shoulder. "You can count on me, Novice."

"Onmiel is fine," I counter, giving her a stern look. I hate being called "Novice" because it reminds me that's what I *am*, even though I'm the best damn librarian here on several critical topics, ancient languages being my specialty.

I hear Zakarias's footsteps fade away as I gesture for them to join me. We leave the lush meeting room and follow Zakarias up the hall toward the archives. I pray I won't be embarrassed and get stopped by the guards if my mentor isn't with me, but it should be fine since I was assigned to this group. The band around my arm confirms it.

Still, as we approach the desk with a burly guardian seated behind it, I cross my fingers that he won't stop me and make me feel foolish.

I breathe a sigh of relief when he gestures us through, handing me a small manila envelope. Pushing glossy double doors open, I step into the archives, turn to my clients and open the envelope. Inside are three round metal pins, embossed with the library's motto. I dump them into my palm and show them to Arliss, Tenebris, and Ascelin.

"These pins go on your shirt. They'll mark you as guests and grant you access to the archives, which are off-limits to the general public. You won't be able to remove the majority of the books in the archives from their shelves as they're spelled to stay put, but you can walk around and view some of the research tools. I'll show you that in a minute. Let's go ahead and put these on."

I pass them out before pointing up the long hall ahead of us. "The archives are generally a quiet area. It's frowned upon to interrupt a librarian who's in the middle of their research. That being said, everyone here is helpful, so if FL Zakarias and I aren't around, you can ask another librarian to assist you."

"What is the point of being assigned to you if you may not be around?" Ascelin questions, eyes narrowed again. So suspicious, this one.

I give her a quick wink. "Even librarians have to pee sometimes, First Warrioress."

She snorts as if the idea of stopping anything to urinate is totally ridiculous.

I begin leading the group past a long row of books as I point fifteen stories above us. "Every floor up to the fifteenth is full of books and study rooms with the exception of the fifth floor, which is for librarians on assignment. It's living quarters as well as a garden. While Zakarias and I are assigned to you, I'll live at the library twenty-four hours a day."

"Zakarias won't?" Arliss questions, glancing up at the barely visible archives' ceiling.

Smiling, I shake my head. "As FL Zakarias's Novice, it's my role to clean up at the end of the day and to be on call for whatever you need. If something comes up, I'll notify him and he'll be here within fifteen minutes. We are dedicated to finding you answers." I look around at the group. "Let's finish up a quick tour, then I'd like to dive into everything straight away. You're welcome to explore the archives on your own if you want to."

Tenebris, who's been looking around at the books in awe, glances down at me, eyes the color of whiskey focusing with sudden intensity. "Thank you," he growls, and it's so low and sensual, all I can imagine is that big head between my thighs, thanking me for coming all over his pretty mouth.

Gods, I've got to get it together.

"You're welcome, Tenebris," I purr instead before turning and striding up the hallway. The row of books ends at a gigantic circular table, an ancient map of Lombornei that's been at Pengshur since it was built.

"The Magelang Map has lived at Pengshur for nearly ten centuries." I point to the wooden platform around it, a space between it and the map allowing for librarians to sit and study it. As we watch, a First Librarian seats himself, pinching in on the map's leathery surface to zoom in on a particular part of Lombornei.

I keep my voice low so I don't bother him. "This map shows the location of every person, city, and town on the continent, and is often used in research."

Arliss steps to the opposite side of the map and hunches over it, grinning as he plops a finger onto the map's surface. "Oasis."

Ascelin scoffs. "We could scarcely find you, yet if we had come here, we'd have found your precise location. That is frustrating."

Arliss shrugs. "I was trying to attract scholars with dirty minds, Ascelin, not beautiful vampiri First Warrioresses. I've always allowed my location to be shared with Pengshur."

I'm trying to keep up with their banter, but I'm obviously missing something. "Everyone's location is shared with Pengshur," I correct gently as Ascelin looks over at me.

"What about Rama's sky city, Paraiso?"

The blood freezes in my veins as Tenebris growls and looks at a stack of books, drifting away from us to examine their spines.

I had hoped not to cover the topic of Rama with them because there's so much that's unknown about what's going on, and because she had very little to do with Pengshur—I thought. ML Garfield's comments this morning have me thinking there's more to it, but I'm not sure yet.

"Even Paraiso," I acquiesce, leaning over by Arliss to scroll the map in my direction and spell it to zoom on the coast of Vinituvari. "It has been there for several weeks now, although that's not unusual."

"So, you kept tabs on her?" Arliss's deep voice is curious, blue eyes focused on mine even as Ascelin glances at Tenebris.

"I wouldn't call it tabs," I hedge. "Merely a curiosity, although I know there were some librarians here who watched her movements far more closely. But again, this province was unscathed by her, thank the gods."

Tenebris shoves his hands in his pockets and starts walking up a row of books as I resist the urge to call for him. Instead, I look at Arliss and Ascelin. "I had hoped to avoid this topic, given you and Tenebris were trapped in the maze. It's clear he doesn't want to speak about it, so I'm curious why you brought it up in front of him?"

Ascelin shifts back at my direct line of questioning, but tactful sincerity is a hallmark trait of a good librarian. The vampiri shares a look with Arliss, but he remains silent as she turns back to me. "We do not avoid the topic of Rama simply because we were imprisoned by her. Things are...complicated." She says nothing else, though. I can't help but wonder what part of their story they aren't sharing, and if it might have implications for our research.

I have a million questions, but Ascelin turns and strides up the row of books after Tenebris.

As she goes, Arliss grins and stares at her ass. When I catch him looking, he huffs. "What?"

Letting out a beleaguered groan, I leave him and trail my monster clients up a row of books, wondering why my first assignment couldn't have been something nice and easy. It scares me a little bit how something deep in my heart is thrilled about that.

CHAPTER EIGHT

TENEBRIS

I had forgotten how books smell. I had them in my room in the maze, but not this many. It's different.

As I walk slowly up the long row, perusing the beautifully bound leather titles, I can't resist leaning in to scent them. Gods, I love that smell. Without thinking, I reach for one entitled *On the History of the Mermaid Clans*, wondering if I might learn about my sister-in-law's people in it.

When I tug at it, it doesn't move. Right. Spelled. The female librarian mentioned that. It's disappointing though because I'd love to take that book and curl up with it for a day, to lose myself in its pages and not think about my real life. Part of me desperately hoped that coming to Pengshur meant I could hide from reality while Ascelin and Arliss sort out what Diana needs.

But then a wave of guilt slaps me in the face. I owe it to her to focus on finding a cure.

The female librarian stops next to me, looking up with a soft smile. She whispers under her breath, snapping and moving her fingers in a series of motions, and then she pulls the book I was looking at from the shelf and hands it to me. At the bottom of the spine, a golden number appears, embossing itself on the faded surface. She presses her forefinger to the number, and it glows gold for one brief moment.

Looking back up at me, she grins. "Had to catalog it on the list of books for this project. And to remember where to return it to once you're done." She gives me a wink before indicating we should follow again. Tucking the book under my arm, I rejoin the group. Ascelin and Arliss trail behind me.

The librarian smiles and points out to both sides with long, skinny arms. "The archives sunburst out from the Magelang Map. From there, there's a secondary ring that circles the archives' center. After that ring, the sunburst continues. Ten concentric rings make up the Pengshur archives. The public section of the library is even larger than that, housed in the building next to this one. From anywhere in the archives, you can follow the yellow arrows inlaid into the floor and get to the public side."

She turns and begins to walk backward. "It's unlikely a book we need will be on the public side, but it has happened from time to time, so we'll check publicly available books once we make our way through the archive collection." The librarian turns, and we follow her silently until we reach the outer edge.

I never imagined Pengshur would be so enormous. There must be millions of books here. I'd like to disappear and wander the ornate rows for a while, smelling them all.

The female stops in front of a tall door, its chunky golden handle reflecting bright sunlight coming in from somewhere.

She points at the handle. "These reading rooms line the outer wall of the archives, going up the first three stories. If a handle is gold, then the room is available. If it's black," she points at the next room over, "then someone is using that room. You can find a room you like, and I can assign it for the duration of your stay, or if you'd like me to pick for you, I'm happy to do so."

She swings the door open, and we get a look inside. The floor is a zigzag pattern of beautifully inlaid wood and a large wooden table takes up most of the room. The far side has a round window to the outside, and each side of the room is lined with empty shelves. A fireplace in the corner gives it a cozy, hidden library vibe—if I was feeling into such a thing.

"We do not care which room we get, Novice," Ascelin growls.

"Onmiel," she corrects. Ah, that's her name.

"I didn't think so," she chirps, "so I'll assign this one because it's got sufficient space to spread out." She steps into the room and places her hand flat on the wall, closing her eyes as she whispers yet another incantation. It's odd to me that she seems so unfazed by us, whereas her mentor was practically terrified. Maybe she just doesn't know much about monsters.

Her whisper is low, her voice throaty. It lacks the femininity of Rama's, but there's something far friendlier about Onmiel. Her ears are ever so slightly pointed, delicate and long. She must have monster blood somewhere in her lineage, although I don't sense that just looking at her. She appears human enough.

Arliss and Ascelin follow me into the room, and Ascelin perches herself on the table. "I am anxious to begin. Is there anything of the library we have not seen that we must?"

"Oh," Onmiel continues with a helpful smile. "There's plenty more to see, and if you were here for fun, I could spend two days showing you around. But I know you're ready to help your friend. What is her name, again, so I can address her properly?"

"Diana," Ascelin murmurs, and for half a second, I think I see tears in her eyes. But that can't be. I've never seen Ascelin cry. I don't think she even knows how. The tears are there and gone in a flash, but there's an obviously distressed expression on her angular features.

Loud footsteps break through my thoughts. The male librarian shows up with an armful of books. He places them gently on the table and nods at Onmiel.

"Tour's all done, we were about to begin discussing the translation," she tells him, her expression expectant.

He looks around, and I realize once again he's afraid. The unmistakable scent of fear rolls off him, reminding me of chasing marks with Noire in the maze. I suck in a deep breath, not really meaning to, and he shrinks back a little.

Ascelin joins my side and takes a book from the stack, examining it before she places it harshly back down. "You saw us kill in the maze, did you not?"

The male nods, and Onmiel joins him, a resolute partner by his side.

Ascelin senses the same thing I do: this male is deeply afraid of us. She sneers, letting her fangs descend as a drop of venom makes its way hastily to the floor. "You know what we are capable of, Zakarias. Perhaps it would be best not to dilly-dally."

He gulps audibly, but rounds the table, giving us a wide berth as he sets a book down in front of Arliss. "Our primary tome on carrow, Arliss. If you can tell me what you're looking for, I'll examine it for—"

"No need," Arliss interrupts, taking the book and heading for the door. "I'll be back later." Without another word, he leaves the room, jerking the door shut behind him.

Ascelin and I know he's a carrow, but I can't imagine what sort of research he needs to do. I ponder it for a moment, but then exhaustion sets in.

Onmiel turns to Ascelin. "Show me what you've got that needs translating, and I'll begin right away."

There's so much to do, and so much that hinges on us healing Diana. We've got to figure out what the second half of her prophecy means, and how to heal her at the same time. I'm sure the two are connected, and there's every chance the news won't be good.

I can't do more bad news right now, even though I'm struggling to find enough emotion to care about anything at all.

I sit in a chair in the corner and open my book, watching as Ascelin and Onmiel take seats at the end of the table closest to me. Ascelin pulls a piece of paper from her pocket and carefully hands it to Onmiel. "Long ago, the vampiri received a prophecy that our king would give his life to help a direwolf and that the direwolf would then allow the king to be born anew. That part of the prophecy happened during our escape from the maze. My king's spirit lives inside Diana Ayala."

Onmiel is silent, but it's easy to see the wheels of her mind turning. "I need the first half, written in its original language, if you can."

"Of course," Ascelin purrs. "Give me paper and a utensil and I will write it for you."

The librarian stands and opens a drawer in the bookshelves, bringing out pen and paper for Ascelin, who continues, "It turns out there was a second half, received by a vampiri seer, but it is in an ancient language even she did not know. She is hundreds of years old," Ascelin grumps. "It is unfathomable to me that this language is so old, she could not understand, but here we are."

Onmiel opens the paper and squints, then looks up at Ascelin.

The vampiri grimaces. "Because she did not know the language, she could only write it phonetically as she received it."

Onmiel sighs and sits back in her chair. "And there's no video or anything from when this person received the prophecy, I assume? Was it the same person who received the first half?"

"No, and yes," Ascelin growls, tapping razor-sharp claws on the desk.

Onmiel reads the words aloud, but they don't sound familiar to me either. She turns to Ascelin with a frown. "Do the words sound remotely vampiri to you at all?"

"No, so your guess is as good as mine, Novice."

"Onmiel," the librarian corrects once again.

Ascelin shoots me a grin, and I realize she's just fucking with the cheerful librarian.

I can't find it in myself to care as my thoughts turn to my dead mate and the loss of her touch.

"*T*enebris." *A sultry purr caresses my ears, my cock stirring slowly to life. How the fuck can it be interested in something right now? Everything hurts. Was I just fighting? A haze clouds my vision while a tight pull yanks at my chest.*

I reach down to feel for a wound but find something metallic attached to my pectoral muscles. I don't feel worry, though. I just feel...safe.

Someone says my name again, and her tone encourages me to move. I sit up and notice I'm in bed and the sheets below me are a black cool satin. They feel good against my skin. A blooming, warm sensation spreads in my chest, and my heartbeat picks up. It's almost like a sense of knowing that something important is happening to me. I can't seem to clear the haze in my mind, but I'm focused. Focused enough to swing my legs over the bed and find the woman that voice belongs to.

I register long, dark hair and elegant, angular features first. In the back of my mind, there's a niggling moment of uncertainty and surprise. A prickly sensation pokes at my chest, and that worry dissipates.

Desire unfurls in my gut, and my balls draw up tight against my body, my cock throbbing. My fangs descend as my focus narrows on the stunning woman in front of me. She's older than me by a bit, and it's so intoxicating I can barely stand it.

"Come here," I command, knowing, somehow, that she'll comply. The heady, hot sensation in my chest intensifies until I feel like I'll die if she doesn't come close. What does she smell like? I've got to know. Right fucking now.

Red lips part into a sensual smile, and she stalks gracefully across the space between us until she's almost close enough to touch. She stays just out of reach, though, almost teasing me. That won't do; it won't do at all.

Growling, I snap out with one hand, grabbing her wrist and yanking it to her lower back. I splay my fingers over the curve of her ass and pull her between my thighs.

She lets out a growl to match mine, this spitfire of a woman whose soul seems to call to me.

"Mine," I snarl as I bury my face in her throat and suck in great, heaving breaths of her.

"Yes, Tenebris," she purrs. "I am."

. . .

The squeak of a chair moving across the floor snaps me out of that memory. I can barely catch my breath. I don't even want to think about what came next. I can't go down the path of remembering how we bound each other.

Standing, I focus out the circular window. The city of Pengshur bustles below, people going about their daily lives, enjoying, loving, and experiencing as if my world didn't end a week ago, as if everything I loved isn't gone forever.

CHAPTER NINE

ONMIEL

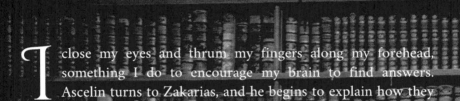

I close my eyes and thrum my fingers along my forehead, something I do to encourage my brain to find answers. Ascelin turns to Zakarias, and he begins to explain how they can tackle the research together.

In the window, Tenebris stands silently, appearing lost in thought.

I stroke my pointer finger down my nose as I think. I've never translated something outside of its original language like this. Finally, I decide to read it aloud and send it to the other librarians here who specialize in obscure languages. Maybe one of them can point me in the right direction.

Whatever this language is, I've never heard anything like it. That's unusual, but there are so many variations and dialects of languages, it's not totally unheard of. Most librarians who focus on languages begin with just a few and then work on tackling the rest. At this point, I'm proficient in about twenty-five languages, but there are hundreds more to begin studying.

I stand and open another drawer, pulling out a small data tablet. Now that we have power back, this will be far easier. A week ago, I would have had to seek each librarian out in person to do this.

Reading the prophecy aloud, I send it to the identification codes of several librarian friends, including a few Novices like myself.

After that, I look at Ascelin. "I need to do some research in another wing of the library. Will you be alright here for an hour or so?"

"I'll go with you," Tenebris growls from the window, turning into the room as Ascelin's frown fades. He doesn't wait for an answer, just prowls out of the room without a backward glance.

Zakarias looks up at me, but he's careful not to bely any of his feelings as he looks back down at the stack of books on the desk.

Ascelin nods, too-white eyes narrowing. Having gained her consent, I leave the group to meet Tenebris. Light filters down from far above us, illuminating his face as he stands in front of a row of bookshelves, muscly arms crossed.

I've always been an empathetic person; I'm excellent at reading people. It's part of why Zakarias loves me so much. He's a brilliant librarian, but he lacks the people skills that come more naturally to me. Which is very obvious to me given how distressed he seems around our current clients.

"Are you alright?" I question the big alpha, who drops his arms, schooling his face to neutral.

"I'm fine, Novice," he growls.

"Onmiel."

"I'm fine, Onmiel."

"You don't seem fine," I press on. "Whatever's bothering you, I probably can't fix it, but if you want to talk about it, I'm here. Okay?"

"That another service provided by the library?" His voice is wounded and sarcastic as his blank expression becomes a glower.

"Not hardly." I laugh. "Most librarians are awkward at best and antisocial at worst. You've probably noticed that with FL Zakarias. I've always been a little different, I guess. I'm just saying, if you need a friend, I'm here for that."

When he doesn't immediately respond, I resist the urge to offer a hug. If anyone ever looked like they could use one, it's the monstrous male standing in front of me. I remind myself that he spent years in the maze. He was a child there, if I've done the math correctly after researching Pack Ayala. Tenebris would have had to be...ten, maybe eleven when Rama threw the Ayala brothers into the maze?

The little I know of the Ayala Pack is that they're a band of thugs, and they controlled the resource-rich province of Siargao, and thereby, the rest of Lombornei. Still, I can't imagine a child trapped in there with all the rest of the monsters.

"Come on," I encourage, waving a hand over my shoulder as I walk along the outer rim of the library. "You'll be an excellent assistant for an hour."

"Didn't say I came to assist you," he grouses.

I chuckle. "Oh, but you did. Some of the books in here are heavy as shit, and you've got super big arms. I can carry more back to the room if you'll help me." I turn to walk backward as the hint of a smile flashes across his handsome features. It's gone as quickly as I notice it, though.

He doesn't agree, but he doesn't take off into the stacks by himself either, so I'll consider it a win. Ten minutes later, we're nearly to the other side of the library and back down a row of books on ancient languages.

"Okay." I rub my hands together. "It stands to reason that if a vampiri received the prophecy, the language is some ancient form of vampiri, even though Ascelin didn't recognize it. It's as good a place to start as any."

Tenebris doesn't answer, but holds out his palms. I begin stacking books in them, trying not to stare at the way his biceps bulge as I weigh him down. I spell a dozen more off the shelves and hand them to him, and I don't miss the way his eyes light up as I fill his arms.

Gods, he's a nerd. I just know it. I'm about to tickle his nerd fancy, then.

I grin. "Most of the books in the library are made out of bovine leather, something like ninety percent." I waggle my brows. "But a lot of the older books are bound in skins from all sorts of monsters, including direwolves."

Ten scoffs, but looks down as I continue loading him with books. He's holding twenty or so at this point.

He looks lovingly at the stack, a curious expression on his face. I nibble at my lip before speaking because it's not really my place, except he looks almost entranced. "You know, you could apply to become a Novice here, if books are your thing. Which they seem to be based on the way you're staring."

He lets out a harrumph, but doesn't immediately answer. I give him a long moment, even shooting him a helpful wink of encouragement, but he looks away.

"Alright, then," I chirp. "Time for coffee and chocolate, and then we'll go back to the research room and dive in."

"Coffee and chocolate?" His tone is flat, and it's not lost on me that maybe he hasn't had a coffee or chocolate in a really long time. But if I'm anything, it's an optimist.

"A chocolate a day keeps the doctor away." I shrug.

"Not how the saying goes," he grumbles, but he hoists the book stack higher and follows me without further complaint.

Ten minutes later, we've visited the library's cafe and picked up coffee and snacks for the whole team. It might seem frivolous to do that when they're researching something so pressing and important, but they don't realize Zakarias and I truly will be here at all hours until their answer is found. We're either researching or assisting clients all the time.

A librarian's work is never done. Learn in order to guide.

That's our motto for a reason.

When we return to the room, I hold the door for Tenebris, who stalks through and sets the books carefully on the desk. I follow him with the drinks and food, placing it in the middle of the table as I look at Ascelin and point. "That one's the Type-A latte, a vampiri barista made it when I asked what you might like."

She sneers but takes the drink and sniffs as I hand Zakarias his usual. He takes it without looking up as I place his favorite scone next to him on a plate. It's my job to keep him well-fueled and in possession of everything he needs to do his job well for our clients.

"Thank you, Miel," he mumbles as he flips a page, shoving his reading glasses higher up his nose.

Tenebris is already seated at the far end of the worktable, thumbing through a book absentmindedly. His dark brows furrow as he scowls but continues to flip the pages.

This assignment is going to be hard and prolonged if I can't break through to these folks and get them to open up a bit. I sense Zakarias and I have about half the information we need to really find an answer, but I'm determined to chisel away at their reticence with my sunny-ass disposition until I get what I need to figure it out.

They'll never see me coming.

CHAPTER TEN
TENEBRIS

O nmiel lays out a plan of attack, handing Ascelin and me both books on languages. She tells us what to look for. I admit it feels like hunting for a needle in a haystack.

Still, I lose myself for hours in the pile of books in front of me, only putting one down if the librarian requires it for something. She has an obsessed look on her face, and it makes me wonder if I looked like that to Noire all the times he let himself in my room to interrupt my reading.

Of course, he didn't know I was reading books sent to me by Rama, and he never questioned where I got them. Even I didn't realize what any of it meant at the time. How I'd wake up one day and know she was fated by the gods to be mine.

That thought produces a stabbing pain in my gut, so I stretch my arms over my head, letting my head fall back as I flex from side to side.

When I shift upright, Onmiel's eyes flick from my core up to my face. She bites her lip thoughtfully but looks over to Ascelin. "Ascelin, do you know how these words are pronounced when they were received? There's not a recording, but did you get this parchment directly from the person who received the prophecy?"

Arliss strolls back into the room with a cell phone in hand. "Nope, she was riding my thick cock at the time, but you may call Firenze to ask. He was there with the woman who spoke the prophecy."

Ascelin sputters and swipes at Arliss with her claws out. He sidesteps her with a smirk as he dials a number on his phone.

Onmiel doesn't miss a beat, taking the now-ringing phone, even as her pale eyes slide back to me. When the phone connects, she explains who she is and what she needs, but all I can think about is how she's speaking to my brother Jet's mate. Somehow, in the time my mate was taken from me, Jet managed to land two of his own.

I grit my teeth at how unfair it feels. I know nothing in life is fair, I was aware of that from a young age, but knowing what remains of my pack is all mated now has me wanting to rage and burn the library to the ground.

I was distraught when I killed Rama. But now, I'm angry.

I'm angry at her, at my pack, even at myself.

Why did she drug me?

Why did she put me in a position to be here, now, without her?

I'll never get answers to any of that, and when grief chokes me so hard I forget to breathe, I decide I'll leave and walk the library for a while. Just as quickly, I know I won't because Diana needs us, and anything I can do to save her, I should do. I will do.

Onmiel's voice breaks through my thoughts. "You'd like to speak with Tenebris?"

I give her a warning look, begging her to read it, and she gives me a thumbs up as she sits back in her chair.

"He's stepped out of the room for a moment, but I'll let him know to call you back later. Alright?" She hangs up, and Ascelin shoots me a knowing look.

"Take a walk, alpha," she encourages. "I will continue with the librarians and Arliss."

I can't think around the pressure in my brain, my focus narrowing as I shove my chair back and stand. Black dots crowd my vision as Onmiel stands and looks at me, her expression disconcerted for the first time since I met her this morning.

Her tone is low and comforting. "There's a garden on the exterior edge of floor five. If you go right, take the first elevator up. It's beautiful there. I think you'd like it."

I can't even summon a response, but I practically run from the room as memories flash and crowd my brain.

Rama on her hands before me, taking my knot so sweetly.

Rama calling my name for the first time before sliding a silky robe off her delicate shoulders.

Rama slipping her hands into my pants to stroke my cock while she whispered all the dirty things she wanted from me.

I sprint for the elevators, smashing the button to call it as I gasp like a fish out of water. I'm fucking falling apart, and right now, I can't summon enough strength to keep going. Not even to help.

The elevator slides open with a whoosh, and I step inside, grateful it's empty. I press the button for the fifth floor, and as soon as the doors open again, I run out, my head swiveling from side to side until I see a sign for the Pengshur Gardens. I don't stop to wonder how they've got a garden in the middle of the building. This whole place is imbued with ancient magic, built centuries and centuries ago.

I take off at a full-out sprint, ignoring the curious looks of other beings as I pass, focused only on getting to the sign up ahead. Passing it in a rush, I burst through double doors and into the middle of an actual forest. It reminds me so much of Siargao that I fall to both knees and gaze around. The foliage is a myriad of brilliant colors. Flowers cover almost every surface. Plants grow up from cracks in the bark of every single tree. It's a wonderland of verdant greenery.

I miss home, or what I can remember of it, anyhow.

Managing to stumble back to my feet, I rip my clothes off and shift into my direwolf. I lose myself to the forest for hours, running through valleys, leaping over logs and small rivers. I smell a larger body of water somewhere, but I don't stop to find it. I run until my legs are shaky and the tension has receded to the back of my mind.

I don't encounter anyone in the forest. Eventually, I find a sturdy, tall tree and decide to shift and climb to the top. I need to rest for a minute, and I'm curious how far up the forest itself goes. I haul myself up the thick branches, careful not to crush the beautiful vines that grow around the tree's wide, thick trunk. When I pull myself through the last layer of greenery and above the canopy, I let out a gasp of wonder.

Thousands of shelves line either side of the forest, soaring many stories up above to a glass ceiling that lets outside light in. I think I read once that Pengshur was famous for many reasons, one of them being the extraordinary gardens. It never occurred to me that any of those would be inside like this.

I sit at the top of the canopy for a long time, watching librarians bustle along the walkways in front of every story's-worth of shelves. Pengshur is a busy place, it seems. There's so much I don't know about it, and I find myself wondering what Onmiel might be able to tell me. Eventually, watching all the movement reminds me I'm not doing shit to accomplish my only mission. With a sour emotion overtaking my mind, I climb out of the tree and head back to find my clothing.

CHAPTER ELEVEN

ONMIEL

We research until the moon is high and Ascelin is cranky as shit. Eventually, I kick my clients out of the library with a kind reminder that they need rest, and most research requests take a few days.

Ascelin snapped at me, literally, but when Tenebris touched her shoulder and reminded her it was time to go, she relented. They seem...close. Honestly, I'm a little jealous. I'd love to be friends with the hulking alpha. He was quiet all afternoon after disappearing for a bit, lost in a stack of books and not engaging at all.

I never watched when Rama televised the hunts going on in the Temple Maze, but now, I'm wondering if I should have because I'm far less afraid of these clients than I should be.

After they've gone, Zakarias turns to me and sinks back into his chair, running his hands through his long braids.

"I should not have dragged you into this assignment, Onmiel," he mutters, more to himself than anything.

My blood chills, wondering if I've done something wrong, but Zakarias looks over and shakes his head.

"They've not mentioned Rama but now they're researching the Tempang's monsters. I've got a terrible feeling about all this," he whispers, his voice so filled with dread that I'm worried he's about to burst into tears.

"A librarian's work is never done. Learn in order to guide," I remind him gently, perching myself on the tabletop as I look at my oldest friend.

For a long moment, he stares at the intricately inlaid wood ceiling, but then he sits up and nods at me. "You're right, Onmiel, and it isn't a good lesson from me to you to second-guess assignments. I had just hoped your first official one would be something thrilling but not dangerous."

"Librarians get pulled into all sorts of situations, don't they?" I counter.

"That's true," Zakarias mutters.

"Why don't you head home, and I'll clean up," I offer.

He eyes the stacks of books left on the desk with a grimace but grabs his bag and heads for the door. I know he'd like to help me, but it's the unspoken rule between Novices and First Librarians—Novices do the grunt work. This means I'll be here a few hours still, reshelving and respelling the books, cleaning the room, and making sure we're prepared for tomorrow. I'll probably be here first, too, because I'm a dog with a bone when I have a mission.

Something niggles at me about this damn vampiri prophecy, but I can't put my finger on it.

The door swings softly shut behind Zakarias, and I pull out my datapad to see if anyone has responded to the group message I sent earlier. I'm still getting used to having the tech again, but I'll admit it's helpful to connect so easily. When I scan my messages, there's nothing new. I let out a huff of frustration, and then I look at the table full of books, reorganizing them by shelf in order from closest to farthest.

Grabbing the first stack, I head out of the reading room and slot the first book into place, whispering the standard incantation to keep it there until another librarian requires it. The magic of Pengshur is something Novices learn in our second year. There are layers and layers to it, and knowledge of Pengshur's spells must be earned. I can spell almost all the books in the archives at this point. There are only a few I can't call—banned books and books in private keeping rooms.

It takes me two hours to put everything away, but I love the library late at night like this. It's quieter than the daytime, although there are always people here; it's literally never empty. But it's peaceful, and after a crazy childhood, I need this peace like I need to breathe air. I've never felt so *me* as I did when I arrived at Pengshur for the first time and was accepted to the Novice program.

Eventually, I manage to reshelve the books we don't need and clean the room for tomorrow. I close the door and pace around the outer rim of the archives until I reach the elevator bank. From there, I take it to the fifth floor. When the elevator door opens, a broad hallway leads left and right, a desk centered in an alcove in front.

"Miel, girl! Spill the beans!" my human friend, Kassie, screeches from behind the desk when she sees me. Her head bobs as she leaps up off her stool and points one finger with rainbow-painted nails at me.

"About what?" I snort.

"About what?" she scoffs, rounding the desk to slap me lightly on the arm. "Those two huge hunks you're working with. I saw the black one take a book and disappear into the fifth-floor gardens. Tell me literally everything. There's been nonstop chatter today."

Nonstop chatter among the first-year Novices, she means. What they don't tell you when you enter the program is that you're not even allowed *into* the damn archives the first year. That year is spent tending the Novice dorms in the next building over and learning about the library's magic. Truthfully, it would be dangerous on the library floor without having a magical baseline. Visitors are allowed in only because they don't know the spells, and they're always accompanied, so they're safe. The archives are filled with magical artifacts and dangerous books.

"One of them was in the maze," I whisper as if Tenebris might show up here at any moment and hear me talking about him.

"Which one?" she gasps, bringing her hands to her cheeks excitedly.

"The hot one." I laugh. "The alpha."

She feigns a swoon and throws herself into my arms, looking up at me with big doe eyes when I catch her. "An honest-to-gods alpha? I die. What does he smell like? How tall is he?"

Giggling, I shove her upright. "Give me the key to my room, and I'll tell you."

Kassie grumbles but disappears behind her desk and grabs a key to room fourteen, my favorite. While I've never been on assignment before, I've often snuck up here and gotten room fourteen for a little shuteye. It's got a great view over the city, and I love to watch the nightlife.

When she levels me with a wry, displeased look, I chuckle.

"He smells clean, and he's probably two heads taller than me. But there's something different about predatory half-breeds," I admit. "There's a quiet focus to them that humans just don't have."

I think back to the way Tenebris stared at the rain just this morning, and heat flares between my thighs. Gods, I love a nerdy man, and beneath his somber exterior, I sense a dork waiting to shine. This library is just the place for that.

Kassie sighs, bringing my mind back to the present. "It's late as shit, Miel. Gah, I can't wait to pull all-nighters like this." She looks so wistful that I have to laugh.

"It's three a.m. you ding-dong. This is hardly an all-nighter."

"Yeah, but you'll be back at it by six, right?"

"Right," I grouse, remembering I should grab a few hours while I can. I give Kassie a quick salute, then head down the hallway to my room. When I open the door, there's a rush of wind and I'm yanked immediately to the side. Someone tosses me against the wooden wall. Pain bursts at the back of my skull as I bare my teeth at my attacker.

A low chuckle echoes from across the room as a standing lamp flicks on.

Ascelin.

She's now perched under the window, smirking as she crosses her thin, muscular arms.

I rub at the back of my head. "How'd you get in here and what the hells are you doing?"

"Warning you," she says, crossing the small room to get back in my space. "Stay away from Tenebris."

I choke out an irritated laugh, ire filling my chest as I try not to yell at her. "That'll be hard to do seeing as how we're working together to get you answers."

I try to force myself to remember this woman is a killer. I've heard stories of her eviscerating men—and women—with her bare hands. She's dangerous and unscrupulous. Somehow, though, I'm just really fucking irritated.

She collars my throat, shoving me against the wall a second time. "I mean stop considering him sexually. It is clear you find him attractive. But that sentiment is not returned."

Ah.

I open my mouth to respond, but a second figure pushes through the door.

Arliss. The bulky male turns to look at me with a grin, shoving his thumbs in his belt. "I see. Ascelin has already begun her interrogation."

"Not an interrogation," she snaps. "An interrogation would involve blood and torture. This is a kind warning."

"Kind, huh?" I scowl. "You could just ask me for a moment to speak, but in any case, you don't need to worry. My only priority is translating your prophecy so Zakarias can assist in the healing piece. Your friend's life is on the line, and I'm cognizant of that."

Ascelin lets out a low, threatening growl, venom dripping from translucent black fangs onto the ornate parquet floor. "See that you do, girl. Because—"

Arliss steps in front of me, blocking my view of Ascelin as he leans over me, throwing one arm above my head, his palm flat on the wall. Brilliant blue eyes scan my face, lingering on my mouth before they travel farther down.

It's a sexual perusal, nearly an offer. And I'm not at all interested. He's hot, but not my type in the slightest. Even so, my body reacts to the proximity of such a virile, sensual male so focused on me. I clench my thighs together, and Arliss grins. Ascelin peeks around his broad shoulder, her all-white eyes narrowing. This is the strangest interrogation I've ever heard of. They either want my deepest, darkest secrets or a threesome.

Maybe both.

Arliss lets out a low, rumbly growl, breathing deeply as he presses his body closer to mine. "Mmm, that's right, librarian. You could use a good fucking, couldn't you? How long has it been, my sweet?"

Snorting, I peer around at Ascelin. "Is he serious right now?"

"He is always serious about sex. He is a manwhore," Ascelin huffs. "As I was saying."

"Your message grows tiresome, Ascelin," Arliss growls. "Let us instead convince this pretty young thing to come to bed with us. Perhaps we can show her a good time, and then the moon eyes she has for Tenebris will be turned upon us instead."

Good *gods*. These two.

Ascelin rolls her eyes. "I'll remind you, Builder, that one ride on that cock was enough for me." She gives Arliss a reproachful look. Not that he notices because he's still staring at my mouth.

Builder? I wonder why she calls him that...

Milky eyes flick to mine. "And *you*. Stay away from Tenebris or you will not like the side of me you see."

I don't bother to agree with that. I'd like to be his friend if I can. Sometimes you meet someone, and your soul recognizes them immediately as someone you have to have more of. I felt that way the moment his golden eyes looked my way. It doesn't have to be sexual. In fact, it probably won't be. He seems caught up with other priorities. But being friends sounds great.

Ascelin slips in a puff of black smoke out my door, leaving me with Arliss as I resist the urge to grumble under my breath.

TEN

"It's so curious how completely unafraid of us you are…" he muses. "Is it foolishness or are you truly that brave?"

My lips curl up into a grin as I meet his lazy perusal. "Very little frightens me, carrow."

His eyes flash wide for a moment, and then they narrow. "You can't possibly presume to know I am one simply because I'm interested in them."

"You are, though. Aren't you? That's why you want the books?"

"What makes you think I am?"

I reach up and stroke one long finger down his square jaw, grinning.

"All carrow mark their successors with a practically invisible tattoo along the jawline. I couldn't see your tattoo in the Solarium, but it was visible in our working room. Were you aware you had it?"

A tic starts in his jaw, his muscle pressing against the pad of my finger. I drop my hand to my side. "You didn't know…" It's less a question and more a confirmation based on the frustrated look he wears.

He glances away, his expression clouded. He strikes me as a male who doesn't let others see a vulnerable side. It's on the tip of my tongue to comment on it, but even *I* know when to keep my mouth shut. Usually.

He shakes his head, long braids swaying before he turns a dazzling smile back on me. Thick, black fingers come to my hair and tug softly. His gaze becomes molten desire.

"What other secrets do you hide, Novice Onmiel?" He's practically purring, but I resist the urge to shut him down too harshly. If he wanted to talk more about the topic of his power right now, he wouldn't deflect.

I press both hands to his chest and attempt to push him from me, although he's too fucking big for me to move him very far. "Zakarias gave you our most well-known book on carrow, but there are a few lesser-known items I think might be more helpful. I'll make sure to bring them tomorrow. Plus, I'm always happy to answer questions, based on what I know. Monsters are kinda my thing."

"No matter." He shrugs his big, round shoulders and takes a step back. Both hands slide into the pockets of his tight jeans. "Back to the topic of Tenebris, be wary of the vampiri. I am the last person on Lombornei to ever dissuade two consenting adults from fucking, but there is a reason she is so protective of Tenebris. He's sacrificed more than you can ever imagine."

I haven't known Arliss long at all, but I sense he wears humor like a mask.

"I understand. I'd like to be his friend, if I can," I remind him. Then I shoot him a little smirk. "You can read what's in my heart, carrow, can't you? Take a peek."

Sapphire eyes narrow as he steps closer. There's an uncomfortable feeling inside my brain, like something's worming its way through. Smiling, I will myself to relax, and I concentrate on counting my fingers as his invasion of my mind continues. After far longer than it *should* take, the sensation abruptly ceases. I suspect he's unable to fully control his power for some reason. Either that or he wanted it to hurt.

"Find what you were looking for?" I can't resist another smirk as Arliss crosses his arms.

"You want to fuck him, but you're sincere in your desire to help us. You'd be happy to be his friend."

"Indeed," I confirm, giving him two finger guns to make my point.

For a long moment, he stares at me, and then he leans in the doorway and crosses his huge arms, accentuating beautifully muscular biceps. Arliss snorts when my eyes drop to them. "Don't tell me you're not the slightest bit intrigued, librarian."

"Don't need to fuck you to find your muscles attractive," I counter as I lean opposite him. "I suppose I do find you somewhat fascinating. It's clear you're not exactly part of the Ayala pack, and I know you weren't in the maze. How did you all come to be connected, and why? Why don't you know what it is to be a carrow? Tell me all of your secrets, friend."

"I'm going to let you in on a secret, just not one of mine. It may help you navigate the next few days." He laughs. "Ascelin will not tell you this, and Tenebris likely won't speak of it."

My blood begins to freeze and boil simultaneously, starting behind my eyes and traveling down my spine as his gaze focuses, intent and predatory.

He leans in close enough for his lips to brush just over mine, his breath warm against my face. "Rama was Tenebris's mate. She is only dead because he ripped her head from her shoulders to protect his family. If he seems unmoored, it is because he sacrificed everything to protect the rest of us."

My hand flies to cover my mouth as tears fill my eyes. It can't be. She imprisoned him when he was eleven for gods' sakes!

And so it's true—Rama's gone. I can't even begin to think how to react to that news.

Arliss nods and rocks back onto his heels, crossing both arms. "I read his heart sometimes when he's unaware I am doing so. His is shrouded in darkness, Onmiel. You would do well to steer clear of him."

Arliss growls once, then turns and shuts my door, and I'm left alone with thoughts that spin my brain so hard, I slide down the ornate wall to the ground as they batter me.

CHAPTER TWELVE

TENEBRIS

I wake before the sun rises. The townhouse Noire rented belongs to the library but is located a fifteen-minute walk away. Ascelin and Arliss are nowhere to be seen, so I dress and leave. I consider a note, but they'll find me later. This early, the city of Pengshur is quiet, and I marvel at how different the architecture is from Siargao. My home province is all harsh, straight lines, and the over-water houses typical of a riverside city that's slowly sliding into the water.

This city, by contrast, is almost gothic in design. Every structure is ornate and scrolled, down to the glittering white street signs that tell me which direction the library is. It's ironic because the library building is impossible to miss. Where most of the structures here are six to eight stories, the library soars at fifteen or so. It's a beacon in the middle of town, and all roads seem to end at the library.

I roll my shoulders as the sun begins to peek up over the horizon, lighting up the giant white library building. It's stunning. If my life had been different, I would probably have petitioned Noire to let me come here and apply for the Novice program. Even as a pup, I was always obsessed with monster lore and reading every book I could get my hands on. It helped us in the maze, actually, because I knew every monster species' weakness.

That pulls a growl from deep in my chest, all my memories of hunting and killing rising to assault me. It prompts me to do something I started doing after my run last night—cataloging the things about my life that were fucked up because of my ma—because of Rama.

I'm aware it's a coping mechanism, but it's what I've got, so I start with my childhood. I think back to how she showed up at our pack home and slaughtered everyone she could, even the pups. I barely escaped with my life. Her goons caught me and tossed me in a bag in the maze. Noire found me when he woke up in the maze, too. Years later, she orchestrated an attack by another monster pack, and my brother Oskur was ripped to shreds.

Rama has been at the center of every horrible thing that ever happened in my life.

She never comforted me. She never reached out after doing something to hurt me. I screamed and sobbed and grieved when Oskur was killed, and she was never there for that either.

In fact, I barely saw her at all, except for the nightly message about our intended marks, our prey.

But when I turned eighteen, she began sending me books on every topic under the sun: math, monster lore, Lombornei's history. Noire wondered why I was always reading, but she stimulated my mind at a time when there was nothing else to do but the nightly hunt. We were her killers, her captives, her servants.

And then, eventually, I was hers in the only way that really matters to a direwolf male—bondmates.

When my memories threaten to get too sentimental, I remember that all of us Ayala brothers did time in the Atrium, me included, and it didn't stop when I came of age. The Atrium was all about the basest of instincts—sex. It was how Rama's wealthy patrons could touch and experience every sensation, safe from us monsters. It was a way for her to force us to perform in ways we never would have wanted to.

I wonder how my mate felt, watching me touch other women and be touched as well. Did it bother her? Turn her on?

It was fucked up, that's for sure. Growling, I turn my mind to Diana instead. She was the first omega I ever touched sexually, but that was before we all realized she was Noire's bondmate. Jet and I both had her, and gods she felt good. But we had to do it to pull Noire out of an impending rut.

I play our escape from the maze over again in my mind as I head for the library, up cobblestone streets still lit by oil lamps on giant white posts. That's Rama's fault, too, because she cut off the power seven years ago, and that affected literally every being on the continent. She thrived off of complete and total control. But in my short time as her mate, I never found out why.

The list of questions I have for her grows every day, but I try hard to shut off the way my mind wanders to that list.

Instead, I urge it to drift to the monsters in the Tempang, and I find myself wondering what their lives might be like? Vaguely, I remember the Volya who attacked Diana telling us the Tempang was sick. What did they mean, and how can a forest itself be sick? What would Diana and Achaia's lives have done to alleviate that?

The library looms in front of me. I've come directly to the archives entrance, and I'm able to make it through without assistance, thanks to the discs Onmiel gave us. The security guard keeps a wary eye on me. He must have seen me in the maze. I'm surprised we haven't gotten more strange glances, honestly, but I suspect some of the librarians never take their noses out of their books long enough to know what's going on outside of Pengshur.

In a way, the library feels hidden away from the rest of the world, and I like that. I feel like I could hide here for ages, and nobody would find me.

I pass through the entry hallway and the giant map we saw yesterday. When I stop to look at it, I shove down my own hesitation and pinch in off the coast of Vinituvari. Rama's flying city, Paraiso, should be there because none of my pack knew what to do with it. Well, I think it's more that Noire didn't give a fuck, and he never wanted to visit it again.

Arliss *must* be interested in the tech, as much of a collector and inventor as he is. But he hasn't seemed focused on Paraiso either. I haven't thought much about that until right now.

I pinch again at the map, but nothing happens. I guess I don't have the right magic, and that frustrates me. I want to know how the map works, to look at every inch of it. Even more than that, I want to know the library's secrets. Pengshur has been around for nearly two thousand years. The sheer amount of knowledge here is breathtaking.

Snarling, I step away from the map and find the long row of books that leads to our assigned reading room. Before I even swing the door open, I hear Onmiel muttering inside. When I open the door, she looks up with a brief flash of annoyance before smiling. That, at least, looks genuine.

"You're here early," she murmurs, glancing at an ancient-looking scrolled clock on the wall.

Damn, it's five a.m.

"Couldn't sleep," I grumble, sitting next to her. She's perched in the same place she was yesterday, tucked under the window. She sips a coffee and scowls down at the book in front of her.

Today, her hair is a brilliant blue, shocking and bright, although it fades to a pale cornflower at the tips of her wavy, shoulder-length hair. It's striking, but the orange was just as crazy-looking.

She's lost in thought, her glasses on the tip of her nose. She keeps scowling at the book and then scribbles on a spare notepad next to it. I grab the stack of books I was using yesterday and sigh. This work is daunting and tedious. I'd rather go back to the tome she gave me on mermaid clans.

Onmiel looks up at me before throwing her shocking hair up into a loose bun. Tendrils fall down around her heart-shaped face as she smiles again. "I need more coffee, so I'm going to run to the cafe. Can I get you anything, Tenebris?"

"It's just Ten," I correct. Rama and my father are the only ones

TEN

who ever used my full given name, and it doesn't feel right for her to say it. Ten is so much more comfortable.

"Ten," she repeats, poking a pencil through the bun. "What'll it be?"

"I'll come with you," I murmur. "Maybe you can tell me a little more about the library on the way?"

She beams with excitement, pink stealing across her already rosy cheeks as I watch.

"I'd love to do that. What are you most curious about?" She stands and grabs a second pencil, shoving that through her bun as well. I wonder if she realizes there are now two there, sticking up out of her head like chopsticks.

I hold back the snort threatening to break loose and pace for the door, opening it as she steps quietly through. She waits for me just outside as I close the door, admiring the ornate black handle. Everything in this library is so beautiful and old, it needs to be treated gently.

"Tell me about the map. I tried to pinch in, and it irritated the fuck out of me that it didn't work."

Onmiel laughs, a tinkling sound that seems to echo around us as we follow the outer edge of the library and head for the coffee shop. Everything in here smells so good—I catalog old parchment and leather. I try to pick out anything non-bovine, but there's just so much.

"I'm gonna let you in on two secrets, Ten," she chirps, patting my forearm. "First, Novices aren't even allowed in the archives for a year because the magic is potentially dangerous if mistreated." She looks me up and down as if she's assessing me and then leans in like I'm about to hear a secret she can't say aloud.

Without thinking, I angle my head down to hear it because I want to know more about this place. Onmiel's lips nearly tickle my ear.

"I'll teach you how to touch the map if you promise not to do it when anyone's looking."

I shoot upright at that, incredulous. "You would? Even if it's dangerous?"

She shrugs and keeps walking, laughing when I jog to catch up. "I can tell a kindred spirit when I see one. You're curious about the library, which probably means you should apply to the program. If you want all the secrets, I mean." Her happy smile falls, but she plasters it right back on as we arrive at the coffee shop.

It's already bustling with librarians in tunics of all three level colors. I've read a few books about Pengshur. It's nice to have a baseline of info, although the reality of this place is so much more overwhelming than I could ever have imagined.

The Master Librarian who greeted us the first day is in the corner sipping an espresso, and he lifts it, inclining his head toward Onmiel as she responds in kind. She looks surprised to see him here, her eyelids fluttering before she smiles up at me.

I peruse the menu as we wait in line, but when he gets up to leave, there's a tangible sense of relief in the coffee shop. Onmiel watches him go and then turns to me secretively.

"ML Garfield is a super hardass; that's why everybody's thrilled he's gone. He's always been fair to me, but I'm a kickass librarian, so…" She shrugs again, and then it's our turn to order. I turn in the direction the Master Librarian left in, wondering how long he served here in order to get to his current station. He looks old as hells in person, even older than Thomas, my adoptive father.

We place our order and stand to the side to wait, and I lean against the wall as Onmiel taps one foot impatiently, long arms crossed. She's a stick, so different from Rama, who was all luscious curves. Rama was sex personified, the epitome of what a direwolf omega should be.

Onmiel is a pencil in human format.

She looks up at me and plants both hands on her hips. "What?"

"What, *what*?"

"You're staring at me like I'm some sort of maze prey or something."

Her casual mention of the maze has my hackles rising, but something about the teasing look on her face simultaneously puts me at ease. She's messing around with me, and I don't hate it.

She isn't treating me like a victim because she doesn't know everything I've been through. And she's not acting like my life was ruled by Rama and the maze because that's not her style.

I reach out to thunk the tip of her nose hard. "You wouldn't last twelve seconds in there."

"I might surprise you," she says bitterly before giving me a swift, playful punch to the side. I dodge it easily and grip her wrist, shoving it up behind her back as I bring my lips close to her ear.

"Nothing surprises me, Onmiel. I'd have been on you in less than a minute."

Shit.

I didn't mean to say that so seductively, but she straightens, giving me a serious look. Tugging at her wrist, she steps away, and I do my best to make light of my awkward comment.

"See? I haven't even chased, and you're on edge."

Her smirk is back as the barista delivers our drinks. "I'm just saying, I might look like a stiff wind could knock me over, but I'm scrappier than you think."

I grunt to keep from disagreeing but take a sip of the latte instead. The warm liquid burns on the way down my throat, but that burn feels good. It's a reminder I'm alive, and my family's alive.

Mostly.

Onmiel looks up at me with a smile. "So," she draws out the 'o' like she's about to tell me the gravest of secrets. "Arliss propositioned me last night. Is he always such a ho?"

I'm so caught off guard that I choke on the coffee and start coughing my head off.

Onmiel snorts and claps my back a couple times. "Poor thing. You're not used to my humor yet, but you'll come to love it. Everyone does."

There's a lump the size of an airship trying to go down my throat, but I give her a thumbs-up because it's all I can manage.

CHAPTER THIRTEEN

ONMIEL

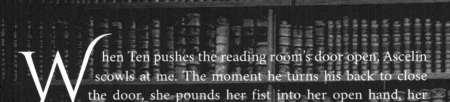

When Ten pushes the reading room's door open, Ascelin scowls at me. The moment he turns his back to close the door, she pounds her fist into her open hand, her nose scrunched angrily.

I hear her message loud and clear; I just don't care. I've watched other librarians be bullied around by their clients just because of a whole "client is always right" attitude. I don't subscribe to that belief. It's like I told her—my primary focus is finding the information she needs. It's none of her business if Ten and I become friends.

I smile at her in the friendliest possible way. "Ascelin, we were here at the ass crack of dawn, and I didn't expect to see you for a bit. Would you like me to grab you another Type-A latte? You seemed to enjoy it..."

She doesn't bother to answer me, instead settling down on a chair. She reminds me of a cat hissing at unwanted affection.

Zakarias comes into the room, waving a quick hello. I set his drink down to the right of his book stack, smiling as he takes his glasses from his vest pocket and places them on the tip of his nose.

And then we get to work, Zakarias, Ten, and Ascelin hunching over the Volya books. I keep at my translation, having gotten a few tips overnight that might help. Hours after we begin, the door swings open, and Arliss shows up, a fresh round of coffees in his hands. He sets them down.

Standing with a smile, I move to the nearest bookshelf and pull a burgundy, leather-bound book off the shelf. I hand it to him with a meaningful look. "Lots of good info in here, Arliss. Let me know if you have questions."

He gives me a momentary look of surprise and clutches the book to his chest, then makes for the door again. I follow him out, the slippery weasel. I don't know why he can't research along with the rest of us, but I'd like to know.

"Where are you going?" I question, crossing my arms in what I hope is a motherly sort of fashion.

He presents me with that same shit-eating grin he flashed yesterday.

"Cut the shit, Arliss." I scowl. "Throw me a bone here. Why do you hide this?"

Blue eyes scan around us before he takes a step closer to me. "There are still those who would control a carrow if they thought they had found one. The only people who know of my existence are Ascelin's pack and now you. I would like to keep it that way because I might be the last of my kind."

"Meaning you can't pass on your gift?" I ask.

His expression falls, and he nods curtly.

"You never learned how? Or what..." I press.

He looks almost sad when our eyes finally meet again. "The carrow gift is a blessing and a curse, Onmiel. No one is meant to carry it forever. I would long ago have passed it on if I could. I need to know everything I can about it, as the one who gave it to me died during the transfer."

I sigh. "That's unfortunate. Most carrow function as mentors for a decade or two afterward."

"I'm aware," he replies in a flat tone. "How is it you know so much about this anyhow?"

I straighten my chin. "My life's work is a study of the monsters in the Tempang and the languages of Lombornei. This is literally what I spend all my time doing."

"What do you mean, monsters in the Tempang?" he presses on.

"You're actually *not* the only one, Arliss. An ancient tribe of carrow lives in the forest, but you'd have to journey there to meet and learn from them. They're highly reclusive."

An urgent look flashes over his face as he clutches the book to his chest. "I'm leaving immediately," he mutters, glancing around as if he's already thinking through the plans.

Angst hits me square in the gut. "You can't remove the book from the library, Arliss. Stay for a day or two and read that and its sequel. That'll tell you everything anyone on Lombornei knows about carrow. They're not friendly to outsiders; you can't just run up to the Tempang half-cocked."

"I don't do anything half-cocked, sweet one," he counters, right back to his old shit.

"Ugh," I groan. "I'm already exasperated by this macho-male horseshit. Can you not with me?"

Arliss throws his head back and laughs, and it carries throughout the section of the library we stand in. I hold back the urge to snip at him to hush. "You are a wonder, Onmiel. You'll be running this place in no time," he chortles.

"Seriously," I encourage him. "Stay a little while longer so you can read the books at least. I worry what might happen if you just traipse into the forest, even if you go in smoke form."

He looks shocked that I know about that. Arliss hesitates, but when he looks down at the beautifully bound book and then up at me, I know I've got him. He'll be staying with us for now, at least.

A wormy sensation of guilt wriggles around in my chest. I should tell Garfield about a lot of what my clients have shared—Rama's death and Arliss being an elusive carrow. But somehow, I find I'm not ready to do that. I want to help them first. If Rama's gone, then the worst of our fears are gone as well.

For now, it looks like I'll be keeping Pack Ayala's secrets.

~

Hours later, everyone's grumpy as shit. I've retrieved lunch for the males and another blood latte for Ascelin, who refuses to say she's hooked, but downs it in two seconds flat. I'll break through that prickly exterior if it's the last thing I do. I get it. She's protecting Ten because he's a treasure, and I see that now.

She's right to do it—Ten is amazing. He was helpful today, poring over the books and picking out bits and pieces of information that might help Diana. He works through the information far faster than Ascelin. He's got future Novice Librarian written all over him if I'm being honest.

I shelve that thought for another day, though, because this group has a big enough mission to accomplish first.

I'd love to help on the Volya front, but I can't speak to the intricacies of their medicine, and Zakarias can do the research better than I can. His background is in ancient healing techniques. Even though I excel in languages, this vampiri prophecy is punching me right in the asshole.

Nothing matches up.

Ascelin snarls and throws her coffee cup across the room. That makes me snarl in response because I'll have to clean the damn thing up. The warrioress leaps upright and paces aggressively in circles around the room. Arliss watches her dispassionately before turning his nose back to his book.

Ten and I can't stop watching her until finally, she breaks out a cell phone and dials a number. "Give me the Chosen One," she growls when someone picks up.

Moments later, her face softens. "Diana, how are you this day?"

I'm in awe at the change in her from one moment to the next.

"How are you feeling?" Ascelin probes, her voice gentle even as she frowns, pinching the bridge of her nose as she fakes a smile.

"Good, good. I am relieved it is a good day." The fake smile falls as she shakes her head. "No, Chosen One, nothing yet. We are putting together pieces here and there, but it is slow going." There's a momentary pause before she grits her teeth together. "Of course, if you feel up to the trip, please come."

Next to me, Ten tenses. When I look over, he's staring at the floor under his feet. Ascelin finishes her conversation and hangs up the phone, sighing as her head falls back and she focuses on the ceiling.

Ten breaks the silence first. "Noire's coming?"

"Achaia is taking them to an ancient mermaid city on the off-chance there is a healing salve of some sort. Once they do that, they will come here."

Ten nods again and then stands, excusing himself. I don't get a chance to ask if he's alright, but it seems like his brother coming is bad news.

Arliss looks up from his book to grin at me. "I can't wait to see you meet Alpha Noire, sweet one. He is *such* a fucking asshole."

CHAPTER FOURTEEN
TENEBRIS

I'm not anxious to see Noire, Jet, or their mates. The reality is that, even though we're desperately hunting for a cure, it's been nice to distance myself from my pack. Ascelin and Arliss aren't direwolf shifters. There's no mate or family bond tugging at me constantly. There's no Noire barking at me or Jet trying to hug me. There's no new sister-in-law to get to know. There's no kissing to look away from.

It's been fucking nice. I've had a few moments where I felt almost normal, aside from the moments where I catalog what a psycho my mate was in an attempt to distance myself from my ragged, painful emotions.

The sudden realization that I'm running away from everything douses me like icy water, and I turn back to the room. I can't run from my broken bond. I can't run from my family. And I shouldn't. What did Noire drill into us in the maze?

Family above everything.

He reminded us of that when we were escaping. In fact, we left the vampiri behind for a time, and half of them got slaughtered as a result. It was *always* Ayala Pack first. My older brother may be an asshole, but I know with certainty he would've burned this entire continent down to get me back if that's what it took.

Steel makes its way down my spine as I straighten and roll my shoulders, closing my eyes as I slump against a row of books. I index what I can scent around me. Leather, binding glue, thread, and paper of all sorts. Beings come and go, some scurrying and some leisurely walking. Echoes of voices make their way into my ears as I focus on the library itself.

This place has been a balm for my soul in the last two days, and I urge that healing sensation to spread to my aching heart. Rage seems to have made its way to the front of my mind in the last twenty-four hours, though, and it's a useful fuel. That and Onmiel's easy, immediate friendship.

When I get back to the room, it's tense, but she shoots me a glance, clearly asking if I'm alright. I nod softly, smiling a little before I seat myself next to her and look down at her work.

"Tell me about this," I encourage. "I need a break from the Volya stuff."

Her eyes sparkle and light up as she points down at the book and her paper. It's a list of symbols so intricate I can barely follow the scrolled lines and curves. When she opens her mouth and reads the first few lines aloud, I'm shocked at how stunning the language is. It's lyrical and beautiful, and I could listen to her speak it all day long.

"What is that?" I breathe.

Onmiel grins again and taps her pencil on the table before shoving it into her bun. Now there are three. Does she know? Is she that absent-minded?

I resist the urge to yank them all out as she starts looking around for another.

"This is Korsenji," she murmurs, stroking the page lovingly. "It's the language of the harpies, most of whom reside in the Tempang. You'll find the occasional harpy elsewhere, but they're highly territorial and very rare."

"Rama had one," I say without thinking. Diana told me that

before we came here. A harpy told her how to find Arliss, and that information eventually led us to where we are today.

Onmiel gasps aloud. "Incredible. Hundreds of years ago, we had a harpy librarian, and she made this book for the library. Only a handful of people have ever studied it, though, because it's so incredibly complicated." She looks down at Ascelin's paper, the prophecy looming up at us from the fading sheet.

"I thought it sounded a bit like Korsenji, but now that I'm putting them side by side and matching the prophecy with the rarest of pronunciations from the book, I don't think so."

She sits back in her chair, huffing out a breath as she twists her bangs up and tucks them into the bun. She finds the pencils then and slaps me on the shoulder. "You didn't tell me I had three pencils stuck in my hair? Did I look like a doofus all day?"

I smile and look back down at the intricate language, the realization hitting me that finding the language this prophecy is written in is like finding a needle in a haystack.

Ascelin and Zakarias stay til midnight, poring over every line in every book we have about the Volya. As it turns out, there's information squirreled all over the library. There are close to three hundred books for them to go through, and even stacking by relevance, it's a daunting task.

Eventually, Ascelin gives up and tosses another coffee cup at the wall before leaving. Arliss follows her out after shelving the book he's been reading all day. He and Onmiel share some sort of look before he gives her a mock salute.

Zakarias works with us for another half hour before giving up, and then Onmiel and I are alone in the reading room.

She turns to me after yawning for the third time. "You should get some sleep, alpha. If you can?" She's referencing how I mentioned this morning that I didn't sleep well last night, but I'm wired after a day of drinking coffee. I never had coffee until she gave me one, but I think it's safe to say I'm hooked.

"I'm going for a run," I muse aloud, thinking of the gardens up on the fifth floor. I felt like myself for a moment there, shifting into my direwolf and letting all that predatory focus eat up the emotions of my human body. Direwolves don't feel any *less* than their human forms, but they're able to focus on simply living, and that's a welcome distraction.

Onmiel gives me a thumbs-up and turns back to her work, so I leave and go upstairs.

Hours later, my head feels a little clearer, and I find myself wondering if she got to bed at a reasonable time. The plucky librarian seems to have no regard for her own wellness at all, something I can relate to because I haven't felt much of that lately, either.

I have a hard time falling asleep, with my mind picking and organizing all the information I learned today. There's got to be a cure for Diana somewhere or a faster way to get to it.

A sudden need to talk to her hits me, and I pad out to the kitchen of our rental to find Ascelin's phone. Diana picks up on the first ring. "Asc! Oh, Ten!" Her face is drawn and pinched, black circles resting under her eyes.

She's dying. It's obvious.

Noire appears behind her, squinting at the phone before he smiles at me. "Good to see you, brother," he growls.

"I wanted to check on you both," I murmur. "Diana, how are you feeling?"

Her half smile falls as she tucks her long hair over her shoulder. Noire's eyes move to her neck, his expression so pained that I almost hang up then and there. He presses his lips to her skin as her eyes close, and she sinks back like he's the only thing that can bring her comfort.

"We will fix this," I growl at them both. "You won't lose each other the way—" I stop before I can say the rest because I don't want to talk about it.

"Thank you, Ten," Diana whispers. "We did manage to get a coagulant from another mermaid kingdom with Achaia's help. So far, it's working to at least stall the bleeding, but I feel worse. Any luck with the research?"

TEN

I run one hand through my hair, running over everything we've learned about Volya so far. Eventually, I shake my head.

"There is something like three hundred books on Volya, and we're going over them line by line. Sometimes there are just mentions in a book, not more than a sentence or two. It's slow going, but if there's information to be found, we'll find it."

Noire growls as he pulls Diana into his lap and lays them both backward so I'm now looking at them from above. It's easy to see Diana's exhausted from this simple conversation. Her eyelids flutter shut, and she falls asleep as Noire looks at me.

"I need you to work faster, Ten," my pack alpha growls. "If I lose her, there will be no containing my rage. I'm starting to understand Father a little better, how insane he was after Mother died."

I think back to our asshole of a father. He was never kind to my three older brothers, but he doted on me a bit. Being the youngest had its perks, I suppose. But whatever goodness there was in him died with our mother. He never recovered.

That's how I know Noire will turn to the damn dark side if he loses Diana.

"How are you handling things?" Noire's surprisingly gentle question brings me back, his stare probing, even though he's hundreds of miles away.

How am I handling things? My mate was a fucking asshole, but I miss her. My only bright moments are the times with Onmiel when she treats me like I'm normal and life is normal, like every woman I love isn't dead or dying.

I don't know how to put all that into words, though, so I shrug. "The librarians are nice. They barely take breaks to sleep. At a minimum, they're extremely committed."

Noire nods, lost in thought, before he turns back to me. "We'll be there in another day or two. Elizabet is working on some concoction for Diana. As it is right now, I can't risk moving her too much. She's so fragile, Ten. The strongest person I know is reduced to almost nothing in such a short time. I feel like I'm losing my mind."

I can't think of anything to say to that, so I give him an apologetic look before leaning in the doorway to the kitchen. "I'm headed back over to the library now. Onmiel thought she cracked the code on the prophecy, but it was another dead end."

Noire growls. "At this point, I could give a fuck what the prophecy says unless it's about healing her."

It seems to me it's likely all tied together, but I can't say for sure, so we say our goodbyes, and I hang up. When I set Ascelin's phone down on the countertop, I sense she's in the room. Turning, I find her leaning in the doorway, watching me in silence. Even at this hour, she's fully clothed in her warrior garb, complete with a knife strapped to her thigh.

"You ever *not* ready for war, Asc?"

She grimaces, gritting her teeth before she speaks. "How was she?"

"Not good."

"How much time do we have?" Ascelin's eyes are filled with tears, a reminder that so much has happened in the last several weeks. We faced off against the vampiri for years in the maze, although Noire protected me from that as much as he could when I was younger. But then the vampiri king, Cashore, gave his life to save Diana, infusing his soul into hers. Now, Diana has two vampiri partners who protect her like she's a goddess.

It's fascinating, and I find myself wishing I had time to learn more about their culture, and to talk to Cashore through Diana, to learn how things might be different in a pack of blended monsters.

But any of that'll have to come later.

"I'm going up to the library," I tell Ascelin.

"I will join you," she says, her voice so soft I can barely hear her. We leave the apartment and walk to Pengshur in silence.

When we arrive at the reading room, I growl. I can smell Zakarias inside, but there's none of Onmiel's bright, friendly scent. And no coffee.

Swinging the door open, I enter to find the male librarian head down, so focused that he doesn't even notice us enter. When I seat myself across from him, he looks up to greet us.

"I was able to speak with my partners at the Pengshur Healing Hospital. They are ready to act on anything we might uncover, so that is good news."

"Where's Onmiel?" I ask before he gets the chance to say anything.

He smiles kindly. "Miel would work herself to death if I let her. I asked her to grab a few hours of rest. She will be here again later."

Misery settles in my gut as I turn to Ascelin. "I need coffee. Want your latte thing?"

"Most certainly," she grumbles as she perches elegantly on the edge of her chair and opens her book to the last page.

I leave the reading room, irritated that Onmiel isn't here. I hope she comes back soon.

CHAPTER FIFTEEN

ONMIEL

Gods, I'm grateful Zakarias insisted I get a few hours' sleep because I feel like a new woman. The persistent caffeine headache I'd been nursing has finally dissipated, and my limbs don't feel like they weigh two tons apiece.

I've been so focused on translating this prophecy, and it's easy for a librarian to neglect their sleep schedule. It's worse for Novices since we carry extra responsibility during an assignment. Zakarias's schedule isn't much better than mine, but he's getting at least four hours more sleep every night.

I take an extra minute with my hair, curling the blue ends a little. Ugh, it's growing out again. My natural white color is nearly translucent at my scalp, which makes it look like it's floating. So fun because it appears I'm going bald when in fact, I can barely keep my crazy hair in check. It's always grown inexplicably fast like this. I hate it.

I look around my assigned room, gazing out the window onto the streets below. The city of Pengshur seems so happy with everybody bustling around. I swear, this really is the most peaceful place in all of Lombornei. Pengshur is its own insulated world, although ML Garfield's comment from two days ago still rings in my head.

If it appears that way to you, then I'm doing my job.

I should probably check in with him, but so far, there's really nothing to report about the monsters. I know Zakarias has been giving him daily updates, but I can't tell him Arliss told me that Ten killed Rama. It would be a horrible breach of trust, and if she's really dead, then the secret can certainly wait.

I'm still conflicted in my emotions about that. Direwolf bond-mates are rare, and it's often said that losing one results in insanity in the other. How Ten puts one foot in front of the other is sort of amazing. Unless being mated to that psychopath wasn't all roses. But it's not like I can ask him...

Now that I know the horrible news about Ten and Rama, I'm more determined than ever to be a good friend, despite a rapidly growing and very inappropriate attraction to the muscular alpha. It can't possibly be a good time for him to start a relationship, and friendship is fine with me. It really is.

But is it? A little voice helpfully pipes up in my head. I grab the ends of my hair and twist them around my fingertips. Maybe there's a day in the future when Ten will have moved past his horrible loss and be ready to date. And if that day ever comes, maybe he'll remember the sexy, nerdy librarian who tried really hard not to stare at his super nice abs. And his super nice shoulders. And his super gorgeous ass.

I'm hopeless. At least, that's the conclusion I come to as I dress and grab my bag, heading downstairs for the reading room. To my surprise, Ten stalks out with a scowl. When he sees me, he grips my shoulder and directs me away from the room.

"Ten, what's going on? Are you okay?"

"Need coffee," he snarls, not letting go of my arm. He's clearly upset about something, but I don't want to push him, so I let him hold me like a wayward child all the way to the coffee shop. Eventually, I pry my elbow out of his grip and give him a stern look.

"You could ask pol—"

"That room is unbearable without you," he huffs. "Zakarias is trying to make small talk, and Ascelin snips at him every time he

TEN

does. It's so tense. You're my barrier, so come help me fuel my new coffee addiction, and then come back and barrier for me."

I scoff, my mouth dropping open. I'm a *barrier?* I zip my lips shut as I ponder my response, but ultimately, I realize this is a good thing. I'd like to be Ten's friend, and if he counts on me, and if I can bring him peace? I'd love to do that.

Ten is a tense, seething presence at my side when we reach the ordering station. I order for the both of us, Zakarias, and Ascelin, too.

"What about Arliss?" I question as Ten scowls.

"Arliss can go fuck himself," Ten growls, crossing his arms.

The half-minotaur barista snorts, a gold ring in his nose moving with his wide, hairy muzzle. I used to find him hot until I met Ten. The barista rings us up to my library account, and then we turn to wait for the coffees.

Ten's silent, and I can practically feel the tension rising in him based on how his eyes move from side to side. He's assessing every being in here. Is he thinking of them like the marks in the maze?

When his breaths become shallower and his fists ball, I step close to him and place both hands on his immense pecs. Amber eyes flick immediately to my hands, then to mine, as I croon.

"Easy, alpha." I keep my tone low and friendly. "You can always come to find me upstairs if you need me." That's not technically true. He shouldn't be upstairs in the Novice quarters, but I've never been all that great about rules, something Zakarias has had to remind me about many times.

"Zakarias said you needed sleep."

"I did."

"I didn't want to bother you."

"You never will. Just come to room fourteen and sit with me. I snore like a hog, but I'm told it's adorable."

One corner of Ten's mouth curls up, pearly-white fangs descending as his pupils dilate. Is he thinking of me like prey? Gods, I wish he was imagining me in bed. But I'm one thousand percent certain that's not the case. He hasn't even told me yet that he killed his own mate. Maybe he never will.

Amber eyes focus on me as the black pupil recedes. He strokes absentmindedly at the back of my hand with two fingers. After a few minutes of ridiculously intense eye contact, his breathing slows.

The barista bellows out my name, breaking the moment. Ten yanks his hand back but grabs the drinks. We head back to the reading room, but when we arrive, Ascelin and Zakarias are in the middle of a heated argument. Well, it's more like Ascelin snapping her creepy black teeth at my delicate mentor while he cowers in the corner.

Ten breaks them up immediately, shoving Ascelin so hard she flies across the room, although she lands with incredible grace. It's sort of fascinating if it weren't so terrifying.

"What's going on here?" I demand, looking from Ascelin to Zakarias and back again.

"We are running out of time," Ascelin roars. "The Chosen One is dying, and unless you help us find a cure, she will be dead in a week!"

I pad quietly across the room, grabbing Ascelin's hand and putting it against my chest. My heart pounds in my chest as Ten moves to stand behind me, a comforting presence, although I know he's focused on his friend.

"I will never stop until we find a cure for her," I reassure the distraught vampiri. "I can tell you love her so much, and this is really fucking scary for you."

Ascelin yanks her hand away. "Nothing frightens me."

"Losing people does," I whisper. "That frightens everyone."

No sooner have I said it than I realize what I just said, and I worry for Ten. But I carry on, even though I've just stuck my whole leg in my mouth. Opening my arms, I throw myself onto Ascelin, hugging her tight. "It's okay to be terrified, First Warrioress. But FL Zakarias and I are by your side, and I have a bit of good news."

There's a heavy pause, and then Ascelin buries her face in my shoulder and weeps like a child. I can't purr like an alpha, but I don't have to because Ten joins us, wrapping his big arms around us both. A rolling, deep rumble echoes out of his chest, vibrating against my shoulder and Ascelin's.

Gods, I've never heard an alpha purr. But I can one thousand percent admit it's sexy as hells. The noise vibrates through my entire body, my nipples pebbling as I resist the urge to clench my thighs together. Although, the sobbing vampiri woman in my arms puts a quick damper on my libido.

I hold Ascelin for a long time, and when she shows no signs of stopping, I step back and slap her lightly on the cheek. "Get to work, sister. Let me show you what I'm talking about."

Ascelin nods, wiping at both cheeks before she rounds the table to her seat again. She doesn't apologize to Zakarias, but he comes to stand next to me, looking over my shoulder as I flip my book around and turn it to her.

"See this language here?" I point to a line of angular markings in the book. "There are seven variations of this language. If your prophecy is not one of these seven, then it can only be one thing."

"What thing?" Ascelin bristles, even though we're narrowing down.

"Volya," I say in a strong voice, hoping I sound confident and professional. "If it's not one of these seven, it can only be Volya. Or I suppose it could be a language nobody's ever heard of, but that seems unlikely. Prophecies aren't typically delivered in unknown—"

"Onmiel," Zakarias murmurs. "That's enough, child."

I look over at Ascelin, and she's slumped in her chair, looking utterly despondent.

"Of course," her voice is an angry hiss. "Of course, it would be those fucking monsters. What are the odds of that being the case? And why did we not start with the Volya language?"

It's my turn to sigh and lean back. "Nobody knows the Volya language except the Volya. It has never been written down in any book in this library. I know because I asked to learn it when I started my studies, and I hunted high and low for it. It doesn't exist."

"We're going to have to go to the Tempang," Tenebris says, standing upright and crossing his arms.

"Godsdamnit," Ascelin mutters. "Tell me something I do not know."

~

Midnight comes and goes, and Zakarias has a breakthrough—an ancient text references a woman who was healed by a medicine man after a Volya attack. He sends a message through the library's system for any additional books that might reference the event.

Ascelin calls Diana and Ten's brother to let them know, and there's an almost tangible change in the feel of the room.

We break for the evening, but after Zakarias and Ascelin have gone, Ten remains.

He stacks books alongside me, and it doesn't surprise me in the slightest that he stacks them correctly.

Grinning, I look up at him. "After all this shit is done, and assuming Diana is okay, you're going to apply to the Novice program, right? You're doing this better than most second-year librarians."

Ten gives me a slight smile, then picks up the first stack as I give him a quizzical look.

"What?" he rumbles. "It doesn't feel right that you're busting your ass to help us. Plus, I don't sleep well anyway."

"Okay." I laugh, grabbing a second stack. "Then I'm going to teach you how to spell them back in place, and how to spell them out. But don't tell a soul I taught you because the magic is dangerous."

Ten's face splits into a huge, broad grin, and he puts his free hand on my lower back. I struggle not to sink into his warmth. Gods, I'm so sad he's had so much trauma and he's dealing with that. My heart is broken for him, but my pussy just wants to rub herself all over his face.

We make our way into the stacks, and I check each spine for the number, holding up my hand to Ten. "We make a fist like this." I wrap my fingers together, keeping my thumb on top of the other four. "And then we whisper the correct incantation to locate the book's spots. *Libris Actuis Localis.* You try it."

Ten makes a perfect fist and repeats the spell, and the number on the book's spine glows brightly. Without me even having to tell him, Ten follows the sensation that pulls us to where the book belongs. When we get there, he gives me a triumphant look. It's heady and beautiful and overwhelming because this is what he could be if given the proper environment to shine in.

I point to a shelf that doesn't look empty when he starts to appear confused, dark brows pulling into a deep vee above his striking eyes.

"Now it's *revertere ips manerit.*"

"Can I say it?" Ten questions, looking around to make sure nobody's near us.

"Go ahead." I give him a conspiratorial wink.

When he repeats it, not quite correctly, nothing happens.

"Mah-nair-itt," I correct. "Not Man-urr-itt."

"Got it," he says, his fangs descending. Ooh, so he's feeling some kind of way about this little lesson if the fangs are a sign. I know enough about shifters to know it happens in a time of strong emotion. I love it. I'm going to convince him to join the program if I have my way, which I pretty much always do.

He repeats the incantation, and the books on the shelf slide apart. The one on top of his stack levitates and then shifts upright, slotting itself in its spot. Once it's in, the glowing number on the spine stops.

Ten turns to me with a little whoop of excitement.

You can take the dork out of the librarian, but you can't take the librarian out of the dork.

I grin and gesture for him to continue. It takes us an hour still, but we get all the books put away, and by the time we're done, Ten seems refreshed.

It's more than that, though. He seems good for the first time since I met him. He seems happy. It might not last because grief is a funny thing. It's not linear, and it's never really done. I know. Grief and I are close friends.

But if it's good right now, then it's still progress.

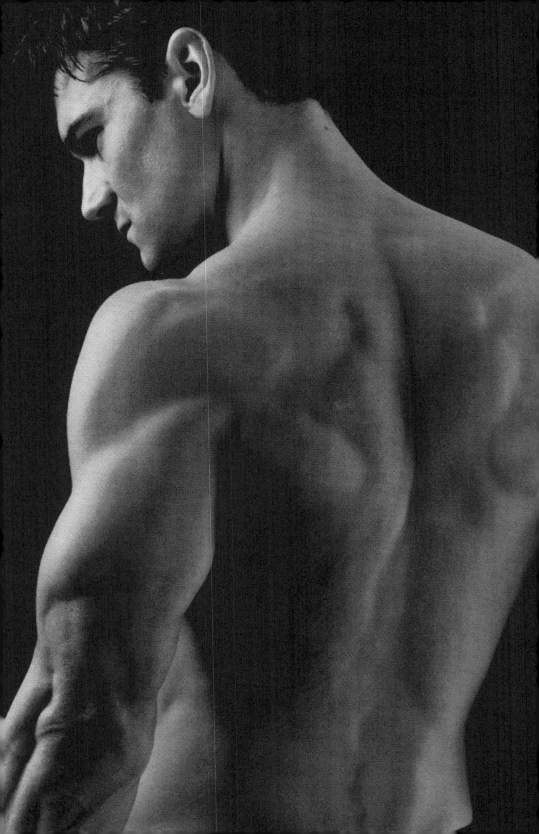

CHAPTER SIXTEEN
TENEBRIS

I should be exhausted, but I think I'm too wired and hyped on coffee to go lay down. Even Onmiel seems energized by having taught me something.

I look down at her. From my height, I can see the top of her head since she's so short. "Wanna go run with me in the garden?" I'm not sure what makes me ask it, but I think I'll be able to get a little rest if I do that.

Onmiel rubs the back of her neck but looks up with a wry smile. "As much as I'd love that, I think you mean in direwolf form, right?" She points down to her long, thin legs. "Athletic as I am, I'll never be able to keep up with you."

"You can ride me," I purr, not meaning for it to sound so incredibly sensual. But it does, and she stops in her tracks, crossing her arms as she narrows her eyes at me.

Onmiel's nostrils flare. She looks like she's trying not to laugh. "That sounds very sexual, Tenebris."

"I didn't mean it to," I say quickly, hoping I haven't made her feel incredibly awkward. "It would be fun, come on. It's not some big secretive direwolf thing. If I was still around my pack and there

131

were pups, I'd give them a ride, too. Consider yourself a direwolf pup."

That seems to mollify her, even though it buries a dagger in my stomach.

My pack. Our pups. My friends.

All dead.

All dead because of Rama.

I hold back a growl because she'll never hurt anyone again. My heart paid the price, but Lombornei is safe.

"Okay." Onmiel's agreement brings me back to the present, and I smile.

"You'll come with me?"

She scrunches her sloped nose and nods. "Yeah. I'm going to wrap my hand around all your neck fur, though. That doesn't sound comfy."

I do laugh at that because if she thinks that'll hurt an alpha like me, she doesn't know as much about us as she believes she does.

"Come on." I gesture for her to join me as I head back toward the elevator bank, debating if there's time for more coffee before the run. I'd better not, though. I should get some sleep before the rest of my pack arrives, assuming Diana is stable. Pack? Court? I'm not sure what we're calling ourselves these days, but I've heard both terms used.

Onmiel is a bundle of excitement all the way up to the fifth floor, and when we get there and enter the gardens, she grins at me. Then her cheeks turn pink as she tucks a strand of brilliant blue hair behind her ear. "You, uh, need to get undressed, right?"

Pulling my shirt over my head, I toss it on a nearby bench and grin. "Yep, unless I wanna walk out of here naked."

She grumbles something under her breath, but when I reach for my pants, she turns from me and walks away a few steps, looking studiously anywhere else.

"Alphas don't give a shit about nudity, Onmiel. It's sort of a side effect of shifting all the time. Someone in the pack is always naked."

"You might not, but I do," she chirps back. "I'll ogle you, and I don't want to be weird."

"Ogle me, huh?"

"Yeah." She laughs. "You're hot, Ten, but friends don't ogle their naked friends. I mean, not any more than is absolutely necessary."

I hear her heart pounding in her chest, galloping along at full speed as she works herself into a lather about my nudity. It's funny to me because I don't even think about it. Nudity doesn't equal sex for shifters, although I suppose if Onmiel were to actually stare at my dick, it might feel that way.

I shift into my direwolf and cross the small walkway, nudging her in the back with my nose. Like this, I experience her differently. When she turns, there's a surprised but joyous look on her face. She says nothing but reaches out to stroke both of my ears, which brings her chest nearly flush with my face. She smells...good.

Better than good. She smells sweet but a little tart.

When she scratches behind one ear with a little laugh, I butt her chest with my head and lie flat. She gets the message and gives me one final look. "You sure about this? I'm going to come away with handfuls of hair, so it's your funeral if you agree to it."

A low growl rumbles from my throat, and she takes my meaning, hopping lithely onto my back. She rocks her hips as she gets situated, squeezing me tight with both knees as her hands rest at the base of my neck. I take off at a slow canter, like a horse, to get her accustomed to the movement.

Onmiel leans forward over my shoulders and wraps her arms around my neck, and godsdamnit, she does wrap both fists in my fur. It pinches, but my direwolf is thrilled to have her on us. Alpha packs are affectionate with close-knit friendships. I've missed that, and he has too.

I run for a solid half hour before finding the crystal-clear lake I found that first day. Dropping to the ground, I shrug Onmiel off as she laughs excitedly.

"That was amazing, Ten! You're so fucking fast, I'm totally jeal— oh gods, what are you doing?" she shrieks when I shift out of direwolf form. My direwolf wants to play with her, to tease her, because he recognizes a kindred spirit.

Her cheeks flame red, and her eyes dart immediately to my cock, which hangs heavy against my thigh. I'm half-hard, knowing a female's examining me. I don't know if Onmiel's aware she is, but when I clear my throat with a haughty grin, she crosses over and slaps my chest.

"I told you I wasn't going to be able to not look. It's your fault for making me do it. I think you did that on purpose," she snaps, crossing her arms as I pick her up, and throw her over my shoulder.

"Don't gaslight me." I laugh. "I didn't force you to look."

It's nice to be playful, and it makes my direwolf happy—something he hasn't been since we ripped Rama to shreds. I jog straight into the lake and throw Onmiel bodily into the water, laughing as I dive under it to watch her.

She flails before finding purchase on the rocky bottom, and then she stands up with a glower as something blue runs in rivulets down her arms. "You are such an *ass*, Tenebris Ayala! Damnit, I just dyed that, too..."

Grimacing, I swipe two fingers up her arm, watching goosebumps cover it as I lift them to show her the dye. "I'm so sorry, I was just playing around, but I fucked up your hair."

As I watch, the dye runs in intense rivers down her hair. She gives me two middle fingers but dunks herself, shaking her head side to side as she runs her fingers through her long hair. When she comes back up, I gasp in surprise. Where her hair was a vivid royal blue before, it's now a shimmery, opalescent white. It shines like a pearl as she grimaces, pointing up at it.

"Do I look like an old lady?" She must hate the hair, based on the way she seems to expect me to hate it.

I take a step closer to her, picking up the ends and taking a look. Up close, it's actually every possible shade of the palest pastel, almost like a real pearl.

"I've never seen hair like this, Onmiel," I murmur. "What are you, if not fully human?"

"Nobody's ever seen hair like this," she grouses. "It's stupid to deal with. That's why you've known me for three days, and you've already seen it be two different colors. And I don't know what I am, sadly."

"It reminds me of my brother's mate, Achaia's, pearls. She's a mermaid queen, you know."

I splash Onmiel, who sticks out her tongue in a raspberry.

"So, what'll your hair color be next?" I turn on my back and float lazily around her. She's careful not to let her eyes drift to my crotch, where my half-mast cock still pokes out.

"I was thinking neon green," she smirks. "I'm already pretty noticeable in the library, but nobody'll be able to miss me with that."

When I think of how ever present she is in the library, I have to grin. I suspect even before we arrived, Onmiel was at the library as much as humanly possible.

There's a sudden movement, and I shift upright just as she throws herself on top of my head, dunking us both. Water shoots up my nose as I growl and remove her, although she's wrapped herself around me as she yanks at my hair with both hands.

Calling on my direwolf's strength, I lift her off me and toss her fifteen feet across the pond.

For half an hour, we play, but I notice my friend is starting to fade.

"Time to get you home," I mutter as I walk out of the lake. She doesn't even stare at my crotch before yawning and following me.

"Shit, we've got to be back in a few hours," she moans. "You want to just come sleep on my window seat? Or we could maybe get a room assigned for you."

For half a moment, I debate the merits of this plan. I'm not looking forward to the walk home, and I do have to be back here soon. But a bedroom with another woman? I don't know if I'm ready. But when my direwolf growls at me, I nod.

"Let's go. I'll stay with you."

"Good," she murmurs, her eyelids drooping. "You can shower because there's literally a fish scale on your forehead. Herk!"

Laughing, I peel the scale off my skin and flick it into the lake, shifting so she can get on top of me again.

The entire run back to the elevator bank, my direwolf preens at having Onmiel ride us. He likes her.

≈

Half an hour later, we've showered separately in the small room assigned to her. It's nothing more than a tiled bathroom, shower, and a small bed with a chair in the corner. A big, round window overlooks the city outside, with a bench seat underneath it. I sit there as she comes out of the bathroom, clothed, toweling her incredible hair.

When she smiles at me, it warms me from the inside out, and I pull my knees to my chest as I watch her.

"What?" she questions me with a suspicious smile, tossing the towel aside. "You look like you're about to ask me about the secrets of the universe or something."

Something deep inside me breaks, standing here with her. I want her to know me, to really know me.

"You don't treat me like a victim," I start, not sure I really want to go into this, but also desperate to talk about it. "Why is that?"

Onmiel grabs a fluffy gray sweater and pulls it onto her thin shoulders, flopping down across from me on the bench seat. She gazes out the window for a moment and then turns to me.

"I never watched what happened in the maze, but I heard about it, of course. The librarians and Novices used to talk a lot about all the maze's monsters. I don't pry because if you want to talk about it, you will. And I don't treat you like a victim because I've been a victim, and everybody pussyfooting around you does you no good."

"When were you a victim?" I growl, shifting forward as I lock my eyes on hers. A victim? Who hurt her? My direwolf prowls inside me, pushing an uncomfortable pressure into my chest. He hates this.

"It was a long time ago," she shrugs. "But everybody walked on eggshells around me after, and I hated it. Eventually, I left home because of it."

Gods, I've got so many questions about that.

"I'm sorry," I say instead, resisting the urge to pull her into my arms and run my cheek along hers. It's what I'd do for any omega in my pack, but I don't want her to think I'm being forward.

"Do you want to talk about the maze?" she asks softly.

For a long minute, I lean back against the smooth, burled wood and watch the city of Pengshur begin to come alive. Gods, we really do need to be back to the reading room soon.

"Another time," I growl finally, looking over to where she waits, her expression hopeful and then disappointed. "You need sleep, Onmiel."

"We need sleep," she corrects with a laugh. "You're welcome to sleep in the window or on my chair, or you can sleep in the bed with me. I sleep deeply, and like I said, I snore like crazy, I'm told."

A sudden possessive alarm trills in my brain. Who told her she snores? Who was here when she was asleep, watching her, protecting her?

I shove that thought away and nod, crossing the room and falling onto the bed, facing the window.

She lays down facing me and shoves a pillow between her knees, grabbing another one and clutching it tightly.

When I give her a look, she shrugs. "Can't help it. I'm a pillow whore. You should see the sheer amount in my actual apartment."

We fall silent as I smile, watching her eyelids droop. As she begins to nod off, I keep watching. I think she's asleep, but she reaches out and places a hand on my chest.

"One day, will you tell me why you looked so broken the day you arrived?"

I force myself not to look shocked. I felt broken. I am broken. Although every day seems to be a little bit better.

"One day, I will," I whisper.

CHAPTER SEVENTEEN

ONMIEL

My alarm goes off at some godsforsaken hour, and I flutter my eyelids open with a groan. A soft snore reaches my ears, and I flip over before remembering that Ten slept with me last night.

The early morning light illuminates his tan skin and dark brows. Chocolate waves are still slicked back from the shower, although one piece sticks straight up, giving him an almost comical look.

Gods above, he's so fucking handsome.

I wonder if I should leave him to sleep, but then I imagine the look on Ascelin's face when she asks me where he is, and I tell her he's passed out in my bed. Huffing out a laugh, I consider it, if only for the sheer pleasure I'd derive from fucking with her. I know she's killed people—a lot of people—but I just can't hold back when it comes to her. I like her, and I'm going to force my friendship on her despite her reluctance. She'll give in.

They all do.

Almost as if he can feel me willing it, Ten's eyes open, dark pupils widening as they filter the increase in light.

"It's morning," I whisper. "Unfortunately. Coffee?"

"Coffee," he growls, fangs peeking out from behind his lips. He

ANNA FURY

rolls onto his back and reaches for my headboard, stretching out long as he points his toes and lets out a pleased growl.

Gods, help me, but I can't stop noticing the huge morning wood pressed against the front of his jeans. I think that thing would break me. It's so damn big. I read a shifter erotica once. They've all got a knot at the base that swells. That must feel like birthing a baby.

"Onmiel, what are you thinking about?" Ten laughs. "You're staring at my junk."

I don't know when we turned the corner from tentative friendship to sexual innuendo, but we've passed that corner, and we're hurtling toward the next one.

"I was just thinking a knot probably feels like you're giving birth if you're not an omega."

"Oh, I don't know about that." He laughs, rolling onto his side as he props his head in one hand. "My brother, Jet, is mated to a vampiri warrior and a mermaid queen. She takes both of them together. In the same hole."

I scoff. "Bullshit."

"Unfortunately, I've heard them. But in any case, you'll get to ask her yourself later," he replies, his tone suddenly wry. Amber eyes move back up to mine. He looks hesitant. "You'll love Jet and his mates. Achaia is fierce and kind. Renze and Ascelin together are hilarious. Diana is amazing, too. My whole pack is incredible. But my brother Noire is…" He seems to struggle to come up with a word for his eldest brother.

"A dick?" I offer helpfully. Ten sits up and stretches again, rubbing one big hand on the back of his neck.

Gods, I'd love to help with that.

"It's more than that." His voice is quiet, and I wonder if it's hard for him to talk poorly about his brother, being the pack alpha and all. "Noire is calculating and devious. He's always looking ten steps ahead. Just be wary of him. He'll use anyone to get what he wants, and he has everything to lose right now. He'd burn Pengshur to the ground if he thought that would get him an answer for Diana. He

140

threatened Garfield with that before we even came. He'd do it, Miel."

A chill skates down my spine, imagining what that sort of male might be like.

"We better get him answers, then," I confirm.

Ten nods, but he looks lost in thought. We dress, leave the room, and head downstairs.

When Ten swings our assigned room's door open for me, I smirk when Ascelin's the only one present. She snarls as I enter with Ten right behind me. He's oblivious to her ire, but I hold back a smile as she turns apoplectic with rage. I can tell because her face gets a little grayer, all the dark blood rushing to it as she bites her lip to keep from screaming at me.

Instead, she turns to Ten with a lofty grin. "Tenebris. Your brothers will be here shortly. Are you ready?"

Oh, checkmate. The point goes to Ascelin because that news took all the wind out of my proverbial sails.

Ten stiffens, and I shoot her a shitty look. I open my mouth to say something, but Zakarias and Arliss come into the room together, mid-conversation.

"—sure we will be able to handle whatever—"

"I am certain you are not ready for Alpha Noire, First Librarian," Arliss snarls. "But you had better get ready with answers fast because he will not hesitate to use whatever means necessary to persuade you." Arliss uses air quotes to punctuate the word "persuade".

I think I see what's going on here. Ten warned me in the same way this morning. All that aside, I'm not here to let Zakarias or myself be bullied around by anyone. We are on the same mission as the Ayala Pack, and we are making progress, albeit slowly.

"We've got this handled," I interject, breaking Arliss's attention on my mentor.

At the same time, the door swings open, and a giant male steps through, pitch-black eyes flicking from face to face before landing on mine.

This could only be Noire. He looks slightly older than the male just behind him, even though he's a tad shorter. He's broader, though, all stacked muscle and an air of superiority. There's a sneer on his face, sharp fangs poking out from his upper jaw. He cocks his head to the side, and a flash of terror streaks down the back of my neck.

This male is a predator in every sense of the word. When Ten said Noire would burn the library to the ground without remorse, I found it hard to understand, but not after seeing him in person. Behind his steely, focused gaze is an air of insanity.

Noire is a male on the knife's edge of something, and I don't want to be in his path when he snaps.

"Brother," Ten murmurs, pulling me away from the door and behind him.

Noire doesn't move from the doorway, but the two males behind him push inside the small room, which now feels stifling. Next to me, Zakarias sounds like he's about to hyperventilate.

The second male looks like Noire but is a little taller, a little lankier. This must be Jet, the pack's strategist. Next to Jet hovers a slender vampiri male, blond hair braided away from his forehead and ear on one side in an intricate series of braids. They hang down his back on one side. He's a First Warrior like Ascelin if I read the braid pattern correctly.

So that must be Renze, one of Jet's two mates.

When nobody says anything, my mind wanders to such an unusual pairing. I've rarely heard of direwolves mating outside their species. But for Jet to take not only a vampiri but a mermaid queen. I wonder how it's changed their pack dynamics, if at all. Of course, I've wondered the same thing about Ascelin and her connection to Diana. It seems like the maze brought them all together in unforeseen ways, and I'm curious wha—

"Where are my fucking answers?" Noire keeps his voice light, but there's an intense undercurrent to the question.

Zakarias steps forward to stand next to me, wringing his hands. Gods, I hope he stops that. If there was ever a male not to be prey-like in front of, it's this one. "Alpha Noire, allow me to int—"

"I don't give a fuck who you are," Noire snaps, his voice rising in timbre. "I sent Ten here for one reason and one reason alone. Garfield assured me you were the best team, yet I've heard no good news. So, where the fuck are my answers?"

I watch the other brother's eyes flick around the room and refocus on his pack alpha. There's a long beat, and then Noire's eyelashes flutter against his tan cheeks.

Are they communicating through a family bond? They must be. If Jet is the strategist and the "nice one", according to Ten, I assume he could be talking his brother down. Or trying to.

"We're close," I lie. "We've made progress, but we're piecing information together from hundreds of different sources."

Black eyes narrow on me.

"Don't lie to me, girl." The promise of violence is heavy in his words. "Work yourselves to the bone if you have to, but find my fucking answers. You don't want to see me at my *persuading*, as Arliss said."

Oh fuck me.

"We won't need to go there," Jet breaks in, his tone calm but decisive. He glances over at Zakarias and me. "Because the librarians are going to fix this, right?"

"Of course," I tack on smoothly. "We are dedicated to finding Diana an answer." I purposefully mention the omega herself, even though she's not here. I want to remind this pack alpha that it's not him we're doing it for; it's his mate. That we know she's important, and our focus is on her.

"Good," Jet says, shrugging his shoulders. I watch the vampiri slip an elegant hand around Jet's waist and squeeze. The direwolf sinks almost imperceptibly into that touch.

It's fascinating.

Noire laughs bitterly, gesturing around the small room. "All of Pengshur at my disposal." Sarcasm drips from his tone, despite the hundreds of books in stacks around the room. He doesn't know or care about the organization system I've got going on here, how I'm cataloging every scrap of information we find.

My mouth goes dry as his focus moves to Ten. Noire cocks his head to the side, his frown deepening as he widens his stance.

"Of course, alpha," Ten purrs. And then, "That's not necessary, Noire."

What's not necessary? Watching this pack all together is like watching a well-oiled machine function at high capacity. I heard from colleagues who watched the nightly hunts that the direwolves were the veritable kings of the maze. Despite just four of them being there, they only lost one brother in seven years of hunting the maze's dark halls. Or so I heard. Ten hasn't mentioned a pack enforcer, and that's the primary role I don't see filled here.

Although having two vampiri certainly counts. I'm dying to ask about the dynamics, but now hardly seems the time.

"I said no, Noire," Ten snaps, reminding me there's a whole conversation happening that the rest of us aren't privy to. Zakarias simmers with tension next to me. I reach out and place my hand on top of his.

Ten continues in a respectful tone. "Go to our rental, alpha, please. I'll wrap things up and meet you there. I'd be happy to share what we've uncovered and what we're still hunting for."

Noire lets out a snarly, pissed-off rumble, but I hear the click of boots on the floor. The door opens, and footsteps tell me at least one person left.

There's a sigh, and when I look around, Ten, Jet, and Renze are still in the room. They exchange a look. Renze's dark lips split into a grin, translucent black fangs clearly visible. "Best to follow him, lest he rip a limb from Garfield to make a point."

Gods, if Noire is on his way to see Garfield, I think Garfield needs a warning. I step to the nearest comm and send him a message. Jet leaves with just a quick nod to me, disappearing out the door quietly.

"Firenze." Ascelin purrs, slipping across the room in a stream of black smoke. "How I missed you." I'm shocked to see her throw her arms around Renze and give him a big hug. They're all smiles, and it's then I realize not much is known about the personal habits of vampiri warriors. I could spout a dozen facts about the First Warrior relationship, but I don't think I realized there was a true friendship there as well.

Arliss strides to the door and reaches out, pulling Ascelin out of Renze's arms. The tall vampiri grins, but Ascelin slaps Arliss on the cheek. Despite that, he doesn't let her go. Instead, he grips her chin and turns her to face me.

"Look how beautiful she is, my sweet. Let us tempt the librarian. She could use a good fuck after meeting Noire. You've had an eye on her since we arrived."

Gods, he is insufferable.

"Fuck off, Arliss," Ten barks, pulling me back behind his larger frame. "She's told you no a dozen times at this point."

I peek around to see what happens, and Renze winks at me. "It seems I have missed quite a bit since being parted from my First Warrior partner. Asc, let us retire to our temporary rooms. I have many questions for you, friend."

"Ugh," Ascelin groans, slapping Arliss again. "Enough with your tiresome games, carrow."

"You love me," Arliss sniggers, squeezing her butt before shoving her away from him and into Renze's arms.

Then, to illustrate a point about who he is, I suppose, he disappears into a wisp of black smoke and out the door.

"Fuck me," Ten sighs. "This is going to be a long day."

He's right about that.

CHAPTER EIGHTEEN
TENEBRIS

The rental's kitchen is crowded with this many people in it. Jet and Achaia cook fish while Renze and Ascelin hover around Diana. They seem relieved to be together again as a First Warrior duo. Diana's sitting at the head of the table, watching us in obvious misery.

I don't know where to turn first, but I wish Onmiel was here. I'm awkward around my family; I want things to go back to how they were before the evidence of Diana's illness was so present in front of me.

Crossing the modern-looking kitchen, I sit next to her. Noire hovers behind his mate, holding a cup of water and reminding her to drink.

Renze gives Diana a look. "It is time to change your bandages, Chosen One."

Diana's eyes flash white. The vampiri king, Cashore, speaks from inside her in a deep, commanding tone. "It is nearly time for me to return to my Zel, First Warrior. Do not delay me."

Noire bellows, but I can see he's resisting the urge to grab Diana by the throat and shake her to get at Cashore.

"Is this new?" I gasp, looking over at both vampiri.

Renze nods. "Cashore seems to believe it is time for him to move on, but we do not know how to extricate him from Diana without killing her. I have never heard of something like this. His spirit may very well be giving her strength."

Diana gasps, eyes rolling back to the normal, vivid blue. "Gods, he's strong," she complains. She shifts forward, and Noire sets the water on the table, pulling her shirt off her shoulders as I avert my gaze from her high, round breasts.

As my eyes travel down her ribcage, misery sinks into my stomach. Both sides of her core are lined with gaping slash wounds. The skin around them is black and mottled, poisoned.

Renze leans forward and applies a pink salve directly onto one of the wounds as Diana hisses and immediately begins to cry. Noire grits his teeth tightly as he strokes her cheek with the back of one hand. She cries all the way through the treatment, gasping when Renze has finished. Noire gently closes the wrap around her, and she falls back against the chair.

"Is this the treatment Zakarias found, or what you got from the mermaids?"

Achaia joins us, her brilliant green eyes flashing as she looks from me to Diana. "The mermaid treatment was a simple coagulant we often used. The sea is full of sharkfolk, even more than mermaids. Can't have lots of blood in the water." She gives me a wry grin as she grips the back of Renze's chair. "It can't do anything for the poison, though."

"What news from the library?" Noire barks, black eyes practically drilling holes into my own.

I sit up straight under my oldest brother's heavy, angry gaze. "Nothing new to report. The librarians have combed through about half the books referencing Volya, and they're ninety-five percent certain the prophecy is also Volya, but no translation exists."

Noire curses under his breath as he looks over at Jet. "So, we make a plan to capture one of the bastards so they can fix this."

"Perhaps that is exactly what the prophecy would have us do," Ascelin murmurs. "There is no way to translate it. Our only option is to ask the Volya themselves. There is almost no way for this plan to work."

"We've done it before," Diana reminds her. "But I can't ask you to risk your lives, especially with Cashore trying to dip out."

Ascelin leans over, rubbing Diana's hand with her own. "You will always be the Chosen One, Diana, even once Cashore has left you to be with Zel. That will never change. You will always be our queen."

A heavy silence falls over the group as Diana looks over at me. "Can we change the research focus to Volya defenses? We need to know what we're up against if we're going up there."

"Of course," I agree. "I'll ask Onmiel tonight."

"Onmiel?" Noire's voice is light, but there's something animal about how he says her name.

I fully expect Ascelin to have a sarcastic remark, but she's entirely focused on Diana, still rubbing the back of my pack omega's frail hand.

For a moment, the kitchen is silent. Somehow, despite the fact I killed Rama and freed our continent, it feels like that was just the beginning of something bigger. I can't stop thinking about how the Volya said the Tempang was sick, and I have to wonder if Diana's somehow tied into all of that. Maybe that's what the prophecy is about.

The moment breaks when I stand. I've got to talk to Onmiel. I've got to tell her everything I haven't shared because if there's any chance that information could save Diana, we have to take it. I wouldn't have thought my killing Rama had any bearing on our research, but I just don't know anymore.

When I turn to leave, Noire bristles through our family bond, his direwolf snapping angrily at me.

I spin in place, giving him a reassuring look even as I refuse to bow to him. I've lived a lifetime in the last two weeks. He may be my pack alpha, but the days are long gone when Noire can lord his power over me.

"I'm going back to the library to speak with Onmiel," I say

quietly. "I'd like to share all of this with her in case it sparks an idea. I'll be back in a little bit."

Again, I expect Ascelin to make a derogatory comment, but she looks up at me, her white eyes filled with tears. My pack is falling apart as Diana's health fails. I always knew the pack alpha and omega were its heart—that was why my father losing his mind was such a devastating blow for us. But to have sacrificed my mate and still lose everyone else? I can't.

When nobody says anything, I leave my family behind and jog back toward the library. Onmiel isn't in the reading room or the cafe, so I make my way upstairs to her room. When I call her name, she doesn't answer, but I hear a soft, low whine.

Her voice sounds pained. Oh, fuck, gods. What if she's hurt?

Without thinking, I shove my shoulder against the door, knocking it half off its hinges as I barrel into the room.

The first thing I notice is that she's naked, an enormous tattoo covering her entire back. The second is that she's wearing giant cat-eared headphones, eyes squinted tightly closed. Now that I'm in the room, I can hear faint music.

Oh gods, she didn't hear me come in. She rocks back, impaling herself on a gigantic ribbed dildo stuck to her headboard.

My cock stiffens as she rocks forward off the dildo. I see it's coated with her juices. This entire room is soaked in the candy-coated, tart scent of her pheromones. I should leave. I need to. I—

My brain goes to my dead mate, and I feel like an asshole. But I've spent a lot of time in the last few weeks attempting to retrain my brain to remember what Rama was to everyone else.

There isn't a kinder person in the world than Onmiel.

I spin this around, trying to make sense of a deep, building attraction between us. I want to lower myself onto the bed and take charge, to press her back onto that dildo and take control until she breaks apart.

But it would ruin our friendship because I'm fucked up about killing my bondmate.

Suddenly, Onmiel's eyes spring open, and she screams, reaching for a sheet to cover herself as I throw my back against the wall and look away.

"I'm sorry!" I shout. "I thought you were hurt."

"I'm not hurt. I'm masturbating!" she yells back, wrapping the sheet as she grabs the dildo and shoves it under a pillow.

"Fuck, I'm sorry," I groan, willing my cock to lie flat. Instead, it throbs harder at the idea of me joining her in that bed, maybe tossing her against the headboard to fuck her.

Rama liked that, being manhandled by me.

Gods, I'm so fucked up. I feel like I'm cheating on my dead mate while also being attracted to my closest friend. And I'm still standing here like a creep.

I look up at Onmiel, her white hair glowing like a light in the small room. "I'm sorry, Onmiel. I needed to talk to you, and I thought you were hurt."

She huffs and stands, letting the sheet drop to the floor as she places both hands on her hips with a scowl. "You said nudity wasn't a thing for shifters, so I'm going to embrace that and act normal. Hand me my clothes, would you?"

I blink as I try not to stare at her beautiful godsdamned figure. She's thin and athletic whereas Rama was all curves and soft skin.

Both of Onmiel's dark red nipples are pierced through with bars. There's not a single hair on her entire body, her swollen pussy visible as I struggle to swallow. Slick honey drips down her thighs.

I hold my breath.

"Ten," she murmurs, breaking the moment as I drop my eyes. I'm standing on her godsdamned clothing.

I drop down, grab the tee and jeans, and hand them to her. When our fingertips touch, I bite the inside of my cheek to resist grabbing her and pulling her to me.

I've got to get the fuck out of here before I do something I'll regret. Locking my eyes on her face, I give her what I hope is an apologetic look, but she turns and shimmies into the jeans. I can't help myself, crossing the room to run both hands carefully down the tattoo on her back.

"What are you?" I murmur as the tattoo shocks me.

"You know what this is?" She turns her head over her shoulder, and the look on her face is so sorrowful that I want to pull her into my arms and comfort her until it's replaced by the usual joy. Instead, I do what I swear I'd do with any omega in my pack; I lean down and rub her cheek with mine, purring softly.

"Prisoner tattoo," I mutter. "Achaia had one, and they had to cut it off to release her mermaid form."

"Gods, that's fucking awful. There's a serum to remove them, but it's an ancient magic. Only a few species of beings know it exists."

"Is that how you know?"

Onmiel sighs, making the tips of her breasts brush against me. But when she looks up, her face is distraught. She's forgotten about the nudity because whatever she's sighing about must be something terrible.

"I don't know, but sit down, Ten," she encourages, pointing at the window seat. "There's a lot about myself I haven't shared, but I'd like to now."

Fuck.

CHAPTER NINETEEN

ONMIEL

I'm simultaneously sweating and freezing to death. Sweating from the masturbating and the embarrassment of Ten seeing that. I was legit about to scream his name because it's totally fine to jack off to my hot friend whose pecs I want to lick.

But I'm freezing because I'm about to share something with him I've only ever told one other person at the library.

Ten grabs the T-shirt I've forgotten about and pulls it over my head.

"If your tits keep touching me, I won't be able to concentrate. I'm sorry."

I blanche and pull my arms through the sleeves, crossing them as I look up. "Ten, I—"

He throws his palms up in the air. "I shouldn't have barreled in here. It was an invasion of your privacy, and I'm sorry I did it."

I nod, but I'm not really sorry. I wish he would have joined in. Was he standing there for long? What did he think?

Crossing the room, I flop down in the window seat and pick at a hangnail as he sits down opposite me.

"Gods, I'm really nervous," I whimper. Ten laser focuses on me, his head cocked to the side, and then he reaches out, grabbing my waist and pulling my entire body between his legs. I'm facing him, seated between his knees, our bodies so close together.

He leans down and rubs my cheek with his, a soft, rumbly purr rolling out of his chest. With one hand, he strokes my sweaty hair back behind my ear. "Alpha packs are physically affectionate. Does this bother you?"

"No," I murmur. The reality is that as a single librarian, I have very little physical contact. Even a hug feels damned good.

"Tell me everything, Onmiel," he whispers, his fingertips drawing a path from my ear down my chin.

I suck in a breath and look out the window. "I don't know what I am, and that's the truth." Patting my shoulder, I glance over at the handsome alpha. "I've had the prisoner tattoo for as long as I can remember. Typically, it keeps the person from remembering anything about their life. Unless you tattoo yourself, which I did."

Ten pulls me a little closer, his forehead pressed to mine as his purr intensifies.

"I killed someone." The words are so godsdamned hard to say that I can barely get them out, and I don't miss the way he stiffens like a board. What he'll think of me now is anyone's guess.

Now that I've said it, everything comes out of me in a flood of words.

"I don't remember most of my life, but I remember killing my sister. It was an accident, but I had some kind of power I couldn't control. It ripped my family apart when she died."

Ten gasps and moves his hands to my thighs, which he squeezes once.

"I'm sure I'm not human. Not fully, at least. When Zura died, I couldn't stay home," I sob, the tears streaming. "So, I placed the tattoo on myself, leaving just enough memory that I would know what I'd done and wouldn't try to remove it and risk hurting someone again. I left," I add as the tears become a torrent. "Because I couldn't stand the looks on my family's faces, knowing I killed her."

A gut-wrenching sob leaves me then, both hands coming to my

face as Ten sits stiffly across from me. I can't even focus on his rapid breathing.

"If you want to get the fuck out of here, I get it," I shout. "I'm a murderer, Ten. I'll still help you find a—"

Ten's warning growl stops me—its tone low and menacing. Memories of Zura's death flood my brain as the tears continue to fall, wetting my shirt as I debate my next move. I shouldn't have told him. I should—

"I killed my bondmate, Rama." That's all he says, and he says it simply like he's telling me what sort of latte he had this morning.

My eyelashes flutter as I struggle to focus on him around the tears.

"She was a psychopath; I know that," he admits with a shrug. "But she was mine. Still, she did things that I couldn't live with. She hurt everyone I loved, and she would have destroyed this continent. I killed her because she couldn't be allowed to hurt anyone else." He looks up at me as the first tear falls down his bronzed cheek. "I had to choose her or my family, and I picked my pack."

I don't even know how to respond because Arliss told me that, and I don't want to throw him under the bus, except I can't to lie to Ten.

"Arliss told me the day I met you," I whisper.

Ten growls and pulls me into his arms, our bodies pressed tightly together as he wraps his arms around me. "He's such an asshole, so I'm not surprised."

"We're both fucked up, aren't we?" I whisper into his neck as he strokes my back, careful not to touch the tattoo itself.

"I don't want to be," he admits quietly, his lips tickling the shell of my ear. "I want to be normal if that's even possible. You've built a life here," he reminds me. "Despite your tragedies. You have a good thing in Pengshur."

Usually, I agree, but I can't stop sobbing as I remember my sister's death and how it all happened so quickly, yet in slow motion at the same time. I can't even remember what she looked like anymore, or my family, for that matter. I just know I hid myself away so I couldn't hurt anyone else. Never again.

For a long time, Ten holds me. And he cries, too. We fucking cry until we're cried out, and he still holds on like I'm his lifeline, purring the entire time.

Eventually, I look up at him. "You came here for something less dramatic tonight. What was it?"

Ten's eyes are puffy from the tears, but he rubs my cheek again.

"I have more information from my pack. I was hoping sharing it might spark an idea. Diana's dying, Onmiel. She's fading fast."

Extricating myself from Ten's big arms, I stand up and grab my pack, giving him my best librarian look. I've got to focus on something, anything other than my dead sister and Ten's dead mate.

He swings his legs off the window bench, leaning over them with an elbow on each knee. Whiskey-brown eyes focus on me as a little spark returns to them. "You think we need a coffee?"

I nod.

I'm going to ask for a shot of tequila in mine.

CHAPTER TWENTY
TENEBRIS

As we walk to the cafe, I fill Onmiel in on anything we haven't explicitly told her already. I relive the Volya attack while avoiding talking about the moment I killed Rama. I rehash everything the Volya said, although some is a little fuzzy to me because I was so focused on the mechanical spider my mate was drugging me with and finding out why she would do that.

Onmiel is quiet as I share what they've tried with Diana healing-wise and how Cashore is trying to leave her.

When we order and I've blurted everything out, she turns to me with an incredulous look.

"You did all of this while dealing with your own grief?"

I give her an uncomfortable look, agreeing. We shared so much earlier, but I don't want to rehash it now. It all feels too tender, and I'm not ready to talk about that part again.

Onmiel seems to realize that, though, because she reaches out and holds my hand, standing quietly while we wait for our drinks. When she lays her head against my shoulder, I wish I were shorter so I could put mine on top of hers. In the short time I've known the plucky librarian, she's wormed her way right into my soul. I think she might be the best friend I've ever had.

Our coffee arrives, and we head back to the reading room.

"Noire wants to go up to the Tempang, capture a Volya, and force them to heal Diana."

Onmiel gives me a thoughtful look as I open the door to the reading room.

Noire, Jet, and Ascelin stand inside, Noire with his arms crossed as he glares daggers at us. Pitch-black eyes move from my face to the coffee in my hand before he sneers at me.

"So, this is how you're trying to save Diana? Getting coffee with the librarian…"

It's obvious Noire's about to fly into a godsdamned rage, but I'm too old for this shit, and I'm a head taller than my older brother at this point. Straightening my spine, I let out a warning growl as Jet takes a step closer to us, ready to pull us apart if we fight.

Ascelin appears from somewhere and quietly moves Onmiel out of the way as Noire bumps me with his chest. Despite his slightly shorter height, his pack alpha dominance bowls me over. Our family bond is tight with seething anger, even though Jet's trying to remind us we're all working toward the same end goal.

"I'm going to say this once, Noire," I tell him in a calm, collected tone. "Onmiel and I are here almost twenty-four hours a day, poring over books and research to find an answer—any answer. Sometimes, all we find is a singular line with information, and that leads us to the next book. I haven't slept more than two hours since I got here, so don't press me."

Noire lets out a bellow of rage that knocks several books off their shelves. Onmiel winces as they fall to the ground, spines cracking. I resist the urge to slap him for his irreverence.

Snarling, I grip Noire's throat and pull him even closer, snapping my teeth at his face. "Simmer the fuck down, brother. You're being an asshole, and I won't stand for it. I'm doing everything I can to help you save your mate while grieving the murder of my own. Don't say a godsdamned *word* to me about how hard we're working."

Onmiel hisses in a breath and rushes to my side, too quickly for Ascelin to grab her. She shoves her way hard between Noire and me and looks up into my eyes. "Ten!"

I don't look away from Noire, who's glaring daggers at me. Onmiel rubs at my chest. "We don't have to talk about this, Ten," she murmurs. "Let's just get started, okay?"

My eyes flick down to hers as I nod, glaring back down at my big brother. Onmiel turns, still standing in front of us. I dare Noire with a scathing look to do anything to hurt her. I swear to the gods, I will pull him to shreds if he touches a hair on her head.

"What are you?" he snaps instead, noticing the way her hair is so white that it's incandescent in the low light of the reading room.

Onmiel lets out a low chuckle, her tone wry. "I don't know. I sealed my identity in a prisoner tattoo a long time ago. But it doesn't matter now because we need to help your mate, and Ten has just filled me in on your possible change of plan."

Ascelin snarls. "Did you place Achaia's tattoo, then? We were told there's nobody left on this continent aside from the Tempang's monsters who know how to do this..."

"I've only ever placed one," Onmiel murmurs, rubbing at her shoulder. "The one on my own back. Can we get back to work, or is this critical to finding help for Diana? I don't know what I am or why I could do it, and I have no way to find out. I'd rather not even focus on it now."

Noire says nothing, leveling her with a stare that's dropped grown men to their knees. But Onmiel doesn't wither underneath it. Instead, she gestures for us to follow, even as Noire mutters under his breath about us wasting time.

"Not a waste, I promise," she chirps, walking backward as we head toward the center of the library. When we arrive back at the expansive Magelang Map, I know exactly what she's thinking.

She points to the map and then looks at my brothers expectantly. "The Magelang Map has lived here for centuries, and it'll show the location of every person on Lombornei if you know how to use it." When Noire shrugs, she rolls her eyes and carries on. "So, if you want to find a Volya, we can use this map to locate them. Volya don't leave the Tempang, so they'll be in that area of Lombornei."

Noire's face lights up when he realizes what she's saying. He leans over the map as she pinches in, and the paper face of the map appears to zoom in closely on the edge of the map closest to the province of Deshali.

All I can think about is how I'm dying to know what magic powers the map. Who made it? How does it work? And how can I learn it…

Gods, I hope she doesn't zoom into the city of Nacht because if I have to see my mate's dead body on a map, I'll lose my shit.

Thankfully, Onmiel scrolls the map along the edge of the forest near Nacht. "From what we know of Volya, they live deep inside the Tempang, but if you know anything about the ones who hurt Diana, we might be able to use that information. There are several Volya clans we know of," she clarifies.

Jet straightens, sucking at his teeth. "They called themselves the protectors of the forest and said the Tempang was sick. Does any particular group deal with that?"

Onmiel shrugs. "Most monsters of the Tempang are secretive, and many have never left the forest or interbred with humans. If we don't know of the species, it won't be listed on the Magelang. But we've also been reading a lot about the Volya in the last few days. From what we've gathered, it's not so much a certain clan but a particular class of Volya who care for the forest. Unfortunately, caring for the forest could mean a lot of things."

Jet grumbles as I lean over the map. "What if we had a name?" I murmur. I sift through vague memories from my time with Rama as she planned those final days. Somehow, I was lucid, but not. I was there for her, for our mating. I was there as I watched her bring years of plans to fruition, but my emotion was totally focused on her and her alone.

I wonder for the hundredth time what was in that godsdamned spider she poisoned me with.

"Lahkan," I say, the name coming to me as Onmiel hunches over the map. She murmurs an incantation as she pinches in, and the map zooms across the Tempang to a point where the land curls around the sea like a finger.

"Godsdamnit, they're at the far end of the fucking continent," Noire rages, his voice echoing out over the books. Onmiel and I turn to shush him at the same time as he gives us withering looks.

On the map, a small label indicating "Lahkan" hovers over a village. The map won't zoom any closer than we've got it, but the beast who hurt Diana is *right there.*

"We can't run off half-cocked, Noire," Jet warns in a low, gentle tone. My pack alpha is about to lose his shit, seeing the name of the male who hurt Diana right in front of us.

Noire's glittering dark eyes focus on Onmiel. "You've got twelve hours to tell me anything we need to know about the Volya. We're leaving for the Tempang after that."

Arliss appears out of nowhere, clapping Jet on the back. We whirl to face him. I haven't seen him much, and he's just strolled in like he never left.

"If you're going to the Tempang, I'm going with you," he announces. "Was going to go alone, but if I can be helpful to Diana at all…"

"Bullshit," I snap. "You haven't opened a book to help us the entire time we've been here. Why are you coming? Because it's not to help my pack omega."

Arliss scowls at me but eventually shrugs, even as Noire balls his fists. I can tell he wants to pound Arliss into dust, but the reality is Arliss is really fucking strong, and I don't know who'd win that fight. Jet told me they fought once, and it only ended because Arliss had some sort of health episode. Even that is related to Rama because she poisoned him, too.

"I have my reasons for going, but just like on Paraiso, when our goals are aligned, I'm on your side."

Onmiel gives Arliss a shriveling look. "If you want information about what we discussed, the Volya will not help you. When you get to the Tempang, you'll have to part ways."

Arliss narrows his eyes as he points to the map. "Be a dear and show me where I might find what I'm looking for, librarian."

CHAPTER TWENTY-ONE

ONMIEL

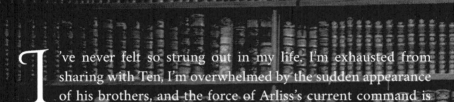

I've never felt so strung out in my life. I'm exhausted from sharing with Ten, I'm overwhelmed by the sudden appearance of his brothers, and the force of Arliss's current command is practically tangible.

"Stop with the magic," I bark at him, his power scratching at the edges of my mind. I haven't told anybody about him being a carrow. For all I know, this whole group is already aware, but if he's going to fuck around with me in front of everyone, I'll happily toss him right under a bus. Dickhead.

The uncomfortable sensation dissipates, and I shush him aside with one hand. The pack parts, and I lean over the forest on the other side of the Tempang, the northeastern corner. Whispering an incantation under my breath, I pinch in on the map. Just like before, it zooms to a lake. I didn't look for a particular person; all I know is that carrow live in that area.

Pointing to the spot, I glare at Arliss. "That's where you'll find answers, as long as you've paid attention to the resources you've been given in the last two days. You cannot simply show up and hope for the best."

Everyone is silent as Arliss inclines his head at me, not saying another word. Eventually, he looks over at Tenebris. "You freed me when I could not free myself." His voice is low, almost kind, as he talks. "If you want my help, I will lend it for a time. Once it's done, I'll move on."

Ten cocks his head to the side. "We need every extra hand, Arliss. Thank you."

Something momentous is happening here, this reforging of alliances between the mysterious carrow and the direwolf pack. Behind everyone, Ascelin stands in silence, her cell phone tightly gripped in her hand. It rings, and she jumps but picks it up with urgency.

"Chosen One, are you well?"

White eyes move to Noire, who grabs the phone and starts purring.

"What do you need, omega?" His voice is sultry and comforting, all sensual, dark promise. He listens for a moment before growling softly. "I'm coming, Diana." He tosses the phone back to Ascelin. "She's not feeling well. Let's go home and change the bandages again."

Pitch-black eyes turn to Ten. "I'm counting on you, Tenebris."

He strides off into the darkness without looking back, Ascelin a dark shadow silently trailing him. The other alpha turns to us with a soft look, his dark eyes locked onto Ten.

"How are you, Ten?" His voice is deep and concerned, but Ten takes a step closer to me.

"Fine," Ten barks. He doesn't sound fine, and the skeptical look on his brother's face indicates he realizes that, too. He smiles softly at Ten, though, and doesn't ask again. Instead, he turns to leave.

When everyone's gone, I catch Ten's eye.

"Your family's intense."

He snorts out a frustrated laugh. "Intense isn't the half of it, Onmiel." When he falls silent, I look back at the Magelang Map, wishing it could give us some sort of clue as to how to help Diana.

"We've got to be missing something that can help her, Ten. I just feel it." I mutter the words to myself more than him. At the end of the day, Zakarias and I are working hard to find answers, but I'm starting to worry it's not going to be enough. I know Zakarias checked in with ML Garfield after Noire showed up earlier. It almost feels like the whole library is tense and quiet as it waits to see what the violent alpha might do.

Ten crosses his big arms and leans up against the map as I try not to stare at the corded muscle of his enormous forearms. I've noticed in these last few days that shirts don't fit him. He's just fucking huge.

"Hear me out," I start. "This will probably sound unconventional if you haven't been around the library for a while."

Ten chuckles and bites the inside of his lip. "Well, I can't wait to hear this, Onmiel. Spit it out."

"Okay," I start. "You know it's common for librarians on assignment to work insane hours. Sometimes, you get really stymied doing that. There's a secret-ish room in the basement where we go to dance and do other stuff. It doesn't have a real name, per se, but it's pretty much the breakthrough room."

"Is this like a dungeon, or..." Ten looks like he can't decide whether to laugh, cry, or run away.

Does he think it might be like the maze? Oh, hells no.

"Not like the maze," I rush, hoping it doesn't seem like I'm asking him to do something that might remind him of where he came from. "I'm not explaining it well. Why don't we just go, and you can see. It's a way of opening your mind to other possibilities."

"And we haven't been there before now because..." His voice trails off.

"I think we thought we had more time, to be honest." It's a shitty answer, but it's the truth. We knew Diana was badly hurt, but I don't think Zakarias or I even realized she's hanging on by a thread. And maybe she wasn't when they came here, but it seems obvious she is now.

Ten stands tall and gives me a look. "Let's go, librarian. If we need to do this thing to have some kind of a breakthrough, let's do it."

171

Nerves jangle around in my stomach as I shift from one foot to the next. "Okay, but I want to warn you, the breakthrough room is a little wild."

"Wild?" Ten looks down at me with a mischievous glance.

"Yeah, it's, umm. Well, people pretty much let loose in there."

"So…drugs and fucking?"

A nervous cackle makes its way out of my throat as Ten places a hand on my lower back. "I'll be fine, Onmiel. Sex and drugs don't bother me. Remember the whole nudity conversation?"

I do, and to be honest, we've already seen one another naked. Not that I'll be getting naked in the breakthrough room, but still.

"We'll go and hope Noire doesn't come back to hear we've left our post to go do this. But I swear, it's led to some of the biggest research breakthroughs to ever come out of Pengshur. It's worth a try."

"Diana's worth it," he confirms, following me as I hang a left around the Magelang Map toward the opposite side of the library.

"We've never even come over here," Ten muses as he reaches out to stroke a row of books.

I'd love to stop and tell him all about these, but Diana's situation is dire, and I can't help but feel we're missing some brutally obvious connection.

We make it all the way to the outer rim of the library before stopping in front of a flat expanse of wall. I feel around the edge of a nearby painting, depressing a small red button as the wall swings on a hinge, opening like a secret lair from a superhero book.

Ten grinds his teeth as I step in, and when I turn, his eyes are locked on the dark hallway. Immediately, I wonder if this is like the maze, and it's too horrible to ask him to do this.

"There's another way," I offer, stepping back out.

Ten growls and takes my hand. "Come on." He pulls me back into the hallway and follows it toward the steady beat of music. The hallway is lit by the very lowest of lights, but Ten guides me like he's done this a million times. It makes me wonder if he was like this in the maze—focused, protective, and unafraid.

And how does he feel about the fact that the person who imprisoned him was later revealed to be his bondmate? I can't fucking imagine, but I squeeze his fingers tighter to let him know I'm here for him.

At the end of the hall, we come to a glossy black door, much like the rest of the doors here at Pengshur. Rounding Ten, I swing it open, and we move forward onto a platform that overlooks a giant subterranean club. A dancefloor takes up most of the middle, a deejay spinning electronic music from a stage in front of us.

I point to the outer rim, where small alcoves are built in. Ten follows my gaze.

"Those are research alcoves. Sometimes, librarians will bring their team down here with their work."

"Or other things," he murmurs, his eyes moving with focus to the alcove next to the one I just pointed at. The U-shaped leather alcove is currently hosting an orgy, and I half expect to find Arliss in the middle of it.

Ten lets go of my hand and crosses his arms. "Now what, Future First Librarian Onmiel?"

I laugh at him calling me the title I'm desperate for, but it's also hot because I can imagine him saying it in a seductive way in a bedroom conversation. But then I remember everything we shared earlier, and sobering reality crashes down on me.

"Time to dance," I chirp, pulling Ten down the stairs behind me. When we get to the bottom, one of the other Novices runs up and throws herself into my arms, pulling away, only to gape at Ten in surprise.

"Is this the hot alpha from the maze?" she whisper-hisses as Ten and I both stiffen. Without pulling her eyes from him, she digs around in her pocket and presses a small bag into my palm. "Find me later if you want to have some fun."

I roll my eyes as she gives Ten a suggestive wink, then slips off into the darkness.

"Friend of yours?" Ten's voice is dry, although I can see he's holding back a smile.

173

"Fellow Novice," I shrug, showing him the small bag she handed me. "But this could be fun. They're nose spices. They help you relax, allowing your mind to do the work of getting around your roadblocks."

Ten looks skeptical as I barrel on. "It's super common down here, although you'll almost never see them upstairs. It's a break-through-room-only sort of thing." Gods, maybe he thinks I'm a druggie now.

His striking eyes move around the room, narrowing as he takes it in. He looks uncomfortable as fuck. I'd give my left arm to know what he's thinking.

"I wish we had a family bond," I grumble as I cross my arms. "I'd love to be able to talk to you without having to shout in this loud-ass room."

Ten's gaze flashes back to me as he nods at the packet dangling from my fingertips.

"Let's do it."

"Are you sure? There's absolutely zero pressure to," I remind him.

"What can I expect?"

"You'll feel happy and high for a few hours, and then you'll be back to normal."

"Alphas burn hot, Onmiel. It might not affect me at all."

Alphas burn hot. Godsdamn, everything he says turns me on, even though he's not trying to.

For a long moment, I don't respond, but Ten's smirk widens. I swear I think he's messing with me on purpose, but it's probably just wishful thinking.

I break the moment as I lift the bag up, pulling the tiny draw-string open.

"Bend down here," I shout, pinching powder between my fingertips.

Ten leans down, his forehead almost touching mine.

"I'm going to blow this in your face, okay?"

"Do it," he growls, his long fangs poking at the edge of his lower lip.

I blow softly, the purple powder coating his nose and mouth. His tongue slides out to lick at where it covers his lips, and then he takes the pouch from me. Ten repeats my action, and I breathe in deeply, pulling the drug into my system as I wait for the moment it hits.

"It takes a minute to hit me," I laugh, "but most people feel it within about fifteen seconds."

"I've got nothin'." Ten laughs, and then that smile falls, and his chest rises and falls more rapidly. I watch his pupils widen until they take over nearly the whole pale amber of his iris. Ten's fangs descend from behind his upper lip, poking into the lower one hard enough to draw blood.

He reaches out, gripping my throat in his hand as he pulls me flush with his chest. There's a wild, focused look in his beautiful eyes as he squeezes me so hard that I struggle to breathe.

"Is this a fucking aphrodisiac, Onmiel?" Ten's voice is ragged and on edge, throaty and dangerous.

Oh shit, oh fuck. I hope I haven't just dragged him into the basement and given him an aphrodisiac. He'll think I'm doing it on purpose.

I hate the direction this is going.

"I've never heard of it being that," I gasp out. "We have other shifter librarians, Ten! Oh gods, I'm so sorry!"

His grip loosens as his lashes flutter. Ten shakes his head and grumbles something under his breath, but I can't hear it over the din of the music. He looks behind me at the packed bar and even more crowded dance floor, and then the drugs hit me.

"Come, Onmiel," Ten growls, pulling me toward the music.

And come I do.

CHAPTER TWENTY-TWO

TENEBRIS

I'm high as fuck, focused on one thing alone—the music. Deep, throbbing beats pull me by the dick to the dancefloor as I drag Onmiel behind me. I'm horny and uninhibited, and every-thing feels so good as long as I don't focus on the room itself.

This place is a dark stone grotto. It's the maze all over again, and that fractures my mind so hard the only thing I can do is focus on a second thing—my librarian. She's high now, too, her pupils a galaxy of black with starbursts of gray at the edges. She positions herself in front of me and starts dancing.

The music is fast but sensual, pulling and swaying as we rock to the beat, not touching but not looking away from one another. She grabs my hand and spins herself, cackling the whole time. I struggle against the urge to pull her lithe body to mine to feel her.

Mate.

The word flits through my mind, there and gone like the stab of a knife.

Rama.

I remember Rama screaming my name the first time I took her, how she fell to pieces on my knot.

No.

Not now.

And never again.

Growling, I step away from Onmiel and rock my hips to the music. I've never danced. I've never even heard music like this, and it's so fucking beautiful. Sensual. The notes smash down my spine like the strike of a hammer, jolting my body with their intensity. The drugs make it feel like the music is coming from within my body, taking over every nerve ending as sensations too numerous to process war for my attention.

My head falls back as I rock and sway. It's like fucking but not, and everyone around us is doing it, too. This is a sea of writhing bodies.

I look back up. In front of me, Onmiel dances with the female librarian from before. They hold on to one another, swaying seductively with their lips hovering together. If my dick wasn't already as hard as the stone walls around us, I'd stop to watch them move. Onmiel grabs the other woman's throat and pulls her in for a kiss, her pink tongue slipping between the other librarian's lips as she sucks it.

A groan falls from my throat as I reach down to adjust my cock. I'm going to fucking knot myself, high on these drugs, and watching the intensity of the room play out. I don't know if the nose spices are an actual aphrodisiac or if my inhibitions are just gone, but there's nothing but an intense sense of pleasure as I move to the music.

Hands circle my waist, and I smile, but then I realize Onmiel is making out with the other librarian, so it's not her hands on me. I'd bristle, but I'm too high to care. All I know is one hand slides up my shirt, and the other reaches down for my dick, and I let it happen. It feels so good as I leak precum like a godsdamned waterfall.

A second hand joins the first, traveling down into my pants as the drugs push me higher until all I can do is focus on the hands now stroking my cock with even, measured pulls.

Onmiel's scent flares in the tight space, and when I look up, the other librarian is gone, and Onmiel is focused on me. Her beautiful gray eyes are locked onto the hands in my jeans as I pant, my mouth open. The pleasure builds, my balls tightening as I throb into the hands of a faceless being.

Gods, this is so fucking hot. Onmiel stares at me like she's ready to worship me, and I want it.

I rip my pants open, my cock falling out heavily as there's a whispered "yes" from the being pressed to my back.

Onmiel gasps. Is she enjoying this show? I focus on her because I can't focus on this pitch-black room that reminds me of the maze and my dead mate. I focus on the pleasure because my mate was a complete asshole, and she doesn't deserve my time or energy.

She never deserved it.

I find myself wondering, again, if a mate bond can be broken by magical means. I think I want that.

Because the woman in front of me is watching me get jacked off, and all I can think about is how I wish the hands were hers.

I want her. Gods, I do.

When I look down and realize the hands now stroking me with expert tugs are a man's hands, I grimace and pull away. It's not my preference, and while I don't care who fucks anyone else, men don't interest me.

There's a soft whine behind me, but the hands disappear, and then I'm standing in front of Onmiel. She drags her eyes back up my body, her breath a rapid staccato as her nostrils flare. Strobe lights send a rainbow of colors across her face, white dots ringing what remains of her iris. I could fall into the black pools of her pupils and swim for hours.

You want me, I think. *And I* want *you, too.*

It's a realization that spins my head as a waitress shows up with a tray full of shots. I grab two without thinking, stalking forward to hand one to Onmiel.

She licks the salt at the rim and then throws the glass back, tossing it to the floor as her muscles begin to tremble.

Oh, sweet girl, I could eat you alive.

Instead, I press my chest to hers, purring as I lick the edge of the glass, gathering the salt on my tongue. Then I wrap my fist in her beautiful long hair and yank her head back. The back of her skull hits my palm, and her throat bobs. Every predatory instinct I have screams at me to rip at it with my teeth.

My direwolf wants her blood, my cock bobbing between us as I lean down slowly. I drag my tongue up her neck once, depositing the salt. And then I lick and suck my way back up it, pulling her skin into my mouth as I groan around the sheer taste of her.

Sunshine. Tart candy apples. Pure pleasure.

Take her, a voice whispers at the edges of my mind as I startle, but I'm too high to sort out who. It feels like a problem for later.

Onmiel goes limp in my arms until I clamp my teeth around her throat and bite hard. My direwolf preens in my chest, eager for more, even as surprise burrows somewhere at the back of my mind.

I shove that away. I can't dwell on the past. I can only focus on the now. And my now is looking really fucking good.

Onmiel's hips rock against my thigh with steady, even punches, her hands gripping my arms as I bite and suck my way back down her neck. I'm a hair's breadth from coming all over her clothing, so I release her hair and move that hand to her upper back. The other goes to her ass as I help her grind on me.

I rock slowly to meet her. It's a sensual dance, her clothing rubbing all over my cock. We don't look down. We don't need to. This euphoria is so all-consuming that I can barely breathe around the intensity of it.

Onmiel gasps as her cheeks turn pink, her plump lips falling open as she begins to shudder and moan.

My gods, she could come like this, I realize.

Do it, a voice murmurs again in the back of my mind, even as a memory wars with that intention.

Snarling against that push and pull, I shove my hand down the side of Onmiel's pants and push the front far enough down to slide my cock between her thighs. The moment it slips through her slick, soaked heat, we both groan. Her hands come to my T-shirt and twist as she holds on to me. This isn't the ideal height, though. I'm too tall, so I grab her ass in both hands and wrap her around my body, my cock rubbing her clit with every roll of my hips.

Onmiel presses her forehead to mine, her lips almost touching mine. And she never looks away. Not as her body coats me in slick juices. Not when her breath begins to rise, her muscles tightening in my arms. Her scent floods my nose, so heady and beautiful that I salivate.

She doesn't even look away when that pleasure crests, and she floods my dick with her sweet honey, throwing me into an orgasm so hard, I lean back to roar. My bellow is lost in the crowd, melding with the beats as she leans forward and screams into my chest, clenching her thighs around me as her orgasm prolongs.

Moments later, we come down, and I can't decide if I should throw her to the ground and fuck her or leave and take a freezing shower. Everything smells of her release. She's nowhere near sated, and my direwolf knows, prowling in my chest as if he can't stand not taking more.

He's never been this active, this present in my entire life. I've never read about this in a book. Our wolves are a sentiment, not a separate being.

Take her, I hear again.

Oh, my fucking gods, is it him? My direwolf?

Good. Very good.

Shifters' animals don't speak to them; they don't have a voice.

Pleasure rumbles through my system, a sudden, intense desire to start this all over, but Onmiel pushes out of my arms, zipping up her pants even as I whine, watching all that honey disappear from my view.

She slaps my chest, looking up at me with a thrilled expression. "Ten! I've got an idea."

CHAPTER TWENTY-THREE
ONMIEL

I'd be a godsdamned liar if I didn't admit to still being halfway high, but that gorgeous fucking orgasm opened a door somewhere in my mind. I didn't intend for it to escalate to that, so I'm going to move right along like we didn't just dry hump until we came all over each other.

But I've got an idea. An honest-to-gods idea. I practically sprint from the breakthrough room, up the stairs and down the long hall, and back out into the library. Ten rushes out behind me, and then we're flying together through the aisles, passing the Magelang Map and hooking a hard left. We come to the exit.

Ten gives me a quizzical look. "We're leaving the library? Why?"

"Not the library, just the archives," I whisper-hiss in excitement. "I'll tell you on the way. Come on."

He doesn't ask anything else but opens the wooden doors as I sail through, pointing down another burled wooden hallway to a second set of doors.

"That's the public section of the library. Anyone can visit there, and there's no magic keeping the books in place."

Ten looks ahead. I barrel on. The public section looks a lot like the archives, but it's larger. It's also dead this late, although we pass the occasional librarian as we head for a giant circular staircase in the middle. Stopping at the bottom, we look up.

"At the top of the public section is an archive of gifts. Anything anyone has ever gifted the library lives here."

"And you don't have access to this in the archives?" Ten's voice is confused as we start trekking up the stairs, moving quickly from one inlaid wooden step to the next.

"It's not connected because everything is cataloged when it's gifted. Master Librarian Garfield is our ML now, so he's responsible for cataloging each gift and deciding if it needs to be in the archives or not. Sometimes, the decision is that it's not dangerous, not secretive, or not librarian-only information, and so the item or book remains in the public section."

Ten catches on quickly. "So, you're saying the library could have been gifted something that ML Garfield just didn't think was important enough to put in the archives."

"Could be." I look up at the sexy-as-sin alpha, hoping he's as embroiled in this as I am and definitely not thinking about the way we almost just fucked.

Ten's beautiful eyes are focused on me, narrowed with intensity. His nostrils flare. He's still a little high, I can tell. Shit, I am too, but it's fading fast as my excitement builds.

"It's totally possible there's nothing to find here," I caution.

Ten puts one hand at the base of my spine, urging me faster up the stairs, even as my muscles begin to tire.

"We have to try," he murmurs.

We make it to the eighth floor and rush to a circular bookshelf in the middle. There's a small reading room on the inside of the ring that people can sit in and peruse the books.

"How do we find anything about the Volya here?" Ten's tone is morose as he strokes the spine of one of the books.

"This is where the library's magic comes in handy." I chuckle. "While there's no magic keeping books on shelves in the public section, I can use my magic to hunt for what I'm looking for. Like this…" I place my hand on a spine and murmur an incantation, and the book wiggles a little bit but doesn't move.

I point at the spine. "If this one had contained a reference to the Volya, it would have popped out of the shelf."

Ten grins. "Teach me. I'll help."

I quickly show him the incantation, and we start at opposite ends of the bookcase. For half an hour, we go through the books one by one, and then we move to the next row and the next. It's arduous, painstaking work until Tenebris comes around the corner with a triumphant grin, a black leather-bound book in his hand.

"This one popped out." He shrugs, his grin growing larger as he hands the book carefully to me. My hands shake with excitement as I press a button on the bookshelf, and a panel swings open, revealing the small reading room inside this column of bookshelves.

"This place is amazing," Ten mutters. "I could spend years uncovering all the library's secrets."

"I hope you will." I laugh, entering the reading room and taking a seat at the tiny table inside. Ten props himself on the edge of the table, crossing his legs at the ankle as he watches me. His pupils are still blown wide from the drugs, his breathing quick and shallow.

"One day, when all this bullshit is over, I hope I get the chance to come back, Onmiel." There's such a serious look on his face. I can't help but wonder if he means for more than the library. It feels like he's saying he's coming back for me, too, and while that gives me hope, anguish settles in my chest, curled like a cobra waiting to strike at my heart. I don't deserve him, this perfect, amazing man who feels like he fits me so easily.

It's a cruel, fucking twist of fate that I'd find the him at the most imperfect time.

"I don't want you to leave at all," I whisper, not even meaning to say it out loud.

Ten looks down at the floor, and I ponder apologizing for making this awkward, but instead, I turn to the book and begin flipping through its pages.

When he says nothing, I want to slap myself for opening my

dumb mouth. I push the thought aside, focusing on the book in front of us.

"It's an account of the gifts given to the library in the last ten years," I murmur as I carefully look through the various lines. I point out the columns to Ten as he leans over. "This is ML Garfield's handwriting, so you can see here and here where he noted what the gift was and who gave it, if that's known."

"People give anonymous gifts?" Ten's voice is low and curious as he leans over me to examine the page more closely.

"It's less common," I share. "Most beings are happy for the library to list them as donors. Occasionally, we'll receive something that just shows up on the doorstep."

"Seems sketchy," Ten grumbles.

I can't think of anything to say to that. Ten spent seven years locked in a dangerous maze, fighting for his life. I'm sure everything unknown could present a danger there. It must be hard to stop thinking that way.

Frustration sends a pinch of pain between my eyes as I growl. Ten slides down into the chair next to mine. "Let me, Miel."

My eyes dart up to his. "You've never called me *Miel*." I can't resist the grin that splits my face.

Without missing a beat, he keeps flipping the pages, concentrating on the book, although the very edges of his lips curl into a smile. "That was before you came all over my cock while high on nose spices."

Oh, fuck. Fuck. Fuck. I thought we were going to just pass right on by that. I mean, I'll never forget it, but I don't want him to feel pressured. I nibble at my lip, but I can't think of a damn thing to say once again. My cheeks must be redder than cherries right now.

"Found it!" Ten chirps, setting the book carefully down. He points to an entry from eight years ago.

"Unnamed Volya gifted the library with a vial of blood. Remanded to ML Garfield for safekeeping." I look up at Ten. "We don't know if Volya blood would be an antidote for Diana, but a good physik might be able to craft something from it. I know that much from helping Zakarias with medical research."

Ten stands with a little whoop. "Let's find Garfield now. We've got to get this vial immediately."

I huff out a breath, thinking. "The library has a physik on-call, and Garfield is sometimes in his office very late. Let's try that first, and if he's not there, we'll buzz him on the messaging system."

Ten gives me a hopeful look. "I'm going to call Noire and let him know we might have an option before we haul Diana up to the Tempang."

I smile as I look back down at the book, running my fingers across the beautiful ink. Ten grabs his phone and dials his brother, talking in excited tones as I flip through the rest of the book, making sure nothing else has been mentioned about Volya. Finding nothing, I watch Ten instead.

Realizing I should update Zakarias, I stand and go to the screen buried in the back of the circular bookshelves, calling up the messaging app. I'm still awkward with the tech, but I can figure out the basics.

Grumbling under my breath, I punch in Zakarias's code and force through an urgent message detailing what we've found. I wait, listening to Ten answer a barrage of questions from his brother. He hangs up as I stand in front of the comm screen. Zakarias sends a message back moments later.

Buzzed ML Garfield to meet at his office. Coming now.

Ten looks at the message and beams at me. "We have hope for the very first time, Onmiel. Thank you." His beautiful eyes drift down to my lips. Gods, I wish he'd kiss me. I can imagine just how good it would be when he looks at me with that predatory gaze.

"Ten," I whisper.

He doesn't acknowledge he's heard but plants one palm above my head on the wall as he leans in.

"What are you doing?" I manage as he tugs my head back with a hand in my hair.

"Alpha packs are affectionate," he murmurs, bringing his nose to my neck and inhaling with a soft, pleased groan. "I'm excited and relieved, and I want to connect with you."

I can't ask the question I want to know the answer to, which is that this seems like more than an affectionate hug. There's an underlying sexual current to this that's so strong that I could easily drown in it.

My heart pounds in my chest. It's so damn loud I know he can hear it. "Are you like this with your sisters-in-law, then?"

Ten chuckles, low and throaty, as he purses his lips. "We rub cheeks and hug, but if I scented Diana's neck like this, Noire would remove my head."

Why are you doing it to me, then? That's what I want to ask.

Except the answer is obvious to me now. He's attracted to me the same as I'm attracted to him. The bigger and more important question is, is he ready for something? I'm going to wager *not* after murdering his bondmate in the last month.

"I wanna chase you, Onmiel," he breathes out. Tawny eyes flash with need before dropping to my mouth. His lips part, his fangs descending. His nostrils flare, and he sucks in a deep, slow breath. Time slows to a halt, and sound muffles. There's nothing in this moment but the male in front of me, looking at me like I'm the sun at the center of his universe. I want that with every fiber of my being.

But fierce realities batter me, reminding my heart that he's still grieving, and he's still a little high, and to initiate something with him now isn't right. I press myself harder to the shelf, trying to get away from the overwhelming *everythingness* of Ten when he's focused like this.

He must sense my hesitation because his eyes shutter. He presses off the wall with an unhappy frown and turns toward the opening. "Ready to go?"

Fuck no! That's what I want to shout because I'm desperate for more of that connection with him. But now that neither of us is riding that all-encompassing, drug-aided high, I'm more cautious of anything that might be taking advantage of him.

Instead of voicing any of that aloud, I sigh. "Come on, alpha. Let's find the Master Librarian and see if we can save Diana with this blood."

CHAPTER TWENTY-FOUR
TENEBRIS

Warring emotions spar in my mind as we leave the public section of the library, passing back through the long hall toward the archives. I know where I'm going now, so my focus is on Onmiel, who's silent by my side, her strides long and purposeful.

I want to stop and toss her up against the wall, to have a conversation about everything that happened in the breakthrough room, just now, and everything that's been building up between us.

Friendship. Support. Partnership.

Something *more*.

In my chest, my direwolf presses against the breastbone, anxious to break free and touch her. He's never been so active in our connection. Shifting was always a thing I could do, but in direwolf form, I was always *me*. Direwolf shifts always reflect our emotions, but they don't have their own separate thoughts.

But mine seems to, all of a sudden. He has his own preferences, and his choice is not to beat around the bush but to start something with her right now.

And then there's the achy place in my chest that misses my dead mate. That can't stop thinking about how I killed her. I can't forget how she pleaded for mercy in our bond, but having that connection meant I could also feel that seedy undercurrent of lies beneath her plea. It was like ash filling my mouth and choking me. If I had given Rama mercy, she'd have stabbed all of us in the back a moment later. I know that. And I've worked hard to remind myself of that, hoping it would somehow shred the stupid bond I share with her. It still hurts.

My direwolf quiets as the memory of Rama takes over my thoughts. Did the serum she kept me drugged with hurt him? How does he feel about that? Why is he making his desires known just now?

But now isn't the time to explore what's going on with him. I'll eventually return to Pengshur and research if other alphas have experienced this. I'll ask my brothers and my adoptive father, Thomas, too, but it's new. It's…weird.

When we arrive at the entry to the archives, Zakarias is there with an excited look on his face.

"Well done, Onmiel! My goodness, I am so thrilled to have a real lead." He looks up at me. "Fingers crossed, alpha."

I give him an understanding look, and then I follow them both through the center of the library, passing the Magelang Map and out to the other side of the archives. We'll exit the archives and then—

There's a sudden hiss and the sound of scales slithering across wood. I freeze, grabbing Onmiel's arm.

Zakarias turns to us with a confused look.

I glance around urgently. "Is there a naga here?"

I killed two naga in the maze, and I'm coated with their death mist, a pheromone that'll announce to any others that I'm not to be trusted. Smelling like that pheromone is a fucking death sentence. If there's one here, it'll try to kill me.

Time slows as the doors to the archives open, and sure as shit, a godsdamned naga slides through, speaking with another librarian. He's huge with a large, round, black body. His humanoid upper half is crested with the round hood common among his kind.

TEN

We all pause. The naga's head whips in our direction. His slitted eyes meet mine, snakelike, flat nostrils flaring as his tongue slips out, flicking the air as he tastes it.

"Onmiel, run!" I shout as I shove her and Zakarias away from me and sprint in the opposite direction, hoping to distract the naga as I shift into my direwolf.

An ungodly roar shakes the bookshelves around me.

I hear Onmiel and Zakarias's panicked screams as the shelves start to fall, the naga giving chase.

"King killer!" he shrieks. It's deafening as I try to lead him away from my friend.

He's nowhere near as big as the naga in the maze, but it took our entire pack to kill that one, and we barely survived it.

I race around the outer rim of the library, hoping to pull him into the hallway leading back to the public area; it's emptier than the archives. There are faint, far-away screams as those in the archives flee the fury of the raging naga. He chases me without giving thought to the library itself. I hear the splintering of wood and the tearing of books from their shelves.

An entire bookshelf flies past my head, tumbling over itself as the naga catches up, his whispered hiss right behind me as I push my direwolf harder.

Away from her, my wolf rages in my chest. *Then fight.*

I barrel through double doors and into the hallway before a swipe of black claws knocks me into the wall. I'm up before my feet even hit the ground, pushing off the wall to leap at my attacker, slashing my claws across his chest and face before sprinting away.

He roars and raises up high on his long body, his chest shaking with anger as he rattles the tip of his tail. The hood behind his head flares open wider, revealing a red and black scrolled patterned tattooed along the inside. This specific pattern marks him as a naga scholar, but any naga is dangerous.

His eyes blink slowly, his forked tongue tasting the air as he slithers quietly up the hall toward me.

"You killed him. You!" He points a black-clawed finger at me. "King killer. You are a king killer."

I scream for my brothers in our bond, praying they can feel me from this far but also hoping Onmiel called them. If I can keep him talking long enough, Noire will get here, and I won't have to do this on my own.

I hear footsteps pounding behind the naga.

I can't answer him in this form, and there's no fucking way I'm shifting to talk this out.

Fight, my direwolf growls.

Crouching, I flick my tail from side to side. The naga coils, preparing to strike. He balls his fists as his upper body sinks lower, preparing for maximum impact.

Behind him, the double doors swing wide open, and Zakarias runs through. Onmiel is right behind him, her pale face flushed, gray eyes wide with terror.

"He won't recognize you!" she screams at Zakarias, even as her mentor barrels toward the naga, waving his arms to get its attention.

The naga whips around, and I take that moment to strike, leaping onto his hood and slashing. I rip and tear my claws down the back of it, trying to get around to his neck. His hood is a series of massive muscles, flaring as he bucks and writhes, his body ripping and curling.

I hang on for dear life as he flails around the hallway.

There's a grunt. Onmiel screams. A glass window shatters as the naga's body goes halfway through it. I'm tossed to the wall, sliding down as he lets out a rattling war cry. Onmiel is pressed against the wall to my left, twenty feet from me. Slitted, furious eyes move from me to her. He's no longer the male she might have known. The pheromone that coats me has turned him into a wild beast with no logic left, save to kill in revenge.

There's an immediate shove in my chest, and my direwolf takes over, all consciousness narrowing to Onmiel, who looks horrified as she edges toward the door with a knife in her hand.

Good girl, I think, *for grabbing that from somewhere.*

The naga strikes like a flash, but I catch him right before his teeth sink into her, clamping my fangs around his throat as I sink deep into the muscle. His arms come around me, and he whips from side to side, smashing us up against the ceiling, down to the floor, against both walls and then the plate-glass windows. I hang on, refusing to let go as I crush his throat, praying Onmiel's out of the way of his writhing coils.

Screams echo around me as pain blooms in my core. He's digging his claws in, trying to rip me from him before he dies. Then there's a flash of shock, and blood fills my mouth. Ascelin hisses from behind the naga's head. My eyes dart up to my friend and the knife she's just driven into the naga's skull.

We fall to the ground in a heap as the naga's rolling movements slow. But my direwolf never lets go of his throat, not until the last drop of rich blood spills over my muzzle. Not until the rapid beating of his heart slows, and I'm coated in sticky, smelly naga blood.

The screaming intensifies. My direwolf recognizes the voice as Onmiel's. We quickly assess the enemy, ensuring it's dead before he'll let go of its throat. I faintly hear my brother, Ascelin, and others all shouting, but Onmiel is my only focus. I shift, naked and covered in blood, and look for her. She's running to me across the floor, slipping in pools of slick blood.

I fly to her, ignoring the pain in my sides, grunting when she throws herself up into my arms, squeezing my neck so tight I can barely breathe. In my chest, my direwolf purrs, bigger and louder than he ever has before.

"Are you okay?" I grit out in a hoarse, anxious voice. I try to pull away to get a look at her, but she's gasping for air in my neck, sobbing as she wraps her legs around my waist like a vice.

"Thought I lost you," she cries. "Gods, Ten, I was so fucking scared for you." Her crying escalates as I stroke her hair, sensing my pack joining us. Noire scratches at the edges of our family bond, checking in with me. I don't answer.

Onmiel safe, snaps my direwolf, grabbing my attention.

"Tenebris!" Noire commands aloud. "Look at me!"

I glance over, my eyes flashing with anger as my older brother scowls. The hallway is a fucking wreck. Every window is broken, blood dripping from every visible surface. I'm cut to hell. People stand all over, staring at the smashed wood panels and artwork that's fallen to the floor.

Onmiel safe, my direwolf snarls, leaping inside my chest as I gasp at a sudden streak of pain from deep in my belly.

"Take care of this, Noire," I command my older brother, turning with Onmiel in my arms.

"Where the fuck are you going?" he shouts after me as I pass quickly through the archives, Onmiel still clutched tightly around my neck. I head for the elevator bank, ignoring the increasing pain in my side as I mash the button for floor five. I drip blood all over the elevator and hallway, but all I can focus on is getting her somewhere private, cleaning her, examining her.

Need make sure she safe, my direwolf presses, less urgently now that I'm obeying his desire.

Onmiel's door still isn't locked after how I entered the room earlier, so I sail through and into her bathroom, ripping her clothes from her lean body as I turn on the water. When I try to set her down, she shakes her head and clutches tighter to me.

"I need to examine our wounds," I whisper, and with a sniffle, she drops out of my arms. She turns immediately, rooting around under her cabinet, presumably for a first aid kit. I reach for her waist, pulling her to me as I drag us both into the shower.

Pain wells up hard and fast as I whine and slide down the wall with her in my arms. The endorphins that fueled me through the fight are leaving now, and in their wake is bone-snapping pain.

I run my hand over every inch of my librarian, and she's covered in scratches, but she's unhurt otherwise.

We protected, growls my direwolf, slinking back deeper as he leaves me, content that we kept her safe.

"Ten, you need a doctor," she cries softly. "You need stitches."

"No," I say, pulling her to straddle me while I bury my face in her neck. Her scent calms me, wrapping me up in a comforting, warm blanket as my muscles slowly relax. "Sit with me," I growl.

"Okay," she whispers, resting her head on the side of mine as the water streams down us. "Let me wash this blood off you, at least?"

I grunt out my disagreement as I hold her tighter, relishing the connection. Pain wells up so hot I resist the urge to scream. I'll heal fast; I'm an alpha. But the naga got me good with his claws. Already, my body is knitting together the worst of the injuries from the naga's claws, but it fucking hurts.

I have very little time before Noire barrels his way up here and drags me back down to answer his questions. But right now? Right here? My focus is on the librarian who has so quickly become the light at the end of my tunnel.

For ten long minutes, water washes us both clean, and then Onmiel insists on scrubbing every bit of blood from my body. I lie in the shower, slumped, as I watch her hands move over my skin, touching and probing at the wounds. I could lie here and watch her touch me for hours, I realize.

I know what you look like when you come, I think. And what's more, I want to know what you look like when I'm knotted inside you and pleasure hits. The rush of her being in danger has me feeling possessive and protective. She's safe, and now I want to fuck.

I do. I want her. I've half-ass fought it since we met. The timing is bad. I'm still broken up about my mate, and I'm on a mission to save my pack omega. The timing is *shit*, actually. But when has this world ever given me good timing on anything? The answer is never. My life is what I choose to make of it.

But the reality remains. Despite all of that, I want Onmiel, and it's that simple to me.

When she's done, I take the soap and bring my hands to her neck, lathering as I grip her throat, using my fingers to wash away the last remnants of blood. I move to her shoulders, swirling my fingers over her beautiful skin. When I bring them to her breasts, cupping each one as I pinch and pluck at her nipples, her head falls back, hips moving in my lap.

Growling, I drag my fangs up that slender column of her neck, following the sting with my lips and tongue. Onmiel sighs happily until a banging at the door indicates my brother has, indeed, arrived.

Noire doesn't bother to wait after the knock but enters Onmiel's space and hovers in the doorway with his arms crossed. I snarl when she tries to cover herself, but I don't move us.

Noire smirks at what he sees before his dark eyes fall on my wounds. His voice is surprisingly neutral as he looks at me. "It's a shitshow downstairs, brother. Take a moment, but we have a pile of trouble to deal with."

I growl, and he understands, leaving us as the water in the shower begins to run cold.

Onmiel looks up at me, her expression sad but resolved. She leans in and rubs her cheek along mine before planting a soft, tender kiss on my jawline. When she stands and exits the shower, I can't pull my eyes from the tattoo on her back or the gentle swell of her ass. She disappears into her room to get dressed as I realize I have no fucking clothes up here, and mine are downstairs covered in blood.

Another figure appears at the door, and I hear low voices. Onmiel appears in the bathroom doorway again with clothes for me.

"We keep some on hand for librarians who run out. You're probably too muscular to fit in these, but it's better than nothing." She hands me the items and turns into the room.

My direwolf preens at her words, and despite the urgency to get downstairs, I just can't stop godsdamned touching her.

She pulls a shirt on, her movements stiff and jerky when I press myself to her back, wrapping an arm around her waist. She's hurting and scared, and I want those emotions to dissipate. I want her usual joy and happiness because it's infectious. I want her laughter. I want all the pencils in her hair, to watch her bite the tip of one as she pushes her reading glasses up the bridge of her nose. I want all that like I want to keep breathing.

Purring, I bring one hand up between her small breasts and kiss the side of her neck over and over.

"I would never let anyone hurt you," I growl into her ear. "I will always protect you."

She turns in my arms, and while I can sense she wants to say something, she holds back.

Outside the door and down the hall, Noire clears his throat. Onmiel senses my change of focus and slips out of my arms. She pulls her pants on and threads her fingers through mine.

"Let's go, Ten."

Nodding, I let her pull me from the room, even though all I want to do is hide away and bury myself in her light, in her happiness.

Her, my direwolf rumbles. *Onmiel mine.*

CHAPTER TWENTY-FIVE
ONMIEL

I've never been so terrified in my life. I've known Evizel for years. While we've never been friendly, I wouldn't have pegged him for a killer. The only way that would happen is if he scented someone who had killed another naga.

Oh, gods. I know there were naga in the maze, so I come to the only conclusion I can. Ten's killed one. If I had watched the fucking hunts, I'd have known that, and I could have warned him. I could have stopped all of this. It's not a commonly known fact about naga but I knew it. Guilt chokes me so hard I gasp for breath.

Another one of Ten's secrets uncovered, I suppose. He's like an onion I keep peeling back the layers of. And every time I get to a new level, I find deep wells of hurt. I can't imagine knowing your mate was fine with allowing you to deal with so much godsdamned agony.

I can't let go of his hand as we leave my assigned room and meet his brother again. Noire gives me the first less-than-hateful look I've seen since I met him. "The Master Librarian wants to speak with you immediately."

I struggle to swallow around the lump in my throat. Half the library was ravaged when Evizel went crazy. I can imagine exactly what ML Garfield wants to talk about. I could sob for the thousands of books we'll have to patch together after his rampage.

We're silent as we enter the elevator bank and return to the first floor. Librarians run every which way as they examine the damage and pick up stacks of books and fallen shelves. I can't think about that right now. Because now that I'm not so utterly focused on Ten getting killed, I'm remembering how Zakarias ran to stop Evizel.

My heart begins to pound as we round the outer edge of the library to the hallway toward the public sector. The double doors fly open, and an elderly librarian presses through, retching onto the floor as my heartbeat picks up fast.

"Zakarias!" I shout as I run through the doors.

Behind me, Noire growls at his brother. "She'll need you. Go."

I'll need him? What for? Oh fuck. I can't help the sensation of falling as I run through drying puddles of sticky blood toward ML Garfield, who's huddled with a dozen other librarians in front of one of the many shattered windows. Every one of the long plate-glass windows is blown out, giving us a view into the darkness outside.

Garfield's dark eyes turn to me when he sees me coming, and he puts up both hands to stop me. "Wait, my child. Let's talk."

I rush past him to where the others are peering out the window, talking in hushed tones. Below us is the Sunken Courtyard, a deep pit that many librarians use for meditation. It lies mostly under-ground, and it's four stories below the first floor of the library.

I fly to the window and lean out. Below, at the bottom of the pit, Zakarias lies face up, lifeless eyes staring at the sky as raindrops begin to pour out of the middle-of-the-night clouds.

No.

It can't be.

A wail leaves my mouth even as I claw at the edge of the window, cutting my hands on the glass.

"Somebody help him! Help him!" I shriek, even though I know he's gone. I feel like I'm reeling and falling as I scream. Big arms pull me in close, a rolling purr vibrating against me as I scream over and over and over.

Zakarias is dead.

~

Time loses all sense of meaning for me as people come and go. It takes a godsdamned crane to move Evizel's body. Every surface is coated in blood and a sticky scent I know is his death mist. Anyone in the room when he released it is now covered, including me. We'll probably never be able to have another naga librarian because the entire library will be a trigger for them.

Gods, Zakarias is *dead*.

I let out a cry of anguish as Ten pulls me closer. There are voices all around us, his whole pack, I think. Noire's there, of course, but Ascelin, Jet, and even Arliss show up.

A huge figure drops to a knee next to us, and when I manage to drag my eyes from Ten's shirt I see Jet.

His dark eyes are kind as he gives me a soft smile, handing me a bottle of water. "Drink something, sweetheart. Ten's gonna get you out of here. You don't need to be here right now, okay? We will handle this."

I nod and stand. My brain is frozen in time, remembering that moment Evizel's body spun over and over in the room and sent everything flying. And that brings me back to the memory of my sister, Zura, dying. It's the only memory that haunts me on a daily basis, and what happened tonight has that imprint front and center.

Tears stream down my cheeks as I look over to see Noire's mate, Diana. I haven't met her in person yet, this woman who's at the center of bringing Ten to Pengshur. It's obvious who she is, though, with the way Noire hovers so closely by her side.

She's speaking with Ascelin, pointing at something. I think she's helping to direct the workers who now flood the hallway.

My mission demands my attention, and I push out of Ten's big arms long enough to find ML Garfield. Tapping him on the shoulder, I wipe the tears away from my cheeks.

He turns with a somber, consoling look, pushing his glasses farther up his nose.

"We were meeting you tonight about a reference in a book. Did Zak—did FL Zakarias tell you the details about the blood?"

Garfield gives me a quizzical look but then sighs. "You are an excellent librarian, Onmiel. You do not have to do this tonight, but I understand your need to fulfill your duty." He reaches into his pocket and pulls out a small vial of what appears to be blood. "I knew the day would come that you'd ask for this. I hope it helps."

I can't even comprehend his cryptic message as I take the vial and approach Diana, handing it to her and Ascelin. The omega looks half-dead with dark circles under her eyes. Ascelin watches her with something akin to terror on her face.

"I don't know if this will help you, but there's a solid chance. It's Volya blood. If there's an antidote to be found at all, it'll be here. A good physik can use this to help you. Zakarias had the connections to help you with this, but—"

Relief splashes across Diana's face as she clutches the vial to her chest, her face pale and drawn.

"Thank you, Onmiel. I'm so sorry we haven't met," she whispers. Her voice is frail and hoarse. She's wasting away; that much is obvious.

"Call a healer immediately," I direct Ascelin. "They'll be able to tell you in twelve hours if it'll help. If not, you can leave for the Tempang tomorrow."

The elegant vampiri nods, but I can't stay here any longer. I don't have to because Ten sweeps me up into his arms for the millionth time today, and we leave everything behind. I hear Noire call him, but he doesn't bother to respond, although I know he could in the family bond they share. Instead, he goes right back up to my room, pulling me into his arms and tucking my head under his chin.

"I'm so sorry, Onmiel," he whispers into my hair, stroking my back and side as he threads his legs through mine. "I'm so fucking sorry. If I hadn't—"

"Stop," I command him, sitting up as he props himself up against my headboard. "You fought for your life in the maze. What Evizel did put you in danger, and I was fucking terrified for you. What he did isn't your fault. You protected everyone, Ten. You—" I can't go on to say anything else because I'm so overwhelmed with the memory of Evizel snapping at me and Ten leaping in front.

"You could have died," I whisper. *And Zakarias is dead.*

My face crumples, and I hate it. I'm not a weak person. But this day has taken me on an emotional rollercoaster from hells, and I don't have any expectations of handling that well. Ten purrs and pulls me flush with his chest, wrapping his legs around mine as our foreheads touch. The tip of his nose brushes mine, our lips so close.

Oh my gods, is he going to kiss me right now? After everything that happened?

My lips part because all I want is to feel good.

Ten growls, brushing his lips across mine as his golden eyes bore into my soul. What is he thinking, feeling, wanting? I'm dying to ask but terrified to.

A knock at my broken door pulls a growl up out of his chest, but he stands and deposits me gently in the pillows, stalking to the door before he moves it out of the way.

"May I see her?" It's ML Garfield. Oh, fuck me. I don't want to fall apart in front of the Master Librarian, not any more than I have. I leap out of bed, but Garfield comes into my room, shaking his head. "Do not rise on my account, NL Onmiel. There is something I wanted to give you, a letter that came with the blood gift from the Volya."

"Why not give it to me earlier?" I question as I take the faded cream envelope from him. There are no markings on the front.

"It was neither the time nor the place," he says in a kind tone, turning to look at Tenebris and then back at me. "When the blood was gifted to us, I made sure the letter and blood didn't need to remain together, and so I gave the blood earlier since you made a remarkable discovery for your clients. The letter is purely personal."

"You're being obtuse," Tenebris growls, taking the letter from me to examine it.

Garfield sighs. "I knew there would come a day I would give this letter to Onmiel, and that day has finally come."

"You're making no sense," Tenebris reiterates, pointing to the door. "We'll deal with this tomorrow. Tonight, she needs rest."

Garfield nods. "There is no rush, Onmiel. But when you have questions, find me."

All the strength leaves me then, and I sink back onto the bed as Ten sets the letter down on my bedside table.

"You want to read it tonight?"

"I haven't known it existed for years and years, and my mentor is dead. Nothing in that letter can change what happened today. I'll read it another time."

Ten gives me a look and slides back onto the bed, pulling me into his arms. He starts purring, and I'm lost to the darkness, falling into a deep and dreamless sleep.

CHAPTER TWENTY-SIX

TENEBRIS

I hold Onmiel for hours until the sun is high in the sky and finally dipping again. She sleeps the entire time, snoring softly with her fists wrapped in my shirt. I use that time to think because what we're doing, this isn't friendship. This is so much more, and I'm struggling with how I've gone from being destroyed over killing my bondmate to wanting another woman in a relatively short time.

My direwolf sits up and growls when I think of Rama. He begins to pace in my chest anxiously.

Hurt. She hurt. His voice is deep, his words broken. I've never heard of anything like this.

Who's hurt? I question, wondering if I can speak with him and if we can have an honest-to-gods conversation. I've never heard of a shifter being able to do this. Our wolves are more of a sensation than anything.

Hurt me, he snarls into my mind. *Bondmate hurt me. Cruel mate. Bad mate.*

A sense of wrongness washes over me in waves that choke the breath from my lungs. There's so much anguish that threatens to break loose. I have so many questions. How did she hurt him? What exactly did she do? And why? Did she know my direwolf was different? Would I have eventually become another experiment to her? Did the fucking bond matter at all? Does it even matter now? If I start something with Onmiel, will the bond tear it apart?

I'm unsettled that I don't have an answer for any of that.

Onmiel shifts in my arms, stirring, and when I go to move away, my direwolf startles and pushes up against my ribs. *Take. Hurt go away.*

Wait, is he *still* hurting? I ponder the question, but he doesn't answer. Onmiel's beautiful eyes pop open, going wide when she looks at me and scoots back. "What's wrong? You look worried..."

"Nothing," I murmur, standing to go to the window and look out. "You've been asleep all day, Onmiel. Are you hungry? Can I get you anything?" My direwolf preens in my chest as I rub at it, wondering what the hells is going on with him.

When she rises and stretches, joining me, I sit in the window seat.

"Have you ever heard of an alpha's direwolf having a separate consciousness from his?"

Onmiel startles, glancing to where I'm still rubbing absentmindedly at my pecs. "Is that happening to you?"

I confirm with a slight nod.

She sighs, gritting her teeth. "Maybe a mate bond thing?"

Hearing her say the word mate sends me growling and my direwolf preening for attention. Onmiel blanches. "I'm sorry to bring her up, Ten."

"You don't have to dance around that topic with me, Onmiel," I reassure her. "He didn't start speaking to me until *this week*. I find that significant."

She folds her arms over her knees and pulls them to her chest, away from me. My direwolf snaps in my chest, hating how she folds in on herself. Gods, he's going to get insufferable shortly.

"Maybe that takes a while to develop after you mate someone," she whispers. "I've never heard it mentioned about shifters, though. They just...shift, I thought. Can Noire do this?"

I shake my head. "Noire's never mentioned it. Jet hasn't either, although I suppose they probably wouldn't have bothered to cover standard mating procedures with me given how things happened."

There's a sudden pang of sadness, a sense of loss when I think of all the growing up I missed out on in the maze. I came of age there, my eighteenth birthday punctuated only with me being chosen by Rama to kill the mark that night—an elderly woman thrown in for some stupid fucking reason, I'm sure. I'll never forget her terror or my promise to make it quick and painless.

She thanked me before I broke her neck.

If I'd been living a normal pack life, on my eighteenth birthday, my brothers would have gotten me rip-roaring drunk and pierced my cock for my future mate. I find myself wondering how they would have done it. Most alpha piercings are highly elaborate.

I did end up getting hammered drunk the night of my birthday after I killed that night's mark. Jet rubbed my back while I puked my guts up in the toilet and sobbed for hours. Rama was the source of all that pain. She must have known I was hers, then. I'd come of age, a fully adult direwolf male in his prime. But she never came for me. She never did a godsdamned thing to help.

Even when I came out of the stupor after being captured in that final fight to escape the maze, she never apologized. Not a single time. She just carried on with our connection as if all our history was something she didn't need to bother to address. I was so bond-drunk and drugged up that I couldn't even fight it. I fell headlong into mating her without another thought.

I don't think I could regret anything more than I regret that.

My cell rings, and Onmiel falls quiet. We're dancing around a conversation about my dead mate and just how much Rama does or doesn't have control over my present.

"Noire," I growl out my brother's name.

"We're at the hospital with Diana." His tone is gruff. "The physiks and healers are working on a serum based on the blood, and it's looking good, but we'll be here all day. Please thank Onmiel for us until I can come in person."

"Done." I smile softly at her. She can hear him because he talks so damn loud into the phone.

"How is she?" His voice quietens.

"It's hard," is all I say, but Noire gets it. Of course, he does. He led our pack through seven years of hell in the maze. Seven years of bullshit brought on by my godsdamned mate. A switch flips in my brain. She might have been mine in a fated mate bond, but I didn't *choose* her, and if I could undo that fucking claiming, I would. Rama might have belonged to me spiritually and emotionally in ways that matter, but I do not choose her *now*, and I won't let her control a single thing about my future.

It's freeing to think that, and my direwolf curls up contentedly in my chest, seemingly pleased we're on the same page about her.

Noire and I hang up. I look out the window to see the library's flags at half-mast, indicating a death of their own. Onmiel watches the flags wave softly in the breeze, her face tense.

I hate to see that look on her beautiful, delicate features. There should be only joy and excitement.

A ping makes her jump, but she unfolds herself to cross the room and read the screen on the library's tech. She blanches, her hand coming to her throat before she crosses the room to me.

"There's a releasing ceremony for Zakarias tonight. ML Garfield wanted me to know."

I can't resist bringing one hand to her hip as the other tilts her chin up, pulling her between my thighs. "Do you want to go?"

"Of course," she whispers, but her voice wavers even though she lifts her chin. She moves her hands as if she'll put them on me but seems to think better of it. I hate it.

"Don't hold back around me, Onmiel," I demand. "Just be how you always have been."

She nods but doesn't touch me, and my direwolf yowls in my chest. His position is crystal clear, at least. Taking her hand, I guide it to my chest. "Can you feel him, Onmiel?"

He purrs and presses against my chest, threatening to force a shift so he can touch her, but I suspect she can't tell any of that.

There's a cracking sensation deep in my chest, surprising me with its intensity. I fall off the window seat and onto my knees. Pain and shock slam into my brain as my shift takes over in a flash of light. It happens so fast that I'm standing there in direwolf form before realizing I've fucking shifted.

Holy fucking hells.

He took over. My godsdamned wolf took over.

Onmiel takes a tentative step back as I huff and pant, struggling to understand how he was able to control me. It's unheard of. It's not possible. Except, he just did it.

I work hard to get up to speed fast, trying to sense his intention. I don't want her to be in danger; she's been through enough. But I don't read malice from him, and I'm in too much shock that he forced the fucking shift to do much about it. He wants to be close to her. I see her through his eyes, but I'm disconnected, somehow. He's in total control, pushing her with his nose back to the window seat.

She sits with a soft smile, stroking one of his ears as we shove our nose in her lap and inhale. Gods. Oh, fuck. This is probably the last thing she wants, for a giant direwolf to scent her this way. Does she know how sensual this is for us, for him? Her scent explodes against my senses, filling the forefront of my mind with promise.

My direwolf sniffs his way slowly up her body, reading her hurt, her despair. He rubs his enormous cheek along hers with a mournful whine then lays his head in her lap, his ears flat. He purrs the whole time, and I don't bother to try to stop him or attempt to take control. I'm reeling that he could do this, and I'm in complete wonder that it didn't frighten her in the least.

Ours. He growls in our bond. The bond that's always silent because shifter wolves aren't a separate fucking consciousness.

Except mine suddenly is in the last few days.

We sit for a long time, my direwolf purring his heart out for Onmiel. She strokes our fur, ears, and nose, and her scent morphs into something more peaceful. Eventually, I make my presence known, telling him I'd like to be in my human form again, and he allows me to shift back as she looks up with a wry grin.

"Guess he really wanted an ear scratch, huh? This is new, right? He pushed that?"

I suppose she picked up more of that than I thought.

"Yeah. It's new. I've never heard of that. He just...took over."

She looks up with big eyes filled with tears. "I think he thought I needed him, maybe? We'll find answers for you, too, Ten, if that's what you want. Fingers crossed the serum works for Diana, but today, I need to focus on Zakarias's releasing ceremony."

I pull her into my arms, unable to keep my damn hands off her. Everything about her pain calls to me. I've always been like this, though. I can't stand to see a gentle person or child in pain. Noire's always said I'm too nice, too empathetic, but secretly, I know he believes it's a strength. He admires it, not that he'd admit it aloud.

"I'll come with you," I grit out as I run my hands over Onmiel's lithe, tense figure. Little by little, she relaxes, arms crossed and chin laid on top of them as she looks up at me from my chest. "If you want me to," I add, worried she might not want me there. Zakarias wouldn't be dead if I hadn't been in the library.

"I always want you to," she murmurs, pale eyes locked onto mine. We say nothing, but I shift her higher as I touch and stroke her, my direwolf preening at the attention, at the way she's relaxing in my arms. But it's more than that because an undercurrent of desire threads through her usual scent, and I'm hard for her.

"Onmiel," I growl, hauling her farther up until her breasts are crushed to my upper chest, and I'm looking up into her face.

"What is it, Ten?" Her voice is soft, almost desperate, as she hovers above me. Does she even know her hips are rocking against my upper stomach?

I know what you look like when you come, I muse again. *I've seen you fuck yourself on a godsdamn replica of an alpha cock. You want me.*

I slide one hand up her back, over her shirt, so I don't agitate her tattoo. The other comes to the back of her head, and I pull her close, close enough for my lips to brush hers.

Onmiel goes tight and loose all at the same time as she tries to push back, her expression worried. "Ten, are you su—"

214

I silence her concern with my lips, nipping at her plump lower one as I tug it gently. A soft whine greets me as I grip her jaw and force her mouth open wide. And then, I let myself go. All the thoughts and worries I could have in this moment disappear as I slick my tongue over hers, tasting her silky heat.

"Open for me," I purr when she's still too hesitant. She's wrapped up in her brain around what's happening, and I want her to let go.

Gray eyes flash with need, and then she relaxes into the kiss. Heat streaks along my limbs and pools in my groin. I can't do tender, so I unleash, biting and nipping, feral in my need for her.

Onmiel claws at my chest as I plunder her mouth, growling because I want to be inside her in every way possible. I want her joy, her release. I want to drown in her honey. And she smells so fucking good right now, so sweet and bright. So godsdamn needy.

And it's all for me.

Sitting up, I shift myself so she's straddling me. Onmiel's lips are swollen and red from the attention, and I attack them again. I want her marked and smelling like me, and every time I suck at her tongue, my direwolf focuses more intensely.

She drips arousal through her jeans into my lap, coating me as our bodies clash together. I need more of this delicious friction, more of her sweet pussy kissing my dick. I need her to come at least once before we leave for this horrible fucking ceremony.

Growling, I shove her jeans down. I toss them aside and then she's rocking her soaked folds up and down my hard length. I can't tear my eyes from the sight as I grip her throat and kiss her again. I'm going to come so fucking hard like this, finally kissing her.

This connection, this is everything.

When I slide a hand around her ass and coat my fingers with her sticky arousal, she jolts in my arms. But the moment I slip two fingers into her ass and stroke, she explodes all over me. My name falls over and over from her lips, and hearing it sends me headfirst into mind-obliterating pleasure.

I clamp my fangs around her neck, biting hard as I come, coating her with release as my balls tighten and throb. The thick knot at the base of my cock begins to expand even though I'm not inside her.

"Fuck, Ten," she gasps. "What do I—"

I cut her off with a growl, directing her hand to my knot, the swollen area at the base of my cock. She can barely get her fingers around it as it swells, but the sensation of her gripping it, her fingers tight and warm, is enough to get me off again as I snarl and snap and throw my head back with a yell.

Onmiel strokes my knot, aided by my much larger hand until my cock stops spurting cum all over the damn place. She shuffles back off my lap and looks down. It's fucking messy, but I don't stop her when she begins cleaning me with her tongue. She licks her way around my knot as I groan, feeling it harden again. When her lips kiss a trail up my throbbing dick, I chuckle and pull her back into my lap.

"You keep doing that, and we won't make it out of here, sweet girl. Alphas have sky-high libidos. I'll go all night if we're not careful."

Onmiel laughs, and it's finally joyous, but uncertainty returns far faster than I'd like it to.

"What is it?" I encourage. I want no miscommunication between us, no being unsure of feelings. All I had with Rama were false-hoods. I won't accept it now, and I don't always read social cues well after spending my formative years in the maze. I need transparency.

She nips at her lip. "I just...is this all too soon for you, Ten? We have chemistry, absolutely. We have friendship. Is this the best time for..." Her voice trails off as she gestures to the mess in our laps.

"What we have isn't just friendship," I remind her. "We built it on friendship. We built it on trust. We built it on godsdamned coffee, Onmiel."

She bursts out laughing at that, giving me a wry grin before she slips off my lap and discards what remains of her clothing. My dire-wolf preens at the sheer amount of cum she's coated with. It drips from her lean stomach muscles and down her swollen pussy lips onto her thighs.

She grins at me. "Well, I guess if it's built on coffee, who can argue that?"

"I'm serious," I say, pulling her to me as I rise. "We can take this slowly if that makes you more comfortable, but make no mistake, Onmiel, I want to take *everything*."

The look she turns on me is pure heat before her eyes flash away. "We're not done talking about this, Tenebris."

Gods, hearing her say my full given name makes me hard, and my cock leaps, bobbing against my thigh as she holds back a grin. When we met, I told her to call me Ten, but hearing the whole thing now has me aching with need.

"You using my full name gives me sexy professor ideas," I admit. "I'm a simple male, Onmiel. I want simple things. I want to be cuddled. I want to feed each other and run in the moonlight. I want to be fucking adored by the person I *choose* to spend my life with." I purposefully don't use the word mate because there's too much recent connection with that word, and I refuse to choose the woman who wasn't any of the things I want for myself.

Onmiel's smile grows wider, and she crosses the room, grabbing a spare set of clothes in my size out of the closet. "I ordered these for you when it seemed like you wouldn't be going to your apartment anymore."

"Why would I?" I laugh. "When I can stay here and have cuddles for days? And talk books. Don't forget the books."

"Never forget the books," she agrees with a laugh, pulling on dark jeans and an umber tunic. When she reaches for the sky-blue Novice belt, I take it and tie it around her midsection.

Her happy expression falls, but I've smothered her enough today, so I pull on my clothes in silence, watching her. She goes to the mirror and dabs a little color on her cheeks, pulling her still-white hair up into a messy bun on top of her head. When she pulls tendrils down over both ears, I can't resist kissing my way along the side of her neck and down her shoulder.

"I can't stop touching you," I admit. "You draw me in like a gods-damned magnet, Onmiel."

"You must have a thing for dorks," she laughs. "Like recognizes like?"

I grin because most people wouldn't assume my scholarly tendencies based on my appearance, but I genuinely am the ultimate nerd. Give me books and coffee all day long, throw in some kids to be goofy with, and life is perfect.

I like quiet, too, although I suspect there's not much of that in my future.

CHAPTER TWENTY-SEVEN
ONMIEL

I'm literally overwhelmed with emotion, but Ten joking with me like every other day brings some levity to it all.

And that kiss.

Gods.

I'll never recover from it because it was even more incredible than in my numerous fantasies about him. Ten is a masterful kisser. He's commanding and in charge and totally aware of every reaction, every feeling. Kissing Ten was an emotional epiphany followed by orgasming like a damn waterfall.

I honestly needed that, and he knew it. I'm a little more relaxed now, despite what we're about to do. My brain is reeling with all the information we've uncovered in the last twenty-four hours, but I'll dumpster dive through it later. I can't deal with it right now. I'm just grateful that I'm not dealing with it alone.

My face is puffy from all the stupid crying, so a quick swipe of mascara makes me look human again. I've cried enough to last me a lifetime in the last twenty-four hours. I'd like to be done with that. My sister, Zura, is top of my mind as I finish getting ready to lay my mentor to rest.

Ten's standing in the doorway, enormous arms crossed as he

watches me, and despite how pleased he looks, there's a worrying, niggling part of my consciousness concerned about our connection. It's so good, so right, so godsdamn *deep*. But I don't want to be the rebound or someone he latches on to because I'm *alive*. I want something real, and I think that could be what's between us, but it'll take revisiting the conversation another day.

Today isn't the right time.

He must sense my hesitation because he crosses the room and rubs his cheek along mine. "I'm here for you, Miel. Just you." His words are a balm to my cracked, bleeding soul as I lean into his touch and sigh. I want to let go and really sink into this more-than-friendship thing, but I'm scared.

"We're going to address this hesitation later," Ten growls in my ear, nipping softly at the skin just below it. "And I'll keep reiterating to you what I said earlier. I want to know where this goes, sweet girl."

Godsdamn, I'm loving my new moniker. I want to get a T-shirt made with that on the front and wear it every damn day. Librarian praise kink chic. That's my new thing.

We make it back out of my assigned room, and reality hits again. The library is noisy, and people scurry back and forth. Many have been crying if their puffy faces are any indication. I groan as Ten's hand comes to my lower back.

"We'll deal with this later," he reminds me. "Let's honor Zakarias now."

"His mate, Okair, will be there," I whisper softly. "We'll have to pay our respects to him."

Ten nods but takes my hand. "Do you want me to stay out of sight? Do you think it would hurt Okair to meet me?" He means because of his role in Zakarias's death. But the reality is there's nothing easy about death, and hiding Ten won't change that.

I shake my head in disagreement, and we don't speak as we leave the library. Outside, hundreds are gathered in the street, holding candles as they walk toward the square where all releasing ceremonies are held. Ten doesn't let go of my hand, and eventually, most of his pack joins us, walking behind as we pace through the somber, stone, quiet streets of Pengshur to the very last square at the edge of town.

I've always loved this square. It's in the older section of town, and the shops here are quaint and cozy. Zakarias and I spent hundreds of hours picking through fabrics, shopping for antiques, and having coffee with Okair. That's why they settled here, even though it was as far as he could possibly be from the library.

Okair stands on a raised platform, his thin shoulders hunched as he openly sobs. Dark hair flops in waves over his chocolate eyes, red-rimmed from crying. In his hand is a small box. I know when he lights it, it'll morph into a beautiful lantern. Once his is released, we'll all release ours. Someone comes around and hands us releasing boxes.

Master Librarian Garfield stands next to Okair in his formal navy tunic, one arm around the younger male's shoulders as he cries. His anguish rings out around the cobblestone streets, seeming to echo off the buildings until it sounds like the whole city mourns Zakarias's loss. I realize every-fucking-body in the entire square is crying, including me, and when I look up, Ten is too. He's not distraught like me, but tears roll down his handsome face as he watches Okair.

Is he remembering everything he lost in the maze? I know one of his brothers died there; I remember hearing that much from the other librarians who watched the nightly hunts. Maybe he's even thinking of his mate right now. Oh gods.

I'm hit with a sudden hatred for the woman the stars picked to belong to him. She let him languish in the maze. She let him kill and be hurt, this sweet alpha who cries for a male he barely knew. If Rama were here right now, I'd rip her godsdamned head from her shoulders for ever causing Ten a single moment of pain.

Fuck her. May she rot in all seven hells for the rest of eternity.

Garfield gives a moving speech that I instantly forget, and then Okair sets off his lantern. I watch it catch the wind and billow up, hovering just above him before it makes its way slowly up into the night sky. As one, the crowd lights their own lanterns, sending them up to join Okair's. I know my librarian friends are here, but I can't summon the energy to find anyone.

For a long time, the square is silent. We stand until the last of the lanterns have blown away on the breeze, and then the crowd dissipates. ML Garfield catches my eye and gives me a solemn wave, leaving Okair's side as people begin to form a line to express their condolences.

"Onmiel, how are you holding up?" Garfield has a reputation for being shrewd and almost cruel, but he's been so kind that I'm starting to think of him a little differently.

"Everything hurts," I reply honestly as Ten pulls closer to me. "But we'll honor him every day."

Garfield nods as Ten's brothers join us. Noire gives me a quick once-over, then glances at the Master Librarian. "Onmiel's work resulted in a serum that's helping my mate as we speak. She's the best she's been since she was attacked. We have your librarians to thank for that."

Garfield gives me a pleased smile and claps his hands together, a tear traveling down his weathered, pale cheek. His voice is the hint of a whisper when it comes out. "Zakarias would have been so proud, Onmiel. You were his favorite, you know."

I choke back a sob, leaning against Ten as he begins to purr for me, crushing me to his side as the crowd slowly disappears. Garfield turns from us. "Forgive me. I've spoken with Okair, but I'm going to retire early. I've got some arrangements to make regarding our other loss."

Evizel. Gods. I'd forgotten about the naga librarian who was just as beloved as Zakarias. Evizel had been here for ages and ages. Garfield takes his leave, and Ten turns to speak with his brothers. Eventually, they leave too, and then it's just Ten and me.

"You want to speak with Zakarias's mate?" Ten's voice is cautious and low but understanding.

"I do," I murmur. "I have to tell Okair how fucking sorry I am.

They were like my family, the first people to befriend me when I came here."

Ten falls silent, guiding me to the now-short line of beings waiting to speak with Okair. I watch him as he greets each one, and it's not lost on me how this process isn't for the family of the person who died. A wake is for the people who feel the need to say something or give their final goodbye. I've been on the receiving end of these things; I know how fucking awful it is.

My mind wanders to Zura and everything that happened after she died. I'm sure there was a wake then, too, but I can't remember. The prisoner tattoo keeps a huge majority of my memories locked away. I kept just enough of them to remind me how I never want to access that power again. It's for the best.

My heart is broken anew for Okair and Zakarias by the time it's our turn. There's almost no one left. When Okair sees me, he breaks down, pulling me into his arms as he squeezes me so tight I struggle to breathe.

I squeeze him back, crying over and over about how sorry I am. I don't even know how long we do that, but I sense Ten standing off to one side as he watches us.

When Okair and I part, his eyes darken when he notices Ten.

"You're the alpha Evizel was chasing, aren't you?" Okair's voice is flat as he grits out the words.

Ten nods and steps closer to us. "I'm so sorry for your loss, Okair."

Okair sucks in a deep breath as if he's steeling himself to rail into Ten for being the cause of Zakarias's death. But then all the fight goes out of him as he looks from Ten to me. "It hurts so bad, Onmiel. I don't know how I'll go on without him."

Ten croons, his purr strengthening as he joins us, placing one big hand on Okair's thin shoulder. He says nothing, but I know he's trying to comfort the other male, even though he doesn't know him. He's doing it for my benefit, I suspect.

Okair looks up at Ten as tears stream down his face.

"People don't leave you forever, Okair. Part of them will always remain." Ten clears his throat awkwardly.

My blood freezes in my veins. I feel like I'm going to be sick, bile rising in my throat at Ten's words about losing people and how we're never done with them.

There's silence as Okair watches us, but finally, he snuffles and reaches into his pocket, handing me a small envelope. It matches the one Garfield gave me earlier, a fact I struggle to comprehend. What is with this shit?

"Zakarias held this for you at your request. I thought you might want it back now that he, that he..." He loses the ability to say anything else as I take the envelope and tuck it into my back pocket. It's thick like there's an object inside.

"Thank you," I mutter as another mourner pushes into us, anxious for their time with Okair. I give him one last hug before Ten and I turn to leave.

It was foolish to think I could have him. Rama had her hooks in him for years. That doesn't dissipate in a week of friendly nerd banter.

People don't leave you forever, part of them will always remain.

Those are the words that came straight out of his mouth.

I'm such a godsdamn fool.

CHAPTER TWENTY-EIGHT
TENEBRIS

Onmiel is stiff and silent as we leave the nearly empty square. This part of Pengshur is beautiful and old, and I'd love to explore it with her sometime, but right now, she's...hurt? Is that what I sense?

It must have been my words about losing people. I meant what I said to Okair, but losing people doesn't keep us from seizing happiness. I had hoped that would be meaningful to her in a positive way, but if anything, she looks more visibly distressed by the moment.

"Onmiel," I murmur, putting my hand on her forearm to stop her. When she turns with a hurt look, I tilt her chin up and press myself close to her. "How did you take what I said? I want no miscommunication between us, so tell me."

She crosses her arms, but I don't let go of her chin. She's going to tell me if I have to stand here all night and wait for the truth.

"Miel," I whisper. "Talk to me. Don't hold back. Not from me."

"The way you talked about how you felt when she died..." Onmiel's voice falls off as her eyes meet mine. "I've felt that before when I lost my sister. I felt it to a degree, losing Zakarias. But I've never lost a fated bondmate, Ten. It's only been a few weeks for you."

"You never had a fated mate who tried to destroy the world, either," I counter. "I was a fucking mess after I killed her, that's true, but—"

Onmiel interrupts me. "You said we're never done with those we lose. I can't come second to your dead bondmate, Tenebris." She pulls her chin from my fingertips with a sigh. "I'm not saying you need to pick her or me, Ten. Gods, I'm not that person, I swear. We have a real connection and incredible chemistry. That's true. I'm just saying maybe you need time to truly grieve Rama, even if she was a total asshole."

I bark out an angry laugh at her summary. "She *was* an asshole," I clarify. "She hurt everyone and everything I ever loved. She hurt me over and over, even after she knew I was hers. She never fucking apologized, and the moment she had me in her clutches, she drugged me until I stood there and almost allowed her to murder my brothers and their mates. Does that sound like what a bondmate should do? Because if it does, I don't fucking want it. I don't *choose* her."

Onmiel blanches. "I don't want to fight with you, Ten. I just don't want to pressure you or get my heart broken because I'm gonna level with you right now—I'm falling for you. For better or worse, I'm halfway in love, and I don't think I'd recover if we got serious and you weren't done grieving her."

Her words are a splash of cold water, followed by the slow burn of delicious heat in my core. My direwolf preens about what she said. In love? She's falling in love?

Am I? We talked about taking this slowly, but could I be in love with Onmiel?

When I don't immediately answer, she rubs my forearm. "It's a lot, and I shouldn't have laid that on you. I need a night to myself to think. Why don't you stay with your pack tonight? Check on Diana. Find me in the morning, and we'll talk, alright?"

I can only nod as I mull over her words. When she walks off into the fading light, I watch her go, but I'm still rooted to the spot. She's falling in love?

Her admission sends warmth curling through my chest, wrapping around all those places that have hurt since I killed Rama. It's like she's banishing all that darkness little by little, simply by virtue of being who she is.

I walk through Pengshur's quiet streets. The whole city seems to be mourning its loss.

Half an hour later, I arrive at our rental. Diana's back from the healing hospital, and finally, she looks improved. She rises gingerly out of her chair to rub her cheek with mine when I come in the door. Ascelin shows up next, throwing her arms around me as she hugs me in silence. Ah, my other friend—I've neglected her lately.

Jet comes around the corner with Renze's arm slung around his waist. "Brother, we've missed you. Is Onmiel alright? She's not with you?"

Something in my chest bursts with joy that they ask about her, that they seem to hope she came with me.

"She wanted a night alone," I admit. "There's a lot going on."

"Ah, you had a fight with the hot librarian, then," Ascelin comments. "Come in the kitchen and tell us everything." Behind her, I see Arliss at the stove. I'm surprised he's still around, but I suppose he's staying true to his word to remain until our task is done.

I suspect Noire will bark at me to spit it all out, and I'm not anxious to rehash the last forty-eight hours, but all he does is pull Diana into his arms and give me a shrewd look. He kisses his way up Diana's neck as she leans into him, our family bond awash with bright joy. For the first time in a while, I can feel Diana's pack omega strength underlying and supporting the rest of us.

Arliss enters the room and sits across from Noire at the opposite end of the table. I get the sense they've been arguing over which end is the head.

"How is our favorite librarian?" Arliss croons, biting into a piece of white bread as everyone sits at the table. It looks like they were just finishing up a late dinner. Achaia pops up out of nowhere and sets a plate down in front of me as I thank her.

I've been so blinded by grief that I've failed to really absorb how strong my pack is now—a mix of shifters, vampiri, and even a carrow, not that he considers himself part of us. I feel like I've had my head in a deep hole for ages, and I'm just realizing how much has changed.

There's still an achy scar in my chest when I think about Rama, but it's faded, sandblasted away by Onmiel's joyous friendship.

"Brother?" Jet presses me again, laughter apparent in his dark eyes. "Wanna tell us what's going on?"

That encouragement is all it takes to open the floodgates.

Our whole story spills out. How I connected with her, how she discovered the blood, and what happened with the naga and Zakarias. The conversation we just had. Once I open my mouth, it feels so godsdamned good to share with my pack that I can't stop. I haven't had a pack since I was seven, not one that consisted of anything more than my three brothers.

By the time I'm done blurting it all out, Arliss and Ascelin are giving one another joking looks.

"Time to pay up, vampiri," Arliss purrs, kicking Ascelin under the table.

I give them an irritated look; I hate to be a foregone conclusion.

Diana leans over to grab my hand, pulling it into her lap as she strokes my forearm. That's when I realize just what being part of a happy, full pack is like. I don't remember this from my youth, but this touch, this connection? That's what shifter packs do. I fucking missed it. I missed out on it for all of my formative years.

Godsdamn that woman I refuse to call my mate any longer.

"Ten?" Diana's voice is tentative as she scratches the back of my hand. "This is sort of the moment where Onmiel needs a grand gesture. She needs you to chase her, to show her that you want her and that Rama is in your past—and will remain there."

I look around the table to see my whole pack nodding.

Even Noire gestures to the food in front of me. "Finish eating, brother, and then get your woman and bring her here. I'd like to thank her for saving Diana's life. And I'd like to get to know her."

TEN

Smiling, I look down at the food as my pack starts talking around me. It feels good to be with them like this. Arliss and Ascelin needle one another back and forth. Jet is watching his mates make out with one hand down the front of his jeans. Diana and Noire laugh with everyone as we poke fun at Jet.

I'll finish eating and go find Onmiel. Making that decision feels good. And for the first time in a long time, I'm not waiting for the other shoe to drop.

CHAPTER TWENTY-NINE

ONMIEL

I return to my assigned room and sit at the window, watching Pengshur at night. There's a bustling market just outside the side entrance into the archives, but even that seems slightly less busy this evening. The death of a librarian is a big deal to the whole city, and most vendors respect that by keeping the night market low-key.

I'm exhausted from the day but too wired to sleep. When I look around, all I see is Ten every-fucking-where. I see him sitting in the window seat, curled around me in the bed, naked on my shower floor with his soapy hands on my tits.

Godsdamnit. Figures I'd meet the right man at the worst possible time. The red flag of his dead mate was so damn big, waving right in my face, but I happily chose to ignore it because the connection was just *there*. It was so *right*.

I'm the biggest dummy in all Lombornei.

Growling at my own stupidity, I look at the letter Garfield gave me. I'll open it, but not here. I've got to get out of the room. I want my apartment and my blankets and my great view. I need comfort.

It's not lost on me that what I really want is Ten, but I refuse to call him. He's probably enjoying time with his family, who he's barely seen since they arrived, focused as we've been.

Grabbing the letter, I stuff it in my pack and leave the library, heading for my apartment.

When I arrive, I throw open all the windows, letting the sights and sounds of Pengshur at night filter in through my open windows. I make a coffee in my tiny, pink kitchen, grumbling about how much less excellent it is than the ones at the library. And then I wonder if anyone is around to make Ten a coffee because he loves late-night coffee.

I physically slap myself and then take the letter out onto the balcony and fall into one of the plush, oversized chairs that overlook a busy square. Vendors selling to-go booze shout out at the passersby, and it's all I can do not to scream down to them that someone died today. Shut the fuck up and go home! Apparently, this part of town has no qualms about disrespecting the heaviness of the day.

Life goes on; I know that. It always goes on because life is for the living, not those who are already gone.

Grimacing, I tear the envelope open and pull out a single aging sheet of paper. It's folded in half, the heavy handwriting visible from the exterior. When I open it, I choke on my coffee, hacking and slapping my chest until I can set the cup down.

It's my godsdamned handwriting.

I blink rapidly, and then I read the letter in fucking disbelief.

H*ey, you! Hey, me? That's wild.*

I'm sure you're wondering why you wrote yourself a letter and ML Garfield gave it to you, right?

Grab a coffee and settle in. This is a crazy story, but I promise it's 1000% the truth.

You're a Volya, Onmiel. That's what the prisoner tattoo is keeping in. You hide yourself because of Zura's death, which you hopefully remember.

If you're reading this letter, it's because you had a need to know more about your past. You asking for the vial was the only condition under which Garfield was allowed to give it to you.

I'm sure this all seems very vague, but you spelled your tattoo in two ways. Drink the vial, and you'll remember everything. Just don't drink the second one unless you're ready for the tattoo to come off...

P.S. *There's a vampiri traveling orb hidden under a loose floorboard in the bathroom. Just in case you need it...*

S*igned, yours truly (literally)*

Scoffing, I sit back in the chair and sip my coffee in disbelief. This is my fucking handwriting. But me? A Volya?

I close my eyes and sort through my memories. But my fucking memories are vague on purpose. Vague remembrances of loving parents and siblings. The only memory that's aged well is the accident that killed my younger sister. That was my fault, and it's something I will never ever forget or get over. That's why I spelled myself the way I did. I wanted to be clear on how I killed her, even if it was an accident. I couldn't risk losing control by digging up my past, and I wanted that guilt to stay with me.

Zura died because of me. Nobody else ever needs to.

Slowly, pieces move and shift into place, and I realize I gave away one fucking vial of blood to Diana. What if, by finding out more about myself, I could know precisely how to cure her?

Oh, fuck! I shoot upright. If I could at least remember, I could translate the godsdamned prophecy.

Ugh, there were two vials. The letter references two vials.

Suddenly, I remember the envelope Okair gave me at the releasing ceremony. I snatch it out of my back pocket and open it with shaky hands. Is it possible I really planned this far ahead on the off-chance I'd need to know my history? What kind of fucking kismet is that?

Inside, a tiny vial of bright red blood shines, sinister in the low, late-night moonlight.

I reread the letter a dozen times, but it's pretty straightforward—drink this to regain my memory. Memories I locked away for a good fucking reason, I'm sure. But having those back means I can finish my mission and ensure that Diana's healing works. It means I can help figure out what the prophecy says.

I can help Ten achieve his goal because all of this will close a chapter for him. And maybe, selfishly, I hope another future chapter will open where he and I get to write our own book.

The steps are simple.

Drink the vial.

Translate the prophecy.

Save Diana.

Closing my eyes, I pinch the stopper off the vial, steeling myself before I throw it back and swallow.

To my surprise, the blood doesn't taste like anything at all, but it burns like hells on the way down. I fall to both knees as I choke on it, my throat on fire. Then my back feels like flames crawl across it as the blood works its magic to release one layer of the scrolled black prisoner tattoo. Inch by inch, the magic streaks like predatory nails down my back, removing the dark spell I used to conceal myself in human form.

I fall to the ground, gasping for breath as the pain lances down my back. It's so insanely hot and hard that all I can do is scream and writhe on the porch, gripping the railing as the magic releases. The agony goes on for minutes that feel like hours, yanking and pulling as it unlocks whatever I locked away.

When the stabbing sensation recedes, a soothing, cooling feeling replaces it, coating my back in what I can only imagine is the healing nature of my own blood on a wound inflicted by me.

Sobbing, I roll over and pull myself back up into my seat, wiping tears and snot away as I steel myself for the memories.

They come back in a flood, choking and drowning me as I relive my entire life in a flash. I was right to hide myself away for the last eight years.

I'm a monster. I'm a godsdamned monster.

CHAPTER THIRTY
TENEBRIS

I've barely finished dinner when Jet cocks his head to the side.

"Someone's coming, running. I think it's Onmiel."

I'm up and to the front door, swinging it wide as Onmiel barrels through, her face pinched in terror. She stalks past me, shoving me aside as she runs up the hall toward the dining hall, calling for Diana.

Diana appears in the entryway, looking concerned, then weirded out when Onmiel drops to both knees and shoves Diana's shirt up. She inhales deeply over the healing wounds and then falls onto her butt, shaking her head.

"Fuck. Godsdamnit!" She leaps to her feet and looks at Noire. "The blood won't cure her, not permanently, because it's not from the Volya who injured her. The only reason it helped her at all is because it's mine. Lahken's my father, and he's a healer, so I carry some of his ability."

"Wait, what?" Diana and Noire roar at the same time as my entire pack crowds around her. I go to her side and reach for her, but she shies away from me, turning and lifting her shirt to show my brother her tattoo.

241

"Oh, fuck. Not that shit again," mutters Jet as Achaia sinks back into his arms with a wary look.

"I'm a Volya," Onmiel snaps. "I spelled myself to stop from remembering horrible shit I did when I was younger and couldn't control my magic. I spelled myself so I couldn't hurt anyone. But I left myself a letter in case I needed to remember. I left it as a safeguard in case my family ever needed me for something. An emergency parachute of sorts."

"And how does this have anything to do with Diana?" Noire snaps.

Onmiel reaches into her pocket, grabbing a piece of paper which she hands to Noire.

"The vampiri prophecy, remember? The second half? We learned it was written in Volya, but I couldn't translate it. I removed the first layer of my tattoo so I could figure out what it said." Her eyes go wide with unshed tears as she looks up at me and then back at Diana.

"When the dead come to life, the king will sacrifice the queen. A common enemy must die. Only then will there be peace."

"You must be joking," Ascelin hisses. "Do we assume the king's sacrifice means Diana?"

"The Volya who injured her marked her," Onmiel whispers, her voice hoarse. "He could have deposited a killing poison with his claws, but he did this so she'd have to find him to get well. He did this, knowing you'd venture back to the Tempang. This was his last-ditch effort to call Diana to him, so he must assume she's the queen or the common enemy."

"And we are certain he could mean no other sacrifice, no other enemy?" Ascelin sounds doubtful but horrified as she looks around the room.

"The Volya are peacekeepers," Onmiel whispers. "While dangerous and reclusive, we are responsible for the peace and safety of the forest. Lahken has never fought anyone, not in my entire life. If Diana was marked like this, he thinks he needs her for something.

It's hard to say if it's this specific prophecy, but it was given to you, so..."

"He said the forest was sick, though," I counter. "Could there be some enemy there?"

Onmiel shakes her head. "Many beings in the Tempang have enemies, but the Volya generally keep the peace. They simply don't *have* enemies."

"What if *you're* the enemy?" Noire purrs, his voice low and calculating, bringing me right back to our time in the maze. "You said you did terrible things, things bad enough to hide yourself here under that godsdamned tattoo."

"I'm a monster; it's true," she whispers, crossing her arms as she slumps into the wall for support. "I won't deny what I did, but when I left, my family begged me not to go. I thought it for the best, but that hardly seems like something you'd do with an enemy."

Diana turns from us, her hand over her mouth as if she can't even fathom the words to say while she flees the room.

Onmiel looks to Noire urgently. "Gather your things. We'll leave in the morning, and I'll go with you. You can't approach my father with Diana like this. He'll think nothing of tossing her right in the Gate of Whispers, and then you'll be fucked."

"The what?" Ascelin snaps, both hands on her hips as she glares at the librarian.

"The Gate of Whispers is the mother of all life in the Tempang. It's..." She waves her hands around like she isn't sure how to explain it. "The gate is our deity, created by the old gods who ruled the Tempang when the rest of the continent was nothing but dust."

Noire ignores that and leans in close, even when I push myself between him and Onmiel. He pokes his head around me, not caring at all that my big body blocks him from her.

"Hear me on this, Volya. If Diana receives so much as a scratch during this adventure, I'll burn down the entire Tempang and your family with it. There is nothing I won't do to see her fully healed."

"As you should," Onmiel agrees. "I'd do the same if I were you. But all I can do now is give you a fighting chance, right?"

Noire looks at Onmiel as if he can't tell if she's telling the truth or not, but after a tense moment, he turns from us and follows Diana into the depths of the house.

"You sacrificed your personal well-being to give us the truth," Ascelin voices. "I am in awe of you, librarian. Thank you."

She nods. Ascelin turns to Renze with a meaningful look. "Let us prepare, First Warrior. We have much to do."

My pack parts ways as Onmiel turns to me with a resigned look. "We could have gotten to the truth so much faster, Ten. Gods-damnit!" She stomps her foot and shakes her head, huffing.

"Are you alright?" I keep my voice low and soothing as I resist the urge to pull her into my arms and kiss the tension from between her brows. My direwolf paces in my chest, scratching and yowling at me to smother Onmiel in affection, to fuck that anguish away. I still haven't mentioned his development to my brothers. Somehow, it feels like it's between Onmiel and me.

When I can't hold back any longer, I reach for her waistband and pull her flush with my chest. "Are you *alright?*" I reiterate.

"I'm not," she mutters, looking up as she finally places both hands flat on my chest. "I'm not alright at all, but I will be."

"I'll be there every step of the way," I reassure her. "And my dire-wolf. He's losing his mind right now about the stress rolling off you."

Onmiel's plump lips part into a dejected smile. "No exploding out of there. It'll be okay," she whispers, rubbing between my pecs as he preens deep inside me. She looks up at me with a hopeful expres-sion. "Run with me in the moonlight before we embark on this awful fucking quest?"

I nod as I open the front door and pull my shirt over my head. "You think your father won't stop to listen to you?"

"I'll make him," she confirms, following me into the darkness. I get naked and shift into my direwolf, who immediately presses his head between her pert breasts, purring his godsdamned heart out as I lay down, belly to the cobblestones.

Onmiel crawls on top of me, fisting her tiny hands in my fur as I take off. We run up the street and out into the countryside. I run for a solid hour before I slow, stopping at a small overlook before I shift into human form again. Pulling Onmiel into my arms, I seat us so we can look down at Pengshur, the library a glittering white landmark in the middle of town.

"I'm there every step of the godsdamned way, Onmiel," I say again to drive the point home as I pepper kisses down her neck.

"I meant it when I said I was a monster," she mutters from her spot between my thighs. "The things I've done, Ten…"

"More than your sister?" I press, rubbing at one of her knees as she sighs, pulling them up tight to her chest.

"Isn't that enough? Killing your loved one? You did it to save people, Ten. I did it because I was hotheaded and foolhardy, and I thought I could control a power I barely even understood. She died because I was a fucking idiot."

"And you've made yourself pay the price ever since," I remind her. "You can't change that, Onmiel. You can only move on."

We fall silent as the moon reaches its peak. Eventually, she starts yawning. "I've got to go home and pack. I'll be back bright and early."

"Want some company?" I lick and suck my way along her exposed shoulder as she shudders in my arms.

"I just…I need a minute, Ten. I'm fucking reeling, and I just need a few hours to grab some sleep and hopefully wake up with a clearer mind. My brain feels like it ran a hundred miles today."

"I understand," I whisper, even though my direwolf howls at the idea of being parted from her for even a few hours.

Eventually, she starts to nod off in my arms, so I shift and run back, dropping her at the archives. She gives me a sleepy wave goodbye, and then I jog back to the apartment. I pack and shower and lie down for a few hours, knowing she'll be back soon.

Rough hands shake me awake what feels like mere minutes later.

"Ten, get up. We've got problems." Noire's voice is gruff and irritated. I leap out of bed, shaking the sleep out of my limbs as Ascelin appears in the doorway with a baleful look in my direction.

She reaches out, handing me a slip of paper. When I open it, I recognize Onmiel's handwriting.

Ayala Pack -

I've gone ahead to the Tempang. I'll admit to not sharing the whole truth yesterday. You journeying into the Tempang is practically a death sentence. Even with me to escort you, the reality is that my father won't wait to hear about Diana or the vampiri prophecy. He'll toss her into the Gate of Whispers without a backward glance simply because the gate has been calling her.

If I go alone, I can talk to him. I'll get a vial of blood for her, and I'll share the prophecy with him. We'll find another way. But I can't risk you.

Any of you.

Meet me at the edges of the Tempang if you must. But whatever you do, don't fucking come in, I beg you.

Ten, I'm sorry it had to be this way. This is the only chance I have to protect all of you and heal Diana for good.

I'm a half day ahead of you, so chances are by the time you read this, I'll already be well on my way to getting a cure for her.

See you soon,

Onmiel

. . .

T he roar that leaves my chest shakes pictures off the wall as they fall to the ground, shattering. My muscles tense, and I grit my teeth. My direwolf rages in my chest, and finally, I can't hold him anymore. I scream as I fling myself back against the wall.

My direwolf explodes out of my chest, taking over as Noire grunts in surprise. I shove past him and sprint downstairs and out the door. He rages, demanding answers in our family bond. I ignore every command, running to Pengshur.

I barrel through security and into the archives, running every fucking level to be sure. There's nothing left of Onmiel but her lingering scent in our reading room and her assigned room on the fifth floor.

She fucking left. I can't believe it.

Except, I can. She's put her personal safety and well-being behind everything else to find a cure.

I sprint back to the house, shifting as I barge through the door. Inside, Jet hands me a pack, giving me a wry look.

"Now that's out of your system, we going to get your girl?"

"Right now," I snap. "We go for her right fucking *now*."

"Good," Noire growls as he comes around the corner. "Because Arliss is here with his ship, and it's time to go. And I want to know what the fuck happened with your direwolf. You weren't trying to shift, and it happened anyway. Care to fill me the fuck in?"

"Later," I growl. "We've got a long ride ahead of us, even in Arliss's airship.

"Not later," Noire commands. His tone slaps me right in the face, tightening our bond until I struggle to breathe around it. He's gotten so strong since mating Diana, and that's obvious to me now. His pack alpha demand is almost impossible to ignore.

Turning, I roll my shoulders and growl. "We'll have plenty of hours on the ship to talk about it, brother. Not fucking now." Fury rolls in waves off me, my direwolf pressing up against my breastbone. He's furious and terrified. He wants Onmiel, and I'm losing control fast.

Noire's black eyes narrow, drifting down my body. He steps forward, and I'm vaguely aware of Jet and Renze coming closer. I don't know whose side they're on, but I let out a warning growl anyhow. Noire steps until we're nose to nose, then he leans in and scents me. It's an invasion of my space, and the resonant growl that erupts from my throat is a warning from my wolf to his.

Get the fuck away from me.

He shifts backward. "On the way, then, Tenebris. But rest assured, I want answers. Do you pose a threat to my mate like this?"

I snort at that. The last thing I want to do is hurt her. But my wolf is ready to rip into Noire for getting in my fucking space.

"Let's go," I bark.

Noire nods, dismissing me. I stalk back into the street where Arliss now sits in one of his giant mechanical airships. Double doors swing open as I strut inside and look ahead.

I'm coming for you, sweet girl, I think to myself. *And when I get you back, you're never leaving these arms. I didn't tell you I was obsessed with you, and I only hope I get the chance.*

CHAPTER THIRTY-ONE

ONMIEL

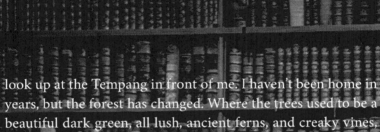

I look up at the Tempang in front of me. I haven't been home in years, but the forest has changed. Where the trees used to be a beautiful dark green, all lush, ancient ferns, and creaky vines, they're different now: they're visibly sick, black, and decaying. When I left, the forest was reeling from Zura's death, but it was still a healthy place. This is something different entirely, and I have a sneaking suspicion, *somehow*, I'm the reason why.

Sighing, I pull my pack higher over my shoulder and begin walking. It's a long way to the Volya village in the far northwest of the Tempang, but it won't be long before Father learns I'm back and retrieves me. It's the one thing I can count on.

The moment I cross from Deshali land into the forest, an eerie sense of foreboding snakes down my spine. The forest is dying. Not just sick, as I was told, but on its deathbed. I choke back a sob, wondering if my magic is responsible for all this. I don't have access to it, not in this form. I can only access it in Volya form, but I won't risk that unless it's a last resort.

If it turns out that I caused this when I killed Zura, Father will never let me leave. I'll have to stay here to fix what I broke. My only hope is that I can barter my life for a cure to Diana's illness. I can't let Ten's pack come into the forest; I've got to get to my father first.

Almost as if on cue, leaves rustle in a clearing up ahead. A gigantic, weathered figure appears. He's nearly ten feet tall, all long, spindly pale limbs, still cloaked in oatmeal-colored robes. His wide mouth, full of sharp teeth, is pursed disapprovingly. His rahken, the wide, flat bones that cover where a human's eyes would be, are angled together. Horns rise up behind them. His are the biggest in our clan…

I remember being proud of him as a child.

"Daughter," my father murmurs in ancient Volya. "You have returned."

"I didn't know," I say, inclining my head as I join him in the clearing, a single tear tracking a path down my cheek. "Is this me? My magic?"

"It is far more complicated, Onmiel," Father hisses, his voice soothing as he folds his hands in front of his waist. Even the wooden crown on his head seems to be fading, the wood dark and chipping at the edges as if it's already dry and dead. His wings look paper-thin, folded to his back and held slightly off the ground.

"Why not come for me?" I question. "You knew where I was going. If I did this, why not come for me?"

Lahkan lets out a laugh, but there's no mirth to it at all. "I will show you, daughter, why we could not leave. You will not believe your eyes when you see the horror that has haunted the Tempang since your departure. Come, let us go home. There is much work to do."

"Wait," I hedge. "I need something. I'll stay and help fix this no matter what, but you hurt a friend of mine, an omega. There was a prophecy about her, and I need your blood to heal her."

Father pauses and gives me a curious look. "Her life is hers to guard, Onmiel. If she comes and asks for the cure, I will provide it if you wish. But know this, Diana Ayala and the other queen were called by the gate herself. I will sacrifice them if I must."

My father glares at me, and there's ripe condescension on his angular, pale face before he gestures for me to follow. "Come, Onmiel. The forest will let us know if your friends arrive. In the meantime, there is something you need to see."

Gods, I hope it takes Ten a day or two to get here. That'll mean I've got that long to sort this out before I have to tell him I can never leave the Tempang again. Because worst comes to worst, Father would toss even me into the gate if it meant fixing the forest. Forest first. That's the Volya mission. Anything for the forest.

Even if it means sacrificing the future queen of the Volya clan.

CHAPTER THIRTY-TWO
TENEBRIS

I stand at the front of Arliss's boxy airship, tapping my foot as I stare out the glass-paned side window at our rented townhouse. He's taking his godsdamned time prepping and I'm ready to get on the road. He and Ascelin are in the middle of a standoff.

"My lap would make an excellent perch," he purrs, rubbing the top of his thigh suggestively. Asc gives him the middle finger and sits in the co-pilot chair, propping her feet up on the front. Arliss frowns at the mud on the bottom of her boots, but when her black brows lift, he says nothing.

"Cut the shit and get going," I snap. "She's ahead of us by hours. She could be in danger."

Arliss turns in the bucket seat and crosses his legs, bringing both hands to one knee as he gives me a condescending look. "In danger from her own family, Tenebris?"

I don't have an answer for that because I don't know if Onmiel is in danger. I just know she's risking herself for my pack, for people she barely knows. She's the most selfless, kind person I've ever met, and I'm dying without her here.

My hands tremble with the physical need to touch her, so I press them to the glass and look out, my forehead touching the cool surface as Arliss spins toward the front and puts the airship in gear.

Behind me, my pack lounges on the hovercar's benches. Diana lays down on one, her head in Noire's lap as he strokes hair away from her sweaty forehead. Jet, Renze, and Achaia occupy another, huddled closely together as they watch Diana with worried expressions despite their light chatter. Their black velzen, Rosu, lays at their feet and watches me, his long tail swishing lazily from side to side. I haven't seen him until right now, but somehow, I find his presence comforting.

My wolf recognizes a kindred spirit in the young predator, not that he looks young anymore. Several weeks ago, he was equivalent to a medium-sized dog. Now, he's about the size of a small pony. He's growing fast as hells, an indicator of the general sentiment of danger around our pack. His growth rate is in direct proportion to how often he feels his people need protecting.

If Onmiel were here, she and I would talk about that, and she'd have some quippy remark about velzen from a book I've not had the chance to read yet.

Why didn't you just take me with you, I think. It's not lost on me that I had a mate who wasn't fully honest with me. I don't want it to be like that between Onmiel and me.

I chose her, but now she's gone, too. What's worse is that she didn't feel she could tell me the whole truth. And I'm so fucking sure it's because she thinks it'll protect me in some way. She knew if she told me her plan, I'd insist on going with her.

Because the reality is that it happened fast, but I'm fucking obsessed with the beautiful librarian. I'm obsessed with everything about her. Her wild, white hair, gorgeous gray eyes and dorky expressions, her love of coffee and terrible rhythm when she dances.

My direwolf whines in my chest, and the noise echoes out of my mouth as I press my forehead harder to the glass, willing the airship to develop warp speed and spit us out at the mouth of the Tempang. I've got to get to her.

"Ten." Noire's voice is pure pack alpha command. He wants to know about my wolf now that we're on the way. I knew he wouldn't drop it, but I find myself not wanting to share. Noire's command has never bothered me, but right now, it rankles. Deep inside, my wolf paces and snarls. He dislikes Noire's command, and that unsettles me. I've never had trouble listening to my brother before.

When I turn, my eldest brother gestures to my chest, his dark eyes narrowed.

"What happened upstairs?"

He's referencing how when they told me Onmiel had gone ahead without us, my wolf forced a shift and took over, running the city looking for her. I let it happen, crazed with fear and need.

"My wolf has developed his own voice," I admit, crossing my arms as I lean up against the glass.

The airship is silent as everyone absorbs my words.

Jet's eyes narrow as he internalizes what I said. "As in he has thoughts that are separate from yours?"

"He speaks to me," I confirm. "It started when I came to Pengshur."

Now, both my brothers are staring at me like I've got a dick sprouting out of my forehead.

Noire looks over at Jet. "You ever heard of something like this?"

Jet shakes his head and leans back, nudging Renze with his shoulder. "You?"

Renze cocks his head and looks at me like I'm a scientific specimen. "I have not, but that does not mean it isn't more common in alpha history, perhaps. We could venture to the vampiri court and ask our whisperer, but it would take time away from our mission. Something to consider once we have healed the Chosen One."

"Can you speak back to him?" Diana's voice is weak, but she shuffles upright and slumps against Noire's shoulder.

His eyes fill with worry as he wraps an arm carefully around her. She seems worse today, even though she improved yesterday and the day before. Dark red circles underscore both blue eyes, her cheeks sunken and her breathing shallow. She's on death's door, and if she reaches that threshold before we get to our destination, Noire will pull this fucking airship to pieces and kill everyone.

"Did he speak to you about Rama?" Arliss's question catches me off-guard, but I confirm it. The dagger that usually stabs me when I think about my dead mate is less noticeable now. She might have been fated to be mine, but I didn't choose her, and she was terrible in every possible way. I don't choose her now, and even if she were standing in front of me, I don't think I'd want her.

When I don't expand on my answer, Arliss shrugs and turns fully around to face me. "Since Diana's brother, Dore, was under the influence of the same drug as you, I asked Elizabet to run tests on it. Dore is still locked up at my compound, and I need to understand if his mind will ever be salvageable."

Diana is quiet at the mention of her twin. I'm equally perturbed. Dore was Rama's right-hand lieutenant, but she drugged him the same way she drugged me.

"And?" I wave my hand to encourage him.

Arliss's blue eyes flash with focus. "It was a hallucinogenic. It would have kept you and Dore in a perpetual state of struggling to focus. What's worse is it would have left you both susceptible to her suggestions."

I can't say I'm surprised at that. When the mechanical spider injecting the drug into my chest broke, the brain fog was a bitch to get clear of. Dore was probably on drugs for years. He may never recover.

What I am surprised at is how it doesn't feel like the betrayal it was. I grieved, then I got mad, and now I'm numb to the horrible shit Rama did to me. That was a past me, and I don't want to focus on that now.

After a quiet moment, I expand on my confirmation. "My wolf says she hurt him."

I shrug as I turn to look back out the window. Nobody speaks, but the airship is tense. Noire and Diana are bondmates. He knows the depth of that devotion, the intense need to protect and care. Diana would kill anybody who posed a real threat to Noire, that's the conviction of a bondmate. That my wolf feels our bondmate hurt him is unfathomable.

Need her, my wolf growls in my chest. *Need Miel.*

I know, buddy, I try to console him. The airship behind me is silent as a grave. Nobody knows what to say about him or what it means.

My entire pack, smart as they all are, is stunned into silence.

CHAPTER THIRTY-THREE

ONMIEL

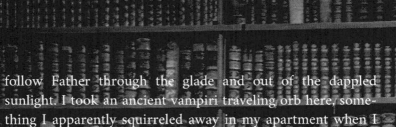

I follow Father through the glade and out of the dappled sunlight. I took an ancient vampiri traveling orb here, something I apparently squirreled away in my apartment when I first arrived at Pengshur. Gods, I really did plan for every eventuality, assuming I'd have to come back here one day and relive my fucking godsawful memories.

The forest's sickness seeps into my very bones like a disease. The Tempang used to radiate peace and vibrant, verdant health to me. Now, every tree, every branch, every vine looks defeated and angry.

My father, Lahkan, comes to a stop in front of a broad tree, placing his weathered, pale hand on it as he murmurs an incantation under his breath. The tree's bark parts and opens into a doorway, glowing a sickly green from the inside out. Traveling trees should glow brightly.

Father's horns slump in defeat when he sees the way I stare at the tree.

I choke down a sob as I follow my father inside the small opening. Once we enter the tree, the space seems to expand, another glowing doorway opening on the tree's now-cavernous interior. I follow him through a series of passageways. Traveling trees are all one giant, interconnected organism that only Volya have access to. They allow us to move quickly all over the Tempang. As moderators and peacekeepers, it's imperative to our success to reach any of the forest's constituents fast.

Our footsteps are barely audible against the smooth bark floor of the tree's hallway. Ahead of me, Father's strides are sure and quick, but there's a slight limp to his gait that wasn't there when I left the forest.

"Father, are you injured?" My voice echoes in the hollow chamber as he looks over his shoulder, his flat profile visible as he shakes his head. It's so familiar. I've seen him look over his shoulder thousands of times. Being here with him hurts deep in my chest. Zura always took after him in looks. Looking at him now is like staring into her face.

Shame and grief sweep me up in a torrent.

"Simply getting older, daughter," is all he says. If he can sense my inner turmoil, he doesn't address it.

When it's clear he's not planning to expand on the topic of his limp, I reach for his hand and tug it, stopping us in the hallway so I can look up at him. Volya have no eyes, just the flat, wide rahken bones that cover where eyes would be. Our rahken allow us to better connect with the sentiment of the forest, connected as we are.

"Father, what's going on here? Please, talk to me."

Lahkan sighs and squeezes my fingers, which might be the most affection I've ever experienced from him—Zura was always his favorite, they were so similar in personality and appearance.

He shakes his head, his enormous horns nearly reaching the sides of the traveling tree's hall. "It will be easier to show you, child, because once we begin discussing this, you will have many questions. I would rather just show you everything."

It's a cryptic answer, but he turns, indicating the conversation is over. I follow him in complete silence for another five minutes, and then he takes a sharp right. This path leads to the far northwestern reaches of the Tempang, an area filled with dangerous, ancient creatures. Kurasao ice dragons, giant spiders, and some of the more ferocious centaur tribes. Even the Volya rarely venture there.

Goosebumps rise along the surface of my skin as Father stops in front of a door to the exterior and turns, a wrinkled finger pressed to his lips. "Quiet, child."

I nod, my stomach tumbling into knots as the traveling tree opens, depositing us into a part of the forest I haven't been in since my sister and I were much younger. This part of the Tempang should come with its own warning. It borders the area where my people live, but the creatures who make their home here thrive *only* here.

I follow Lahkan out of the tree, rubbing anxiously at my elbow as the door seals closed behind us. In human form like I am now, I'm nothing more than a snack to the sorts of monsters who inhabit this sordid corner of the Tempang. Not to mention Father doesn't look to be in great shape to defend me. Volya can be dangerous, and we all know how to fight, but Father is definitely well past his best fighting years.

The jungle in front of us is burnt and blackened, even the earth beneath our feet is scorched. Vines hang from the trees, but where they used to be a dark, healthy green, they now glow as if lava runs through them, red fire peeking out from cracked skin. But that can't be possible.

Wrong. It's so fucking wrong. I suck in a breath, but it barely fills my lungs as I take in the devastation around me.

I whip around, the sensation of fingers on the back of my neck so real, so tangible, I'm certain someone will be standing there. But there's no one. Father grips my wrist and pulls me to his side, snaking around the traveling tree and pulling me up a black dirt path to the top of a small hill.

Below us, a valley opens up. My mouth falls open. There used to be a river here and a vibrant forest that spilled over the banks into the water. Now, every tree is torn down and the earth is scorched every possible shade of brown. The earth itself is cracked open, streams of what looks like lava running underneath the dirt.

I clap my hand over my mouth. Father points down into the valley. At one end, there's an encampment, and all sorts of monsters mill around. I watch as a group of centaurs stomps at the water's edge. They turn from it, and everything is wrong. They don't look... normal. Flesh hangs from their bones, their movements jerky. Beyond them, the valley is filled with a dozen different monster species—species that normally never come close to one another if they can help it.

No matter the species, they move in that same, herky jerky way. Skin hangs from visibly protruding bones. Fire seems to run underneath their muscles, dripping down their limbs to pool wherever they step.

I open my mouth to ask my father what in the seven hells I'm looking at, but he puts his hand over my mouth, indicating I should be quiet. I follow his gaze to the opposite end of the valley where forges blow flames sky-high. There's a clanking sound, and even though it's far, I can barely make out centaurs pounding metal with giant hammers.

Weapons. The motley group below us is making weapons. But why? These monsters never congregate together, much less form any sort of army. The Tempang doesn't work that way. Every monster species has a territory of sorts, and most don't overlap in the slightest.

My father looks down at me, his face set into a mask of sorrow. He scoots back on his stomach before standing, gesturing for me to follow. I glance once more at the dark valley, filled to the brim with unrecognizable monsters. I don't know what this is, and I've never seen anything like it.

I jog quietly after my father, a sense of relief flooding me when the traveling tree opens and then seals shut behind us.

"What's wrong with the forest?" I demand of my father. "What were those...things?"

My father turns to me with a hardened set to the bones that split his face in half.

"The undead, Onmiel. The undead are ravaging the Tempang, and we cannot stop them."

~

I stare at my father in obvious confusion, struggling to comprehend what he just revealed.

"Undead? What do you mean? How can that be?" My blood chills as it pounds through my veins, so loud I can hear it in my ears. My breath comes in stilted gasps, my lungs struggling to move oxygen through my veins.

Lahkan indicates we should get going, and I follow him as he moves quickly through the tree's hallways.

"My warriors are ready to speak with you when we return home. We have much to catch up on, Onmiel. I wanted you to see this first because it is nearly unbelievable."

My mind is still reeling from what we saw in that glade, bodies dripping fiery blood, skin and flesh hanging from their bones. Red, visionless eyes.

I miss Ten.

The thought is there fast and flashes away as I hold in a groan. There's nothing I want more than his big arms to comfort me. I want his inquisitive mind to dig into this with me. I want him by my side. But also, I want him as far as humanly possible away from those things.

Father's being cagey, and as much as I'd love for Ten to be here to back me up, I'm terrified for the Ayala Pack to come to the forest.

I'm not a fool; I know they're on their way. There's no way Ten would let me go willingly, but I have to try to fix this. Diana is running out of time. But so is my forest, and somehow, it's my fault. I know it. That knowledge is curled around my heart like a snake waiting to strike. Father hasn't said as much, but I know he will. I can feel it.

All those thoughts dissipate when the traveling tree opens again, depositing us into a familiar, shady glen. I look up at the trees above, noting how unchanged they seem. This part of the forest still looks healthy and sentient, like we passed through an invisible barrier, and the Tempang here is still happy. The trees are a brilliant green, their leaves shimmering in the early afternoon light. Moss covers their trunks up as far as my eyes can see. It's exactly like it was the day I left.

I struggle to swallow around the lump in my throat.

There's noise ahead as Father exits the tree, his pale robes swaying softly behind him. He tucks his wings tightly to his back and his hands into his sleeves as he heads for our village.

I gulp as I watch him go. Somehow, my magic is the cause of this. I feel it in the way the trees here seem to tighten and shrink back at my presence when I step out of the tree.

They know something.

They recognize the same evil in me that I unleashed when Zura was killed. It was an accident, but my power is nearly limitless and totally uncontrollable. The Tempang may look like a simple forest—however, it's anything but. It's alive in its own way, and it's the Volya's mandate to protect *it* and the Gate of Whispers.

Closing my eyes, I concentrate on the gate herself. Before I hid my true form away behind my tattoo, I could always sense the gate and her connection to the Tempang. Now, when I focus on finding her in my mind's eye, I see nothing. I feel nothing. Running both hands through my long hair, I huff out a breath of frustration.

"I'll fix this," I mutter under my breath, placing my palm on the closest tree trunk. It shudders slightly under my touch. I jerk my hand away, looking up to see the tree's leaves quivering in the wind.

The forest is afraid of me.

I violated its trust when I tried to control and channel my unusual ability to communicate directly with the gate. That violation left mayhem and death in my wake. I deserted the Tempang to protect my clan, but it seems all I really did was leave behind a mess. I didn't face what I did, and that mistake has haunted everyone I love since.

Sick nerves bundle in my stomach, threatening to make me

vomit. I hear my name called in a sharp tone and then a softer one. "Miel? Miel!"

It's my mother's voice, and that, at least, makes me feel good for the first time. My mother is one of my favorite beings in the entire world. She and I have always been so similar, whereas Zura was more like Lahken.

When I turn from the tree, I see my mother's slim, elegant figure dashing up the path, sunlight filtering through to shine on her. She hasn't aged a day, her broad mouth curved into a joyous smile as she runs to me.

I sprint from my spot, arms open, and jump up into hers the moment I'm close enough. Our bodies clash together, and because I'm so much smaller in this form, she wraps her arms all the way around me, crushing me to her chest. I inhale my mother's scent, all woodsy sunshine, like the forest itself is infused in her very skin.

"I have missed you so much, daughter," she whispers, swaying from side to side as if rocking a small child.

Laughing, I wipe the tears away and lean back to look at her. There's such evident joy on her face in the way she's smiling and how her horns are curled up high behind her forehead. I've always loved her horns. Where Father's are shaped broad and wide like a bull, Mother's slide back along her hairline like some kind of gorgeous, curly arrowhead. All Volya horns are different, but hers are so beautiful to me. Zura and I used to drive wooden aircab toys along her horns as children, playing loop-the-loop on the bone.

Zura's were just like hers, maybe the *only* way they were alike.

I suck in a slow, steadying breath. She sets me down and grabs my hand in hers.

"What happened here, Mother? It's my fault; I know it. The trees don't want my touch."

Her happy smile falls, and she nods. "It is not your fault, Onmiel, but we do believe your magic caused what's happening. Come. Father is with Kraven. We will celebrate your return over dinner, but for now, there is much to catch up on."

Kraven.

There's a name I haven't heard in ages. My former betrothed until I killed my sister and called off our engagement.

Mother pulls me by the hand toward the village, stroking my long, white hair with the other.

"You look good, Onmiel. Better than good. You are striking in this form, and your soul is peaceful. Tell me everything about your last eight years."

"Time for that later," I murmur as our village comes into view. Volya already gather around, gasping in shock when they see me. Most faces are angry, although they school them neutral as we approach. This is not a joyous homecoming, no matter how pleased my mother is to have me back.

I killed a clanmate, broke an engagement, and fled the forest, leaving behind whatever this current devastation is. I had no idea, but I suspect they don't want to hear about that.

We enter the village in silence. Mother keeps her hand firmly in mine in a silent show of support. It gives me a moment to look around at the village I grew up in.

It hasn't changed a bit. Multiple levels of beautiful wooden cottages are built into the broad efek trees. Dangling ropes and ladders connect each home to the next. The village appears to be the same size as it was when I left. I would have expected a few more houses by now, but maybe there are less children.

"Onmiel."

A masculine, gravelly voice breaks through my thoughts, calling my attention to what's in front of us. Mother halts, her claw-tipped fingers still threaded through mine.

My former betrothed stands in front of us.

Kraven.

Gods, he's still attractive despite the years that distance us. He's now taller than Father by half a head, long horns spreading wide before curling backward in what I'd call lazy circles that end in vicious iron-tipped points. He's packed on the pounds since I left, far more muscular than the gangly young male who courted me all those years ago. I used to daydream about stroking his horns while we fucked, but that seems like a lifetime ago.

That was back when Kraven smiled, if only for *me*, during stolen, secretive moments deep in the forest.

He's not smiling now.

Father tucks his hands deeper into the billowy sleeves of his robes, scowling over my shoulder. I hear footsteps, the crowd dissipating as he turns that scowl back to me, letting it fall away. He looks so tired, the rahken bones that cover the top half of his face sagging as if he doesn't have the energy to even keep that expression.

"Daughter, now that you have returned and seen the creatures, we need to tell you what you have missed."

"What you *caused*," Kraven corrects, crossing his enormous arms.

Okay, then. There's a significant amount of blame in his tone. I need to catch up fast.

Lahken glances at his second-in-command with an exasperated look.

"We are losing this war, Lahken," Kraven says softly. "She needs to understand the severity."

"Spit it out, then," I snap, disliking how the blame has fallen on me without me having a clear understanding of what's happening. "I'm back to help, so tell me everything."

"Come," Kraven snarls, turning from us and hunching slightly, his muscles flexing before he leaps up onto the first floor of the main Clan House.

Mother sighs but pulls me into her arms, leaping to follow him since I can't do it in this form. Father joins, landing gracefully on the front porch of the Clan House, where he holds his most important meetings.

"Thanks," I huff when Mother puts me down. There are a lot of ladders in my future since I can't leap between tree houses the way my clanmates do.

I walk into the enormous structure, a place I haven't been in almost ten years, not since Zura's death, not since the Volya leader-ship council voted not to kill me for my crimes.

It was an accident, they agreed.

Not that it made anyone feel any better.

Which is why I took myself out of the equation by leaving.

The Clan House is built into the middle of a massive, broad *efek* tree, its branches winding through the soaring, open room. A long, wide table in the middle is covered with maps and weapons, small vials of blood and other serums scattered here and there. They must have been working to heal someone before I arrived.

Kraven lays a map flat on the table's edge, pointing to the part of the forest Father and I visited earlier. "The demon queen rules there now, creating the monsters Lahken took you to see. They're infecting the forest piece by piece, and while the Gate of Whispers is doing everything she can to prevent them, they are a virus. We don't have long before the queen takes the gate, and then we're well and truly fucked."

I blink around the incredible amount of information he just shared, opting to start at the beginning.

"Demon queen? Taking the gate? What in the fuck?"

Kraven turns to me, the set of his rahken angry and resentful. "That is what we call her, Onmiel, yes. When Zura was killed, and you spoke to the gate, we didn't realize, but your power brought her back. You reanimated her, and nobody realized until it was too late, and you had gone."

I fall backward into a chair, looking from Kraven's handsome face to my father's and finally my mother's.

"Is it true?" I whisper. Every muscle in my body quivers, my lower lip following suit. Tears fill my eyes and threaten to spill over. Zura's alive? I brought her back?

My mother will tell me the truth without blaming me.

"Zura's alive?"

"No," Mother murmurs, shaking her head as her horns sag. "She is simply *returned*, child. She is reanimated, she is sentient, and she is preparing for war."

CHAPTER THIRTY-FOUR

TENEBRIS

"We're here." Arliss's voice cuts through the tension in the hovercar as I pace its length for the thousandth time. Ascelin vacates her seat next to him and pats it for me. I lower myself into it so I have the best view of the forest ahead of us.

Rosu pads up from the back and lays his head on my knee with a soft whine. I look down, surprised again at how fast he's growing. His fuzzy, long head covers half my thigh at this point.

I stroke my fingers between his doe-like black eyes as he begins purring. Inside my chest, my wolf responds in kind. He's always recognized the velzen as a friend, but it seems now more than ever, he appreciates the comfort.

We fly low over the scorched earth of Deshali, Rama's home province. Achaia leveled it with a war cry when Rama imprisoned her, and the ground doesn't appear to be recovering at all. I know there should be a pang in my chest, knowing we're closer to where we left her dead body. But instead of the grief that used to hit me, I feel only sorrow for the way things were between us.

I no longer want what she forced upon me.

Ahead of the airship, the Tempang Forest looms.

A dark, gloomy sense fills me as I look at it. Onmiel asked us not to follow her in. I'll give her anything in this world she wants, but that's one request I can't grant. It terrifies me to think of her going in to get help for us without a care for her own safety.

Then again, it doesn't surprise me at all. Onmiel is too selfless for words.

Gritting my teeth, I look at the edge of the forest, a depression settling in my soul that she felt the need to take this on by herself.

In my chest, my wolf stirs and whines, pressing against my ribcage to the point of discomfort. He's as worried for Onmiel as I am, whining and licking his lips in my mind's eye.

Behind me, Diana and Noire begin to argue. Noire's voice is barely above a snarl.

"I'm not risking taking you in there, omega. I'll go with Ten, Arliss, and Ascelin, and we'll return with a cure."

"Like hells you will," she barks. "If you're going, I'm going, and that's all there is to it."

Rosu hovers at my feet, letting out a soft mewl as he plops his shaggy butt on my shoe and focuses on the disagreement. Achaia and Renze join me to watch the show.

"Diana," Noire growls, standing to his full height as I turn to watch their showdown. Even near death, Diana's strength rolls off her in tangible waves. Despite being in obvious pain, she rises and butts against Noire with her chest, a deep growl rumbling from her throat. Her direwolf is bigger and meaner than Noire's, which is really saying something. Jet told me that when they fight, it's no-holds-barred. Their bonding triggered a strengthening in them both.

Diana isn't afraid of Noire; she never has been. Not even when Rama dumped her in the maze to be killed by us. We did hunt her, but nothing turned out the way we expected it to.

"We're partners, Noire," she reminds him, the harsh look on her face morphing into something more delicate, more pleading. "If we can't fix this, if we can't find a cure, or if Onmiel isn't successful, I want to spend every possible minute with you. You can understand that, can't you?"

I've never heard my brother whine, and I've never seen him crack under pressure, but he looks ready to fall to pieces as he collars her neck and pulls her into his arms, burying his face in her throat.

"Diana," he moans, his voice broken as I gulp back my own anguish. Watching them reminds me of those final moments with Rama, how I felt our bond fray and snap and shatter. I thought I'd die, then. Even now, it hurts to see another pair of bondmates and to know their bond is good and strong.

The only reason I'm even put back together is the woman who came into the Tempang to face monsters on behalf of my family.

I can't let Onmiel take this on by herself.

Arliss says nothing this whole time, but per usual, he's in our corner so long as it serves him. I'm aware of that, so I don't count on him. I know he's after information on carrow, and Onmiel told us a tribe lives here in the Tempang. It wouldn't surprise me if he deserts us at the earliest opportunity.

He sets the airship down gently several hundred yards in front of the forest, looking over at me with a wry expression.

"Don't want to take my ship in there and risk losing it. It might be our only means of escape." He says as if this is sage advice, but I suspect Arliss doesn't know that much about the Tempang. I, on the other hand, have been studying it since I was a child. My monster fascination began by learning everything I could about the forest, and it's never stopped.

"Arliss," I begin. "If the forest wants to take us, there will be no escaping. You cannot even begin to fathom what lives in there."

"Don't need to," he grumbles back. "I'm helping you, and then I have my own mission, remember?"

"Hopefully, those two things remain aligned," I growl. He might be traveling with us, but Arliss isn't technically part of our pack, no matter how close he and Ascelin seem to be at times.

As if to illustrate that point, she reaches out and aggressively slaps the back of his head.

He snarls and whips around, but all it does is anger her. She snaps her teeth at his jugular, and he leaps back just in time to dodge a slice of her claws.

They might as well be middle schoolers smacking each other around but secretly in love. I don't have time for this shit right now.

Slinging my backpack over my shoulders, I pound on the hovercar's doors. If the little I know about the Volya is true, they'll find us the moment we cross into the Tempang.

Rosu slinks out of the hovercar and stands quietly by my side, his dark eyes focused on the forest ahead. Jet, Renze, and Achaia join us. Achaia glances around at the blackened earth, her expression sorrowful. Renze leans close to her ear and whispers something. I watch her vivid green eyes close as she presses her cheek to his lips, seeming to seek comfort. Rosu twirls around them, winding through their legs or trying to. He's getting too big for that, and he nearly knocks Achaia to the ground when he tries.

It doesn't stop her from giggling or making cooing noises at the mammoth velzen.

I'd swear he's even grown since we entered the airship, but I don't know what's really possible for a vampiri velzen. He's part guard dog and part cat, but he'll be a warrior if he needs to be.

Noire exits the hovercar holding Diana's hand, although she looks ready to drop. Black circles under her eyes give her a ghostly appearance. She has hours, maybe a day or two max. My wolf can sense it.

Noire's eyes follow mine, and despite Diana growling at him, he picks her up in his arms and cradles her to his chest.

I can't watch how beautiful they are together any longer, so I turn and head for the forest, Rosu by my side. My wolf is anxious to get in there, to shift and run and rip the entire Tempang to the ground to find Onmiel. I don't think I'll breathe easy until I find her in one piece. And then I'm going to toss her over both thighs and spank her ass until it's raw for leaving me like she did.

My pack follows in our usual formation, and I have to say it gives me strength to have us all together. The Tempang is full of monsters, but the worst ones are right here, and they're on my side.

I stop in front of the thick treeline. It's almost like the forest can only grow to a specific point, and although it tries to spill over onto Deshali land, it just can't. Every root, every limb, every branch stops in a line as if held back by an invisible forcefield.

Jet growls next to me, "You want to do our usual formation in there, Ten?

He means how I'm always in front, he and the vampiri cover the middle, and Noire brings up the rear.

Through our family bond, I poke at him. *Think Noire can focus on the rear right now?*

Jet's solemn eyes come to mine before he calls out over his shoulder. "Noire, stay in the middle with Diana so the vampiri can help protect her. I'll take your usual spot."

Noire says nothing but pushes through our small pack, surrounded by the vampiri. It's a testament to how sick she is that he didn't bother to fight Jet's suggestion. Jet gives me a worried look, his chocolate eyes flashing with concern.

"I will join you," Arliss croons, following Jet to the back. I'm sure he'll be looking for the first godsdamned opportunity to leave us, but I can't find it in myself to care.

I turn to my pack with a warning look. "Whatever happens, listen if I give you a command, alright?" Noire gets a serious, pointed look from me. "Even you, brother. In the Tempang, consider me your alpha. I know things about this place you can't fathom, and that could save us. It's fucking dangerous. Worse than the maze, even."

Noire's eyes are narrowed as he considers my words. Finally, he inclines his head to the side. "Noted, baby brother."

He hasn't called me that in ages, not since I broke double digits. But something about it warms my heart. For all that Noire is a fucking asshole, he was there every step of the way for me. He made a big deal out of every birthday by getting me rip-roaring drunk, even in the maze. He pushed through unbelievable odds to get me out of that hellhole. And then he crossed a continent and staged a coup to release me from her clutches.

Love you. I murmur it into our family bond so all my brothers and their mates can hear. I haven't had a chance to get to know Achaia well, but I'm including her because she's family now. And I hope there's a near future where I get to know the mermaid queen who saved Jet from his own demons.

There's a moment of silence, and Noire shifts Diana in his arms. She's practically catatonic, her lips open as she breathes through her mouth.

"Let's go," he growls. "We don't have much time."

I reach out to stroke a stray blonde lock from Diana's cheek. If she were upright, I'd rub my cheek along hers, but Noire's right. We've got to get moving.

I take the lead, stepping from Deshali land into the forest as my pack follows me. There's no visible barrier, but the moment we cross into the Tempang, the scent of ancient forest slaps me. There are trees growing out of trees, mushrooms as tall as I am, and vines slithering on their own across a barely-there path.

"Careful not to touch the vines; step over them," I caution. "They'll grab you if they feel you."

The vines can sense the vibration of our footsteps, but as long as nobody touches their surface, we'll be alright.

I'm focused, keeping an eye on everything around us. Still, my thoughts go to Onmiel. I'm fucking pissed she left and terrified she'll get hurt. We were building something, something important. I want to know where that 'something' will take us.

I lead for half an hour before I sense something is following us. I can't hear it or see it, but my wolf knows it's there. I let the pack pass until Arliss and I are eye-to-eye.

I cast a look around, but I can't see anything obviously amiss. My direwolf paces anxiously, though. Arliss seems to have come to the same conclusion I have, based on the look he gives me.

"Can you shift into carrow form and do a quick circle."

He hands me his pack and shifts into a slip of black smoke,

dashing off into the trees. We continue to move forward quietly, but the sense that we're being followed doesn't leave me. If anything, it builds until there's pressure in my chest, and I'm resisting the urge to shift and attack. Around us, the forest has gone silent.

A sudden crashing sound puts us all on high alert. Noire barks for us to be steady in our family bond.

"It's Arliss," Jet hisses just as the bulky carrow bursts from between two trees in human form.

"Run!" he bellows, taking off up the slim path as I hiss at everyone to move. But what bursts through the trees just after Arliss makes my heart skip a beat. My wolf snaps against my breastbone the second we see it.

It's a centaur, but there's something horribly wrong with him. Muscular flesh hangs from his bones as rivulets of fire drip from fissures in his black coat. The rivulets drop from his belly as he takes a step toward me, and then the fire spreads to the trees, soaking into the nearest vines even as they struggle to move away from it.

A flash of realization goes through my mind. The Volya said the Tempang was sick. Is this what they meant? I've never heard of anything like what I'm seeing.

The centaur's crimson, cracked lips split into a sneer as he grips a long, jagged spear tightly in his hand. The tip of the spear drips with the same smudgy black essence as his body.

No touch, screams my wolf inside before urging me to flee from this being.

The centaur and I face off as I pull a dagger from my belt, lifting it high in hopes I can give my pack a head start. We can't outrun him without shifting, but despite the state of him, I suspect we won't make it far.

I relay all this to my brothers just as the centaur lunges, striking out with his front hooves as I dart to the side.

Up ahead, Ascelin and Arliss yell for Onmiel, hoping she's close enough to hear us. The centaur's head never turns to focus on them, though. Fuck, there must be more.

He slashes out with the spear just as he kicks rapidly with his front feet. Hooves dig into the tree above my head, chipping giant chunks away as I slice at his stomach, watching the muscles split under my blade.

The centaur rears backward with an ungodly roar, nipping at his own side as black sludge drips from my knife.

As I watch, the goo begins to travel up the blade itself toward my hand.

Oh, fuck.

The centaur laughs, even as his slippery-looking intestines begin to spill from the gash in his stomach. I turn and fling the knife, burying it between his dark, glittering eyes.

Initially, he doesn't even react. After a tense moment, he yanks the knife out and glares at me, gaze full of bloodlust.

When I turn and run again, his laughter rings out behind me.

Go, my wolf screams in my chest.

~

Hoofbeats pound behind me but I don't dare turn and look. I smell water ahead, my entire pack sprinting toward it. Maybe we can lose the monster there.

I burst through the dense undergrowth into a clearing to see Noire diving through a small waterfall. He disappears behind it along with the rest of my pack.

Good, they're hidden.

My wolf bursts out of me, forcing a shift, at the same time the centaur clears a fallen tree and slams to a halt, gripping his long spear.

No touch, my direwolf snarls. *Wrong. Male wrong.*

I crouch low, waiting for my brothers and the vampiri to emerge from behind the water. I did a shit job of paying attention to what weapons, if any, we brought. But I can sense my pack distributing them behind the curtain of water. Thank fuck for Jet and his ability to plan for almost any scenario.

There's a flurry of activity in our pack bond, and then Jet and Noire refocus on the monster.

The centaur takes a few steps toward me and bellows, lifting his spear high. He throws it with shocking force. I'm able to sidestep it but he darts forward at the same time, swiping at me with a knife that's appeared in his other hand. I dive to the side and roll around him. He grabs the spear from where it thunked into the ground and turns. The force of his turn pulls guts and a plump, swollen organ through the hole in his side. The dark mass falls to the ground and then slithers off into the trees like it's sentient.

The fuck?

I've never heard of anything like this in all of my reading. I'd heard the Tempang was dangerous, but this? This is something unnatural. I don't know how to fight this.

Before I can say anything in our family bond, a percussive blast echoes across the pool of water in front of the falls. The centaur's head explodes into a black mist.

I fall back and away from him, rolling to ensure none of the offal reaches me.

Ascelin, Jet, and Noire run to my side. Asc holds a big-ass gun. She must have gotten it from Arliss because it's not from our pack.

She grimaces and holds a hand out for me. "Are you alright, Ten?"

I take her hand and nod, shifting and pulling to a stand.

Noire rounds me and steps to where the centaur's headless body now lies, crumpled in a heap on the ground.

"Don't get too close," I hiss. "It's infected or something..."

As we watch, the centaur's body begins to sink in on itself, almost like it's disintegrating in front of us. The black slime that covers it pools into long, thin strings and then begins to slip over the ground, disappearing into the forest.

Ascelin hisses and clicks out a string of words in vampiri before whistling for Renze. He jogs out from behind the waterfall and joins us to watch the last of the centaur disappear.

Moments later, the trees at the very edge of the clearing begin to fade from brilliant green to gray and finally black. They're dying right in front of us.

Jet and Noire watch the scene unfold in silence for a minute, and then Noire turns back to the waterfall.

"Let's get ahead of whatever the fuck this is and try to find the librarian. We need higher ground to make camp if we don't find her before dark."

He strides off toward the waterfall and re-emerges with Diana in his arms. He's followed by a concerned-looking Achaia and a frowning Arliss, who must've stayed hidden to protect Diana.

We fill them both in on what just happened, but what can we even say? Something monumental is happening here, and even though I've never been to the Tempang, I know this isn't normal. Even in the maze, I never saw a monster take a hit like that male did and keep moving.

An hour later, we haven't seen another centaur. We haven't seen any sort of animal, but we've managed to find another clearing with steppe-like, defensible outcroppings that should be a good spot to park for the night.

I'm frustrated that there's been no sign of Onmiel, but I don't know much about Volya. I don't even know where to start to find her.

Need little woman, my wolf growls. *Need Onmiel.*

I know, I say mournfully, rubbing at my chest. *We'll find her; I promise.*

He growls and curls up in my chest, falling asleep almost immediately. It's an odd sensation to feel his rumbly snores when I'm awake. It's almost like his consciousness is separating further and further from my own. I still don't know what to make of that.

When the hair on my nape lifts, I whip around to see Arliss unrolling a backpack across the steppe from me. Blue eyes are narrowed to the spot where my hand is still on my chest. Not much is known about carrow either, so I don't know what he's doing, but he's doing something. Examining me, maybe.

A scratchy sensation pokes at the edges of my mind, and I

suspect it's Arliss fucking with me, somehow. I'm not in the gods-damned mood, so I let out a warning growl and unroll my own pack as far from him as possible.

Achaia and I gather wood, then start making a campfire. Jet drops to his haunches next to his mate, his dark eyes focused on me. "What do you make of the centaur, brother? You're the best read of any of us. Can we expect more of th—"

He's cut off by a gut-wrenching squeal. It's shrill and pained and then cuts off with a gurgly squelching noise. Our pack is up and in formation in two seconds, Diana and Achaia protectively placed between me, my brothers, and the vampiri.

There's a moment of silence, and then the bushes just below our flat outcropping explode in a flurry of motion. A dozen wild boar flee something just behind them, another centaur. No, two.

Fuck.

They haven't seen us yet, but it's just moments before they do.

A muscular chestnut female throws her spear, and it lodges in the gut of one of the boar, who goes to the ground in a cloud of dust and blood, squealing. The centaur grins triumphantly before looking up to see us. We're a solid twenty feet above the ground, but that puts her just six or eight feet below us.

She and the second centaur, another male, step closer to where we are and grin. At their feet, the pig screams as black sludge drips from the spear and sinks into its wound. It shudders, its cries growing more pained by the moment.

I don't take my eyes off the centaur.

Noire barks commands in our family bond. We're ready to fight our way out of here if we have to.

Then the trees part again, and more horse-like men and women join the two staring at us. The boar rises from the ground, its body now covered in tar, dripping rivulets of fire onto the forest floor. It turns beady red, flame-filled eyes on us, and snarls.

Rosu returns the angry noise, dropping to a crouch.

Oh, fuck.

CHAPTER THIRTY-FIVE

ONMIEL

The sun is just starting to fade. Gods, I miss Ten so fucking much. A shadowy figure appears in the doorway to the Clan House just as Kraven opens his mouth to deliver more bad news, I bet.

"The shifters have arrived. They are being attacked by Zura's centaurs."

"No!" I shout, leaping from my seat to run to the edge of the treehouse.

Kraven appears next to me with an angry huff, throwing one arm in front of me. "Stop, Onmiel. You can't possibly help with this. I will retrieve them, whoever is left alive."

Without another word, he leaps from the porch and sprints off into the forest, a host of warriors behind him.

In a panic, I turn to my parents. "I've got to go help them; I can't let the forest kill them. I came here for this pack!"

"We know, Onmiel," Father reminds me. "Kraven will find the queens. Be patient, child."

"Not your strong suit, I know," Mother says in a gently chiding tone. "Those who are meant to join us will."

I hate that fucking saying. It's a nice way of saying sometimes people die, and so when you never get to see them again, you weren't meant to.

Growling, I yank at my hair as I jog out of the Clan House. I trot along the front porch and move quickly down the long ladder. It's thirty feet from the plank platform to the forest floor, but I make my way to the traveling tree where they'll have to emerge.

I'm fucking pissed I couldn't keep up with Kraven, and without being in my Volya form, I can't open the tree, either.

The pack would have had to enter the forest at the Deshali border, even though I begged them to wait for me. I fucking knew Ten wouldn't, and now they're in danger. I had hoped I was far enough ahead of them to take care of things before they arrived. It seems I was very fucking wrong.

I pace back and forth for a full quarter hour, terror clawing at my insides. There's a wooden creak, and the traveling tree splits wide. Two figures tumble out, fists flying so quickly I can barely see who's who. I leap out of the way as two bodies fall into the glade. I recognize Ten's mop of waves immediately, but Kraven's hands are around his neck as he throttles him.

I open my mouth to shout at them to stop, but the rest of Ayala Pack and my father's warriors spill out right after them, the traveling tree zipping closed behind them. Noire pops upright with Diana in his arms. Ascelin leaps forward but slams to a halt when Noire's arm flies up, catching her in the chest.

"What are you—" she shouts but follows Noire's nod.

Kraven's on the ground now, one of Ten's hands around his throat as the other yanks on Kraven's horns, smashing his head to the ground.

"Where is she?" Ten bellows.

Gods, he's going to rip Kraven's head from his shoulders.

"Ten!" I shout. "Ten, stop!"

Ten's head snaps to the side, eyes narrowing as his nostrils flare. The whiskey color of his irises is fully black. I've never seen him like this, out of his mind like a wild predator. He looks at me like he wants to eat me alive, and for the first time since I met him, I'm afraid.

Still, he's *Ten*. My Ten. And he's here.

He leaps gracefully off Kraven and looks at me. My father and the other Volya run to join us. Kraven leaps up in a flash to continue the fight, but Ten pays him no mind. Despite my fear, I run the short distance between us.

"Sweet girl," he growls, opening his arms wide as I leap up into them, his warm, comforting scent wrapping around me like the very real hug. He crushes me to his chest, both arms around my waist, as he purrs loudly, burying his face in my neck. He gulps in breath after breath like he forgot my scent and just needs it again.

"I'm sorry," I whisper. Was it just this morning I left Pengshur to come here and get ahead of him?

"You're in trouble," he huffs into the skin just below my ear. "So much fucking trouble, Onmiel."

I hold back a chuckle because Ten hauls me higher up into his arms and turns from everyone, stalking toward my mother and father, who stand shocked as they watch me wrapped around the big shifter. There are social norms when greeting Volya, but none of those seem to matter right now. I'm just so fucking relieved he's here and he seems to be in one piece.

I open my mouth to say something, but Ten continues past my parents as if they're not there, through the throng of onlookers and across the middle of the village. He heads straight for the Clan House in the center and leaps up onto the first level, stalking to the center, where he sets me carefully down on the broad table.

Ten's eyes don't leave mine, his dark pupils still wide as he steps back, never breaking the heated look. He backs up until he hits the wall, letting his head fall back against it as he licks his lips. "Why'd you leave?"

"Ten, I—"

"I mean, why'd you leave *me*, Onmiel? You can't possibly have thought I'd let you come do this alone."

"I hoped I'd have a cure and be out by the time you came for me,"

I admit. "The note explained the gate's prophecies. It's dangerous here for Diana and probably Achaia, too!"

Ten waves my explanation away, pushing off the wall to stalk back across the space between us. He shoves my thighs wide and plants himself between them, gripping my throat with his thumb pressed to my lower lip.

"We'll sort that out together," he commands, his voice going hard and low. "Never leave me like that again. Do you understand?"

I nod, submerged in Ten's dominance. I could no sooner deny him than my next breath, and when he leans even closer, using his thumb to press my head back, I let it fall.

His other hand is there, waiting, and his long fingers dig into my hair, wrapping it around his fist as he holds me caught in his arms. I squirm as his hips press to mine, the long outline of his erect cock rubbing against my clit.

Gods, I missed him *so* much. It's stupidly crazy to miss a person so much when you've known them for such a short time. And it's even more stupid to miss someone who just lost their mate in the last few weeks.

A squeak and a sigh fly out of my throat when Ten's lips come to my neck and bite hard enough to draw blood. His soft, warm tongue follows, sending a trill of nerves jangling up my spine.

"I need to hear your agreement, Onmiel. Say 'yes, alpha.'"

"Oh gods," I moan. This is so hot. I'm having one of the worst days of my life, but I'm so relieved and overwhelmed and amazed he's here, and this demanding tone is too much. "Yes, alpha," I state simply, grinding my hips against his. He leans further over me, pressing me against his forearm, and holding me up with his immense strength. I'm caught, and there's nowhere I'd rather be than right here.

Beautiful eyes come to mine again as he presses his lips gently to mine. "Never, Onmiel," he reiterates. "Rama never considered me a partner. She lied, schemed, and planned. She hurt me, *and* she hurt my direwolf." His voice breaks as he continues. "You aren't her, and I thank the gods every day for that. But if you leave me behind like that again, I'll wear your ass out so hard you won't sit for a week. Are we clear?"

Oh, fuck. Oh gods. He feels like I left him behind, the same way it sounds like Rama did. I didn't even consider that when I left. I left to *protect* him. Tears fill my eyes.

I open my mouth to reassure him that I would never, ever do that to him, but he closes his lips over mine, his tongue probing deep, and I lose all ability to think. Nothing exists outside of the exquisite dance of Ten's lips on mine, his kiss full of desperate need as he clutches me closer. One hand is still wrapped in my hair, and the other slides down my back and into my pants.

His fingers press all the way down to my ass, and he settles them there as his kiss grows more frantic until he's eating me alive, our bodies wildfire against each other. It's like we can't get close enough; it's like we need to become one in order to be whole. I've never been so fucking gone for a man like I am for him. It's exhilarating. It's *terrifying*.

Ten rips his mouth from mine and shoves me back, removing his hand from my pants but grabbing my waistband and yanking it down. The move sends my father's maps and papers flying, but Ten growls and jerks me to the middle of the table, crawling on top of me like a predator, his eyes on my breasts and stomach.

He drags them back up, pupils back to full black. With a snarl, his fangs descend, and he yanks my jeans all the way off, tossing them aside.

My gaze darts to the left. My parents or Kraven could show up at any moment. I never introduced anybody. His godsdamned brothers are right outside, but—

"Eyes on me," Ten commands, holding my gaze with his. He dips low, shoulder blades contracting as he buries his face between my thighs and sucks hard at my pussy lips. He pulls gently before sliding his tongue between them and sucking again. I've never had a male eat me out this roughly, and I'm dying from the overwhelm of Ten's stubble as he rubs his chin along my inner thigh and buries his tongue inside me.

My head threatens to fall back, but he growls, gripping my ass hard as he spreads me wide and turns his attention...lower.

All I can do is cry out as fireworks bundle and build in my core, my hips desperately thrusting to meet him. But I'm caught in his hands, forced to submit as a cry echoes out of my throat, his name falling from my lips as I struggle to breathe.

Soft lips suck at my pussy again before his tongue circles my clit, and when I gasp, Ten goes wild. He bites and sucks and tongues my clit until I explode in an inferno of ecstasy, screaming my fucking head off as I wet the table—and my father's maps—with a spurt of release.

Ten groans and grips my ass so hard I can feel bruises forming, but when his tongue spears deep inside me, and he shakes his head side to side like a godsdamned animal, I come again.

And then I come a third time when his mouth closes gently on my clit and rubs in soft, tender circles.

After wrenching three heartstopping orgasms from me, Ten sits up and slides a hand to possessively cup my sex.

"Never again, my sweet librarian," he growls. "Never leave me like that again." He utters that last command in nothing more than a whisper as I throw myself upright into his arms, wrapping my entire body around his again. I want him so much, to give him the same pleasure he gives me. I need to touch every inch of him, but I can hear shouting outside.

Ten pulls back from me, smiling as he strokes my hair over my shoulder. "I should never have given you space after we ran last night. I won't make that mistake again, Miel. Am I clear?"

Tears fill my eyes as the emotions from today hit me all at once. Devastation at leaving him behind, relief that he's safe. Determination to save Diana. Horror at what I left behind when I fled the Tempang all those years ago.

"Ten, there's so much to catch up on. There's more than Diana's prophecy. It's so much worse here than I thought," I whisper.

"I'm here for you," he reminds me. "Now, let's go back out there as a united force and get Diana healed. That's my second priority. You are my first."

If I didn't think my heart could physically burst in my chest, I know now it can. And if I didn't think I could fall in love so quickly, I've now been proven wrong because I'm in deep with Tenebris Ayala.

And that scares me more than anything I've ever done in my entire life.

CHAPTER THIRTY-SIX

TENEBRIS

My wolf paces in my chest, needing more of Onmiel. He's possessive and demanding now that we're here and she's within reach. It's just like the last few days in the damned library—I can't keep my hands off her. I'm obsessed, and as I follow her down the ladder to the glade in the center of the Volya's village, I find myself trying to remember if I was obsessed with Rama like this. And if I was, was it chemically induced, or was it because of the bond? I don't even care anymore.

I'll never have answers to that, and it doesn't even matter at this point. It's just that, while Onmiel wants me with every fiber of who she is, she's still worried about my dead mate. I can sense that the same way I sense she's struggling with whatever happened between this morning and right now.

There's a tense, anxious set to her trim shoulders as we approach the group to find Noire bellowing at two Volya.

It doesn't take a genius to guess what he's roaring about, but his dark eyes snap to me as he clutches Diana tightly to his chest.

"If you're done fucking the librarian, tell these motherfuckers to heal my godsdamned mate before I burn the entire Tempang to the ground."

Diana's no longer awake. She's slumped to his chest, her arms and legs limp as if her life has already drained away. I don't think I've ever seen Noire so unhinged.

Now that I'm not focused on reconnecting with Miel, I fall into my usual place in front of my pack. I don't give a fuck that this is her family. They've done nothing but put mine in danger, and I won't stand for it.

The two Volya turn to face us. One's a male, and one's a female. And based on the devastated look on the female's face, I'm guessing she's Onmiel's mother. Still, Miel addresses the male first. A wooden crown rises up between his curled horns, symbolizing him as the Volya king, then. Her father. I vaguely remember him from the last fight with Rama, but at that point, Rama was my only focus. This male is nothing but a blur in my memory banks.

"Father, please," Miel murmurs, dropping her head in deference. "I'll stay and fix this, but help Diana. I'm begging you." Her tone is respectful and cautious. I fucking hate it.

The Volya king frowns, the flat rahken bones that cover his eyes dipping in the center to form a vee. He may not have eyeballs, but there's no mistaking the disappointed, angry set of his expression. Sharp teeth gnash together as he considers Onmiel's plea. He glances over at the big fucker who came to get us and promptly insulted our entire pack.

Asshat.

"We've come a long way," I purr. "You *will* do this for us." I refuse to believe there's a future where we let Diana die.

The Volya male who fought me on the way here bristles and snarls, but there's a chorus of answering, furious hoots and growls from my pack.

"I'm not asking," Noire shouts again. "I'm telling you to fix this unless you want to have a feral fucking alpha rip this entire village to shreds."

The Volya king cocks his head to the side. I do recognize him now. He was there when everything went down with Rama. He didn't bother to try to save her, despite working with her, which makes me angry. All he wanted was to snatch Diana and Achaia and drag them back here. I pull Onmiel closer to me, ready to protect her if I need to.

Next to me, she shivers. She's giving off a nervous, anxious energy. I place my hand on her back, not taking my eyes from her father. After a long, tense minute, the king turns and gestures for us to follow, heading to the gigantic treehouse we just came from. The queen pauses for a moment, her focus on Onmiel. Her rahken are slumped in what looks like worry, but it's hard to be sure. Onmiel says nothing, and the older female turns to follow the king.

Stay focused, Jet reminds us in our family bond. *Stay alert.* I'm in front like always, sweeping my head from side to side as I watch for any signs of an attack.

A dozen Volya warriors surround our pack, but it doesn't matter. We've fought against worse odds, and I'm ready to if we need to do it again now. Curious faces, young and old, peek out from houses built high into wide trees surrounding a big, open glade. I notice a huge firepit in the middle. Something cooks on it, but the food has been deserted now that we're here.

The Volya king and queen leap up to the first floor of the biggest treehouse. Onmiel heads for the nearest ladder, and I follow behind her. Noire climbs up behind me, one-handed with the other around Diana's frail figure. When we arrive at the top, Renze and Ascelin flank them. Jet takes Noire's usual position behind all of us, Achaia in front of him. It's not lost on me that at the end of the day, Achaia alone could level this place if she wanted to. I wonder if the Volya are even aware that of all of us here, she's the most powerful…

I set Onmiel down on the wide, wooden plank floor. She blanches when one of the Volya warriors grabs the soaked maps and tosses them on the floor, giving her a disapproving look.

Inside, my wolf preens with pride.

We did this, he purrs to me. *Make her wet. Make Miel ready.*

We'll do it again later, I reassure him, sensing him retreat deeper inside again now that he's not so worried about finding her.

Lahken climbs onto a throne at the head of the table, perched a level higher than everyone else. Onmiel takes a seat next to me. I drop down next to her, dragging her closer so that I can hold onto both muscular, tense thighs. She's trembling and afraid. I'd rather put my mouth on her again to take some of that anxiety away, but she's hovering on a knife's edge, it seems.

"Set Diana Ayala in the center of the table, please," Lahken instructs Noire.

My brother growls, but climbs carefully to the center and seats himself, Diana's upper body resting within the cocoon of his muscular arms.

"It would be better if you were not close to her," the king drolls.

"I dare you to pry me from her," Noire snaps. "Your people did this to her. Fix it."

"Noire," Jet murmurs in a gentle tone. "We did it, alpha. We're here." *Calm the fuck down,* he shouts in our family bond.

My eyes rove continually around the room, watching how the warriors focus on guarding Lahken. Good. They won't be ready for us, if we need to fight our way through them.

Noire bristles, his grip never loosening on Diana, who groans softly from within his arms, clutching his shirt on one feeble hand.

Lahken swirls one hand in the air in front of himself, focusing on Diana. "I did not give Diana this injury; it was my second-in-command. You killed him."

I sense Noire holds back from whatever he wants to say, but Lahken continues.

"He had one mission if our meeting went awry—poison Diana Ayala or the Queen of the Sea to force you back here. We had no choice. We knew the gate was sending out prophecies about queens, but we could not travel the broader continent to retrieve them."

The snarl that rips out of Jet's throat sets my teeth on edge. He's standing on the other side of the table, Achaia wrapped in his arms. Renze is by their side, looking simultaneously bored and furious.

"I don't need a godsdamned history lesson. Fix it," Noire finally shouts. Our family bond is tight to the point of snapping. I want to stand to be ready for the fight that feels imminent, but I don't want to let go of Onmiel. She's practically vibrating with terror at this point. My wolf perks back up in my chest, focused on what's going on around us and ready to take over.

Onmiel stands and steps onto the wooden table, picking over maps and stacks of paper before dropping to both knees next to Noire. I'm on the edge of my seat, ready to rip her away from my violent brother, but when their gazes meet, his is desperate and hopeless.

She reaches up and cups his jaw carefully, rubbing his stubble with the pad of her thumb.

"We did it, Noire. We can fix this. Do you trust me?"

Noire's throat bobs. To my incredible horror, his dark eyes fill with tears that start to spill over onto his tan cheeks. Onmiel wipes them away carefully. Jet's gaze flicks over to me, but I can barely pull my eyes from Onmiel. She wraps one arm around Noire's waist and grabs Diana's hand with the other, clutching it to her chest.

"Go ahead, Father," she encourages.

You could hear a pin drop in the tense room, Lahken saying nothing as he stares curiously at his daughter.

After what feels like a lifetime, he reaches out with one hand, swirling it through the air in an intricate design. It's almost like he's drawing an invisible picture or a rune. I can't see anything happening, but the temperature in the room heats until a bead of sweat rolls down my face.

His movements grow quicker, a low chant leaving his pale, leathery lips. I don't understand the words, but Onmiel nods along with him.

A black mist begins to rise out of Diana's body. It's barely visible at first, but then it collects and pools into a dark sludge that hovers above her like a cloud. The mist writhes and spins like a snake swallowing itself. Lahken's voice grows louder until he's shouting the same words over and over.

There's a loud pop, and the sludge explodes into a fine mist and rains down onto the tabletop.

Diana shoots upright with a gasping scream, swiping at her clothes like she's crawling with insects.

Onmiel scoots out of Noire's way just as Diana turns in his arms, her face pale and drawn, but her eyes once again full of life, full of concern.

"Noire, are you—"

My pack alpha's lips crash into hers as he falls flat on his back, both arms clasped tightly around her. He kisses her like it's the last time he'll ever touch her, and watching them sends stabs of pain through me. I did the very same thing, not long ago, and it was the last time I ever kissed Rama. I hate that I'm even thinking about it. I hate the way she drifts into my brain sometimes when I don't want her there.

I shudder. Onmiel slips off the table and back into her chair, looking at me with a guarded expression.

The room feels tense, everyone silent as Noire and Diana stop kissing.

Lahken rises from his throne and opens long, spindly arms wide. "Welcome to our village, Ayala Pack. We will find temporary homes for each of you, but in return, you will help us heal the forest."

Renze is the first to speak up. I'm sure the second half of the Volya prophecy remains top of mind for him. "Speak plainly. Are you a danger to Achaia or Diana?"

Onmiel's father turns toward him, the bones that form the upper half of his face splitting into what looks like a scowl. It's shocking how expressive his face is despite having no eyes. The look he gives doesn't reassure me. I pull Onmiel closer as his scowl deepens.

"There was an accident, long ago," he begins, addressing the entire table.

Onmiel is stiff as a board next to me, her muscles trembling. I know instinctively what Lahken's going to share. It must be the story of her sister dying because she looks agonized about hearing it.

"My daughter Zura was killed, and in her grief, Onmiel

attempted to use her ability to communicate with the gate to bring her sister back."

"Is that even possible?" Ascelin breaks in. "I have never heard of that sort of power."

Lahken shakes his head. "It is incredibly rare, even for a Volya. Only twice in history has a Volya received the gift of communication with the Gate of Whispers, who is mother to us all." He turns again, his expression a little softer this time. "Very little is known about that power, so none among us could even guide her. Typically, the gate communicates with us through prophecy…" His voice trails off and he pauses, looking at his folded hands.

"Onmiel's request to revive Zura did not work, so when she asked to be allowed to leave the Tempang and find her way among the half-breeds and humans, we were distraught, but we understood." Lahken suddenly looks years older, his horns drooping as he examines his hands again. When he looks up, he releases a sigh that sounds like the weight of the world is on his shoulders.

"We did not realize that Zura *did* return, just not as we knew her. She is undead and is building an army to take over the Tempang."

"What in the actual fuck?" Diana barks out.

"Why?" I question

Lahken nods at the outburst and turns to me. "The gate is the giver of life. I believe Onmiel has more than just the power to communicate with the gate. It's my belief that she channeled the gate's life-giving power into Zura. But we are not meant to return to this plane. Where Onmiel sought to give life, she brought only death."

There's a sob next to me. Onmiel throws her head back and covers her face with her hands.

My wolf snarls in my chest, demanding I pull her into my lap to comfort her. I hold her close, and she goes limp in my arms, tucking her face up under my chin. My wolf purrs loud enough to shake the chair underneath me.

Lahken isn't done. "Zura's former protective power became a formidable weapon when the gate brought her back. She cloaked the Tempang in a barrier. We cannot venture farther than the town just below Nacht. We are stuck here while she attempts to poison the very well from which all life on this continent is derived."

Jet growls from his seat next to Onmiel. "When you say stuck here…does that apply to us now that we're here?"

Of course, he'd focus on that first. I'm so horrified by this whole story and the tension rolling off Onmiel, I can't decide where to focus.

"It does," Lahken confirms. "The barrier has grown stronger. We used to be able to visit Nacht and now we cannot even do that, so none of you will be leaving either, I'm afraid. Not until Zura is defeated."

"So, what's the fucking plan?" Jet presses on, standing as he crosses his arms. "Why haven't you been able to defeat her yet?"

Lahkan sighs again and tucks his bony hands into his long, wide sleeves. Next to Onmiel, her mother is stiff as a board. Her wings are tucked up tight behind her back, her lips clenched tightly together. She stares across the room blankly like she's seeing a ghost.

The asshole of a male who fought me in the tree glowers at Onmiel before speaking, his voice angry and accusing. "We have been able to capture her once or twice, but she is almost constantly surrounded by her guards. If they bite or impale you, or if their black slime enters your body, you become one of them." His rahken stiffen and press against his head. "We have seen it happen over and over."

Jet snarls. "Tell us again why she gives a fuck about the gate?"

The male answers Jet's snarl with a matching one of his own. "We assume she is drawn to its power, since Onmiel channeled the gate's power to revive her. The truth is that we do not know. We know only that she has been unable to breach the surface of the gate to poison it. If she is eventually able to poison the Gate of Whispers, all of Lombornei will fall…"

The giant, vaulted treehouse is silent as we take in what he just said. After a tense beat, Jet glances over at me with a wry frown.

"Why are we always saving the continent, us Ayalas who never even cared to leave Siargao?"

Noire stands from the center of the table, Diana still in his arms. Although, he's holding her close now rather than holding her up. He walks across the tabletop and hops carefully down, depositing her in a chair. Jet, Renze, and Achaia are at his back. He glares over at the volya king.

"I haven't forgotten your part in Diana's injury. You tried to steal her from me once." Noire's eyes glitter with malice as his fangs descend, poking at his mouth. When he speaks, a shiver steals across my shoulder blades at the power in his voice. "Try to take my mate or my brother's mate again, and I'll kill you myself. Are we clear?"

The asshole next to the king snarls, a wide mouth full of cone-shaped sharp teeth snapping in Noire's direction. I bristle instinctively, gripping Onmiel tighter. She's no longer sobbing, but I'm at my wits end with this entire conversation. I'm ready to fight for my pack, banish this threat, and comfort my woman.

It's Diana who speaks first and breaks the tension. "We'll help you if we can, but let's agree now that this is a partnership. It's like my mate said: we won't be your victims. You don't know us, but rest assured, we're more than capable of laying waste to this place if we have to."

"It would do you no good," Lahken murmurs, shaking his head at her. "But I understand your need for a semblance of control. You have my vow, for now, that no harm will come to you or the sea queen."

"You tried to take us once," Achaia barks from behind Renze. "I want to know precisely what you planned to do and why you assumed it would fix anything at all."

The Volya king shakes his head but slumps against the wooden throne and puts his spindly fingers on the side of his face. "The gate demands blood, Queen of the Sea. She has sent prophecy after prophecy out into the world pulling the strings of fate across our continent. When she sends prophecies, the Volya receive a copy. We know the gate foretold Diana Winthrop's connection to Noire. We knew it spoke of sacrificing queens, and that is why we engaged with Rama to bring queens here. The gate demanded we sacrifice queens of land, sea and air, and we were prepared to offer either or both of you."

Achaia's expression goes from shock to fury in the span of a second. Renze's muscular arm slides around her waist, his focus on the Volya warriors as he snarls. All I hear is Rama's name ringing in my brain.

These are the beings who made her what she was, who hurt her and shaped and molded her into a fucking monster. And then they used her for their own godsdamned purposes.

I've heard enough.

I stand, glaring at the Volya king. When I speak, my voice echoes through the otherwise silent room.

"We stay only in support of Onmiel. Lift a finger against my pack, and you will regret the day the gate brought us here. Am I crystal clear?" My direwolf snaps his teeth behind my breastbone, ready to make his point as known as mine.

Volya warriors crowd around the king, but he merely sighs and nods his head in agreement. "Understood, Tenebris Ayala. For now, we are partners in this. Let us take a step back and start with formal introductions. Today has been unexpected and...trying."

Onmiel's body's shutting down, quivering as she looks at her lap. It's easy to see she's overwhelmed by all of this.

"Introductions later," I growl. "We need to regroup."

Lahken nods. "My wife, Anja, will assign you housing. Dinner is being prepared. Tomorrow, the work begins. Onmiel *must* fix this, or we are all doomed."

"Got that," I snap, disliking how he puts the responsibility squarely on her head. My wolf and I have a deep and pressing need to protect her from the entire world, and that includes her father and the asshole standing next to him who's looking at Onmiel as if she's his.

~

TEN

Twenty awkward minutes later, we've each been given a small treehouse of our own, all in a row leading off the main circle of homes in the village. Noire and Diana disappear into theirs without a backward glance. I sense Jet has questions, but I can't entertain them right now. Ascelin goes with Arliss, although the irritated look on her face tells me Arliss is likely to get an earful. I'm a little surprised he's still here, now that Diana is healed.

My pack bond is flooded with emotions ranging from fury to anger to intense focus. It's the maze all over again. No matter what the Volya said, I don't fucking trust them.

Take a few minutes and regroup, Jet purrs into our bond. *We need a plan.*

I follow Onmiel into our assigned house. She hasn't said a fucking word since her father dropped the bombshell of her story. Wordlessly, she grabs a sweater from her backpack and wraps herself up. She studiously avoids my gaze, tucking her hands into the sleeves, her shoulders hunched as she examines the small space. The house is built around the interior of a broad tree, and all the furniture is carved from the interior of the tree itself.

I can't focus on how cozy it is at the moment, though, because she takes a step or two and just stops, her head falling forward. I hear the tears before I see one fall and splat on the polished wooden floor.

My wolf springs out of me then, taking over as we pad across the small space and butt into her. She turns with a fake smile as we shove her down onto the floor and lay our much larger weight on her lower half. My wolf plasters his head to her stomach, purring his heart out as she cries and strokes his nose.

Her arms go up around our head, and then she's clutching onto us like a baby monkey, sobbing. Like this, he's in charge, and he snuffles at her neck and chin, licking the tears away as they pool in the dip at the base of her throat.

She cries for a solid ten minutes, her face red and puffy as frus-

303

tration and fear bleed from her. Eventually, the tears slow and subside, and she's wiped out, exhausted. She shimmies out from underneath us as we rise to stand in front of her, pressing our face to her chest.

"I'm gonna draw a bath," she says finally. "Gods, I'd kill for a coffee."

That makes my wolf huff, and when she gives us a quizzical look, we pace to my pack and pull out a bag of coffee grounds and a stack of filters. I shove at him, pushing him with my consciousness until he lets me shift back into human form.

"Ascelin packed them for you while I was raging around the library."

Onmiel's eyes flutter with worry but she smiles. "She's grouchy as fuck, but I think she loves me." Pale eyes dart up to mine. "Wait, raging around the library? What about the books?"

I do laugh aloud at that. Despite what I just said, she's worried about the godsdamned books.

"I didn't touch the books," I confirm. "I just ran and looked for you. When it comes to Asc, the more she loves you, the grouchier she is," I confirm.

"Like with Arliss," Onmiel whispers conspiratorially, seeming like herself for the first time since I got here.

"Just like with Arliss," I agree. When we fall silent, she begins to worry at the edges of her lower lip. "Tell me about the bath," I press. "How do we do that? Somehow, I imagine you snapping your fingers and it appearing out of thin air because I don't see any pipes around here."

Onmiel barks out a laugh before gesturing at her lithe form. "I don't have that sort of magic. Conjuring a bath out of thin air isn't one of my strengths. Unlike bringing people back from the fucking dead." Her voice goes low and mournful, but I tilt her chin up.

"You only brought her halfway back," I joke. "Don't give yourself too much credit."

Onmiel laughs, despite herself, and lets her cheek rest in my palm. "My family is so pissed."

"And I don't give a fuck about that," I remind her. "Anyone who isn't Ayala Pack is our enemy, even if they're related to you. Don't forget that, sweet girl."

"They're my family, Ten," she corrects, emphasizing the word.

"They might be, but they tried to rip mine apart," I growl. "The maze taught me one important lesson, Onmiel. Trust no one but my people."

She frowns and tucks a long strand of hair over her shoulder. I sense she disagrees, but I didn't come here for her family, and I don't care about the Tempang. I want out of here, and if we have to help them to accomplish that, that's the only reason I'll do it.

She frowns up at me. "I missed you so much, even though I saw you early this morning."

I reach out and stroke my fingers down her throat and along her collarbone. "We should always have been doing this together."

"Now, you're all stuck here," she presses on. "Even Diana, and we know what the prophecy said now. There's a very real chance this goes south for her. Or Achaia. I suppose the prophecy could be about her, even though Jet isn't a king."

"Whatever it is, we'll get through it together," I remind her. "We both need a bath, sweet girl, so tell me how to draw it, and then I'm going to feed you and fuck you, and we'll fix this tomorrow."

"Feed, fuck, fix?" she jokes with a wry look. "You make it sound easy, Ten."

CHAPTER THIRTY-SEVEN
ONMIEL

There's a hornet's nest of thoughts buzzing around in my brain, but I show Ten around the small treehouse. All the guest houses are the same: one main room with a seating area and small kitchen and then a bedroom with a swinging platform bed covered in plush woven sheets and downy pillows.

He follows me into the bathroom, where there's a secondary room with a toilet. The primary space holds a tub carved right out of the wood. This whole place has pipes; they just run up through the tree and aren't visible. I twist the water knob on as Ten laughs about how normal it is. He expected magic, but the guest houses are equipped for non-magical guests. Volya being the keepers of peace in the Tempang means we often entertain dignitaries or royalty from the Tempang's various kingdoms and clans.

It's so strange to be home. The village itself looks exactly how I left it. But my clanmates stare at me as if I'm the source of all their ills, and I am, in a way, even if I didn't mean what happened.

"Do you want to talk about it?" Ten's voice is low and reassuring as he wraps a big, warm arm around my middle. His lips come to my neck as one hand pulls my sheet of white hair over my shoulder, tucking it on the other side.

"I didn't think I'd bring her back," I admit. "I was distraught, and I asked the Gate of Whispers for help to fix what I'd done when Zura died. But nothing happened, of course. I can't use the gate's power. I mean, I didn't think I could. I just know I cried my eyes out and went home, and Zura was still there, shrouded for burial. I left after that to go to Pengshur, and that's the last I heard of it. But they were stuck here, this whole time, fighting her."

"You couldn't have known," Ten reminds me.

"I know that." I turn in his arms. "But everyone here suffered because I lost control of my magic in the first place. Why I thought I could fix anything is beyond me, but I was young and foolish."

"And grieving," Ten presses.

"Sometimes, we do funny things when we're grieving," I comment. Ten doesn't miss the insinuation, leaning up against the doorway and crossing his arms as he gives me a look.

"I'm not grieving Rama."

"How could you not be?" I press on. "It's been what, two or three weeks?"

Ten's lips purse into a thin line, but he reaches around behind me to cut the hot water off. Steady hands pull my shirt over my head and shove my pants down. Then he undresses himself and helps me into the tub, joining me so water splashes up over the sides and onto the wooden floor.

He makes a point to seat himself across the wooden tub from me, muscly arms resting along the side. Gods, he's so fucking beautiful like this. I wanted him the moment I saw him, staring up through the glass roof at the rain.

Eyes the color of the perfect cup of warm, caramel-infused coffee drift to mine. "I want to have this conversation now, Onmiel, because I want you to be clear on my stance. We've mentioned this before, but we're going to dive into the nitty-gritty tonight."

"Okay," I breathe out, my pulse skyrocketing at the way Ten licks his lips. He's rocking a kick-ass stubble that accentuates his square jaw and dark hair. He's never looked hotter to me than he does right now, whiskey-brown eyes flashing with focus as he shifts

in the tub, reaching for a bar of soap. He crosses the tub and strad-
dles me where I sit on a ledge that's built into the inside of the
basin.

Large hands come to my neck as he rubs the soap gently on it,
kneading my stiff, tired muscles with his big fingers.

"The worst thing I've ever done was kill my bondmate. I thought
I'd die from the pain of it. I wished I did, in those first days after she
was gone. Especially when I watched Noire and Diana. They're
bondmates, too," he points out. I could have guessed that, though.
Their love is practically an obsession.

"Was it like that for you, the way Noire and Diana are?" This is
one of the many questions I want to ask but am terrified to know
the answer to.

"In a way," he confirms. "But I was also drugged the entire time I
was with her. I guess she didn't trust that I'd love her without that
chemical addiction, or maybe she just wanted me compliant. I have
no idea what it would have been like if we'd just been two people
bonded by the fates with nothing else between us."

"Will you not wonder for the rest of your life?" I can barely get
the question out as Ten's strong hands move to my shoulders.

He shakes his head with an easy, slow smile. "I won't. And it took
meeting you to realize it." His beautiful eyes come to mine as he
washes my chin and the skin just under my ears. "She never trusted
me, never supported me, never backed me up. She hurt me and my
wolf over and over again with her lies and deceit.

"She came into my home and killed my friends and family, and
then she groomed me like a godsdamned predator until I came of
age. And somehow, this world thought it made sense for her to be
my bondmate. But the reality is that she would never have been my
choice. I'm glad I killed her because I would have lived my entire life
under her thumb, not as her equal in any way."

His gaze locks onto mine with such intensity I can barely
breathe. I want to believe every one of these words because they
speak to the truth I feel in my soul.

He continues. "Mark my words, sweet girl. I have a choice now, and I choose you. Every fucking time I get the chance to, I'll choose you."

I want to believe what Ten is saying with such ferocity that I can barely fathom it. I want him to be my sunrises and sunsets and every moment in between, but there's still a niggling doubt.

"Spit it out," he laughs. "You're still worried. Be blunt, my coffee-loving librarian."

I fist both hands and cover my mouth, almost afraid to say the words aloud. "Do you worry you've gone from being obsessed about her to obsessed about me? Don't you think you'd be better off being alone for a while and learning who you are without a partner and without the maze?"

Gods, I feel like an asshole for asking that question, but it's at the root of what I need to know. I don't want Ten to get hurt; I can't let that happen. Ten is a fucking national treasure, and he should be protected as such.

Ten's eyes narrow, falling to my lips. "I'll never not be obsessed with you. And the reason I'm obsessed with you is because you're perfect for me. If I could have built the woman I wanted for myself out of all my hopes and dreams, it'd be you, Onmiel. Dorky, hot, loves books, enjoys adventure, fascinated by learning, kind, and addicted to my knot."

I laugh aloud at that one, despite his serious tone. "I can't be addicted to your knot; I've never ridden it."

Ten's responding laugh is so deeply sensual that heat floods my system.

"You will, Miel," he growls.

I clamp my thighs together.

He grips my throat and squeezes, pulling me flush to his chest. "My perfect woman, we're going to rectify that situation tonight, and once you've had this knot, you'll stop worrying. I'm going to bury my teeth in your throat and take from you, Onmiel. What do you think?"

I make a choice then, one I desperately hope won't bite me in the ass. I choose to believe Ten when he says he wants me, that he's obsessed with me, and it'll only ever be me. I choose him because I need someone who's 100% in my court, and there's nobody else on this continent who will be there like he will. I choose to put my trust in Ten, simply because he asked me to.

"Give it to me," I growl, throwing my arms around his neck as he begins to purr.

"Oh, my good, sweet girl," he croons. "Are you ready to get dicked down by a big-ass alpha?"

"Gods, yes. We'll see how it compares to my dildo," I snark.

Ten roars with laughter and stands, pulling us both out of the tub and stalking into my bedroom. He tosses me in the middle and climbs on top of me, his cock swinging against his leg as he lowers himself to rub it through my already-slick folds.

"It's bigger than your dildo, Onmiel," he growls. "A whole lot fucking bigger."

CHAPTER THIRTY-EIGHT
TENEBRIS

Onmiel's eyes are hooded with lust, and while I don't feel her in a mate bond, I read her body language like a favorite book. She's relaxed, comfortable. I am her safe haven, and as long as I live, I'll work to deserve her.

She's worried I'm obsessed with her, and she's right to be. I *am* besotted. Deep inside, my wolf preens at having her in my arms.

Little mate good. Make her happy.

I'm done wondering how he's got his own thoughts about the matter. I'd rather lean into his presence and use it to my advantage to get us out of here and somewhere safe.

Yes, our little librarian is perfect, I confirm. He purrs louder at my agreement.

She arches her back, my little hussy, pressing small breasts closer to my face as I nuzzle them with a low, needy growl. I drag my stubble along the underneath of one soft mound before pulling the hard nipple between my teeth. Onmiel hisses, and it makes my balls draw up tense and tight.

I'm finally going to fuck her. I'd be a damned liar if I didn't admit to having thought about this many times since we met. Not that first day or two, but as time passed and we became friends, my brain and my wolf went there so fast.

Thin hips notch and grind against mine, my cock sliding along her wet heat as she teases me. We were friends first, even though we were friends who wanted to fuck. We've never discussed her likes or dislikes in the bedroom, but based on what I saw when I barged into her room in the library, my girl likes a tease.

Reaching my hand around her waist, I flip her onto her belly, loving how she presses her ass back to meet me.

"You're my favorite book, Miel." I stroke my fingers down the length of her spine, watching goosebumps trail in their wake. "I want to turn every one of your pages, sweet girl. I need every one of your chapters to include my story."

She groans when I hover over her and begin kissing and nipping my way up her back. By the time I get to her shoulders, she's keening underneath me.

"Gods, Ten," she cries out. "I never knew book-sex talk could be so fucking hot." She lets out a little whine.

Chuckling, I collar the back of her neck, pushing her down harder into the soft sheets. Her tattoo shocks me, but the pain travels through my system and spreads between my legs, morphing into a heatwave of searing pleasure.

"How do you want me?" I growl into her ear, my voice rough and needy. I'm going to give it to her hard, but I want to hear her ask me for it.

Onmiel pulls her hair over her shoulder, pressing up on her elbows so she can rub her cheek against my jaw. "I want you unleashed," she whispers, her voice tentative but teasing. "I want you wild, alpha."

Laughing, I rear back and grip her hips, thrusting against her slowly, my cock spearing between her thighs as she moans. She coats me in sweet honey, her breaths quick, her eyes squeezed shut as she grips the sheets.

I want to tease her for hours until she detonates on my cock, but I'm losing control, watching her below me.

Growling, I grip her neck and flip us again, pulling her into my lap with a snarl. I grab both thighs and lift her before yanking her down onto my waiting cock, filling her in one deep punch of my hips.

Onmiel's head falls back, lips open in a silent scream as her pussy clenches over and over around my girth. I'm big, even for an alpha.

"Too much," she gasps out. "You're too much, Ten. Gods, I'm dying…"

"I'm exactly right." I laugh, guiding her up off my dick and back down slowly. Her channel relaxes the second time I impale her, her legs quivering as I revel in finally touching her like this. My mind flashes back to doing this with Rama, how she and I were a catastrophic whirlwind in the bedroom.

Will Onmiel like that? Would she like the things I like? Because I like it really fucking rough.

I think Onmiel would enjoy anything I dish out, so I snarl and pull her off my cock, tossing her against the wall as I slip back between her thighs with a hard thrust. She cries out, her pussy spasming around me as her chest heaves.

"You ready for more, my sweet?" I purr, picking up a slow, teasing pace. In, out, in, out. Onmiel wails every time I thrust back in, her hands clawing at my chest as she tightens around me again. "You're gonna come from this tease, aren't you?" I question, growling in her ear as goosebumps spread along her pale skin.

Sure as shit, her head hits the wall as she grits her teeth and screams, and the way her pleasure rings out in our room sends me over the edge. I snap my teeth around her throat and bite, fucking her through one blistering orgasm and into another, her blood filling my mouth as she thrashes in my arms.

I don't come, focused as I am on her ecstasy, but as her release fades, we fall back to the bed with her on top of me. Onmiel's eyes are glittering jewels of intensity in the low light of the cabin. Her upper lip curls into a sneer as she growls at me.

"More, alpha," she demands. "I need a whole lot more of that."

"Done," I snap, yowling when she grips my cock and seats herself on me with a cry of pleasure.

An hour later, I've taken her four times, and the heat between us is just slowing to a simmer. I carry her into the bath and fuck her there, cleaning her as I go, and when she finally begins to drift off in my arms, I watch her sleep.

I don't trust the fucking Volya, and I'm on edge for my brothers and their mates. Safety is an illusion.

Even so, for the first time in a long time, I feel something close to peace with Onmiel snoring in my arms. Deep inside me, my wolf purrs his agreement, and together, we hold her for hours.

~

Brother. Jet's gentle nudge in our bond has my eyes blinking open. I fell asleep with my girl, and it felt good. *You awake? I want to do a little reconnaissance.*

Be there in five, I grumble.

Onmiel is still fast asleep, her pink lips parted as she snores. She's had an absolute shit day, and part of me doesn't want her to see me taking stock of the village she grew up in. These might be her people, but there's clearly no love lost between them after what happened with Zura. The only one who didn't appear to place all the blame on her shoulders is her mother.

I hop quietly out of the treehouse, not bothering to dress. Noire, Jet, and Diana are there waiting. Diana looks amazing, and I pull her into my arms for a quick hug and cheek brush.

"You look good, omega," I huff into her ear. "Healed."

When we part, she squeezes my arm. "I *feel* good, thanks to Onmiel. I'll thank her later." Blue eyes take in our surroundings. She's as watchful as I am. Noire never takes his eyes off what's in front of us. The strength of their connection is almost tangible in our family bond, like they're the bedrock the rest of us are formed on. I hadn't realized that was missing with her being sick. There's something supremely comforting about having it back. She's a peaceful river of honey easing harsh feelings and worries.

Jet jerks his head toward the dense forest at the end of our "street". *Usual formation, I want to circle the whole village and get a sense of what this place is like. I don't trust these fuckers not to try something with the girls again, and I'd rather not have to rip Onmiel's family to shreds.*

I nod and call my wolf. We shift easily and jog toward the outer edge of the village, slinking off into the dark forest. He's happy to be free and as anxious as I am to get a sense of the Volya. Like any potential threat, we need to know everything we can about them. My brothers shift behind me, although Diana remains in human form, padding along beside Jet. Noire is back to his normal position, bringing up the rear.

We walk for almost an hour in ever larger, concentric circles. As far as I can tell, there are no defenses and no traps unless there's something magical I can't see. I wouldn't put it past the Volya after watching Lahken heal Diana with a swirl of his hand. Unfortunately, there's no way for us to know much about their magic.

They seem clean, Jet growls into our family bond. *I don't sense anything amiss.*

Let's go through the village itself, Noire says. *I want to lay eyes on the people. I thought I saw children, and that says a lot about their intent.*

I'd shudder at how callous he is about children, but he's right. Slinking beneath the treehouses, I direct us to the center of the village, where the large fire pit is. Embers burn brightly underneath three large pots that bubble with something that smells delicious. Half a dozen Volya in long, pale robes are cutting vegetables, stirring what's in the pot, and talking in low tones.

One of them steps carefully to the side to make way for me when I appear next to her, but a quick incline of her head seems respectful enough. A child runs from between two houses and joins her. She keeps the child on one side, but they don't leave. Instead, she gives the child a long, wooden spoon and sets her the task of stirring what they're cooking.

"It's soup," a low voice barks.

I turn to see Kraven, that fucker, leap out of the big treehouse in the middle and land gracefully on his feet. He stands and crosses the clearing to the firepit, glaring down at me from his much taller height.

"Well," he snipes, "are you sufficiently regrouped to do something about Zura? Or does it take direwolves longer to get their shit together?"

My wolf snarls just as a softer voice echoes across the clearing.

"Kraven, you're needed by the king." It's Onmiel's mother, who leaps out of the Clan House, too, and crosses to us. She tucks each hand in her opposite sleeve and gives Kraven an imperious look, her chin held high.

I follow it up with an equally snide look of my own, my brothers and Diana coming to my side.

Kraven snarls at me, thin lips splitting to show off rows of conical, sharp teeth. He's a dangerous predator attempting a show of force, and I'd love nothing better than to rip him a new one. But I'm not an idiot, and eviscerating a warrior who's temporarily aligned with us isn't a good idea, no matter how much I dislike him.

When I don't back down, he turns and inclines his horns low at Onmiel's mother.

"My queen," he murmurs, sidestepping her and leaving.

She doesn't watch him go but turns to us with a smile. It reminds me of Onmiel's smile, for all that her mouth shape is totally different. She walks around the edge of our group, seeming to examine us until Diana finally steps in front of all three of our wolves.

"What are you doing?"

The queen grins even bigger and then reaches out to Jet, laying her hand between my brother's eyes. He jerks back, his lips pulled into a snarl, but she pays him no mind.

"Your wolves are strong, which is a good and lucky thing." She turns to me. "Yours feels different, though." With a shrug, she lifts her hand from Jet's face and moves to me. "May I?"

I push forward enough for her palm to connect with my nose.

Her skin is warm and soft, and she rubs gently at the bridge of my snout.

"As I thought," she says in a kind tone. "We have not been very good hosts, so I will attempt to rectify that now. There were many Volya clans; now, very few remain, and those hide far from here. Our clan is the most connected to the gate. We are her guardians and her wards. As such, most of the Volya here have some element of power. Mine is that I read auras." She looks at me, her rahken bones held high. "Your aura is different from everyone else's, and I think that is because of your wolf."

Onmiel's mother leans in closer, her lips nearly brushing my ear. "You are different, are you not?"

My wolf preens but doesn't sense anything amiss about her. I don't bother to shift to answer.

My brothers and Diana pepper our family bond with questions, but I can't focus enough to answer them either.

"How so?" Diana questions.

The queen straightens up and smiles. "Half-breeds descend from the direwolves of the Tempang, who could not shift and live their lives in wolf form. There are many packs, and we have interacted with them many times through the years. Tenebris's reminds me of theirs, although why that should be, I cannot say."

"I was there when he was born," Noire shifts to snap. "I watched him come into this world from our mother's body. What are you saying?"

The queen holds up both hands in apology. "I do not mean he is not your brother. I mean, simply, that he is something other, as well."

I've heard enough. I don't know or even care why my wolf is different right now. I'd like to dive into it, but I want to do that with Onmiel when we're away from all this bullshit, and she's safe and happy. Everything is on hold until then.

I pull away from her mother and head back for the treehouse. I've been gone from her for too long.

Even so, I sense the queen's focus on me as I leave, and it's unsettling.

CHAPTER THIRTY-NINE

ONMIEL

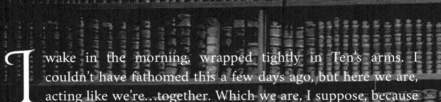

I wake in the morning, wrapped tightly in Ten's arms. I couldn't have fathomed this a few days ago, but here we are, acting like we're…together. Which we are, I suppose, because he chose me, and I decided to take him for a man of his word.

I'd be lying if I didn't admit to worrying that he killed his bond-mate—a bond fated by the stars, according to shifter lore—just weeks ago. But I won't do to Ten what she did. I won't deny him the chance to make his own choices or be an active partner in a relationship. So, despite my misgivings, I'm leaning into what we are.

I'm just praying I don't get my heart trampled on and ripped to shreds as a result. I resolve to enjoy him while I have him because there's every chance that fixing what Zura is doing to the Tempang is an effort that'll kill me…or all of us.

"You're scowling," Ten murmurs, reaching out to stroke his long fingers down the bridge of my nose. "What're you grumpy about?" Chocolate eyes spark with mischief, despite the serious question. His eyes are so godsdamned beautiful.

"I was thinking about Zura," I admit. "How I created her, and what I might need to do to…put her back or whatever."

Ten sighs, but more than anything, it sounds upset for me. The stroking doesn't stop, but he shifts closer and shoves one muscular calf through my legs.

"Want to tell me something about her from before?"

"She liked daisies," I offer. "And she was a daddy's girl. She and Lahken were very close."

Ten frowns. "Wanna go deeper than that, sweet girl? Or is surface level what you've got energy for right now?"

I take a moment. I've just woken up, and the stressors of last night are piling up around me again.

Ten pulls me close to his chest and tucks my head under his chin, his stubble tickling my scalp. A purr rumbles from deep in his chest, vibrating against my skin. It's so comforting, even though I'm not an omega of his people. I feel safe here, wrapped in his arms. Like no matter what bullshit is happening outside the window, Ten will never let anything happen to me.

A sudden, irritated growl joins the purr, and he sits up in bed. "Someone's coming. That big motherfucker who tried to fight me."

"Kraven," I groan, sitting up to pull my clothes on. "He's father's right hand now, I guess."

"We killed the other one," Ten murmurs. "When Diana was injured."

I frown. I knew Etren my whole childhood, and to hear he's gone is a blow. But I can't start counting sins based on what's happened between my clan, the shifters, and the vampiri. I'll be here all day if I start adding up where everyone went wrong, starting with myself.

A sharp rap at the door announces Kraven's presence, and then he lets himself into the front room, despite a warning snarl from Ten. Anxious to put myself between them and ward off any more fighting, I leave the bedroom and incline my head to Kraven in the way of our people—forehead down, sliding my fingertips out and along the horns I don't have in this form.

Kraven returns the gesture, his rahken curving in irritation when he notices Ten emerge from the bedroom behind me. I

TEN

wonder how he feels about all of this. I broke off our engagement to leave the Tempang, but it's been eight years since I saw him.

Kraven's focus moves back to me. "Your father requires your presence in the Clan House as soon as you can. We'll take breakfast there, but we need a plan. Immediately."

Ten presses himself to my back and kisses my shoulder tenderly. "I'll come with you, Miel."

Kraven says nothing, but I can tell he's intensely irritated that Ten's offered to join. With a last withering shake of his horns, he turns from the room and leaves, leaping off the open porch.

"Don't like him," Ten growls into my neck, peppering me with possessive kisses and light nips. "If we were still in the maze, I'd kill him for looking at you the way he does. Maybe I'd have cornered him in the church and ripped him to shreds on the altar. What do you think, my sweet?"

The picture he paints both chills me and makes me wet. That Ten would protect me like that makes me want to toss him on the ground, but I think he's right that he doesn't know how to be outside the maze with normal people, especially surrounded by danger. The library was its own insulated world, but being in the Tempang is different; it's dangerous.

"So, you can tell there's a history there."

"Of course." Ten chuckles. "I bet he doesn't know shit about book spines, though. Or the magic of the Magelang Map. Or how you like your coffee."

"Or where my clit is," I whisper conspiratorially, giving Ten a teasing wink to relieve the moment's tension.

He snickers as he slides a strong hand between my thighs, his thumb rubbing a gentle circle over my still-sensitive mound.

"I know where *everything* is," he says. "And I intend to explore it further tonight. I've only just begun to catalog every inch of you, Onmiel, and I am far from done."

"Deal," I breathe out as I press both hands to his chest. "I'm glad you're coming today. I might be home, but I feel ganged up on here because of what happened." It's hard for me to admit that how I hoped if I ever returned home, it would be under happy condi-tions. The reality is, I left a mess behind me, and it's my job to clean it up. I understand why my clan isn't happy to see me. But it was also an accident, and had I known, I'd have returned far sooner.

"I've got you," Ten reminds me, gripping my chin as he slants his mouth over mine. His tongue probes softly inside my mouth, teasing me because he knows *exactly* what to do with that tongue. I moan as the kiss deepens, the big alpha pulling me into his arms as one hand goes to my throat and the other wraps through my hair.

"Fucking love this hair," he growls, pulling on it to expose my neck to his hungry gaze. Everything about Ten is predatory, but the way he eyes my neck—which still bears evidence of his bite—makes me hot. "I loved it the moment I saw it in the lake." He presses a kiss to the scabs from where he bit me, and I resist the urge to tear up a little bit.

"You think we'll ever get to visit the library again?" I left without a word to anyone, not even ML Garfield. As far as they all know, I shirked my damn duties and disappeared. But this was more impor-tant. Ten's *family* was more important.

A vision of Zakarias and I studying comes to mind, and I almost drop to my knees at the wave of grief accompanying it.

Gods, Zakarias. I'm so sorry it ended the way it did.

"It's hard to imagine what'll come next after all of this." Ten waves one hand around, gesturing out the front door. "But I want to go back there when we're done if you do. I want to explore the library and learn, and apply to the Novice program. Maybe even Novice for you once you become a First Librarian. What do you think about that?"

My cheeks heat when I imagine all the teaching I could do to Ten in my private keeping room if I ever get the chance to make one.

"You've got a deal, sir," I huff out. His lips on my neck turn needy as Kraven clears his throat from outside my treehouse.

Ten huffs but kisses my swollen, tender lips. "We'll continue daydreaming later. For now, let's figure out how we can fix this and get the hells out of the Tempang."

I nod, letting him pull me to the front door. We leap down to join Kraven, who glowers at us both, his rahken set stiffly against his head.

Minutes later, we're back in the Clan House, and the rest of Ayala Pack is filtering in to sit. My father sits at the head of the table, glancing around as Jet and his mates take a seat next to Ten and me. A huge black velzen sits by Achaia's side.

Father turns his focus to me and the pack. "Our time is running low. We need to capture Zura and return her to the grave. When she is gone, the undead army she created will follow her. To kill a snake, you must cut off its head."

My brain swirls with anguish and distress at hearing my sister talked about like this, but I try to remind myself the monster out there killing the Tempang isn't her, not anymore. The Zura I grew up with adored the forest. She would hate what she's doing now.

My brain flits back to a memory of us walking through a traveling tree, laughing about boys. I can remember playing with her in sun-dappled glades and how the forest's animals were always drawn to her protective power. She was so fucking kind, so good. She was the best of us, really.

And I destroyed all of that.

"Do we have other allies?" I question, my voice impossibly small. I try to remember I'm the daughter of the Volya king and that I was fated to be the queen one day when Father passes. Lifting my head, I speak a little louder. "Will others come to help us?"

Kraven shakes his head, arms crossed as he stands behind Father's left shoulder protectively. "Many of the old clans you knew are now decimated. Even the carrow have tried and failed to help us. At this point, most of the remaining monsters have migrated to the northeastern side of the forest, hoping to steer clear of Zura's armies, although we know she sends scouts."

Arliss sits up at the mention of carrow but doesn't voice any questions aloud. His pale eyes drift to me, but when he shakes his head once, I know he doesn't want me to say anything. His carrow tattoo is visible if one gets close enough, but I doubt anybody here would be looking for such a thing.

"We came in at the southern tip of the eastern edge of the forest," Ten says. "Centaurs attacked us. Were those scouts? Or is her army that far? And how are you safe here, so close to where she's building that army?"

Kraven gnashes his teeth. It's obvious he hates answering a question for Ten, but he does it anyway when Father gives him a curt nod.

"The Gate of Whispers protects us and the network of traveling trees. We have a symbiotic relationship of sorts, so the gate will do what it must to keep this Volya clan safe. But even She can only do so much against Zura. She has already attempted to poison the gate more than once."

Poisoning the gate. Oh my fucking gods. I put a hand to my mouth as I absorb Kraven's words.

Ten's big hand wraps around my thigh and squeezes. I let his warmth sink into me, bringing me strength as I lay my hand over the top of his and turn to my clan.

Jet speaks up next. "What are Zura's patterns or schedules? What's our best way to catch her? What haven't you tried yet, in terms of killing her?"

I hiss out a breath. I can't believe we're talking about my baby sister like this. It's her death all over again—that rushing swirl of terror and the sinking pit of realization. Between this and losing Zakarias, I'm fucking drowning.

Father nods. "Zura often remains guarded in her valley. Her scouts go into the forest, and then the armies move to take over lands and turn more monsters. Once her army has captured their conquests, she joins to turn the leaders."

"Turn the monsters?" Noire's voice booms across the quiet room. "I'm gonna need more specifics. Exactly what is she turning them into?"

My father sighs and cocks his head to the side to look at Noire.

"Onmiel's specific magic is an ability to communicate with the Gate of Whispers, as I mentioned. She always understood the gate, even as a young child. But somehow, when she asked the gate to bring Zura back, it worked. But we are not meant to return to this plane when we leave it, and so she came back as something dark. If Zura or any of those she has turned are able to infect you, you are no longer the person you were. You become like them."

"Like a virus," Jet announces. "She's spreading her condition like a virus. But you have to wonder if the other beings are actually dead like her or just hosts for that black sludge we saw on the centaurs."

My father and Kraven give one another looks, and it's clear to me they've not had this train of thought. At the end of the day, I'm not sure it even matters.

I look up at my father, seated at the head of the table. "How can you be sure that killing Zura will stop the spread?"

Father slumps back on his throne, bringing a hand to his forehead as he rubs at the top of his rahken. He looks so tired; I feel bad for even asking the question. "The gate told us, child."

"Through prophecy?" I stand, surprised. I can count on both hands the number of prophecies the gate has given us during my lifetime.

Ten stands with me, one hand on my back below my tattoo.

"Let me see the message."

I sense the Ayala Pack is confused, so I look around at Ten's brothers and their mates. Even Arliss looks fascinated by this entire meeting. He's quiet, for once.

Ascelin speaks up, addressing me. "Why does this appear to concern you, librarian?" Her white eyes are narrowed.

I huff in frustration. "The gate doesn't prophesy with any regularity. She is simply the well from which all life began in the Tempang and from there, the rest of Lombornei. Our clan's duty is to keep peace here in the forest, all of which considers the gate to be our mother."

Renze steps forward. I've barely spoken to the tall, austere vampiri, but he's an undeniable predator, especially focused like he is right now. "What's this about the gate sending a prophecy, then?" He addresses my father directly.

Father sighs, his rahken slumped. "As Onmiel shared, the gate is the original mother of all life on Lombornei. The gate trusts us to maintain peace here. Her prophecies are few and far between, and it has been that way forever. But once Onmiel left, the gate began sending us prophecy after prophecy."

"How many?" My voice barely rises above a whisper.

Kraven turns and focuses on me. "Since you left us, the gate has issued over five hundred prophecies."

I suck in a jagged breath. Five-fucking-hundred prophecies?

"I need to see them," I demand.

"Show us." Noire's barked command stops me in my tracks. I dart a look across the table at him. There's a cruel tilt to his lips, even though his hands are slung casually into the loops of his jeans. The Clan House is silent for a long moment, but then my mother rises and gestures for us to follow. I go immediately, not wanting to waste a single moment.

Mother leaves the main room and walks up a tight hallway behind Father's throne. The hallway empties into a wide, circular room, filled floor to ceiling with scrolls and notebooks. She paces to one wall, and I see the hundreds of notebooks she and I made together over the course of my lifetime. Every one appears to be here, except now, they look full to bursting.

She grabs a notebook from the shelf and hands it to me. She hands a second to Ten right behind me and then more to his brothers.

The book she handed me is bound in dark blue leather with caramel stitching. I remember the day we made it—Zura helped, something she wasn't normally happy to do. She found bookmaking tedious and preferred to make herself scarce when we did it. But on this particular day, she was mourning the loss of a forest nymph, and she helped without us even asking.

Tears fill my eyes at the memory of her long, elegant fingers carefully stitching the pages together.

I open the book to find it stuffed to the brim with hundreds of tiny sheets of paper.

"These are gate prophecies," I whisper, holding one up for Ten to see. Chocolate eyes are filled with concern as he looks at the small page.

From somewhere behind him, Noire snorts.

"You expect me to believe that an ancient gate sends you a sheet of fucking paper with the future of our continent written on it. All of this—" He gestures to the wall of books behind me. "All of this is what's written in our future?"

I shake my head. The gate is hard to understand for anyone who didn't grow up in the Tempang.

Before I can explain that prophecy isn't an exact science, even for the gate, he lifts a page and scowls, tossing it to the ground when he can't read what's on it.

I kneel and pick it up, reading it aloud. "A queen of the land, a queen of the sea, a queen of the air, I demand all three."

His dark brows furrow into a deep vee. "I've heard that before. Here we fucking are, I suppose. Doing the gate's bidding by bringing queens right to you. I've seen enough. We're leaving."

I stomp my foot, frustrated. "You can't, Noire. You don't understand."

Ten wraps one muscular arm around me and turns to face the rest of his pack. Behind them, my parents and Kraven stand casually by the door. Gods, this is exhausting.

My father speaks before I can even begin to explain how I'm viewing this.

"Before the tragedy, the gate only delivered a prophecy every few years. It was rare. We always took what she told us as Gospel because prophecies were so scarce. But now? Many of these prophecies contradict one another. The only way I can explain this is to say that the gate seems desperate to find someone, anyone who can fix this. She is doing everything she can to protect us and the forest, and thus life outside the forest as well."

I rub my chest and think about the gate, wishing I could feel her the way I used to. In this form, I can't feel her at all.

Father grabs a book and flips through the pages. He seems to be looking for a particular prophecy, and after a few moments, he finds it and hands it to Diana.

"I believe this one may be about you, omega." His focus shifts to her chest. "And the spirit you carry which does not belong to you."

Diana takes the page and reads it, her pale face going even paler. She hands it to Noire and gives my father a curt nod.

"Shall we release him, then?" Father continues.

"Can you?" Diana's voice is firm. Noire's arm comes around her waist as he cuts my father a skeptical look.

Father nods. "It is a type of healing, so yes, my power will allow me to release the vampiri king's spirit from you."

"What if we still need him?" Noire asks casually.

"I don't, alpha," Diana's voice is steady. She turns to him and strokes pale fingers down his dark cheek. "Cashore has wanted to go for some time. I think he stuck around just long enough to get me well, but he's anxious to reunite with Zel."

I have no fucking idea what's going on here, but I watch in disbelief as my father takes Diana's other hand.

"He fulfilled his duty to you, child. He received a vampiri prophecy decades ago from the gate. We have a copy of it here somewhere, I'd wager. But now, he is done. Other spirits are not meant to live with ours for very long."

"I understand," Diana says with a soft smile, placing one hand over her heart. She closes her eyes. Noire pulls her closer. I'd guess they're sharing something in their bond, and I wish to fuck I could listen in. The whole godsdamned pack is probably talking right now, and I'm not getting a word of it.

For painful, long minutes, nobody says a word. Then Diana opens her eyes and gives my father a quick nod. "I'm ready."

Father places his hand on her chest and dips his head. Diana's mouth opens, and a voice leaves it—a male's voice—it's sinfully seductive and beautifully deep. It's the voice of a confident male, a leader. Ascelin slumps back against Arliss, and Renze goes white as a sheet.

"My warriors, I will see you in the halls of our fathers. For now, I must find my Zel. Go, thrive, protect. I trust you to guard the Chosen One now and always. I am so proud." The voice trails off, and when I look at Ascelin, blood tears streak down her white skin, black lips quivering as she stares at Diana, whose eyes are rolled into the back of her head.

"Goodbye, old friends," the voice comes again.

Father murmurs low under his breath, and then Diana's eyes snap open. She grits her jaw and places a hand over my father's. When she speaks, her voice cracks on a sob. "He's gone. Th—thank you, Lahken. He's wanted that for a while."

Father removes his hand and squeezes hers once. "It is my duty, omega, and my honor. I know the concept of the gate and her prophecies seems odd to you, but until now, she has never been wrong."

"She'd better be wrong about the sacrificing the queen piece because that's not an option," Noire barks. "Not now, not ever."

My father says nothing but looks around the room with a sigh. "I hope you are right, Alpha Noire, and that, somehow, it will not come to that. But I cannot know the gate's mind, not truly."

Noire's glittering black eyes move to me, and he grins. "*You* can't. But she can."

CHAPTER FORTY
TENEBRIS

et is already barking ideas into our family bond. Ascelin cries
softly behind him. Arliss swoops her up into his arms and
disappears back up the hallway on a wisp of black smoke. If
any of the Volya are surprised to see him morph into a carrow,
they don't show it.

Onmiel looks up at me, and I see the same determined look I
saw on her face in the breakthrough room.

"What do you need, sweet girl?" I pull her close to me by the belt
loops and tuck a strand of pearlescent hair over her shoulder, gripping the back of her neck.

"I'll try to communicate with the gate. Just come with me?" Her
voice is sure and confident. It's the first time she's sounded like
herself since we arrived here.

"We will all accompany you," her father says, but she shakes her
head.

"Just the pack, please. It'll be easier for me that way."

Her mother frowns sadly, but her father nods. Lahken leaves the
room, but Onmiel's mother crosses it and places a hand on her
daughter's lower back, careful not to touch the prisoner tattoo.

"Call for me if you need me, daughter. Alright?"

Onmiel nods and rubs the back of her mother's hand softly. "I will, Mama. I'll be fine; I'll be with the pack."

"I know, child."

With that, the queen sidesteps my brothers and leaves as well.

Onmiel peers around me. "Are you all coming? Or what's the plan?"

"Fuck yes, we're all going," Achaia laughs. "The pack that slays together stays together, right?"

"Ugh," Diana groans. "That's your worst joke yet, bitch."

Achaia snorts out a laugh. "Oh, come on. We've been through the seven hells together. If we can't laugh about it, our only option is to cry, and I'm really, really tired of doing that."

Renze strokes her hair, his expression thoughtful. "Speaking of crying, I would like to check on Ascelin before we leave."

"Don't bother," I bark. "Arliss has it covered."

"Literally," Achaia whispers.

"Fucking hells." Diana laughs. "I'll grill her about it later. I need the deets. For now, Onmiel, we'll follow you?"

"Yeah, of course," my sweet librarian murmurs. "Let's go. It's about an hour from here."

Kraven growls. "I will join you to activate the tree."

Onmiel thanks him, but I have to resist the urge to slap him for his tone.

We follow her out of the village to the main traveling tree. Kraven presses his hand to it, muttering the incantation that opens it wide for us to step in.

For half an hour, we pace through the glowing green pathway inside the tree. Eventually, it spits us out into part of the forest that still looks healthy. Despite that, Onmiel looks anxious.

We remain in pack formation with Kraven on the outside, just in case something happens.

Onmiel is quiet as she leads us through the sun-drenched forest to a clearing. It's nearly as wide open as the street between our row homes back in Siargao. In the middle of the clearing is a giant stone disk with a turquoise, rippling surface. It looks like some sort of otherworldly portal. A matching round pool in front of it is filled with water.

"This is the gate?" I look to Onmiel.

Gray eyes are wide and worried, but she nods and points to the structure.

"The standing circle is the gate herself. The pool in front is where I used to play as a child." Her pale brows knit together in frustration. "Normally, I can sense how she feels when I'm here, and I suppose I do to a degree. But it's muted."

"We'll give you a minute," I encourage her, stepping closer to my brothers. I don't want to pressure her with my presence, and she already looks frustrated.

We stand quietly in the clearing as Onmiel walks a circle around the gate. She dips her long fingers into the pool of water and frowns.

"What is she doing?" Diana questions Kraven as we stand in the shadows of the forest, watching Onmiel.

Kraven sighs. "Onmiel always said she could talk to the gate, but I never believed it until Zura was killed. Who knows what she is doing..."

"I'm starting to see why it didn't work out between you," I bark. I brush past him, slamming my shoulder into his as my wolf lets out a deep snarl.

He flares his leathery wings wide and snaps sharp teeth at me, but I ignore it.

Stalking across the forest floor, I join Onmiel, where she now sits on the edge of the round pool in front of the gate. I stop just behind her, looking over her shoulder. The pool's water is crystal clear. I can even see stones at the bottom of it. It's...peaceful.

"I can't hear her loud enough," Onmiel murmurs, stroking the water with one hand. "Usually, I can hear her talking to me. I can feel distress, but I can't get anything deeper than that." She sighs in frustration and gestures to her body. "It's this godsdamned form, Ten. I can't communicate with her like this."

She glances over her shoulder at my pack. "We need to consult with my father because I don't know how to do this. I think I need his help."

I don't know what to say, so I rub her thigh in gentle circles. She stands on the edge of the pool and brushes her cheek against mine. It's such a direwolf thing to do, so I'm surprised, but I lean into that touch.

I purse my lips for a kiss, and Onmiel grants my unspoken request. Her lips are warm against mine, her tart, candy-apple flavor bursting against my tongue.

"Let's get back," I murmur. "We'll talk to your father and go from there."

She nods, but she's lost in thought.

CHAPTER FORTY-ONE

ONMIEL

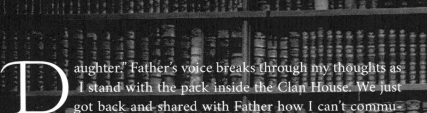

"Daughter." Father's voice breaks through my thoughts as I stand with the pack inside the Clan House. We just got back and shared with Father how I can't communicate with the gate, although I sense her tumultuous emotions.

When I turn, there's a mournful set to his rahken like he's about to deliver yet more bad news. I don't think I can take it.

"What is it, Father?"

"We need to remove your tattoo, child, at least a portion of it. You are too fragile in this form. Perhaps, you could communicate with the gate in Volya form."

My blood freezes, and Diana's hand comes to the middle of my back. He's right. I suspected as much but he's confirming it.

Father presses on without waiting for a response. "Your sister is powerful, Onmiel. If you face her in human form, I am not certain we can protect you, and you are our only chance to win this war. The gate has said as much." He gestures around us at the prophecies laid out on the floor and every other available surface.

Achaia looks sharply up at my father. "I didn't realize you could partially remove a prisoner tattoo. I thought it was all or nothing."

Ten told me that she had one that hid her mermaid form, and they had to cut it off her back in order to free her.

Gods, I can't imagine.

Father nods. "Because Onmiel placed her own prisoner tattoo, she can undo it in layers. She must have removed a layer in Pengshur in order to remember us."

"Right," Achaia presses. "But she doesn't *want* to fully remove it. How many layers are we talking about?"

"There are two more between me and my full form," I mutter, looking up at my father. "You know I can't go back to that form. I was uncontrollable, Father. There are no guarantees I could handle my power now."

"I know, child," he agrees. "But I fear there will come a day very quickly when we will have to return you to that in order to win this war."

I shake my head as I stare up at the man who raised me. "It's got to be a last resort."

"We are there, Onmiel," he whispers back, his voice kind. He understands how dangerous it is to allow me in my natural form. There's a reason I locked myself up under layers and layers of magic.

Diana pats my father on the arm. "Lahken, give us a minute? We need a moment for girl talk."

My father inclines his head and disappears without a word. His words ring through my mind as I watch his pale robes sweep the floor behind him.

Diana sits at the broad table and bends forward over it, giving me a curious look.

"What are you really afraid of unleashing, Onmiel? It's more than just the ability to talk to the gate, isn't it?"

I shudder. She's incredibly perceptive, especially now that she's well. I've watched Diana and Noire since they arrived. They're perfectly aligned in every way.

Would Ten have been like that with Rama under different

TEN

circumstances? The very thought of that makes my heart clench tight in my chest.

I miss him. I wish he wasn't with his brothers right now. Wrapping my arms around my torso, I slump against the table and look at the girls.

"The Gate of Whispers isn't good or evil; she just is. She contains light and dark and every shade of gray in between. I've always understood that about her. When I was a child, I felt I could communicate with her, and eventually, I began to foresee her prophecies before she sent them."

Achaia smiles. "That's badass, Onmiel."

I shake my head. "Nobody thought so at the time except for Zura. She always believed in me, that my power to communicate with the gate was a gift. We loved to play by the gate. We both felt peaceful and comfortable in her presence."

I gulp. What I'm about to share is more than I've ever told anyone. I wish Ten was here to hear it, but now that the girls have encouraged me to share, I don't want to stop. I feel a pressing need to get the words out until I can't even speak anymore.

"Zura and I were playing by the gate one day, and a tiny forest cat was chased into our clearing by something larger. The predator probably saw us and gave up the chase, but the little cat was gravely injured. It basically flopped in the dust and died right in front of us."

"Oh gods," Diana says in a tight tone.

I barrel on because the words are flowing now.

"Zura was hysterical; she was so sensitive to death and particularly anything to do with animals. We were sobbing, and somehow, I just knew that where we had seen death, the gate could bring life. I grabbed the cat and put it into the gate, and I asked her to heal him."

The girls sit rapt, listening to my memory.

"I didn't think it worked at first, but then the cat leaped out of the gate. He wasn't like before, though. His eyes were red and wild. I didn't know what to do. He went for Zura first because she was closest. He ripped her throat out and then took off into the forest. She died in my arms, coughing on her own blood."

343

ANNA FURY

"Fucking hells," Achaia whispers. "You know that wasn't your fault, right?"

"It was, though," I murmur. "I couldn't control my power, and she died because of that. I carried Zura back as fast as I could, and I told my parents everything, but none of it made a difference. Father tried to heal her, but she was gone."

Tears stream down my face at reliving the worst day of my life. "For three days, I sat by her side. On the fourth day, a council of Volya elders agreed I should be allowed to leave the Tempang. Normally, the punishment for what I did would be binding within a prisoner tattoo to lose access to one's powers. I opted to bind myself, and they allowed it. That was eight years ago. I left the Tempang and traveled to Pengshur, and I've been there ever since."

The girls are silent, and I can't help but feel that silence is damning. I turn to go, but Diana lays a hand on my forearm and grips it hard. She rises to a stand, which puts her nearly a head over me. She looks down, blue eyes hard and bright.

"Listen to me and listen good, Onmiel. What happened to Zura was an accident, and you did everything you could to make it right, but you were alone. You are not alone now, do you understand? You're here, and you're one of us, and not a single member of our pack will rest until we right this wrong alongside you." She pauses.

I didn't realize I needed to hear those words so badly until she said them.

"Thank you," I manage.

Diana pulls me in for a quick hug. Achaia rubs my back at the same time. I try hard not to burst into fresh tears, but eventually, I extricate myself.

"I need to talk to Ten. I just..."

"We get it. Go find your alpha," Achaia says. "We're here when you need us."

I nod and leave the friendly women behind, descending the ladder.

I miss the library so fucking much. I felt more alive at Pengshur than I ever have anywhere else—even here at home with my family.

Surprisingly, I hear my mother's voice as I scale the ladder and appear in the doorway.

The view there warms my heart until I think I might burst. My mother sits gracefully at the small table in the main room, Ten seated across from her with his legs folded at the ankle. He's looking down at an ancient, weathered book as she points something out. They both turn when I enter, Ten rising from his seat to cross to me.

He pulls me into his arms, wrapping my legs around his waist as he takes my mouth tenderly, his soft tongue probing the tip of mine. It's the kiss of a lover who knows your body like the back of his hand. It's unhurried and perfect, and I hope there's never a day I can't have this.

"Missed you," he murmurs when we part, despite my mother sitting right behind us. If I've learned anything about Ten in the day since we came here, it's that he doesn't give a fuck what anybody else is doing or who's near us. If he wants to touch me, to kiss me, he takes every opportunity. I've never been more grateful for him than I am right now.

My big alpha sets me down with a devious smile. "Your mother was showing me some of her books from your family library." I have to laugh at that.

"She is a prodigious journaler." I chuckle, following Ten as he sits back down and pulls me into his lap.

"I can't read this," he reminds me, long fingers stroking across the ancient Volya words on the worn, weathered pages.

"I was just translating for Tenebris." Mother smiles. "I hope there will come a day in the future when we can teach him ancient Volya so he can read about your adventures for himself."

There's an achy crack in my heart watching my mother and my alpha connect in a way that's so meaningful to me. I reach out to stroke the book, too, my fingers brushing against Ten's.

"When I was a child, Mother was always writing, always chronicling what happened in the forest. She wrote about peoples' actual lives, and she wrote made-up stories, and this is why I love books." I turn to face Ten, pressing one hand to his chest. "She taught me to bind books, and when I got old enough, I made all her blank ones so she could write. Including this book," I finish in a soft voice, reaching out to touch the familiar pages.

Mother beams as she looks at us. "I am so glad you are home, Onmiel. I know the circumstances are terrible, but there is nothing more heartwarming for a mother than to have her child in her arms once again."

I beam back at her. "After we get through this, I'll make you new books if you'd like?"

Mother claps her hands together, her rahken parting into a mischievous expression. "Perhaps Tenebris can assist you? He should begin to learn some of our ways, should he not?"

"I'd like that," Ten breathes, one big arm tightening around my waist. He tenses behind me and then sighs. "Noire is poking at me. It's time to go, sweet girl."

"I've got to let down some of my tattoo first," I grumble, looking up at my mother. She nods, unsurprised.

"Your father is just worried for your safety, my darling girl," she says confidently, her earlier smile falling. "Zura is incredibly strong, and it would crush us to lose you." She cocks her head to the side. "Do it now, Onmiel. I will remain here with you."

When I falter, Ten strokes his fingers down my side, bringing his lips to my shoulder. "I'm here too, Miel. I'm not going anywhere."

"What if I go crazy?" The question is out of my mouth before I even mean to say it.

Ten grips my chin and turns me in his lap, his amber eyes serious as he gives me a chiding look. "I don't want to hear any more of this self-doubt. You're the strongest person I know. You can do this. For yourself, for me, for your family, and for your forest. I believe in you with all of my heart."

A single tear tracks down my cheek, but he leans in and licks it away with a laugh.

"Will you still have eyeballs?" he chuckles, thumping the tip of my nose as I guffaw, sitting up a little straighter.

"Probably not," I titter, nerves jangling in my belly as I slide off Ten's lap and hold my arm out to my mother. When I look back over at Ten, there's nothing but confidence in the way he looks at me. "Better get your last look at this face," I joke. "It might be different here in a moment."

"I'll still love it, though," he whispers before reaching out to lock his fingers with mine.

Love. Gods, Tenebris Ayala wants me. Could I be any luckier? I don't think so, and that knowledge alone steels my resolve. I will do this, and I will fix what I broke because I need a long life to love him. I need years and years to explore him, to fulfill him, to enjoy him.

I nod at my mother, who draws one long claw across the vein inside my wrist. Hot, sticky blood wells immediately up to the surface, and my magic screams in my veins to be released.

"Careful, child. We will help you stop taking blood when it is time," Mother reassures me.

"You can do this, sweet girl," Ten croons, a purr picking up that fills the room as I squeeze his hand.

My hands shake, but I bring my wrist to my mouth and suck at the wound, blood filling my mouth. The moment the blood hits my tongue, awareness of my magic fills the forefront of my brain. There's a sudden deep awareness of the Tempang, too. Everything sounds louder to me, and it sounds wrong. The bird cries, the animal grunts. It's all...poisoned.

Zura's doing this. She's poisoning the forest, and even though she is my own creation, she must be stopped.

Magic thrums in my veins as I suck harder at my wrist until I feel my mother pull it gently from my teeth.

An uncomfortable, dark sensation worms its way through my mind. The gate. She calls me just like she used to. But where she always brought me comfort, there's now inky darkness. Everything is wrong, and she is so, so afraid.

"That is enough, child," Mother says. I yank my hand from her and put it back to my mouth. More power. I need more power. I need to stop Zura, and my power isn't enough. I need to channel the gate like I did before but in reverse. Where I brought Zura back to life, I need to return her.

I *will* return her.

When Mother draws my hand away again, I snarl, an angry yowl leaving my mouth as my body shifts, pain lancing through me as the prisoner tattoo begins to melt away. I fall to the floor against the pain, but Ten drops down next to me.

"We're here, Onmiel. We're right here, and you are so fucking beautiful. I'm here."

Magic screams through my veins, filling me. I haven't accessed or been aware of my magic in years, and now that I have it back, that heady need for more is a constant ache in my chest. The tattoo feels like glass shards ripping at my back as it fades partially away until all I can do is cry at the pain.

Ten's big arms come around me, his purr filling the room as it picks up in intensity. I want more blood, I ache for it, to release all that magic. To find Zura and take care of this now. My magic and the gate created her, and I'm drawn to her because of it.

"Focus on me, Onmiel." Ten's voice is all alpha command, brooking no argument. His purr draws me out of my desire for blood as he repeats his demand. The world reduces to nothing but Ten—his scent, his purr, the strong, corded muscles of his arms. Everything fades but him, and I feel a little bit like myself again. After long minutes, the pain in my back ceases, and I look up.

Ten's handsome face lights up, full lips curving into a smile. "Godsdamned beautiful, Onmiel. Well done."

I preen under his words, despite my mother standing right behind me. I sense her moving, her hand coming to my shoulder.

"Daughter, I am so very proud of you. I'll give you and Tenebris a few moments. Everyone is gathering outside. Join us when you can."

I nod, turning to her with a soft smile. Her robes billow behind her as she steps gracefully out of the treehouse, leaping off the front platform and disappearing from view.

Ten strokes my hair, wrapping it in his fist as I realize that I'm

348

suddenly the same height he is. I look down, cataloging all the other changes. I'm still humanly pale, although my arms and legs are longer, thinner like the Volya. Long claws tip both hands, and when I reach up, my face is still human, but long horns curve alongside my scalp.

"You've still got eyeballs." Ten laughs. "But they're a brilliant amethyst purple now like you're lit from within by a star. Gorgeous." His voice is reverent as he strokes my hair. "This is the same, still long and white."

"I miss the neon orange," I grumble.

"You can put it back if you adore it." He laughs. "But for what it's worth, the white is fucking hot."

"Good thing I'm hot in all forms," I snark. Ten laughs and reaches his hands up to stroke along my softly curved horns. Heat floods my system as my pussy contracts, a gasp leaving my lips as I curl my hands around Ten's shirt.

"Gods. Oh, fuck, Ten." My voice is deeper in this form, throaty and sensual. All Volya are sensual, sexual beings, but I forgot just how true that was. Even though I was a horny hussy on the best of days.

"Mmm. So they're sensitive." Ten's fingers still stroke and tease my horns as my head falls back, my neck bared to him.

"Bite me," I command, needing more than this horribly inconvenient tease. Now that I'm partially back in my real form, need has me at the point of pain. I need to be filled and used by him. I ache for it. My soul recognizes his, and I won't be happy until I have him. Tasting my power for the first time in years has me drunk and inhibition free.

I have to have more of him.

Ten's mouth closes over my throat, fangs punching through the skin far harder than he ever did in my prior form. It's difficult to breathe like this, but he bites harder, then releases it and makes his way down my throat, licking at the hollow at the base of my neck.

"I'm not gonna make it out of here if we keep this up, Miel," he growls. "You're going to be unhinged in this form, I can tell."

I let out a growl I don't recognize as one hand comes to Ten's throat and squeezes, my mouth hovering over his.

"Need you, alpha."

Ten purrs and drags my body closer to his, not backing down.

"You want to dominate me, Onmiel? Have you forgotten I'm a fucking alpha? That I grew up in a brutal, terrible place? That I could rip you to shreds with my bare hands?"

A possessive snarl leaves my throat as Ten laughs, cocking his head to the side.

"Much as I'm anxious to continue this fight for dominance, people need us," he sighs, taking my hand as he steps back. The long outline of his thick cock is evident against the front of his pants.

I want to drop to my knees and worship it. I want to learn what I can do to him in this form.

Ten yanks at my hand. "Come on, dirty girl. There'll be time for that later. Let's go hunt your sister."

CHAPTER FORTY-TWO
ONMIEL

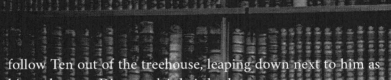

I follow Ten out of the treehouse, leaping down next to him as his pack turns. Diana and Achaia both gape at me.

"You look fucking badass," Achaia says, walking across the space to join us. Like this, she has to look up at me. Achaia walks a circle around us and pretends to fan herself. "How do you feel, Onmiel?"

I have to smile at the perky queen. No matter how dark this adventure gets, she maintains a surprising level of humor. I know she could annihilate the forest if she had to. She's our last resort. Between that and the growing velzen at her side, she's plenty badass herself.

Nearly the entire clan has gathered, so it's probably a good thing I didn't just start fucking Ten upstairs. Gods, I want to. I need to. I'm more predatory in this form, monstrous and dominant.

I recognize a familiar soul in Ten's wolf. It's almost like I can feel him roaring inside Ten's chest, wanting to get out and command me, fight me, and claim me. He wants to chase and take me. I can tell that from the way my alpha stares at me and licks his lips slowly, suggestively.

Noire glares at my father. "So, how do you imagine this going?"

Kraven comes to the forefront of the group and gives us all a haughty, cold look.

"The Dead Queen spends time at a lake near her lands, and occasionally near the Gate of Whispers. None of our plans ever work as expected, so instead, let us focus on a goal. Onmiel's presence is likely to surprise her. Let us use that to our advantage. We will distract her guard to give you an opening. Kill her if you can."

It sounds so simple when he says it like that.

It's anything but.

I haven't seen my baby sister yet, but it's anybody's guess what'll happen when I do. Despite what's going on in the forest, it's hard to imagine being able to kill her, no matter what she's doing to it. Everyone seems to believe I'll have to, but—

Ten's hand comes to my lower back and slips up my shirt, skirting the edges of my tattoo. He strokes me softly and then brushes his cheek against mine.

"I'm here. Here for every moment, Miel." His purr rumbles between us. It's the louder version that happens when his wolf is actively focused on me, too. Something about knowing I have them both at my side helps me focus.

I'm a bundle of nerves as I follow my clanmates and the pack through the traveling tree. We decide to try checking at the gate first, and already, she calls to me. There's a desperate tugging sensation deep inside my chest, so heavy I rub between my breasts to ease the pressure.

In this current form, closer to my full, natural form, I sense the traveling tree's distress. The very ground beneath my feet seems to quiver with anxiety. The forest is sick, hanging on by a thread, and that sickness seeps into my bones.

It's a real mindfuck, honestly. I did this. I thought I was just communicating with the gate, but somehow, I channeled her power and caused this. It's up to me to fix it. We're a small group, but if Father is right, a large army can't move on Zura without being seen.

It makes sense, but given what I've seen so far, I'm still terrified. Whatever magic Zura is using to poison the forest is something ancient and dark. She didn't have that sort of magic when she was alive, so somehow, when I brought her back, I gave it to her. Or the gate did. Or maybe her own protective power just got twisted when she came back. I don't know.

My sins are piling up on top of my head so hard and fast, it's difficult to breathe around the weight of them.

Ten is a silent, steadying presence by my side as we walk quietly through the distressed, dying forest. The trees here are sickly and gray, their leaves either blackened, wilting, or gone. Zura has eaten this land up, and everything about me aches to turn the forest green and healthy again if it's even possible.

I grip my spear as we follow Kraven through a dappled, dark glade. He stops behind a group of boulders and turns, his focus intent.

"The gate is just ahead. Zura's guards usually remain out of sight. We need to capture her quietly." He turns to me. "Onmiel, you'll need to distract her. We'll grab her while she's focused on you."

I nod. The pack is silent. I imagine they're all talking in the bond. I wish I could hear them, but I know they've got my back.

The trees here are scorched and darkened, already destroyed by Zura's magic. I sigh and look around, reaching out to touch a tree before thinking better of it. Everything in this part of the forest drips with the black, sticky tar my sister is using to poison the Tempang. The sludge seems almost sentient, lifting off the trunk to reach for my hand.

Ten tickles my side.

"No touching, Miel. I'm going to shift until we see her, then I'll change at the last moment if you distract her."

Nodding, I grab his pack as he shifts and stalks slowly into the depths of the forest. There are no sounds. No bugs, no small animals. The forest's usual noise is simply gone. Pools of black tar lie all around us. I don't remember seeing this when the pack and I came to the gate before.

Ten's brothers and Diana shift and disappear into the trees with Rosu. Achaia remains by my side with Renze, Ascelin, and Arliss.

Nobody says a word as I lead them through the trees toward the gate.

Eventually, it comes into view. My heart thumps wildly in my chest. The gate's pull is even stronger here, like she's screaming for help. It's all I can do not to run to Her and do something, anything.

Achaia and the vampiri remain out of sight behind me. I round the gate's pool and Zura is there, kneeling at the edge as she swirls one black finger in the water. I suck in a breath at seeing her for the first time.

This is my sister, but not. Her skin is mottled and dark, her rahken missing giant chunks with blast marks marring their smooth surface. Her hair is stringy and limp, her clothing torn and wet.

Her throat is still ripped open from the wound that killed her, and dark slime leaks out of the shredded flesh, sliding down her body and wetting her clothes. She is utterly focused on the pool of water in front of the gate, her black lips parted into a sneer.

I feel like I'm having heart failure. My muscles quiver with the need to run to my sister. I want to pull her into my arms and apologize for turning her into this, this *thing*. The Zura I knew would never want this, would never accept it.

As I watch, black goo drips from her fingertips onto the rocks that surround the gate's pool. The sticky deposits snake along the stones and then slither into the forest of their own accord.

The gate is practically screaming into my mind at how wrong this is, sending a chill of goosebumps flashing across my skin.

Zura, I'm so sorry.

Around us, there's nothing but a terrible and heavy silence.

I take a few more steps around the pool.

"Zura," I murmur.

My sister pauses but shudders. She remains kneeling but swivels her head to face me. A river of lava runs down the crack between her rahken. She snarls and pulls her hands from the gate's pool.

The gate breathes an audible sigh of relief in my mind, but there's still so much tension, so much wrongness in my sense of her.

Zura rises, slow and creaky, her dead bones and muscles unable to move smoothly. Tar drips from her as she takes a step toward me, her lips splitting into a cruel grin.

"It's me, Miel," I whisper. "I'm home, sister. Talk to me, please."

I don't know how sentient Zura even is in this form. Is she driven by a baseless need to conquer? Is she capable of forethought? Is she purely reactive? It's hard to say.

I'm fucking terrified as she descends the pool's steps and takes a few steps toward me. My brain screams at me to flee this danger. I steel my spine, knowing the pack is here if everything goes south.

"I'm so sorry, Zura," I say softly. "I'm sorry for making you like this."

Zura cocks her head to the side, and a look of fury crosses her face. It's there and gone in a moment, and that's when I realize that despite her not speaking, she's scheming. It's obvious in the way her focus shifts around me, like she's sensing the forest and the encroaching danger of the wolves and vampiri.

My sister straightens tall and purses her lips, whistling a string of discordant notes that echo harshly into the quiet forest.

She throws her head back and laughs, and that's when everything descends into chaos.

Spiders the size of aircabs ripple from the bark of the trees behind Zura. They were hiding in plain fucking sight, and I didn't even see them, but as they descend in droves down the trees, black sludge follows in their wake.

Zura sprints for me, raising a dagger high as she shrieks out a stream of curses in ancient Volya.

I'm frozen in fear as I watch her, spiders filling the clearing behind her. Something bursts through the trees behind me, and I hear the pad of footprints.

I pull myself up onto one of the direwolves without pausing to figure out who's who. Rosu lets out a shrill yelp and darts off into the forest with Achaia on his back. Volya warriors tumble through the trees with spiders right behind them.

And we flee. Zura's laughter rings out, echoing off the gate herself.

The spiders give chase, leaping from the trees above and following our path, crashing through the underbrush.

In front of us, one of the Volya warriors runs for the nearest traveling tree. If we can't get to it, we stand no chance.

A spider swings out of nowhere and impales him with the stinger on its back end, disappearing into the underbrush with a great, heaving crash. His scream of pain cuts off on a squelch.

Kraven roars and sprints ahead. Next to me, Arliss evaporates into dark mist just as a black spear flies through him, thunking into a tree ahead.

I scream into the wolf's fur at how helpless I feel. Kraven shouts out a spell, and a tree in front of us splits wide, its glowing green interior a beacon for safety.

Kraven pauses as the vampiri and wolves rush into the tree, not stopping. I'm in last with Arliss and another Volya bringing up the rear. We slide into the tree, but just as it begins to close, a black hand—my sister's hand—grabs the Volya by one of his horns and yanks him backward. The tree closes tight on his leg, trapping him. There's a terrible scream, and then the leg drops to the ground, severed.

Kraven lets out a bellow of anger and tosses his horns against the interior of the tree in frustration.

My heart pounds, my chest rising and falling so fast. I can't seem to pull the breath into my lungs as I fall to the ground and stare at the leg.

Jet shifts and paces to the tree's door, eyeing the leg. "Is it infected? Do we need to get it out of here?"

Kraven turns to him with a scowl but looks at the leg.

I clap a hand over my mouth as they kick at it. No black sludge leaks out of it. Nothing emerges to attack us.

This is all so wrong, I'm physically sick to my stomach.

It's also clear to me what I need to do. I'm the only one who can stop Zura. The gate reassures me through our connection, whispering a chorus of anxious yeses into my mind.

I hop upright and into the depths of the traveling tree. Ten is an angry, seething presence at my back, but he says nothing. Everyone follows as we return to the village and head directly for the Clan House.

My father sits on his throne, speaking in low tones with my mother.

"She's poisoning the gate," I say. "The gate is barely holding on. She told me."

Father shifts back in his wooden throne, one hand over his rahken as his horns slump.

Ten moves to stand next to me, slinging one big arm around my hips. Behind us, I can almost feel the packs' anger. But underlying all of that is the gate's terror.

Father's voice rings clear as a bell across the Clan House space. "You know what you must do, Onmiel. Your true form's power is the only thing left in the Tempang strong enough to stop her. I have to believe you are capable of that. If you brought her here, you can send her back."

I nod. I want to believe that, too. "If you'll help me control it, I'll do it."

"Of course, child," Father says. "Let my warriors recoup for a few hours. We begin again shortly."

I nod and turn to find the whole Ayala Pack staring at me. I don't have words for them right now, though, so I brush past them without saying anything. What could there even be to say at this point?

CHAPTER FORTY-THREE
TENEBRIS

For once, my pack bond is quiet. I think we're all still in too much shock that Zura orchestrated a trap. I'm still buzzing with anger at the memory of Zura streaking toward Onmiel to attack. I'd swung her up onto my back, but I could have lost her today.

We cross the clearing in the middle of the village and head down the side street that houses all the guest homes. I swoop her into my arms, leap up onto the front porch, and carry her through to the bedroom.

She smiles back at me, although it's forced and weary. And that's the moment I know I'm in love with her. Despite Rama and the hold our bond had on me. Despite the fact that I've known Onmiel for such a short time.

She's good and kind and powerful and sexy. She's sarcastic and goofy. She loves books and coffee, and she's been enamored with me since the moment we met. There's a reason for that, a reason she was drawn to me so completely, even when I couldn't see it.

And I almost lost that today.

I fucking refuse to lose her. Not now, not ever. In my chest, my wolf pants with the exertion of fighting and running and the need to cement her to us.

I open my mouth to tell her that, but she takes my hand and points above us with the other.

"Climb with me?"

I smile and follow as she crawls up the tree trunk on the far side of the living room, out a skylight in the ceiling, and up through the branches. Grinning, I hop up and dig my claws into the bark, following her up. There's a beautiful view of the village, but even that disappears into the darkness once we're at the very top of the tree our house is built into. The leaves rustle quietly around us, still healthy in this part of the Tempang.

When we reach the top, I find a small platform built into the topmost branches. It sways softly as the tree does.

"Are these for sleeping?" I join Onmiel as she settles down onto the flat surface.

She gives me a saucy look. "And other things."

Heat floods my chest as my wolf growls.

Careful, friend, I caution him. *You won't fit up here.* He slinks back into the recesses of my mind, comfortable and relieved to be in her presence.

She lies back and folds her arms behind her head. "Every Volya home has a platform like this. We believe the gate made it because Volya souls come from the stars. They enter our bodies at birth, and when we die, we become part of the forest." Onmiel turns on her side, her head in one palm, as she smiles at me.

"Zura and I used to come to sleep up here together when we were children. We used to imagine which stars would be our own children someday." Onmiel's voice goes soft. I sense her thoughts turning dark again. Today was an epic clusterfuck.

I pull her into my chest and stare deep into her beautiful, gray eyes.

"When I was a pup, I watched my father lose my mother. They were bound like Noire and Diana, and while all direwolves hope to find their soul bond in that way...I was afraid of it happening to me."

She strokes her fingers down the bridge of my nose. I nip gently at them, sucking on her fingertips. But I can't start fucking her; I've got to tell her how I feel. I want her to go into what's next with the full knowledge of what's in my heart.

"When I came of age and Rama started sending me books and letters, I didn't get it. I didn't understand the soul bond until after she'd kidnapped me when I woke up in her bed. I saw her, and something just...clicked."

Onmiel's silent. I don't want to hurt her by talking about Rama, but I want her to know how I feel.

"When I started to realize she was drugging me, I felt betrayed, broken. And then Jet showed me what she forced him to do in the maze. All the terrible shit she put him through just because she could." I pause, overcome by all the things he never told me about. I knew the Atrium room was a fucked-up sex-slave palace, but I didn't know the lengths Rama went to just to screw with him simply because she could.

I press on. "Killing her was the worst thing I've ever done." My voice breaks with emotion, but I grip Onmiel's throat gently between my fingers. "And I thought I'd never come out of that grief. But then I met you."

Purring, I reach down and thread Onmiel's legs through mine as she looks at me wide-eyed. Her heartbeat trills fast in her chest. I want to sync it to mine until we're bonded in every possible way we can be.

"You have surprised me at every turn, Onmiel. You snuck into my soul with every look, every joke, every time you needled Arliss, every fucking cup of coffee. I couldn't deny an immediate, incredible connection."

Her throat bobs under my hands, tears filling her eyes as I pull her closer, pressing our foreheads together. I want to breathe the same fucking air she's breathing.

"I'm in love with you," I whisper. "I fell so fucking fast, Onmiel.

And despite what's in our past, there is nobody on this continent I'd rather build a future with than you. I want it all. Your happiness, your joy, your safety."

"Ten, I—"

I silence her with my lips on hers, and where I expected to make this a sweet kiss, the stress and insanity of our day turn my lips hungry. I can't get enough of her, and so I attack her with my mouth, nipping at her tongue and sucking her lips between mine.

"I wanna fill you with my cum and make babies, Onmiel, when we're free of all this," I snarl as my wolf sits up and takes notice.

Pups. Yes.

He's just as sure as I am.

Placing Onmiel's hand on my chest, inside my shirt, I tip her face up to look at me.

"You're mine, in here. My wolf knows it. I know it, and I will spend every day for the rest of my life worshipping you, pleasuring you, and loving you. Wherever you go, Onmiel, I'll be there."

Tears stream down her face as a joyous smile parts her beautiful lips.

"I don't know what'll happen when I undo the rest of the tattoo," she admits. "It could be a fucking shit show. But for the next few hours, make me forget?"

I growl as I flip us, using my knees to spread her legs apart.

"It would be my honor," I growl, dipping down to lick my way up her neck.

I don't know if I'll ever call Onmiel my mate because I don't want her to associate that word with Rama and everything that came before. To me, she's more. Because Onmiel is my choice, and choice is all that really matters.

"You're my fallen star, Onmiel," I growl into her neck, nipping at her sensitive skin as she lets out a soft, needy moan. "You came down out of that sky for me. We didn't know it, but I was on this earth, enduring every day. And every one of those fucking days brought me to you. I'm the luckiest alpha in the world."

Onmiel thrusts her hips hard against mine, greedy for more.

TEN

"I need to claim you, sweet girl," I growl.

"Later," she gasps, struggling when I pull her hands above her head and capture them in one of mine. "After we fix this..."

"Now," I snarl, biting at her neck as I unzip my jeans with my other hand. "Need you tied to me, Miel."

"Gods, Ten," she groans. "Fuck me, please!"

I give her a stern look. "Leave your hands there, little star."

She nods, twisting her fingers together as I reach down and slide her pants off, tossing them to the side. I hover over her waist, breathing her in as she cries out with need. Purring louder, I slide my tongue down into her sweet pussy, circling her clit once as her groan falls off into a pant. Onmiel's knees fall open wide as I feast on her, one small hand sliding through my hair as she grips it in a fist.

"Gods, Ten," she gasps out. "You feel so fucking good!"

I purr as I suck at her clit, pulling it gently between my lips, and then I press both knees down to the ground, holding her with my weight as I attack that sweet pussy. She belongs to my wolf and me in ways Rama never could have.

"You are everything to me," I growl, pausing for a moment to drag my stubbly jaw along her inner thigh. Onmiel's muscles quiver as she tries to rock her pussy up to meet my mouth and can't.

"I'm gonna give you this tongue," I murmur. "I want you soaked for me when I slide this big alpha cock into you. You ready, my love?"

Onmiel lets out something between a plea and a wail as I kiss her clit and then thrust my tongue deep inside her, curling it up to rub against her g-spot. She detonates the moment I do, screaming her pleasure into the quiet night as I purr my heart out. I watch every one of her muscles tense and tighten through the throes of her orgasm, and even though we don't have an alpha mating bond, I imagine she feels my devotion, so I send her my love just like I would if we had that connection.

I suck at her pussy until she's coming again, and when she finally shudders and relaxes, I smile and snake an arm around her waist.

Onmiel nuzzles into my neck before biting me hard, really fucking hard, drawing a growl from my wolf and me. He typically recedes when I'm touching her sexually—it's something for my human form —but that bite, godsdamn.

When I look down at Onmiel, her pupils have overtaken the shocking iris of her beautiful eyes, and there's a feral, unhinged look on her face.

"I need to fuck you," she snarls, darting forward to bite at my lip.

I whine at the pleasure and pain that shoot through my system as she reaches down and roughly strokes my erect cock.

Gripping her throat, I use the arm around her waist to flip her and push her head down into the smooth wood surface of the platform.

My wolf joins me, watching her as she waggles her ass at us, taunting, teasing.

"How about getting fucked by a wolf, Miel…would you like that?" I don't know what the fuck I'm doing, but I know my wolf wants to mount her as badly as I do.

And I'm going to let him.

CHAPTER FORTY-FOUR

ONMIEL

My entire body is a livewire, despite coming twice all over Ten's beautiful fucking mouth. I fantasized about him the moment I saw him that day in the Solarium. But the reality of him is better than every daydream.

And he loves me.

He loves *me*.

The part of me that worried he was moving on too fast, getting too obsessed, is gone. I trust him to know his mind and his heart. I believe every word that comes out of his mouth. I don't know how I fell so fucking fast; I just know it started that day I saw him standing in the library, watching the rain patter on the glass windows above us.

Gods, I hope we get to go back one day. The Tempang might be my home, but the library feels like it's meant for Ten and me.

His voice brings me back into the moment, overwhelmed as I am by everything he shared.

"What do you think, my sweet girl?" he growls. "My wolf wants to take you like the animal he is."

Oh gods. It shouldn't be so hot, but I nod.

The moment I confirm what I want, Ten's big body comes down

over the top of me, his hips pressing into mine, his enormous cock sliding between my thighs. Except when his hands come to either side of me, wolf claws grip the smooth wood. Soft fur brushes against my back, sending a trill of alarm and need through my core. He's half-shifted, and I'm about to be taken by a direwolf.

Whining, I press back into him as he brings his lips to nuzzle my neck. But when his tongue snakes out, tasting my shoulder, my neck, my upper back, it's not Ten's tongue. It's bigger, rougher.

Ten's attention turns hungry and fierce, his teeth and tongue dragging over my shoulders and back as he tastes every inch of me. I rock back as much as I can but half-shifted like he is, I can't fucking move. I can't get him where I want him, but as his thick cock bobs between my thighs, dripping precum onto the wood below us, I snarl.

"Fuck me, Tenebris," I command.

There's a low, confident laugh behind me. His voice is different like this, full of gravel, seductive, wild, and utterly breathtaking. Not for the first time, I wish we shared a bond like Diana and Noire, something to allow me to see inside his mind, to feel his soul.

"Steady, Onmiel," Ten commands. And then he grips the base of one of my horns, squeezing it tight as he yanks me back onto his waiting dick.

I scream at the intrusion—his cock has ridges in this half-shifted form, and they drag along every sensitive nerve ending in my pussy. But then his big claws stroke my horn, and I'm lost. Pleasure sweeps over me in waves as Ten pounds into me from behind, bringing one hand to grip the back of my neck. I'm caught and fucked, and I can't even think around how good he feels.

A low growl lifts the hair on the nape of my neck as Ten leans forward, his hips pistoning as he pushes me flat down onto the platform. He grunts his pleasure as my muscles clench around him, my hips slamming into the wood below me. Ten is everywhere, his lips and sharp teeth at my shoulder as that hand continues stroking my horn. Gods, I never knew it would feel so good to have him touch them.

An orgasm rushes through me like a tidal wave, and I squirt all over his huge cock as Ten lets out a bellow that's half howl and half roar. I tighten around him as the pleasure drowns me, but he's not done. If anything, that release unleashes him, and he fucks me hard and fast with zero regard for how much bigger he is. He's wild and untamed, and then in a moment, he flips me, and I'm treated to a view of Ten.

I gasp when I see him. He could be an ancient werebeast like this. His eyes are narrowed, golden slits, and his snout is fully wolf, leading back to long, tapered ears. But his body is somewhere between—covered in thick, chocolate fur but still Ten's muscular form. But then behind us, a long tail lashes angrily from side to side.

Ten's lips are curled back, revealing enormous fangs that drip saliva down onto my stomach. Everything between us is a mess, and as his slitted eyes focus on me, heat builds between us again.

Clawed hands come to my knees, and he presses my thighs up to touch my chest.

"Mine." The growl that rumbles out of Ten's mouth is barely human at this point. And somehow, I know his wolf is pushing further and further through.

"Yours," I confirm, pushing up onto my elbows as his ridged cock slides along my slick, used pussy. I whine as he nudges at my entrance with a broad, flared head, and then he's sinking to the root inside me once more, his head thrown back as he pants.

He picks up a brutal, punishing pace as he leans over me, his tongue snaking out to lick every inch of my upper body. His big wolf tongue curls around my nipple and tugs, and I'm lost, wrapping my hands around his broad neck as I scream out my release. The world goes starry and black behind my eyes as pleasure robs me of the ability to even speak.

I don't even realize I blacked out until much later when Ten is curled around me in full human form, stroking my thigh lazily.

"Must have been good," he rumbles in my ear, nipping my lobe as he slides his hand between my thighs. "You're still so wet, my fallen star."

I scoot closer to his chest, loving how his chest hair tickles my back. Everything about him is so masculine, so alpha. He's perfect in every way.

"We've got to get started soon," he reminds me. "I insisted they let you get a few more hours rest, but we can't wait any longer, according to your father." Ten's tone turns sour so I flip over to face him.

"I've got this, and even if I don't have it, you'll help me, right?"

He strokes my hair out of my face and smiles. "I'm there for every moment, Miel. Anything you need, okay?"

~

I follow Ten down out of the tree, hating that every step brings me closer to reality and its consequences. All I want to do is hide up in the tree for the rest of my life with him, basking in his love and happiness. But I can't because all this goodness around us is dying.

When we reach the ground, my clan stands there in solidarity. Ten's brothers and their mates are there, too. Even Ascelin and Arliss have remained, although I know Arliss is anxious to visit the carrow and learn. His time might even be running out, but he's staying here instead, and that means the world to me. I give him a thankful look, watching his dark lips tilt up into a smirk.

I don't miss the way Ascelin looks up at him, and even though she plasters a neutral expression on her face, there's a longing in her eyes I can't help but notice. There's more to that story, I'm sure of it. I just fucking hope I fix things so they get to enjoy one another if that's what they want.

Looking at my clan, I notice Kraven is watching the two of them closely, his rahken knitted firmly together at the top. Father steps into my view, laying one clawed hand on my shoulder. He pats it lightly. "Your mother and I will take the women and children to the carrow in the northeast part of the forest. We will make our last

372

TEN

stand there if you—" his voice trails off as my mother joins him, wrapping her arm around my waist.

"We believe in you, child," she whispers in my ear. Father gives me a curt nod. My clan parts around me as Ten shadows me into the clearing in the center of our village.

Butterflies rocket around like vultures in my stomach, eating away at the lining when I think about what I'm going to do.

Ten comes around me, holding my hands.

"I'm here, Miel. The whole time, my love." His whiskey-brown eyes burn a hole into mine as he helps me lift a wrist to my mouth. I bite deeply, sucking at my own blood, and just like before, power fills my veins, thrumming as my head falls back.

The gate speaks into my mind clearer than she ever has.

Come to me, daughter. Take what's mine. Return what's lost. Come, come, come.

I don't remember falling to the ground; I just know that I'm there as knowledge and magic fill my veins, and the world around me starts to change. My parents' faces blur, then everyone begins to scream, and the last thing I see is Ten's worried expression as I let out a guttural, animalistic roar of pain.

CHAPTER FORTY-FIVE
TENEBRIS

E verything happens so quickly. Onmiel's eyes roll into the back of her head, and then her body changes. Rahken form over her eyes as she curls in on herself, screaming and writhing on the ground.

"She is enraged," hisses Arliss as he appears beside me. "I can almost taste her power. She wants blood."

The wrongness of it scratches like nails in my mind, but Arliss has the gift of reading intent. He is reading hers now and does not like it.

"Bind her quickly!" Lahken screams, directing Kraven and the other warriors. They form a circle around us as my pack moves in to surround us.

I snarl and stand over her. She's defenseless like this, in the middle of changing. But Arliss is right; she's not in control. I sense it. Still, I won't allow them to hurt her.

Kraven and the others back up, although he still holds a spear aimed at her. I snap my teeth at him, shifting into my wolf and hovering over Onmiel.

She rolls underneath me, screaming as her body changes. There's a cracking sound, and when it stops, she rises from the ground in full Volya form. She's not any bigger than she was before, but where before she had those incredible striking eyes, now, I'm looking at rahken like her father's and a cruel, thin-lipped mouth filled with razor-sharp teeth. Saliva drips from them as she glances around me at the warriors holding spears pointed in her direction.

A low, menacing growl leaves her lips. I reach for her, horrified at the way she shudders from my touch. She snaps at my hand, so I pause, even though Noire screams at me to get out of the way.

"My love," I try to soothe her. "It's me. I'm here. We're doing this together, remember?"

Onmiel cocks her head to the side but then throws her head back and lets out an evil cackle. It reminds me so much of the way Zura laughed at the gate that I shudder and step back.

A shrill noise rings through the forest. We all pause, and Onmiel goes quiet, her head jerking in the direction of it. She cocks it to one side and then the other, and then a throaty, murmured "yes" echoes out of her mouth.

Someone rushes toward us, shouting, "Zura comes!"

The village devolves into a frenzy of rushing Volya. The king and queen guide the women and children to the closest traveling tree. I can barely focus on that as I beg Onmiel to see me, to hear me.

Noire grabs my arm, but when she sees him, Onmiel lets out a percussive roar that knocks us all flat on our asses. The scurrying around us increases as her arms swing wide and a crack appears in the ground around her, the earth falling away as she separates herself from us.

I stand at the edge, watching the crack widen as the earth carries her away from me.

"Onmiel, please," I beg, reaching out for her. "It's me, my love. Let's do this together."

A distant roar comes again, and then the crashing of hooves.

Noire grabs my shoulder. "There is no time, brother! Zura is attacking!"

I shout for Onmiel, but in the moment I turned to look at Noire, she disappeared. The spot she stood in is empty, and only a rustling in the bushes on the far side of the village gives any indication of where she might have gone.

"No!" I bellow, screaming as my brothers drag me from the clearing.

A herd of undead centaur barrel into the open space, and I thank the gods that all the women and children have already escaped.

Black, sticky spears fly. The Volya warrior next to me falls to the ground, impaled, sludge overtaking his body as he jerks. I don't stick around to watch him become like the rest of them.

All we can do is flee as dozens of centaurs fill the village and chase us all the way to the tree. The traveling tree's door closes, but a black spear lodges in the opening, and tar drips off it, slinking toward us like a snake.

"Run!" shouts Kraven, taking off into the tree's depths. We sprint for a solid ten minutes until we don't see the slime anymore. Kraven stops and turns, but it's Renze who speaks up first. He strokes Rosu between the eyes, but Rosu remains watchful, focused on the darkness of the passageway behind us.

"What now, Tenebris? We hunt your woman and make her see reason?"

I look around at my pack. My brothers stand ready to fight. Their mates look on with resolute expressions. Even Arliss is still here and focused.

"I need you to join me," I say. "We need to find Onmiel and support her. She'll do the right thing. I know she will."

A pair of all-white eyes flash at me from across the traveling tree's hallway. I meet my friend's gaze and give her a look I hope she can read, but when Ascelin smiles, revealing two rows of translucent black teeth, I return the look.

She's with me, I know it.

"We are ready to hunt by your side, Tenebris," she purrs.

Good, I say into our family bond.

"She'll be at the gate," I whisper. I don't know how I know, but I do.

My pack trails quietly behind me, but we're on high alert. That sensation brings me right back to the maze. I'm in front as always, Jet, Renze, and the girls in the middle, Noire bringing up the protective rear. I was never safe in the maze, of course, but with my family at my back, I was never worried either.

I'm worried now, though. Worried for the sexy, perfect woman who captured my heart when I didn't even know that's what I needed. Now, she's lost to her power and its darkness, and it's my job to pull her out of that.

She did the same for me.

CHAPTER FORTY-SIX

TENEBRIS

"We are here," Kraven says coolly, brushing past me when the traveling tree opens to deposit us into a dark, desecrated glade.

I half shift, calling my wolf to the surface; my senses are better like this, anyhow. Noire comes to my side, barely contained surprise evident on his face. Direwolves don't halfway shift; it's just not something we do.

"What's the plan, brother?"

"Find Onmiel. Help her kill Zura. Try not to get killed in the process." The voice that leaves my mouth isn't mine, and I didn't even think those thoughts. It's all him, focused as he is on our mate and getting to her as quickly as possible. We don't wait for anyone as we stalk into the underbrush.

Behind me, I hear Jet's voice in a grumbly, low tone.

"That isn't a fucking plan; it's a death wish. We need an actual plan, Noire."

The thing is, Onmiel doesn't have time for us to plan. I search for her in a bond, but I can't feel her the way I always felt Rama. Still, I continue on because I will never stop looking for her as long as I live.

There's a faint light ahead in the jungle. The occasional tree is still verdant and green, although streams of sticky black tar drip from branches in front of me. They hit the ground and slither off into the forest. Lahken was right. This is our last stand because Zura's magic is right here at the godsdamned gate, the home of life on our entire continent.

I scent the air as we come into the gate's clearing. The shallow pool in front of it is still pale blue and clear, the water undisturbed by Zura. There's no sign of the Zura or Onmiel.

"She is not here," Kraven snarls, grabbing one of his horns and yanking at it in irritation.

Turning to my brothers, I give them a look.

"Standard formation," Noire barks. "Ten, you're up front. Everyone else, fan out in the middle. I'll bring up the rear with Arliss and Kraven."

Kraven turns with a scowl and nods.

"If you find her first, drive her to me," I command, my voice otherworldly as the gate shimmers in front of us.

What I'll do when we find her is anybody's guess. I don't know how to make Onmiel see that she can do this, that she can harness her power and save us all, but I have to try.

My pack splits off into the forest as I scent the air again. There's the crisp tang of Volya magic, so much stronger in this form. I sense my brothers and Diana shift into their wolves, then disappearing off into the forest. Rosu slinks next to me with Achaia on his back.

The thrill of the hunt fills my chest, my muscles trembling with the need to move and seek, to find my quarry and corner her.

I'm coming, Miel, I send out into the universe. I only hope she can hear me.

For two hours, we patrol an ever-widening area around the gate. Frustration is at an all-time high when I catch a whiff of something, my wolf locking onto a scent.

Little mate close. Something wrong. My wolf's voice is an urgent warning in my mind. I'm on high alert for any sign of Zura and her armies, but the forest waits with bated breath. I half expect Zura to pop out from behind the next tree and stab me.

Instead, Onmiel is just ahead. We're deep in the forest, but I smell water. My family bond is awash with concentration as Renze slips in front of us.

When he returns, stopping in front of me, I pause.

"She is up ahead on the banks of a small lake. The Dead Queen is coming; I heard her."

Nodding, I break into a run and pump my arms to get to her, to have time with her before Zura shows up, and we need to be a united force.

I slide to a stop when the edge of a cliff looms ahead of me. Forty feet below, a crystal-clear pool of water shines with the midday sun. Onmiel stands waist-deep, focused on the water below her. Her hand darts into the water, and she pulls out a huge fish, ripping its head off as blood sprays her rahken and horns.

A growl of appreciation for her in predator form rises from my throat.

Mate strong. Mate good, my wolf reassures me.

Arliss appears in a stream of smoke next to me. "She is not herself, alpha. She is agitated and frustrated. Be cautious."

As if she can hear us talking, she looks up to the cliff's edge where we stand. She doesn't seem to recognize me, though, although she doesn't look away as I follow a trail down the side of the cliff, meeting her on the beach.

Stay back, I tell my family through our bond. *Give me a minute.*

"Onmiel," I purr, crossing the pebbled shore and wading into the water.

She backs up with a low growl, ripping into the fish's belly as wet innards spill down her chin.

"My fallen star."

She cocks her head to the side, feral in this form. Anxious energy radiates from her. Arliss was right. She's not in control of her emotions like this, tasting her power for the first time in eight years. I just need to get through to her to bring her back to me.

I take another step. I'm five feet from her. "I ache to touch you," I admit. "You are so fucking beautiful like this."

She drops the fish, wiping blood from her mouth and takes a step closer to me, eyeing me as if she might attack.

"You can do this, sweet girl," I whisper, remaining still.

She comes up to me, almost close enough to touch. I need to show her something to remind her she's mine, that I trust her, and that I always will.

I close the distance between us but don't touch her. Her body tenses and tightens, ready to fight or flee.

I let my head fall back, a sign of trust. A long moment passes, then two, during which Noire bellows at me not to show her my godsdamned neck, not to get killed being a stupid fucker, but a warm tongue dips into the hollow at the base of my throat.

I sense my pack flying down the hill to tear me from her, but I can't be bothered to focus on them.

A ragged groan bursts from my lips as her tongue snakes straight up my throat, sharp teeth closing on my chin and biting hard enough to draw blood.

I resist the urge to yank her to me and have her right here in the water.

"Your power, my love," I whisper. "We need your power. Your sister is coming."

That intoxicating tongue traces a path to my ear, sending goose-bumps along my entire body.

I reach for her, wrapping an arm around her waist.

"Ten?" Onmiel's voice is worried and afraid.

I crush her to me, gripping the back of her neck with one hand.

"We need you, my star." I bring my head up, locking eyes on her face.

She sputters, looking around us. "I, I don't remember coming here, Ten. I'm not in control like this. I—"

"You can be, my love," I encourage her. "Focus with me. I'm right here. You can do this, Onmiel. I know you can."

An angry shriek echoes from above.

Onmiel snarls when a black-tipped spear flies through the air, narrowly missing my head. It clatters off the stones behind us and falls to the ground. Her focus moves to the cliffs above us.

I follow her gaze to where Zura stands, blazing red eyes narrowed on us, the threads of her black dress waving in a non-existent breeze. It's like she's floating through the air, and up close, she's even more horrifying than what I previously saw. Zura says nothing, her mouth opening in a silent scream as she lifts one hand, pointing toward us.

Noire snaps from the beach. "We can't fight off a godsdamned army, Tenebris. Is she ready?"

I press a hand to Onmiel's lower back, but she leaps from me with a hiss before turning to her sister again. She's a predator, utterly focused and drawn to her sister like a magnet.

She's lost to me, even as another spear flies through the air. I catch it and spin, throwing it at the first centaur, who barrels down the rocky path toward us.

It hits him square in the chest, exiting his back with a horrifying squelch. He laughs and pulls the spear from a gaping hole, tossing it lightly in his hands, ready to throw again.

We really can't kill a fucking undead army. We need a miracle.

"Protect Onmiel," I bark at my pack. "Get her to Zura, no matter what." I turn to my mate, even though she's not focused on me in the slightest. "I'm with you," I murmur low enough for her to hear. "We're all with you, Miel."

She lets out an ungodly roar and takes off, sprinting up the path toward the approaching army. We take off after her, and I pray to every god and goddess I grew up with to watch over her alongside me.

The moment it's clear Onmiel's not slowing down, Zura's entire army moves as one, like a flock of birds. They round her, but she pays them no attention as she runs for her sister.

Jet barks a command at Achaia.

She opens her mouth and shrieks, sending a percussive wave that flattens the army in front of us. They fall to the ground, rolling and stumbling as they struggle to rise. Rosu sprints next to me with Achaia on his back, her face screwed up in concentration. We're right behind Onmiel. As the undead begin to rise, my pack and the Volya warriors slash, removing heads where we can. The bodies rise and run, but headless, they can't focus. And more importantly, they can't bite and turn us.

Achaia lets out a second deafening scream, and I crouch while the army falls to the ground again.

Zura leaps to her feet, a spear in her hand, as Onmiel gets close.

Behind me, my pack keeps slashing and attacking, but we're outnumbered by hundreds of monstrous, undead soldiers.

My heart pounds in my chest, the only sound in my ears is my own blood rushing through my body.

A centaur dives for Onmiel just as she nears Zura.

I bellow, but with a wave of Onmiel's hand, he disintegrates into dust.

Oh my fucking gods. Is she channeling the gate's power in reverse?

"*Yes!*" Kraven shouts. "You can do this, Onmiel!"

If she hears his sudden support, she says nothing, focused as she is.

I watch the sisters clash together, Onmiel's larger frame knocking her sister to the ground.

Zura lets out a scream of anger.

Everything is chaos as Achaia levels the army to the ground a third time, only to watch them rise again. More undead stumble out of the forest to join the horde. We can't keep going like this.

Zura slices black-clawed fingers across Onmiel's face, and I watch the dark sludge ooze into the wound. Oh fuck, oh gods. If she infects her, that's it.

I sprint for Onmiel, screaming for her to remember why we're here.

With a wave of her hand, Onmiel disintegrates the row of monsters closest to her. They disappear into a fine mist that coats the ground as she scrambles to fight Zura.

Onmiel screeches and throws herself on top of her sister. When she waves her hand over the smaller woman, nothing happens. Zura doesn't disintegrate like the others.

Zura kicks Onmiel off her, leaping up with a black, dripping dagger in her hand.

Time slows as Zura brings the dagger up and drives it through Onmiel's chest.

Onmiel's rahken lift in surprise, then her horns slump, and she drops to both knees with the hilt of the dagger sticking out from between her breasts.

I roar, my wolf taking over. I grab Onmiel by the neck and drag her from Zura.

Kraven throws an iron net over the Dead Queen, yanking it tight until she falls to the ground in a heap. Around us, soldiers still rage, but Achaia knocks them down, and my pack picks them off.

I half shift and haul Onmiel into my arms. Blood spills from her lips. Her focus drifts past me to the fight. She waves her hand in an intricate symbol, and the entire army explodes into mist.

CHAPTER FORTY-SEVEN
TENEBRIS

Behind me, Kraven lets out a roar of triumph. I can't focus on that, though. Fear tears through me as I look at Onmiel, slumped against my chest.

One of her hands wraps into the fabric of my shirt. "The gate requires sacrifice," she murmurs, her eyes fluttering closed. "A queen of the land, a queen of the sea, and a queen of the sky."

It's the prophecy all over again, and it chills my blood to hear her repeat it now. Is the gate telling her this?

"No, fallen star," I whisper into her ear. "Not today. But we *are* going to return Zura to it."

"Won't work," she mutters.

"It has to," I purr. I stand with her in my arms and look over my shoulder at Kraven. "Bring Zura. Follow me."

It's an alpha command from my wolf, who takes over. My pack follows in silence. Our family bond is full of anguish and heartache for Onmiel. Rosu pads quietly next to me, Achaia slumped in a heap on his back.

I pace through the thick underbrush, ignoring the black sticky tar that follows us like a virus. Despite killing Zura's soldiers, our fight isn't over.

I need to get to the gate and end this. I don't know what'll happen after that, but I can't watch Onmiel die or turn. So, I'm going to beg the gate just like she did. Spare her because she saved everyone.

I send my intention out before we even arrive at the gate, hoping it is sentient, that it can hear me because I belong to Onmiel, that it can see what we're trying to do.

The only sound is Zura yowling and scratching, but Kraven silences her with a backhanded slap, dragging her behind him in the net.

We enter a traveling tree, and Kraven directs us through it. Exiting, we walk until the gate looms ahead of us. Onmiel's body is limp in my arms, the wound in her chest filled with the black sludge from Zura's dagger.

By the time we see it, I know what I have to do.

I stop next to Kraven. "Give me Zura."

He hands me the rope. My pack watches as I approach the gate portal.

How are we doing this, brother? Noire questions into our pack bond. *Let us help you.*

I don't immediately answer. Zura thrashes and screams as I pace to the gate and ascend the steps. When I step into the pool, Kraven rushes to the base of the platform.

"You cannot step into the portal, alpha. It will kill you!"

Noire sprints across the clearing and commands me to stop with the deepest alpha tone I've ever heard from him. Normally, that would cripple me. But now? My wolf shrugs it off and focuses on Miel, limp and dying in my arms. I pull the dagger out of her chest and toss it away.

I'm knee-deep in the pool when I turn to my family, watching their expressions of confusion turn to abject terror.

"I love you all so fucking much, and I'm sorry it has to be this way," I start. "Long live Pack Ayala." I stride across the pool and up the two steps to the Gate of Whispers's big, round portal. I surge through, dragging Zura with me.

TEN

The only sound I hear is Noire raging behind me.
And then, nothing.

~

Asense of calm fills me, the worry about my family left
behind. They will live and thrive, even if it's without me.
Onmiel saved our entire continent. My pack and the
Volya will flourish. I know all of that just like I know my own name.
Somehow, after coming into the gate, I sense it in the way Onmiel
must have.

It's a peaceful sensation, like a warm hug wrapped around my
soul. I'm still half-shifted, my direwolf refusing to be parted from
Miel.

There is no sound, there is nothing but the draw of the gate, and
as I look at it, I hope it can hear me.

I could never leave her, I admit. *I will be by her side forever in this life
and the next and the next. We return Zura to you, but in her last
moments, I want Onmiel to have peace. And you are her peace. I know
that now.*

The surface of the portal we came through shimmers as if the
gate Herself is laughing.

Cool water flows over me, even though I'm not getting wet.
There's a splashing sound, and Zura falls through the gate
behind me.

Without a word, she rises and lifts her hands to look at them.
Sticky, black tar melts off her, tendrils of color returning to her
skin. Worm-eaten flesh heals and reattaches to her bones. Her thin
lips part in awe as all the death flows away from her, and what's left
is beautiful life.

After a few long minutes, she stands, cocking her head to the
side. When she smiles, it's broad and happy, the picture of health.
She puts a finger to the side of her mouth in thought. "You are not
what I pictured my sister with, but it is right. Can you feel it?" She
gestures around us, laughing. It's a lyrical, happy noise, and it sends

an ache through my chest when I think about Onmiel losing her so long ago.

"But we are together now, are we not? Together forever." Zura laughs as if she heard my thoughts, turning from me as my eyes follow her.

I gasp. Where there was nothing around us, we now stand in a pastel forest. It's a mirror of the Tempang, but not. Everything is the color of cotton candy, and as I look in awe, Zura strides off, motioning for me to follow.

"They used to say the gate killed those who entered it. That the old gods who live here are full of wrath." Zura speaks over her shoulder. "But I think Onmiel always knew the truth. The gate simply delivers those who enter it into what's next. What is next for you, Tenebris Ayala?"

I clutch Onmiel tighter to me as I follow her sister. I'm too overwhelmed to even respond to her question.

Zura turns when we arrive at a pale pink waterfall, her focus on Onmiel in my arms.

Where the dagger stuck out of her chest before, the wound is gone. I feel peace when I look at her. I should be heartbroken and terrified. Where has that emotion gone? Did the gate take it? I hug Onmiel tighter.

Zura looks at me. "She was always the best of us, you know. The kindest, the smartest. I wanted to be her when I grew up."

I give her a brief smile, but worry is beginning to push through the peace I feel. Dropping to my knees, I set Onmiel gently on the ground.

Zura joins us, laying one manicured hand on her sister's head. She strokes bloodied hair away from Onmiel's face and sighs. "It is time for me to return to the stars, Tenebris. Tell Onmiel that I forgive her, that I love her, and that we will pick daisies again one day. Tell her I approve."

She reaches out and ruffles the fur on top of my head, pinching one of my ears playfully.

"Goodbye for now," she says. "I will see you in the next life, brother."

I watch as Zura's skin begins to shimmer and flake. Where her hand was, she seems to be disintegrating into thin air. She seems happy about it, humming as she sits with us. It doesn't take long. A minute or two, and Zura is gone. The pastel forest around us is peaceful and quiet, and a sense of knowing hits me again.

When the first bit of Onmiel's skin and mine begins to shimmer like Zura's, I bury my face in her neck to remind her how in love I am. How it's always been her from the moment my wolf decided it. How he slapped me around to help me realize it, and how all I want to do is make her happy for the rest of my days.

I watch us drift away, the colors of our souls dancing and mingling together on a faint breeze. It grows stronger, whipping my hair as we become one and disappear into the sky.

And then there is nothing but peace.

CHAPTER FORTY-EIGHT

DIANA

Noire rushes past me, sprinting for the steps to the gate. Anguish fills our mate bond so completely that I can't breathe around it. He runs smack into Jet's broad chest, bouncing back with a furious roar. I grab his arms from behind, trying desperately to stop him from throwing himself headfirst after Ten into the Gate of Whispers.

"You cannot go!" Kraven shouts, joining me to haul Noire away from the gate's pool.

My mate yanks his arms from me and shoves Jet, but Renze and Ascelin join us until we're all piling on top of Noire, who rages, snaps, and snarls as he struggles to follow Ten.

Oh my fucking gods, Ten. After all of this, after *everything*, he's gone.

I know in my heart Noire will never recover from this.

"Mate," I cry out. "Noire! You can't go! Stay. I need you!" I throw that last bit in as a final resort, feeling like a total ass, but Noire can't follow Ten into the gate, or I'll lose him forever.

A resonant explosion knocks us flat on the ground. I blink my eyes wide, trying to understand what happened, but the forest is silent.

I struggle to sit up, but Achaia pulls me up next to her, squeezing my hand. Even Noire has pauses. In front of us, streaks of green seep out of the Gate of Whispers and up over the edges of its pool. Smoke in every possible color erupts from the gate in streams that dash into the trees.

We're all so shocked that we say nothing.

"The trees," Arliss hisses. "Look at the trees."

My entire pack looks around in wonder as decay and darkness disappear and healthy color returns to the forest.

The clearing around us is silent until a wail rises up. Noire. Goosebumps crackle down my skin to hear the way he howls. His voice cracks, his wolf screaming in agony at Tenebris's loss.

Rosu joins him, raising his nose to the sky, his ears flat as he howls. It's a long, mournful sound that rings out over the stones, covering the forest with all-consuming heartbreak.

Tears stream down my cheeks as Noire slumps to the ground, falling forward onto his knees as great big sobs wrack his giant frame.

The vampiri move aside, and Jet sits back on his heels, gasping for breath with a hand on his chest. I move to Noire's front, plastering myself to him. He doesn't say a word, doesn't even look away from the gate, but tears slide in a torrent down his cheeks.

"Mate." I scratch at his chest, willing him to look at me, to remind himself that I'm here for him, no matter what he needs, no matter what insurmountable thing hits us next.

Ten is gone. Onmiel is gone.

"The king will sacrifice the queen to the gate," Achaia whispers. "Do you think it meant Ten and Onmiel? She was the Volya's future queen, so he'd have been—" Her voice trails off like she can't even finish the sentence.

He'd have been king.

I try to process the idea of it, but Noire's sanity is unraveling in front of me. Big muscles tremble as he pulls to a stand, still not looking at me.

"Not Ten," he growls, his voice breaking, fists balling by his sides.

"Never Ten." I've never heard Noire this broken, this angry. Our family bond is frayed to the point of snapping. Agony floods it until I can't stand it. He's the fire to my water, and together we bolster our pack. But white hot agony streaks through our bond, choking me until I can barely breathe.

Noire is shattered by this, and I don't know if it'll ever be possible to put him or our pack back together without Ten. We've overcome every godsdamned obstacle, every impossible feat thrown at us—first the maze, then my injury, then a zombie queen intent on taking over the whole continent. But this?

This I can't even comprehend.

"The barrier entrapping us is gone," Kraven whispers. "Can you feel it?" He looks around in wonder, but I can't fucking focus on that right now. I don't give a shit.

I don't even know what to do next, but I scramble to think of something. My pack stands silent and shocked, but I'm the gods-damned pack omega. It's my job to support every one of my people.

Even my alpha.

I stroke my fingers down Noire's face, but he still quivers with rage, his black eyes narrowed at the gate.

"Noire." Jet's voice is urgent, and when we turn, his eyes are on the gate, too.

Kraven joins us, one hand gripping a sword as we gaze at the gate's surface, which now ripples.

"What's happening?" I demand of the big warrior.

"I don't know," he grits out. "I have not seen this nor heard of it. Step back, everyone."

Despite his warning, Noire surges toward the gate and manages to fling himself into the pool. I scream for him, but it doesn't make a difference. He sloshes toward the portal as I scramble after him, desperate to pull him to safety.

The pale blue surface of the gate shimmers again, and then a set of broad, leathery horns appear. They push forward and up out of the portal as if whatever's coming out has to duck to make it through. Wavy chocolate hair appears next, and then a figure that would be Ten if he were twelve feet tall and half Volya.

Horns twice the size of Lahken's curl up and away from Ten's forehead. His eyes glow pale blue like he's lit from within by the gate's power. He's clothed in a simple tunic and pants, his form as muscular as ever. Pointed black claws tip his hands and feet. This not-Ten stares silently at us, his enormous chest rising and falling with slow, measured breaths.

"Tenebris?" Noire's voice cracks as he stumbles forward until he's standing just below the monstrous male.

Kraven paces up the pool's steps and stops next to me, the look on his face incredulous as he stares. "The Prime," he murmurs, his voice barely above a whisper. "The king of all that is. The gate has never given us a Prime in all of Volya history. There are only fore-tellings from many generations ago. I never thought to see it happen."

I'm still clinging to Noire as Ten watches us.

"What does that mean?" I hiss. "Is this Ten or no?"

"Yes and no," Kraven continues. "He is your brother, but also the alpha of alphas, the king of vampiri, the regent of naga regent. He is the king of *everything*. He is the gate incarnate. The ultimate protector. The light and the dark combined into one."

Kraven falls to his knees in the shallow pool, his head dipping respectfully.

Ten moves toward us with otherworldly grace. He steps into the pool, towering above us in this form. I sense my pack joining us, but I can't look away from Noire, and he doesn't look away from Ten.

Not-Ten looks down at me, a soft smile splitting his face. "Hello, Diana."

I step forward until I'm next to Noire, threading my fingers through his. "Hello, Ten. Assuming you're still Tenebris of Pack Ayala."

Not-Ten smiles, and it's the comforting smile of a parent to a young child.

"They are all my packs, my clans, my kingdoms." He shrugs as if it's the most obvious thing in the world, but when his glowing eyes light on Noire, I press myself closer to my mate. Rustling behind us tells me everyone else has dropped to the ground, too.

Ten looks behind us and grins at my mate. "You know, everyone else is kneeling for me, Noire." Ten's tone is all lyrical joy as he gives his oldest brother a teasing look. Is this really Ten, this giant beast of a man with horns wider than an aircab?

Next to me, Noire shifts from one foot to the other and reaches out, placing his hand on Ten's chest. "Is it really you, brother?"

Ten laughs. "Yes and no, alpha."

Noire frowns. "How much of the Tenebris I know is left?" His voice is just as commanding as it ever has been, a deep resonance that seeps into my bones and makes me want to show him my throat.

Tenebris laughs again, but it's not harsh and angry; it's more melodic than anything. "Everything you knew remains, brother. There is simply more of me now."

Moving slowly, my mate drops to one knee, never pulling his eyes from Ten. I drop with him, watching in shock as the strongest male I know bends the knee for his youngest brother.

"Only ever for you," Noire whispers, his voice so low it's barely audible. "Only ever for you, brother."

Ten smiles and places a hand on Noire's shoulder. "The gate blesses you and yours, Alpha Noire. I will be there to see all of those happy moments, brother."

A surge of emotion crashes through our mate bond as Noire stands and pulls me to his chest.

Ten turns from us and faces the gate as a second figure emerges. *Onmiel.*

Goddess, I'm so fucking relieved to see her. I sprint forward before anyone can stop me, throwing myself up into her arms the moment she's through.

Noire goes tense in our bond, but I couldn't stop myself if I wanted to.

Onmiel wraps both arms around me and sighs, whispering in my ear. "Being dead was weird for a minute, but I've got some cool new powers. I can feel them."

I let out a hysterical cackle as she lets me down, crossing the pool, and descending the steps with Ten following her. The clearing breaks out into chaos as the Volya surround her and pepper her with a million questions. When she raises a hand, Kraven and the Volya warriors drop to the forest floor again, bowing low.

"That's enough." Onmiel laughs. "Please rise, and don't do that every time you see me. I'm still me, sort of."

Ten wraps his arm around her, snaps his fingers, and then they're both in normal-sized form, although they've still got incredible horns.

Jet slides an arm around Onmiel and hugs her. "We're so fucking glad you're safe."

"Me, too," she whispers, radiant, glowing blue eyes moving to Ten, who gives her the happiest look I've ever seen on a male's face.

"So, the prophecy was never even about Diana or Achaia, then?" Noire questions.

"No," Ten confirms. "It was always Miel, because she is the queen of everything—land, sea, air, and all that lies between."

A bubbling laugh rises out of my throat. That godsdamned prophecy has been a noose around my neck for what's felt like ages. But it's done now, gone.

I watch Ten and Onmiel reintegrate with the group and smile. For the first time in a long time, I feel safe. I'm not dreading what's next. I'm not worried about some madwoman stealing my happiness and ripping me to shreds. For the first time in a long time, I can think about the future.

And that future is intoxicating.

CHAPTER FORTY-NINE
ONMIEL

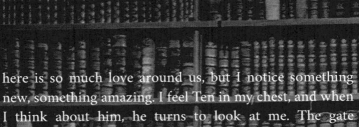

There is so much love around us, but I notice something new, something amazing. I feel Ten in my chest, and when I think about him, he turns to look at me. The gate unleashed us and gave us a gift I could never have imagined having —a bond that allows me to feel and experience him as a true mate should. Every bit of his emotion, his needs and wants? I can sense all of it.

My mate and his wolf have a few things on their minds.

Ten looks at his brothers with a quizzical, almost amused expression. "I need to return to the maze to release the monsters."

At his proclamation, the shifters and vampiri explode in a flurry of indignation. I think Ascelin is the loudest, her brows all the way up to her hairline as Arliss laughs from his spot next to her. It's not lost on me that he has yet to leave us to find his own way with the other carrow, but now that Ten and I are what we are, we can help him.

There's a sense of knowing in my chest, driven home by my sacrifice to the gate. I am her, and she is me. The entire continent is connected to my very bones. I feel a need to protect and cherish everyone and everything. Every monster, every being, *everything*. It's all my family now. Ten and I have a duty to protect Lombornei. The gate is no longer alone; she has us—the first Primes.

Noire is still raging about Ten's maze comment. "You've got to be fucking kidding me," he bellows. "We can't go back there! It's dangerous, and whoever's left has been weeks without food, Ten. You'll be ripped to shreds. Don't ask me to watch that."

Ten laughs, and I join him, taking his hand.

"They will not hurt us, Noire," I reassure him. "You don't even need to come; we'll be fine on our—"

"Like hells," he snaps back, crossing his enormous arms. "If you're going, I'm going."

And like that, it's settled. Nobody seems willing to disagree with him.

A tug pulls my focus in the direction of Arliss. I give the bulky carrow a grin.

"I need to find my parents, and they are hiding with the carrow, Arliss. Fancy a trip to meet your kind?"

There's a tangible look of relief on his face, but he gives me a brusque nod.

Half an hour later, our group emerges from the traveling tree into a clearing. I watch color seep back into the trees here, and I hear a titter. A child hiding in the bushes. A quick flash of smoke surprises Noire, and he growls as a child appears in human form right before us. She's young, maybe six or seven, and seeing her fills my heart to the brim.

"Call your kind," I whisper to her conspiratorially.

Arliss joins me, practically quivering with the desire to finally get answers about who he is.

The child darts off into the trees, and we follow. Moments later, several pops of smoke deposit three carrow in front of us. They see Ten and me, their eyes blowing wide, and they drop to the ground in deep bows.

"Is this gonna happen everywhere?" Noire deadpans. Diana shushes him, and I try hard not to laugh at how quickly he returns to his naturally abrasive demeanor.

TEN

I do turn around and give him a saucy wink. "Yeah, alpha. Better get used to it. You look pretty good on your knees."

Achaia giggles. Noire scowls.

It feels...normal.

There's a crashing sound in the forest ahead, and then my mother breaks through a group of Volya warriors and falls into my arms, sobbing. Father is right behind her, and the moment he sees me, he drops to a knee in deference. His wings tremble with the force of sobs that wrack his spindly frame.

"Father," I murmur.

He rises, and when I open one arm wide, he tucks in for a hug.

I don't know what the future will hold, but I know that this is just the beginning.

∼

Eventually, we leave the carrow to return our people home. Arliss remains with them, but Ascelin comes with us. I'd have sworn she wanted to stay, but even with the vampiri king's spirit gone from Diana, neither vampiri seems willing to stray from her side. To some degree, she will always be their Chosen One, and Cashore's absence doesn't seem to have changed that.

As for me, I don't see a future where Ten and I spend all our time in the Tempang, even though it's the Volya way and the gate is here. That's a conversation for another time, though. For a day, we remain with my family. We rest and eat, and then it's time to free the monsters in Rama's maze.

My very soul tells me to call them home, to set them free and right Rama's wrongs against them.

Noire bitches the entire ride from the Tempang to the verdant, stunning island the maze is built under. He doesn't fall silent until we enter its dark halls.

It's such an odd thing to be inside the dark, damp maze where Ten was a prisoner for seven years of his life. I no longer harbor hate toward Rama for what she did to him, even though I can't

405

understand it. I'm just thankful he's mine to love for the rest of our long lives. The gate has never produced a prime, although it was foretold eons ago. I suspect we will be around for a good long while. It's a good thing, too, because the Tempang needs our help to fully heal.

"I cannot believe we are doing this," Ascelin hisses as we enter a cold pine forest, snow covering the ground. There's a snuffling in the woods, the sound of hooves, and then a gavataur bursts through, its head lowered and a wild look in its red eyes. I read its pain the moment I see it, and my heart breaks for its confusion and hurt.

"Hush, my child," Ten whispers, walking toward the monster. He reaches out and strokes between its eyes. The creature falls back, cocking its head to one side. The pack is tense behind us, but when the gavataur raises its head and lows, I smile.

"He's calling his people to follow," I tell the pack. They look positively terrified, but Noire refused to allow us to come without him. I don't think he wants to let Ten out of his sight, despite the fact that Ten and I are now the most powerful beings on Lombornei. We have every power the gate has ever given. It's near limitless.

I know we'll be good stewards of those gifts.

We spend hours in the maze, collecting what's left of the monsters imprisoned there. The humans are gone, something Noire preens about. Ascelin and Renze are highly unsettled by a trail of manangal that follow us. The moment we lead them out of the maze, most of the monsters take off, with the exception of a basketful of baby naga Ten found hiding in the depths of a heated pool of water. Turns out that when the pack killed the naga queen during their escape, she was pregnant.

It takes us hours to get to the far northwest corner of Lombornei, Rezha province, to reunite the babies with the naga court there. The king and queen bristle when they smell the death pheromone, but being prime has its advantages—namely Ten having time to explain what happened and deliver the babies to their homeland.

Once that's done, we return the pack to Siargao and what

remains of Ten's extended family. He's crushed immediately between an aging omega and her alpha who both sob when we show up on their doorstep.

When they finally let him go, Ten pulls me forward. "Thomas, Maya, meet Onmiel, my mate." Ten grins. "Thomas and Maya raised us after Father died."

My eyes fill with tears when I think of all Ten lost before we met, but Maya pulls me in for a crushing hug, thanking me over and over for returning Tenebris to her.

Eventually, a herd of vampiri children rushes through the house and crowd Ten, dragging him into the street to play with a ball. If they notice he's got horns, they don't comment on it.

Diana joins me as I watch him go, linking her arm through mine. Achaia takes my other hand, holding it to hers as she smiles at me.

"Noire has always said Ten was the best of us: the kindest, the smartest, and the one he wanted to carry on the Ayala name. I never realized it until now, but Ten is the heart of our pack, Miel. You are now, too." Diana's voice wavers a little bit as Achaia lays her head on my shoulder with a little nod.

"Our sister. Our perfect, dorky sister. You're not going to stop being nerdy now, are you? Your love of coffee and books hasn't disappeared, has it?"

I laugh as I shake my head and groan. "Gods, coffee and books sound so good right now."

Ten looks up at me from the middle of the street, his beautiful lips curling into a smile, and I know exactly what he's thinking.

We spend a full day with the pack before taking Arliss's airship back to Pengshur. When we arrive at ML Garfield's office, he doesn't bat an eye, letting us in without a word.

For two hours, we share our story, and Ten requests to be officially allowed into the Novice program. Garfield immediately promotes me to First Librarian, with Ten as my Novice, but when we ask to have Ten fast-tracked out of that ridiculous first year, Garfield declines.

"We can't bypass the process for anyone. We never have in the thousand years since the library was founded."

I laugh because now that I'm the prime, I know everything about the Volya who created the library ages ago and left it in the capable hands of half-breeds they trusted to guard the secrets held here. I'll have to find a new area of focus because I'm now an expert in monster lore and languages. Another gift from the gate, it seems.

When we leave ML Garfield's office, I give Ten a devilish look. "Coffee, my love?"

Ten threads his fingers through mine and plants a scorching kiss on the side of my neck, huffing just below my ear.

"Our first coffee together as mates. I want it, Miel."

It feels like he's talking about far more than coffee, and we both know it.

I don't think I've ever been so happy in my entire life.

CHAPTER FIFTY
TENEBRIS
SIX MONTHS LATER

I've thoroughly enjoyed six months of bliss, traveling back and forth between the Tempang, Siargao, and Pengshur. I don't feel much different than I did before I took Onmiel and Zura into the gate. Even so, things aren't the same. I have an awareness of *everything* now. When I meet someone new, I read their soul like a book, and I know if they're good...or not. I can communicate with and understand any species of monster. Most of all? A deep-seated need to protect and serve everyone underlies each decision I make.

It's an odd feeling, but the need to heal my world is threaded through me as deeply as my own blood. That and Onmiel. She's part of me in a way Rama never was and never could have been. Because at every turn, Onmiel was my choice, all the way to the very end. So much so that I gave my life for hers, and that love allowed the gate to bring us back and make us her partners, her stewards.

I focus on how fucking much I love my fallen star as she sinks onto my hard cock, throwing her head back at the bliss that rockets through our bond.

Our bond.

I didn't realize I gasped it aloud, but everything between us is more heightened since the gate. Every sensation, every touch, every emotion.

"I feel you," she cries, clenching around me as I try not to spill too fast.

Snarling, I grip her thighs and guide her on and off me until we're both a feral clash of fangs and claws. She grasps my horns tight in her fists and strokes them until I unload my seed into her womb, praying it takes root fast. I want a million babies with this woman, and I want them immediately.

Onmiel slumps in my arms as I carry her to the tub, and then I wash her hair, kissing her all over. We eat dinner with her parents in the village in the Tempang, and then I take her to the closest traveling tree.

She sighs as she looks around us. "The forest is healing; can you feel it?"

I growl as I pull her to me. I will never get enough of her. I've been obsessed for ages, and it never goes away. "I feel it, little star," I murmur. "You are an excellent guardian, but I have a surprise for you."

"Is it coffee?" she whispers surreptitiously.

I have to laugh at that. No matter how much coffee we bring when we come to the Tempang to visit, it's never enough. The water here doesn't make the coffee taste like it does at the library, which is where we really consider home.

"Follow me." I laugh, nipping at her ear as I pull her into the tree.

"Anywhere, anytime." She laughs back, tickling my side as we head into the tree's depths.

I take a left turn.

Onmiel pinches me playfully. "Where are we going, Tenebris?" She infuses authority into her voice, but it only serves to draw a purr from my chest. My wolf and I love it when she uses our full name. He's different since the events at the gate, too, but it feels right to me. He was always different from other wolves because I'm different. I was meant for something more. And now? Everything is perfect.

I don't answer but pull her faster, and when the tree opens, and we see my family's smiling faces at home in Siargao, Onmiel squeals with delight. She leaps out of the traveling tree and throws herself into Achaia's arms and then Diana's. Then my whole family shouts as they take turns hugging her. We haven't been home in two months, and Noire says he never wants to leave Siargao again.

Jackass.

But now, there's a look on my brother's face I haven't seen before. Something protective in a new way. When I glance at Diana, I know what it is.

Congratulations, brother, I murmur into our family bond. *Don't be like Father.*

Jet and Renze laugh in the bond. I imagine he's been insufferably proud.

Noire scoffs but preens, giving me a snide look as I watch Diana share the happy news with my mate.

We think Zura's a good name, Diana whispers into the bond. Onmiel's joy at the news is palpable in our family bond.

Noire sidles up to me. "We never pierced you, you know." His alpha purr is pure evil. Jet comes to my side and grips my shoulder. Then they're both manhandling me, and although I could fight them with my newfound strength, I don't. They've been planning this for a while, and I don't want to take the wind out of their sails.

Renze helps Jet and Noire drag me into the kitchen. Onmiel follows with a slightly concerned look on her face. Rosu pads after her, whining at what they're doing. My wolf senses him, reaching out to let him know we're alright. He's remained enormous, a perfect protector for my family when I'm not around.

When my brothers toss me onto the kitchen table, and Thomas rounds the table to hold down my shoulders, Onmiel raises a brow and crosses her arms.

"Family tradition," I snort as Noire unveils his piercing kit.

"Damn, this shit hurts," Diana laughs as she grabs Achaia's hand and heads back up front. "We don't wanna watch!" she hollers as she goes. Ascelin rolls her eyes just as hard and follows the other girls out the door, and then it's just my mate, my brothers, and Thomas.

Thomas deftly yanks my pants down far enough to expose my dick. With a practiced, clinical touch, he holds it by the head.

Noire grins at me as he threads a curved piercing onto a long needle.

The first piercing slips through the skin underneath my cock as I bellow, pain shattering up my core. I thrash, and Noire growls.

"Be still, brother. You know you'll heal fast. Don't be an asshole."

Fifteen horrible minutes later, a row of bars line the underneath of my throbbing cock, and I'm trying not to fall apart at the seams.

Jet slaps an ice pack to my chest and hands Onmiel another. "Brutal, I know. But trust me, brother, when you and Onmiel do the thing for the first time, you'll think you're losing your mind from how good it feels."

"I'll take your word for it," I croak out, reaching for my girl, who slings one arm around me and leads me to the front of the house.

"Nice of you to let them do that," she whispers into my neck.

"Thought you might like it," I say. "I wanna spend a night here and then go home."

To the library, I mean. I'm halfway through my first Novice year, kicking everyone else's ass because I mentee with the best First Librarian ever. Smiling at her, I pull her in for a kiss as my pack cheers from the front steps of Noire's brownstone.

Later that night, after an amazing dinner, Onmiel helps me to bed and checks on my dick. It's hard for her like it always is but bruised and swollen. It'll be better by tomorrow, but for tonight, sex is off the table.

It doesn't stop me from pulling her on top of my face and making sure she gets off a few times, though. Nothing will ever stop me from that. I'm obsessed with my fallen star. And that's never changing.

TEN

The following morning, we say goodbye to the pack and take the new traveling tree right to Pengshur—my second surprise. I've been growing the two new trees for six whole months to make our travel easier. We emerge just outside the library in a grove ML Garfield's been helping me keep secret from Onmiel. When we walk out of the tree and into the busy street, she claps her hands together and throws herself into my arms.

"Ten! I can't believe you did this. You're such a sneak!"

I bury my face in her neck and breathe her in the way I always do when I need to feel grounded. Love spreads along our bond, overwhelming me the way it always does.

"I don't think there's ever been a man who loved a woman like I love you," I whisper, wrapping her legs around my waist as the busy street behind us continues on, oblivious to our happy moment.

She chuckles, kissing the tip of my nose. "I love you, Tenebris Ayala."

"Good," I huff. "Because we haven't fucked in your keeping room yet, and I want that today."

Onmiel throws her head back, glorious white hair swinging as I wrap my fist in it and carry her into the library. Her gaze turns heated as she looks at me, one pale brow curling upward. "I always knew you were a nerdy freak."

I grin. "You're right, my sweet. You've *always* been right, Onmiel, about everything. And most especially about you and me."

"Mhm." She laughs, pressing her soft lips to mine. "Take me there, Tenebris."

"Yes, ma'am." I smirk, heading through the dark halls, through the smell of musty books and the sound of a coffee machine.

Heading home.

+++++

I bet you're sitting there wondering how a fellow book lover came

415

up with something as cool as the keeping room but didn't even let you see it! Well, you're in luck. As soon as I finish the spicy keeping room epilogue, it'll be available to newsletter subscribers!
Sign up for my newsletter to get it straight to your inbox when it's ready!

BOOKS BY ANNA FURY

DYSTOPIAN OMEGAVERSE

Alpha Compound

START THE SERIES

Northern Rejects

START THE SERIES

HOT AND COZY MONSTERS

Haven Ever After

START THE SERIES

Scan the QR code to access all my books, socials, current deals and more!

@annafuryauthor
liinks.co/annafuryauthor

ABOUT THE AUTHOR

Anna Fury is a North Carolina native, fluent in snark and sarcasm, tiki decor, and an aficionado of phallic plants. Visit her on Instagram for a glimpse into the sexiest wiener wallpaper you've ever seen. #ifyouknowyouknow

She writes any time she has a free minute—walking the dog, in the shower, ON THE TOILET. The voices in her head wait for no one. When she's not furiously hen-pecking at her computer, she loves to hike and bike and get out in nature.

She currently lives in Raleigh, North Carolina, with her Mr. Right, a tiny tornado, and a lovely old dog. Anna LOVES to connect with readers, so visit her on social or email her at author@annafury.com.

Made in the USA
Columbia, SC
23 January 2025

3c402520-910c-4680-829f-5050a3362987R01